THE
BLOOD THRONE
OF
CARIA

Empire of the Nightingale: Part III

Roy Casagranda

SEKHMET LIMINAL PRESS

Sekhmet Liminal Press
Published by Sekhmet Liminal Press, LLC
Copyright © 2018 by **Roy Edward Casagranda, PhD**

Roy Casagranda/Sekhmet Liminal Press, LLC
https://bloodthronecaria.com
https://casagranda.com
https://facebook.com/BloodThroneCaria

Publisher's Note: This is a work of historical fiction. Every effort has been taken to make this novel as accurate as research and personal bias would allow. Since this story takes place over twenty-five centuries ago, any similarity to medieval, modern, and contemporary names, characters, places, companies, organizations, political parties, and incidents are purely coincidence. Locales, names, and some concepts are usually written as they were in ancient Greece and Persia.

Book Cover © 2018 Roy Casagranda

Book Layout © 2017 BookDesignTemplates.com

The Blood Throne of Caria/ Roy Casagranda. – 2nd edition
ISBN 978-1-7324775-0-6

Quantity sales. Special discounts are available on quantity purchases by corporations, schools, book clubs, associations, and others. For details, contact the publisher at the website above.

Printed in the United States of America

To Ahsan, Soona, Awatif, and Suzie

For all the victims of patriarchy

Acknowledgements

A special thanks to Banafsheh Madaninejad, PhD, Sina Madaninejad-Casagranda, Roham Madaninejad-Casagranda, Cori McCarthy, Sara Kocek, Joe Schlichting, Sally O'Grady, Gianna Cala-Smith, Chris Kocek, Dave Aretha, Olivia Ott, Sahar Chmais, William Ried, David Wells, Zoe Fox, Jennifer Cunningham, Bobby Spencer, JD Mossburg, Leah Harris, Carrie Conwill, Lillian Ramage, Diana Ceres, Gabriel Chance, Jeremy Scroggins, Sarah Bale, Carolyn Shelley, Janet Brooks, Alden Kahl, and Jess Popp.

Prologue

For at least two and a half millennia, there has been a conspiracy to write women out of history. Fortunately, that conspiracy is unraveling. In 2017, the occupant of the grave of a powerful Viking warrior in Birka, Sweden, was identified as a woman. We already knew that women were not merely cheerleaders to history, but the DNA analysis provided tangible evidence that contradicted the dominant paradigm.

Coincidentally, I was experiencing a similar discovery in my own research. I had set out to write a work of historical fiction in 2014. As I read about the ancient and medieval Mediterranean, I learned the names of 40 ancient women rulers and philosophers. I had never heard of any of them. I have always thought of myself as historically literate, but in that moment, I was humbled. That list is still growing and so is my humility!

One of those women was Artemisia I of Caria. Her story is as brilliant as that of any man's, maybe more so when you consider the misogyny she had to overcome, and yet almost no one outside of Greece, Turkey, or Iran has ever heard of her. *The Blood Throne of Caria*, is my first real attempt at pushing back against this conspiracy.

UNCHARTERED TERRITORY

Writing a novel about Artemisia, was difficult because so much of her story is unknown. Consequently, I had to make up names, events, motives, and chronologies. Another problem I faced was that some of the historical material was contradicted by other historical evidence. As if that wasn't enough, my primary source, Herodotus, lied. For example, Herodotus accuses a Persian Empress of intense cruelty to a rival's mother, but we know that the story he told was recycled from an old myth. When your best source is lying at least some of the time, how do you know when he is honest and when he's not?

And there was a fourth issue at stake: resurrecting an ancient heroine for contemporary readers. The erasure of Artemisia I of Caria from humanity's collective history is as outrageous as getting rid of William Tecumseh Sherman, Mark Antony, or Ramses II. Learning history without its female protagonists, is like going to battle with half a spear.

A CALL TO ARMS

Stories like Artemisia's are sacred and powerful. They inform us of who we are, and they keep our ancestors alive in our hearts, which is precisely why she has been erased from our collective memories. In reality, all narratives are to some degree fictions. We have created a line between nonfiction and fiction and said everything on this side is mostly true and what is on that side is mostly made up. This is the power and danger of historical fiction. It intentionally blurs that line. Moreover, it seems to me that the common discourse is shaped by exciting fiction and not nonfiction. It is as if there is some primordial part of us that yearns for myth over description.

For these reasons, I have chosen to wage this battle inside the historical fiction genre. The challenge we face, however, is that the project to write women out of history is still ongoing. For instance, the misogynistic and racist film *300: Rise of an Empire* (2014) went out of its way to villainize Artemisia. It's not enough to boycott such narratives, and we must do more than simply write corrections. How many people will read the corrections? We must attempt to write captivating narratives with heroines that resemble the women in our lives.

As Walter Mosley so aptly put it, "You don't exist unless you're in the literature, and that doesn't include history books." If we fail to bring those women back, we surrender the past to an inaccurate history. To fully know who we are, we must have access to an accurate herstory. *The Blood Throne of Caria* is my first attempt at feminist historical anamnesis and this novel is my call to arms!

Roy Casagranda, August 20, 2018, Austin, TX

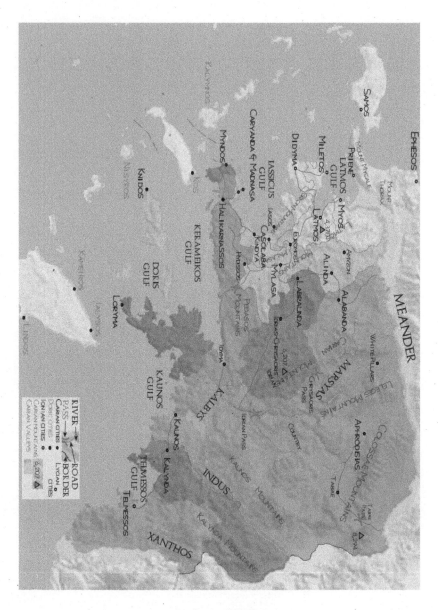

Caria ca 500 BC

Artemisia: Ar teh mee see ya

Book I · The Hollow Throne

Artemisia dashed between the gnarled trunks of an ancient olive grove. She had never been so determined to escape in her thirteen years of life, not even when pursued by her merciless brother. But she knew that she could not outrun Iokaste, three years her senior. So the path she took was populated with frequent tight turns and even a loop. It was elaborate, and it seemed to be working.

Towering above all else was a single massive grandmother of an olive tree. Artemisia imagined that the undulating swirls in the bark were an arcane script chronicling the deeds of the men of Caria. Caria from before the Persians, Dorians, Ionians, Phoenicians, and Lydians; Caria from a time when the White Pillars were new, painted, and glorious. Though no person had carved the patterns in the bark, Artemisia knew that the tree was witness to centuries of history. All she had to do to learn its secrets was climb to its top.

The clanging of iron against iron, and the grunts and screams of men echoed off the trees and drew Artemisia's thoughts to the battle beyond the orchard. Iokaste's breathing got suddenly louder. Artemisia glanced back and discovered that despite her best efforts, her handmaiden was going to reach her.

She ran around the back of the massive tree, towards a large rock she had pushed into place the previous evening. This was her backup plan. The princess wasn't sure she could make the jump. She kicked off with her feet and threw her hands up, barely catching the lowest bough. Despite her weak grip, she shot her feet up as high as she could. Her momentum took her over, until her belly rolled onto the thick branch. Pride throbbed in the scraped skin on her hands.

"Princess Artemisia!" Iokaste screeched as she ran beneath, gasping for breath. "Your father'll be furious!"

Artemisia responded by climbing higher. The branches got greener and skinnier, until she was precariously balanced. *My handmaiden won't pursue me this high. Letting me witness the battle will get her punished. Breaking the branch that I'm standing on, that'll get her executed.* She sucked in a large breath to pay off a long-overdrawn debt, closed her eyes, and listened. Her veins throbbed in her ears and hairs stood on the back of her neck. A man ran up to Iokaste. Though he said nothing, Artemisia was sure it was Myron, her bodyguard.

The battle sounded so close, she wondered if she could touch the men. When she opened her eyes, the first thing she saw was the remorseful grimace of a Labraundian warrior. His eyes locked onto hers and softened, as though he found hope in them. Then his opponent pulled a bloody sword out of his bowels.

Artemisia's stomach sank. She felt weak and gripped the tree harder. "This is what men do?" she asked trembling. "This is what battle is?"

"What?" Iokaste called up.

"It's so horrible." Artemisia continued to speak to herself. "These men are murdering each other! I swear I'll never be so naive again."

"What did you think battle was?" Iokaste's voice was filled with contempt.

"I don't know." Then she saw her father, King Lygdamis, come into view. He led Halikarnassians towards a breach in the wall surrounding the town. In a flash, a spear shot out towards him. The battle became suddenly quiet. She watched with horror as the tip of a spear seemed destined to strike him in the chest. But he stepped back, and with a crash, bashed his shield into the shaft, shoving it away.

With lightning speed Lygdamis cut his assailant's face in half. Artemisia was stunned by all the blood. The soldier dropped his spear and fell to his knees, trying to hold his flesh together.

"Papas!" Artemisia shouted.

"What do you see?" her handmaiden quavered.

"My father has just defeated a man." She was overwhelmed by so many emotions, she could not differentiate them.

"The breach?" Myron's deep voice boomed. "Are the Labraundians still holding it?"

"Yes, but I can see the fear in their faces. Papas is leading men against them." Her voice filled with pride. "The enemy is faltering. I see the White Pillars, the temple of Artemis on the Marsyas, behind them."

"Yes, mistress," Iokaste said as if answering a question. "You should come down now. Such behavior isn't suitable for a princess."

"Why is it that all the women who tell me what's suitable behavior, have never followed their own rules?"

Iokaste sighed.

"How many trees have you climbed, handmaiden?"

Just then a Labraundian, holding the red and yellow labrys banner of his kingdom, charged her father. But before he reached the king, he and his banner went down hard. Behind him was a woman; the left side of her clothing was torn open, exposing half her chest. She held a bloody sword. "There's an Amazon fighting alongside Father!"

"No, mistress, she's not an Amazon," Myron corrected. "The Persians allow exceptional women to fight."

Jealously stole through Artemisia's heart. *If only I were an exceptional Persian, I'd be a warrioress! But alas I'm a Hellene.* She knew better than to voice her thoughts. Experience had taught her that everything got back to her father and that no allowance existed for exceptional women in Caria.

Lygdamis walked through the hole in the wall through a volley of arrows. Artemisia's mind raced. She had heard the men in the court talk about battle, but to see it was a shock. "What sin have the Labraundians committed that we're here killing them?" she called down to Myron. "We're all Carians!"

A long silent moment passed before he answered, "The White Pillars belongs to Aphrodisias. The Labraundians took it. Your father tried diplomacy, but when that failed, as Satrap of Caria, he was forced to come to the aid of one part of Caria against the other part."

"Don't tell her all of that!" Iokaste shouted.

"She's too smart to believe a half truth," Myron retorted.

"That's why you mustn't tell her the concerns of men." Iokaste's voice filled with annoyance. "That mind of hers is always at work. Her father says she's like Pegasos!"

"Pegasos?"

"The winged horse."

"I know who Pegasos is." Myron was irritated.

"I don't know what he meant. Maybe she's too free?" Iokaste went on. "How can she accept her role if we give her too much knowledge? You know she stole Pissindelis' book!"

"We looked through her possessions. It's not there."

"I don't know where she's hiding it, but I'm sure it was her!" Iokaste huffed.

Just then, King Lygdamis reached the top of the wall. Artemisia cried out as he waved his banner: two red bulls charging towards each other on a white background. A cheer rose up from the men pouring through the breach.

"I want a life filled with glory and struggle!" Artemisia shouted as she shot her brown eyes down to her servants below.

"You're a princess!" Iokaste looked back up at her. "You should be plucking those unruly bushy eyebrows and learning to sew! You must learn to accept the role that you were born to, Princess Artemisia, otherwise you'll make your own life painfully difficult!"

Artemisia furrowed her brow and shouted. "I know my place, already! I'm going to be the King of Halikarnassos and the Satrap of Caria!"

That night, Artemisia turned her head sideways and pushed it under the back of her tent, wriggling until she was out. She crawled to the edge of the camp, where she stood and ran. When she reached the road, she looked east towards the gate.

Too many guards! In the light of the full moon, I could never get past them. After thinking through her options, she settled on the breach. There, the dried blood splattered on the broken rocks, looked black in the moonlight. Carefully she picked a way through that allowed her to stay in shadows. Guards slumbered or chatted sleepily about their exploits.

When she was inside the walls, she saw no signs of a living town. It was as if all its denizens had been banished. The town was built as a small grid on the Marsyas River to serve the Temple of Artemis—The White Pillars, as everyone called them. Lit by the moon, tall white roofless columns rose up as if to support the dome of stars above. *How old is this place?* She headed towards the temple, working her way down the streets, counting the corners. The base of the temple was lit with torches and populated by soldiers.

Artemisia sighed and gathered her resolve. She approached carefully, hugging the north end of the street. She could hear voices coming from the temple. *Father must be here.* The cool spring air cut through her crimson peplos, leaving her chilled. She waited until a guard walked past and then dashed across the street and up the stairs. Three ancient roof slabs lay on top of each other. She crawled between them, until she reached a spot where she could spy on the gathered men. Her father and brother, Pissindelis, sat next to four other men.

Artemisia recognized Artaphernes, the Satrap of Lydia, from a visit he had made to Halikarnassos. He was the brother of the Emperor and a Persian. Though her father was also a satrap, the two men were not equals.

"Satrap Artaphernes, if I might?" A middle-aged Milesian waited for the Persian to answer.

"Yes, Polemarch Hecataeus. Speak," Artaphernes ordered.

Ah, that's Hecataeus! If only Papas would send me to tutor with him!

"The Labraundians were in the wrong. "Hecataeus said, "But their men have suffered terrible losses."

"Half of their army is dead, and their allies failed to come to their aid."

Artemisia was shocked at the loss of so many men.

"Ionians see being part of the Satrapy of Lydia as tyranny," Hecataeus went on. "If you grant us our own satrapy, it would demonstrate that those who are loyal get rewarded."

"Yes, yes, your people want a satrapy," Artaphernes rolled his eyes. "What do we do about the Labraundians?" He turned to the other Ionian commander, a man who wore a chiton cut so high his legs were entirely exposed. "Aristagoras?"

"Satrap, my advice is to give Ionia its own satrapy."

"That's not going to happen!" Artaphernes let anger infiltrate his voice. "I want to know what to do with the Labraundians!"

"Sure, whatever you think... give them mercy." Aristagoras' tone was like her brother's—spoiled and resentful.

She caught a glimpse of her brother's bewildered face in the flickering light. *I bet Pissindelis understands none of what these men are talking about.*

Artaphernes shook his head. "King Lygdamis, what do you think? After all, you are Satrap of Caria."

"I'm inclined towards leniency." Artemisia's father shifted his body. "However, there must be some consequence. We should send the horses, women, and children in the Labraundian baggage train to Shoosh."

"Finally, a man who can answer my questions!"

Artaphernes turned towards another man. He was in bandages and appeared forlorn. "King Kandaules of Kalynda, what say you to King Lygdamis' recommendation?"

"We're beaten. I accept."

"So be it," Artaphernes declared.

Just like that! Artemisia couldn't believe how quickly the satrap agreed. *Those women are like horses—loot.*

Artaphernes cleared his throat and locked his gaze on King Lygdamis. "I've another matter to attend to, though it's awkward." He paused. "Emperor Darayavahu has asked me to get a hostage from you."

"From me?" Lygdamis was surprised.

"My brother and I don't doubt your loyalty; this isn't punishment. Your son will be educated in Persia and will come back to you more talented."

Lygdamis hesitated. He looked at his feet. Then spoke. "I...I only have one son."

Artemisia could hardly breathe.

"Master?" Hecataeus waited for a nod. "I vouch for the Satrap of Caria."

"Can I send my daughter, instead!" Lygdamis blurted out. "As you know, my injury precludes making any more children. If you take my daughter, it would allow me to keep my only heir to be trained by me."

Father! Artemisia's heart beat so hard she thought it would erupt out of her chest. But as the betrayal surged through her veins she made a realization. *If I can be sent in Pissindelis' place, then I must resemble something equal to him.* She held her breath, awaiting her fate, glancing at Pissindelis to see he was frozen with fear.

After a long moment, Artaphernes spoke. "I've heard your words and decided that your request is reasonable. Satrap, send your daughter to Shoosh with the women."

Artemisia looked at her father to gauge his reaction. *Relief! Joy! I'm no different than the women and horses. Or am I the prince's surrogate?*

"King Lygdamis, Satrap of Caria, Hecataeus, Polemarch of Ionia, and Aristagoras, Tyrant of Miletos, your friendship is a reward unto itself. You and your men are examples for the empire. King Kandaules of Kalynda, let this be a lesson to you and your people."

Artemisia felt a powerful need to escape. She started to back up but realized she was too noisy. She stopped moving to calm herself. After a few breaths, she backed out. The young princess ran, not caring whether she was seen. When she counted a fourth left turn and saw the breach, she bounded through it like a gazelle, startling the guards. One of them shouted, "Come back, little priestess! Your temple needs you!" Laughter erupted from behind her.

When she reached the outer edge of the camp, she turned back and to her surprise saw Myron jogging behind her. *Has he seen me? What will Father do? Exile me to Shoosh?* When she reached the tent, she slid onto the ground and squirmed under the wool wall.

Artemisia lay in her bedding, staring up at the tent ceiling, her heart still pounding. All was quiet save the footsteps of a guard and the occasional crackle from a dying campfire. *How can I live in exile so far away from Caria... from my family!*

In the morning her father came into her tent. "Artemisia."

"Yes, Papas."

"I'm about to leave. You'll stay here with Myron and Iokaste."

Artemisia wanted to scream, *I know that you traded me for my brother! I hate you!* She dug her fingernails into her palms and forced a smile. "Am I to be tutored by Hecataeus?"

Lygdamis squinted. "How do you know of Hecataeus?"

"Well, you must have a reason for leaving me behind." Sarcasm welled in her heart, and though she wanted to contain it, her words came out contaminated by it. "I doubt you are assigning me to rebuild the walls. I know how deliberate you are. If you were leaving me in Sardes, it would be to mint coins, Halikarnassos to build ships, Alabanda to raise horses..."

Papas, why don't you shut me up? I want you to! "There's nothing in White Pillars save this temple to my namesake. But Hecataeus is here. So, you must be leaving me with him to go to that most brilliant of cities—Miletos. There I should learn philosophy."

Lygdamis' squint turned into a glare. Artemisia wondered why he didn't censor her. She became uneasy under his gaze and hoped it would give way to truth, but it didn't. Instead her father walked out of the tent.

Artemisia couldn't help but grin. Her sarcasm had allowed her a small victory that floated on top of her broken heart like Egyptian linen on a cold winter night.

When her father and the Carian army had set off towards the south, Myron and Iokaste approached. "Mistress," Iokaste started, "your father has instructed us to join the women heading to Shoosh."

"Are they going to Halikarnassos first?" Artemisia feigned ignorance.

"No, mistress." Iokaste's voice was filled with kindness.

"I see. Will Hecataeus be joining us? I'm sure he'll be my tutor." Artemisia was not entirely sure why she wanted to keep up the charade.

"No, mistress. We are traveling to Shoosh."

"What?" Artemisia faked shock as she cried out. She put her face in her hands and pretended to cry. She felt the need to hurt Iokaste—the symbol of her father's authority—but realized that it would serve her better to try to illicit sympathy. In truth her crying was mockery. Yet when Iokaste put her hand on Artemisia's shoulder, she found real comfort in the gesture.

Soon they joined three hundred children and women and set out towards the country of Lydia.

"These women are widows anyway," Artemisia said, as if to somehow mitigate their sorrow. But then she changed her mind. "Surely widows deserve some dignity."

No one replied.

"Women are little more than property to be traded," Artemisia said loudly.

Iokaste shoved Artemisia.

"What a spectacle."

"Artemisia, please!" Iokaste spoke through her teeth.

"I must accept that women and children are something to be owned and traded." Artemisia felt genuine rage building. "I saw an Amazon fighting next to my father yesterday. She proved to all that women can be part of the world of men."

"I'll beat you right here in front of all these people." Iokaste snapped, glaring at her. "If someone hears you say such a thing, you'll upset them."

"That was my intention!" Artemisia scowled but stopped talking.

Soon the women were trudging through the ford of the Meander River. Artemisia looked back from the north bank. "There's Caria, and here's Lydia." It took another seven days for the slow-moving party to work its way through valleys and over mountain passes to reach Sardes, the capital of Lydia.

As they entered the gate, Artemisia was shocked at the throngs of people and opulent architecture. "King Kroisos' glory is evident even now!"

"*Shh*," Iokaste hissed. "I don't know if the Persians like him. Didn't Kurosh the Great kill him?"

"So, this is my fate? I'm to be exiled not only from my country, but also from my voice? Should we cut my tongue out? Besides, how much hate could there be! He was the brother of Kurosh's grandmother!"

"This is why your father has sent you to Persia! You're unruly!"

"Only a cow like you would think that being ruled was virtuous."

Iokaste struck Artemisia in the mouth. The side of her lower lip instantly grew a pea-shaped lump. The handmaiden raised her hand again.

Artemisia tasted blood, and though the pain in her mouth was great, her pride wouldn't allow her to show it. She fought off tears and forced a smile. "You think you can break me?"

The handmaiden pulled her arm back, but Myron caught her. "It's not the way with one such as this."

Iokaste looked puzzled.

Artemisia couldn't believe that anyone would defend her.

"My daughter was like this. You can't beat a prideful person out of their pride. They must be allowed to discover their own path."

"Your daughter?" Artemisia filled with interest.

"Clytemnestra—she died three years ago of fever." Sadness overtook Myron's eyes. "She was fourteen and lit up all of Caria with her smile."

Artemisia couldn't believe that a warrior the size of one and a half normal men, with a horse's chest, could have been a father. Let alone a father moved to tears by the death of a daughter. Though they had been together for two years, Artemisia realized she knew almost nothing about her bodyguard.

Her handmaiden, on the other hand, was the Dorian daughter of a Carian lord. At sixteen, Iokaste was old for an unmarried woman. She had become Artemisia's handmaiden as a gift by her father to Lygdamis, while she was held in reserve for a strategic marriage. In that moment, Artemisia understood why she was so angry. *Now she's been sentenced to a marriageless life, because of my exile!*

Two weeks from Sardes, a Persian soldier blew a horn. Soldiers began to form into ranks with their bows and swords out. Widows and children ran towards them.

Artemisia strained to see what Myron was pointing at, and then she saw horsemen. "Who are they?"

"Phrygian raiders! Run!"

They began to run, but soon the sound of the galloping hoofs grew louder. Artemisia turned to see a raider closing in on her. She realized that he was going to catch her. She stopped running and squared herself off as she had seen her brother do in training. She bent her knees and tensed.

Just as the Phrygian arrived, he reached down with his right hand, but Artemisia dove in front of his horse. A rock caught her in the ribs as she sprawled on the ground. The pain shot out up through her body, but she managed to stand.

And then her feet came up off the ground. A second Phrygian caught her by the arm. Frantically she kicked her legs, though her feet only caught air. The raider draped her onto his lap like a rag kore doll. Her belly bounced on the horse's back; her feet dangled over the side.

She was powerless to do anything but watch the ground race beneath her. She wanted to scream but couldn't manage any sound.

Suddenly she was floating. Nothing was beneath her, not thigh, not horse, nothing. She hurtled forward without wings. Behind her she saw the horse fall headfirst into the ground. His rider flipped up into the air and then crashed hard onto the ground in front of the horse's head a moment after she hit the ground.

Tearing, burning pain came up from her back and bottom as she rolled over rocks and brush. Branches snagged and tore her crimson peplos, while she wondered how long she would travel. Finally, she came to a stop on a small patch of grass. The green gave off a welcome coolness.

With adrenaline surging through her veins, Artemisia knew she had to stand and find Myron. She managed to get to her feet. She saw her would-be captor crawling away from his horse; a spear jutted out of the rear haunch of the screaming stallion. "Hermes! Look at how quickly Myron reacted!" Artemisia shouted, "How much strength would it take to throw a spear that large, that far, and penetrate the hide of a horse?"

Then she saw Myron. He held a sword in one hand and a shield in the other. The first Phrygian rode towards him, his spear held high. He threw it one way and veered the other. Myron deflected the spear with his shield but had anticipated the horseman's course change. He slashed the man's thigh.

The raider rode away. Artemisia looked towards where she had first seen the raiders and saw a dozen horsemen riding north. They had three women with them. "Iokaste!" Artemisia turned and then saw the handmaiden. She was running towards the downed Phrygian. He got onto his elbows, when she kicked him in the face.

"Nothing's broken."

Artemisia was a little delirious and very achy.

"Mistress, I got you a new gown from one of the widows. You took a beating."

"I'm having trouble hearing." Artemisia touched the side of her head. Instead of an ear, she felt bandage.

"A branch tore your earlobe. We stitched it together and bandaged it up."

"I don't remember."

"You passed out."

When they had traveled three days, Myron approached. He held something in his hand. Artemisia studied the man and noticed that Iokaste was not around. He grinned as he offered the object.

"A book?" Artemisia looked at the cover. "*Water Is Best*! It's my book!" She looked up at him bewildered.

"It's your brother's book, mistress."

"That worm can't read! No, he can but can't understand what it means. Thales is wasted on him!"

Myron shrugged.

"So, you took it from me?"

"When the search was ordered by your father, I stole it from you to protect you from his wrath."

Artemisia stared at the massive man sworn to die for her. She had assumed he was her father's lackey, but maybe he was more loyal to her.

"Have I upset you, mistress?"

She knew if she spoke, emotions would pour out. He set his heavy hand on her back, covering much of it. So tender was the gesture that Artemisia was overwhelmed by a strange mix of love and loneliness. She leaned into her guard and laid her head against his massive chest. Without speaking, Myron cupped her in his arm and pulled her tightly.

She felt safe.

When she awoke it was morning, the sun had shattered the horizon, splattering orange in every direction. She had slept cradled in Myron's arm with her head on his chest. The fire was smoldering. Artemisia sat up, shivering and in pain.

Iokaste walked towards them from where the Persian soldier's tents were. Artemisia wanted to call out, *I see that you found the army!* But she caught herself, deciding to save that bit of information for use in some future shouting match.

"Oh Myron, you coddle the princess too much. She's already too willful."

"You're like the trainer who beats his horse," Myron retorted.

Artemisia laughed.

Iokaste sneered and then walked off in a huff.

Later that day the handmaiden's bag fell, spilling its contents. Artemisia decided to help, but as she picked up the various items, she came upon a book. "You have Hecataeus' *Periodes ges*?" Artemisia was surprised. "You can read?"

Iokaste snatched the book from Artemisia. "I can read, you twit!"

"Why don't you talk to me. How many women can read? We could talk—"

"Three women! You, me, and the Goddess Athena! Tell your pet titan your girly dreams! I've no use for you!"

Artemisia knew the answer but asked anyway. "Where's all of this anger coming from?"

"You don't know, you little shiteater? You have ruined my life. Instead of going back to Caria so that I can marry, I'm stuck fucking soldiers!"

"Are you forced?"

"No, stupid, but I'm not going to waste my days as a virgin for the likes of you! You're the one named after the Goddess of Virginity." Iokaste spit, pushed her book into the bag, and then tied it to the horse pack.

"I'm sorry." *How could anything I say or do ever make up for any of this?*

Iokaste and Artemisia spent no time together for the remainder of the trip. Artemisia found herself wondering about Iokaste's position. *The privilege of having a handmaiden comes at a real cost.*

"That night in White Pillars," Artemisia was nervous. "When the Labraundians surrendered, I saw you."

Myron gave the faintest grin.

"You knew I'd snuck out."

"Yes, of course. What sort of guard would I be if I didn't?"

"Did you follow me to the Temple of Artemis?" Artemisia asked.

"Yes, though unlike you, I didn't hide from the guards."

"Why didn't you stop me? Isn't that what father would've wanted?"

"Perhaps," Myron allowed.

"There's no perhaps!"

"You're the most brilliant being I've ever met." Myron's face was filled with adoration. "How many women can read?"

"I listened to my brother's reading lessons."

"Children run from lessons. You snuck into them." Myron's voice was filled with pride. "You stole a book to read it. The Gods gave me to you after the death of my daughter. I'd be interfering with the will of Athena if I were to prevent you from becoming what you desire."

Artemisia found herself liking the large warrior even more. Then she confessed, "I'm worried that the Gods aren't real."

"Oh, that's disappointing."

"Why?"

"If you've doubt…well, all my life I've been guided by them."

Artemisia didn't expect him to take her so seriously. She realized that she hoped he would convince her otherwise. "I'm only thirteen. I could be wrong."

Myron shrugged.

When 141 days had passed, they reached Shoosh. Artemisia was not just bewildered by the incredible length of the journey but also by the shocking diversity of terrain. They had passed though forest mountains, desert mountains, thick blue-green rivers in deep fertile valleys, yellow plains, patches of farms, desert plains, and more mountains.

"Is Shoosh in the center of the empire?"

"At the rate we traveled, it would take another 180 days to reach the eastern frontier," Myron said.

"It would take ten and a half months to journey from one end to the other!" Artemisia could not believe it.

"Well, we were going very slowly."

They looked at the splendid city stretched before them. It reclined on a plain split by a river and crowned by a palace on a massive hill. Several mounds protruded here and there with buildings squatting on them. "The palace could hold Halikarnassos."

"I think you're right," Iokaste agreed.

Myron and Artemisia turned to stare at Iokaste. It was the first thing she had said in two months.

"I bought Hecataeus' book to show you that I'm smart." Iokaste appeared defensive, but sad. "You're right. I should've talked to you. I should've shared his book."

Artemisia hesitated but finally managed, "I'd like it if you did."

When they reached the city's tall gates, an important-looking man walked up to them with his own entourage. "I'm Prince Ariabignes, son of Emperor Darayavahu. Welcome to Shoosh in Sousianeh. You're Princess Artemisia, correct?"

Artemisia began to bow.

"No, it's inappropriate to bow to me. We're nearly equal. I'm a prince of an emperor, and you're a princess of a king, so I should receive a kiss on the cheek. We'll teach you these things. There's only one person in the world that you will ever bow to—the emperor, and then only slightly. Your people?"

"My handmaiden is a noble, and my guard is a commoner."

"She should bow to me, and he should take a knee. Before the emperor she takes a knee, and your man would get on all fours."

As Myron and Iokaste each honored Ariabignes, Artemisia added, "I'm Artemisia of Caria." She immediately felt foolish since the prince had already asked her.

Ariabignes smiled. "Well, the emperor will be happy to meet you. We should rush. He's holding court right now."

After they left with Ariabignes, Artemisia realized that she hadn't said farewell to the widows. She knew that she would never see them again and was sad for the mistake.

Artemisia walked through the streets, her mouth open. The city was dense and loud. The walls were painted in vibrant red, yellow, green, blue, and purple. People wore the costumes of countless nations, most she didn't recognize. "I think someone from every part of the empire is here."

"Yes, I can't believe it!" Iokaste agreed.

"Has our arrival caused you to become my friend again?"

"I'm stuck with you, and you don't know your place, but I am your handmaiden."

When they reached the palace, Artemisia found herself feeling small beneath its towering height. Its walls were red, orange, and purple. The gate opened without command. The scent of incense filled her nostrils. The walls were covered in scenes from an unfamiliar mythology: griffins, archers, and winged maidens. Myron looked down at his ward, his face filled with wonder.

Ariabignes led them to a massive colonnade hall. It opened to the world on three sides but was covered with a massive stone roof. Light poured in from holes in the ceiling, revealing several heavily decorated people standing around an occupied throne. The columns were covered in small green tiles depicting brown and orange archers. Other tiles were decorated with people in their native costumes from all over the empire. Artemisia pointed. "Look there—Lydians, Ionians, Lycians, Phoenicians, and Carians!"

When they reached some invisible line, they stopped. Artemisia bowed, Iokaste genuflected, and Myron went to all fours. Ariabignes walked up to the throne and declared, "Darayavahu, the great king, king of kings, king of all nations, son of Hystaspes, the Achaemenid, commands you to stand before him!"

The prince gestured towards the young Carian. "Princess Artemisia of Caria."

She stepped forward, unsure of the etiquette. She thought that her father would expect her to look down, so in an act of defiance, she decided to approach with her chin up, her eyes locked upon the emperor. She saw on him the faintest hint of a grin.

He was regal and handsome. Muscles bulged from beneath his purple and golden robes. His black curly hair protruded out from under the crown. Between it and his beard was the face of a forty-year-old man. However, she knew that he had been emperor for twenty-two years and so knew that he looked younger than his age. He wore a massive braided beard. It hung down his chest, hiding most of his lower face. Darayavahu turned to his right and looked at five women. Each was ornately decorated and wore an elegant crown. The one with the largest crown stepped forward. "Empress Atoosa, daughter of Kurosh, this is princess Artemisia of Caria. She'll be a guest of the Imperial Court. I wish for you to raise her as our daughter, with all the rights and privileges."

The emperor tilted his head slightly, hinting that Artemisia should walk towards Atoosa.

Atoosa waved for Iokaste and Myron to follow, then put her arm over Artemisia's shoulders. When they had left the Great Colonnade Hall, Atoosa spoke in a whisper. The voice of Darayavahu could still be heard, but Artemisia tuned him out and listened to the empress. "Artemisia of Caria, Princess of Halikarnassos, welcome to Shoosh." Artemisia was surprised by how beautiful the empress was. "I'm Atoosa, daughter of Kurosh the Great and second wife of Darayavahu." She winced and motioned to the woman beside her. "This is Artystoneh, the third wife. I'm giving you a room in her apartment."

Artemisia felt like she was floating.

Artystoneh smiled large. "Welcome to Shoosh. You'll love it here."

The imperial wife's tone oozed with kindness and put Artemisia at ease.

"This is Parmys. She's Darayavahu's sixth wife. I want you to know that you may come to me or any of the rest of the imperial household, whenever you want, for anything. You've all the rights and privileges of my daughter."

A young man in his late teens walked up to Atoosa. He leaned into her and kissed her cheek. "Mother." Artemisia was stunned by his beauty. He offered his elbow.

"Khshayarsha, I'm exhausted and in pain." She put her hand on his back. "Tell your father that Artystoneh will take my place."

"Have you talked to the physician?" Khshayarsha's bronze skin was exposed only on his face and hands, as his long yellow and blue robe stretched to his feet.

Artemisia watched his mouth, delighted as he talked. She wanted to tell someone, *I think I could learn to like it here!*

"Chaxshnay says that I should keep applying the oil, pray, and not listen to the Hellene."

Empresses get sick?

"What does the Demokedes say?" Khshayarsha wore a trimmed black beard and long curly black hair that had been oiled and hung to his shoulders.

"He says that I must do surgery."

"Mother! Do the surgery!"

Artemisia liked that the spicy smell of the teenager's perfume over-ran his mother's flowery scent.

"Thank you. Your judgment is always good. I'll consult the priests."

"Let's talk again at dinner. Prayer's only useful as meditation before acting, not instead of action. I've got to go. You know how father hates waiting!" Khshayarsha's muscles bulged from his robes as he strode towards the Great Colonnade Hall, Artystoneh's hand resting on his arm.

Empress Parmys took Artemisia by the elbow and led her away. They walked down a long corridor, up a set of stairs, and then down a long balcony with six doors that looked onto a courtyard with a pond, trees, and flowers. In one corner was a dairy cow, and in that corner, to her surprise, was a corrugated clay dome with a hole at the bottom. She recognized it immediately—a beehive.

"He's handsome, isn't he?"

Artemisia pulled out of her thoughts and looked at Parmys. She appeared to be in her mid-twenties. She had a permanent look of innocence in her soft features. Her voice was high and lilting. For a moment Artemisia thought about how she should answer. "Yes," she managed.

"There are a lot of handsome young men here."

Artemisia suspected that Parmys was trying to make her feel better about being at the Imperial Court. The young queen opened a door and led Artemisia into a corridor. "What's this long room for?"

"This hallway?"

"What's that?" Artemisia asked.

"It's to connect the various parts of the palace." Parmys was amused.

"Oh, you have an entire room for that?"

Parmys nodded, her eyes wide.

"We just walk through rooms to get to other rooms," Artemisia admitted.

"Oh, what about interrupting people?"

"We're used to it, I guess."

At the third door on the right, she stopped. "This is as far as you'll go," Parmys turned to Myron. "Only women and children should be in this hall, but I wanted you to see where your ward is. My servant will take you to your quarters, down by the beehive. If Artemisia ever leaves the palace, she will take you with her."

"*If* I ever leave?" Artemisia didn't like how that sounded.

The young queen was surprised. "Anytime you wish."

Myron put a hand on Artemisia's shoulder and forced a smile before he left.

Artemisia hated how it felt as they separated. Then they entered a large living area with its six adjoining rooms. The main living area had a large sofa and two small tables, and was strewn with several pillows. "This balled-up creature is my son, Ariomardus. He's seven years old and should be in school, but when word of your arrival reached us, he insisted on being here."

The boy leapt up and confidently walked to Artemisia. He smiled as he looked her over. "You're pretty for a Hellene!"

"Why, thank you." Artemisia wanted to seem grateful.

"How do you know Persian?"

"I speak Persian, Ionian, Dorian, and Carian." She felt awkward for giving too much information.

"You'll teach me Ionian. I want to be able to speak to Hellenes."

Artemisia nodded.

"Enough, Ariomardus. To school!"

He bowed and backed out of the room with a wink.

"He's so naughty. Let me show you your room." Parmys opened a door. In it was a large shuttered window and a small bed. "This is your room. Artystoneh is in the next room, and I'm in the one on the other side of here. We will be eating in a few hours. Make yourself feel at home."

Artemisia threw herself onto the bed and fell asleep before she realized it. She awoke to Iokaste moving.

Dinner was an awkward affair at first. The women and children sat on the floor around a low table, eating as servants brought wine, bread, a soup made with millet and barley, a lamb dish with saffron, garlic, onions, and chickpeas, another dish with pears, cracked wheat saffron, and beef. Then came split rabbits on a bed of radish leaves and sliced sour apples. For dessert the servants brought out cut pears, muskmelons, watermelons, pomegranates, grapes, peaches, and mulberries.

Artemisia couldn't figure out what to eat. She sampled this and that. She learned the names of three more wives: Uxshenti, number one, Phratagone, number four, and Phaidime, number five. She stared at each of Darayavahu's wives in turn and wondered what their lives were like.

Then a young woman of fifteen or so entered the dining area. "Artazostreh, where have you been!" Artystoneh's voice was mixture of disappointment and anger.

"Demokedes."

"Our guest is here." Artystoneh gestured to Artemisia with an embarrassed look.

Artazostreh sat in a chair next to Artemisia. "Hi."

"How are you?"

Artazostreh giggled. "I'm fine, and you?"

"I'm fine."

"Here, try this." She handed Artemisia a piece of lamb.

The Carian didn't know the spices, but the flavors exploded in her mouth. Slowly Artazostreh gave Artemisia food to try. She loved most of it but found some things too strong.

As the wine kicked in, Atoosa spoke. "I've made the schedule for the emperor. I've left myself off. He gets one day off. I don't want him to misunderstand my illness as permission to get two days off. So, I've scheduled each of you one extra day for the next five weeks."

"How bad's your pain?" Artystoneh asked with care filling her voice.

"I don't want to talk about it."

"You don't have to suffer alone."

"I love you for your kindness." Atoosa seemed scared.

Artystoneh frowned. Then she turned to Artemisia. "Atoosa and I are sisters, and Parmys is our niece."

"I see, your majesty."

"Artemisia, please call us by our first names," Atoosa demanded. "You're a princess. You're only to use such formalities with Daraya-vahu."

"Yes, your...Atoosa? It's hard for me to believe that I can call an empress by her first name."

"You heard Darayavahu. You are here with all the rights of an Im-perial princess," Artystoneh interjected. "Besides, you might be here the rest of your life. It'd be ridiculous to carry on in a formal manner."

Artemisia had to fight the feeling that she was a prisoner.

"Really? You're so surprised?" Atoosa asked.

"No, dear aunt, she isn't thinking about the informality," Parmys said. "She's surprised about the 'rest of your life' part."

"Oh?" Atoosa's voice was tender. "This is the greatest court on Earth. The king of all is our emperor. Darayavahu will be remembered as Darayavahu the Great. You are too young for Darayavahu, but who knows, maybe one of the other members of the court will take a fancy to you. Maybe even a prince."

"I'm thirteen." Artemisia didn't mean to seem ungrateful. "I haven't thought about marriage in all my years as much as it has been brought up today."

"Nonsense. You'll be of marrying age in a year or two," Atoosa re-torted. "You must start developing your prospects."

Artemisia shuddered. "I'd thought I'd go back to Caria. It never oc-curred to me that this might be permanent."

"I'm told that the trip took five months?" Atoosa frowned. "You'd take such a journey again?"

"The widows slowed us down. Normally the journey's half as long and even less if one goes to Syria and then by sea." Artemisia knew that her protest was not about the length of the journey, but rather the length of her time in the Imperial Court.

"Well, it isn't as if you have a choice." Atoosa looked down on the thirteen-year-old. "The most powerful man on Earth holds your fate in his hands. Besides, you have a brother. He'll replace your father. It's not as if you will be missed."

Ah, here we are again. I've no real value! Artemisia stared at the empress. "Might I have an audience with the emperor?"

Atoosa smiled. "Of course."

That night Iokaste took the bed. Artemisia decided to protect their fragile truce and slept on the floor.

When a week passed, Artemisia found herself too bored to tolerate waiting for the audience with the emperor any longer. Without telling anyone, she left the living area and headed down to the garden. There, next to the beehive, Myron was exercising with several palace guards.

"My lady." He walked over, sweaty and odorous.

"Myron, I've been confined for too long and suspect my audience with the emperor will never come! Let's go exploring."

"Certainly."

They walked out of the palace, passing several women and men wearing veils. "Myron, have you noticed how the Persians are?"

"I've noticed many things," he said.

"I mean how they are around other people. They never burp or fart in the presence of another. They touch, hug, and kiss, but they are careful about it. The rich veil their faces when in public. They worry about contact with fingernail clippings, bodily fluids, and hair. And they pretend they don't pee or poop."

Myron grinned. "We're also stiff about such matters."

"Not like this!"

"To leave the home, our women must cover their hair," he contributed. "Yet we rarely let them out."

"In Athens it's taboo to even say a woman's name in public," Artemisia added.

"I'm told that you can wear a veil if you like, but you don't have to because you're still young."

Artemisia looked at her guard. "So, do I get to make any choices about my life?"

"I doubt it." Myron's voice was playful but honest.

"Iokaste has been letting me read her copy of Hecataeus' book."

"What have you learned?" Myron seemed sincerely curious.

"He divides the world into three continents: Libya, Europe, and Asia. Libya is connected to Asia at the edge of Egypt. Asia is connected to Europe between the Black Sea and the Caspian Sea. And Europe and Libya almost touch at Tartessus. And then all of the land is surrounded by a circular ocean."

"Very interesting. There's a sort of symmetry to it."

"It seems that way."

Artemisia talked through her thoughts, and Myron occasionally interjected. Soon, however, they came upon a new subject. "There's the matter of Amazons."

"What about Amazons, mistress?"

"I can't tell you how wonderful it was to see that Persian woman in battle alongside Papas. That her clothing was torn and her breast was exposed, was all the more amazing! She was in battle as a woman, nothing held back."

"I can imagine."

"Can I be that?" Artemisia desperately wanted him to say yes.

"I don't know."

"Why don't you know?"

"We've no such tradition in Caria," Myron confessed.

"I may never leave this place." Artemisia stopped walking and looked her bodyguard in the eyes. "It's not that I don't love it here. It's more splendid than anything I could've imagined. I just wish I could choose."

"What would you choose if you could?"

"Without limits?" Artemisia asked.

"Without limits."

"I'd replace my father as King of Halikarnassos and Satrap of Caria."

"As king?" Myron sought to clarify.

"Yes. Queens are always subordinate to kings. I asked if there were any limits."

"So, you did." Myron became contemplative. Then he said, "The most important part of being a warrior is knowing the things that you have power over and what you don't. Things that you can't change you must set aside. A person who can't do such a thing can never be a warrior. They can only become a corpse."

Artemisia was stunned by Myron's words.

"You've that power." Artemisia saw adoration in the bodyguard's eyes. "When your father told you that he was sending you here, you didn't waste time trying to change your fate. Instead you spent your last moments with him being sarcastic."

Artemisia braced for the reprimand.

"Sarcasm was a way to attack as the physically weaker person. It wouldn't change your fate, and you knew it, but it would harm your enemy, as much as could be expected under the circumstances. You accepted your fate, and that's the most important part. Now Iokaste sleeps in the bed and you sleep on the floor and you're not fighting—"

"I didn't tell you about that!"

"I've always been good at reading a person's actions." Myron gave her a knowing look. "In battle it has saved my life on more than one occasion. I know Iokaste needs to put you in your place. I thought about all the ways she could, and I know you! You'd rather read her book than sleep in a bed."

Artemisia stared at Myron. He broke off eye contact, but it was clear that his attention was all on her.

"I'm willing to train you to be a warrior, but when we train you must do as I say. Though you are my mistress in all things, if you accept this, in those moments I'm your master."

Artemisia nodded. "I do believe in the Gods, Myron. You're proof."

"That's much relief to me."

She wasn't sure that she did but wanted to ease his concern.

Artazostreh slouched on a sofa in the living area. Her long black curls were weighed down with oil. She played with a fold in her red and yellow gown.

Artemisia slouched by her side, her hands tucked under the top portion of her peplos. "Zoster, talking about boys is your favorite pastime!"

"Not you?" Artazostreh asked.

"I'm not that interested. From here they just look like barriers."

"You're only thirteen."

"I'm not saying they aren't handsome. Khshayarsha is beautiful! I think it can be said that he is the most handsome man on Earth and few would argue. But I've said all I know on the matter."

"Come with me." Artazostreh smiled as she grabbed Artemisia's hand and led the Carian through the palace. When they reached a large room with three beds, they went in.

"Where's this place?"

"This is Demokedes' clinic. He tutors me in medicine. You'll study with me."

"Oh! Truly?" Artemisia could not contain her excitement.

"Yes, of course. I'm Darayavahu's daughter. No one dares say no to me."

"You can train with my servant, Myron."

"Ah, no thanks." Artazostreh grimaced. "I've no interest in sword." Then she rolled her eyes in an act of feigned mocking.

Demokedes was bald, appeared to be fifty, and seemed unmoved by anything. He gave the day's lessons to both girls without asking Artemisia's name. She was amused, but learned so much, she didn't care.

On the cold winter solstice in 502 BC, Artemisia was on her way to the courtyard to train, when she heard a groan from Atoosa's chambers. "Your Majesty? Your Majesty?"

When no answer came, Artemisia opened the door. The room was dark. Artemisia found a clay oil lamp and lit it. She found Atoosa laying on the ground, unconscious. The Carian ran to Demokedes and brought him to the room. Together they lifted the empress onto a couch.

"You've been my student for two months, but you'll have to do." The physician's demeanor was stern. "I want you to see what is at stake."

Artemisia nodded.

"Help me. Pull open her gown."

Artemisia was shocked. "Master, the emperor might kill you."

"Do it."

Artemisia opened the gown, exposing the empress's breasts. One was bandaged.

He pulled off a bandage, revealing a bleeding ulcer. "See that?" Then he took hold of Artemisia's hand. "Touch here." Demokedes pushed her finger hard on a spot on the ulcerated breast. "Feel that?"

"It's a lump, master."

"This lump and this one here." He moved the hand more. "These'll kill the empress. You must help convince her to have the surgery, or she'll die."

Artemisia choked up.

"The pain is what has caused her to pass out. Close her robes. I'll fetch wine." As he walked away, he asked, "Where are her servants?"

Artemisia closed the gown and then asked the empty room. "How can breasts kill you?" She touched her own flat chest. "They give life to children, but this one will kill the mother? If Hera was real, why would she allow such a thing?"

Demokedes brought wine and left again. As the empress stirred, Artemisia offered her the wine. "You passed out. I found you on the floor."

"You mustn't tell anyone."

"Why? We all know that you suffer." Artemisia's voice filled with distress.

"I don't want them to worry."

"We already do. I've been here for three months, but I know that the whole court is worried. Why won't you listen to Demokedes?"

"He wants to cut off my breast!"

Horror filled Artemisia. "Cut it off?"

"Yes, I would endure much pain, of course, and that's scary, but to save my life, I would do it. It's not my life I'm worried about."

"What else could it be, Empress?"

"Darayavahu. As it is he already loves Artystoneh more than me. Though I'm the second wife and she's the third, in truth she's the first wife. If I cut off my breast, he won't want me. What man would? I'd become the sixth wife."

"Surely love would—"

"He didn't marry me for love. I'm the daughter of Kurosh the Great. I was empress when he married me. He's my third husband."

Artemisia was surprised. Her eyes grew large. "You were empress before?"

"I made Darayavahu emperor. He didn't make me empress. I gave Darayavahu his legitimacy. So much so that though he had three sons with Uxshenti, his first wife. He has made my son the heir."

"Ariabignes?"

"He's Uxshenti's second son. The emperor bypassed the first three sons for Khshayarsha."

Artemisia wanted to be sure she understood. "You were married twice before?"

"I was married to my brother, Kambujiya II, when he was made king of kings."

Artemisia could not contain a shudder.

"Oh, it was only political. We never consummated the marriage. Anyway, when Kambujiya II died, the usurper Gaumata claimed to be my brother, Bardiya, and took the throne. He forced me into marriage and raped me daily. It proved to be a mistake. I'm the insider who helped overthrow him."

Artemisia was stunned. *This woman has seen and done so much. Her will's manifest everywhere in the royal court.* "I know what ails you."

"Demokedes told you!"

"Don't be mad at him. He wants me to convince you."

Demokedes came in carrying a mortar and pestle. He ground up a bit of dried bark and spices that Artemisia didn't recognize. He mixed it with a drop of wine, until it was a paste. Then he globbed the paste on his finger and approached the empress.

She glared at him.

"This is no cure, but it will ease the pain."

Reluctantly she let him put it into her mouth and frowned as she swallowed. "So bitter!"

"I want to ask that you not separate from your servants again." Demokedes turned for the door.

"What? You're not going to chastise me for not listening to you?"

"You've already heard me, Your Majesty. I'm a humble physician. I can't command an empress."

Maybe this is the reason I'm here!

It took another month, but Artemisia finally got her audience with Darayavahu. She ran down the hall with Ariomardus and Artazostreh.

"Father said it's a gift for your birthday," the prince shouted.

Atoosa stood at the end of the hall frowning, her arms folded, bringing the three to a walk. When they reached the empress, she put her arm around Artemisia and walked with them to the Great Colonnade Hall. A group of men stood around the enthroned emperor. Atoosa led the children through the crowd to a large empty space in front of Darayavahu.

"Approach, Artemisia of Caria," the emperor grumbled.

She walked forward, nervous but excited. She wanted to lock her eyes on his, but this time she was too afraid. Artemisia wanted to walk slowly, but felt her feet rushing. When she arrived at the worn spot on the stone floor, she bowed.

"Artemisia of Caria, I've seen you train with your man. Do you wish to become an immortal?"

She knew that immortals were elite Persian soldiers but nothing beyond that. "Yes, Emperor."

The courtiers laughed. Darayavahu raised a hand to silence them. He revealed no hint of mocking. "I've watched you train. He treats you like I would an older boy. I've seen him hit you hard and work you until you almost collapse. Yet you persist."

Artemisia gave no reply as pride filled her veins. She fought off an urge to smile and to rub a bruise on her arm. She avoided the former, but succumbed to the latter.

"And Demokedes tells me that he's training you and my daughter to become physicians."

"Yes, Your Highness."

"My son Ariomardus tells me that you play with him some, but he laments that you spend most of your time with Artazostreh, training or reading."

"He's a most excellent spy, Your Majesty." Artemisia felt betrayed, even though nothing the prince revealed was worth hiding.

"You're most unusual." Darayavahu stroked his long-braided beard. "Your name is Persian, I think. But I don't recognize its meaning. 'Arta' means 'truth,' but what does 'misia' mean?"

"Your excellency, I was never told the meaning of my name, but in the Temple of Artemis in Ephesos they refer to her as the 'Great Mother of Nature.'"

"Have you been there?"

"No, Your Majesty." She replied.

"You're fourteen?" He asked.

"Yes, today."

"You speak like a twenty-four-year-old." The emperor's demeanor was stern and it made Artemisia feel important. "Your interests are those of a man. In Persia we make room for such women. Do you know what the basis of our empire is?"

"No, Your Majesty." She thought that she might but decided to err on the side of humility.

"Tolerance and inclusion. We conquer in war as surely as any military, but the conquered aren't enslaved or subjugated. They're made full members of the empire, entitled to all its benefits." The emperor clearly saw Artemisia's facial expression. "Ah yes, the widows. That's a different matter. Labraunda attacked a member of the empire. They had to be punished."

"I understand the need to punish them, but—"

"I'm glad you approve." Darayavahu smiled as the courtiers

chuckled. "You're an inspiration to my children. I want the whole court to know the reward for ambition. That is why you are here." He held up a finger. "I'm granting you one wish."

"A wish?" Artemisia asked, surprised.

"Anything you desire."

Artemisia's mind raced. *To go back to Caria? To become an immortal? Marry Khshayarsha? Gold? Books? A fleet of ships? Free the widows?* "Anything?"

"If I can provide it, of course."

"I want you to order Empress Atoosa to submit to Demokedes' surgery."

The courtiers gasped.

Atoosa shouted, "Husband, you can't—"

Darayavahu waved his hand, commanding silence. "Your wish is to force the empress to do a surgery that she's rejected?"

"I believe she'll die without it and she suffers so much."

Darayavahu looked at the queen, then pointed at Artemisia, accusatorily. "You could have asked for my favorite horse, the crown from my head, to return to Caria, or to become an immortal, but instead you risk upsetting the most powerful person in the Imperial Court."

Artemisia went down to both knees and bowed her head. "If I've done something wrong, please forgive me, my Emperor. It was what was in my heart."

He tugged on his false beard. "If it was what was in your heart, then I must grant you your wish."

Empress Atoosa sighed hard as she gave the empty mug to Artemisia. The fourteen-year-old poured more wine into it from a heavy amphora. It was difficult to balance, but it was the anticipation of what was coming that made her shake.

Artemisia leaned against the wall. She knew that she had to be strong. Trying hard not to tremble, she returned the cup to the queen. Khshayarsha sat on the sofa next to his mother and rubbed her back.

Artemisia avoided eye contact with him. She feared it would open a qanat. Demokedes had ordered the empress to stop drinking and eating the previous day. Thirst drove Atoosa to drink, but she clearly didn't enjoy it.

Darayavahu came into the room. All, save Khshayarsha, Atoosa, and Artystoneh, bowed or genuflected. The emperor strode to the queen and hugged her and kissed her on the lips. "All warriors go into battle with a good dagger." He turned to a servant and took a scabbard with a golden hilt. It had two lion heads protruding from the pommel at right angles. The emperor pulled the dagger and held it up. The blade was sharp and silver and covered in an Avestan text.

The emperor sheathed the dagger and offered it to the queen. "Empress of Persia, daughter of Kurosh and Cassandaneh, I've ordered you to perform a mission of great importance. I know that you'll serve the empire with the dedication required of you."

She took the dagger and tilted her head down.

Darayavahu bowed and backed out of the crowded room.

People resumed their gossip about politics and the quality of the seasonal food. Artemisia poured another mug of wine. She wondered how many the queen would need.

Until that moment Atoosa had been quiet, but suddenly she became animated. She turned to the princess. "Have you tried this wine?"

"No."

"I insist." She pushed the mug back to Artemisia. The princess refilled it, but Atoosa refused. "You drink first."

Artemisia took a sip. It burst with the flavor of mulberries and pomegranates. It was thick, almost as thick as honey, and nearly as sweet.

"I insisted that you assist Demokedes."

"I know. I would—"

"If I live through this, I can't imagine we'll be on good terms."

Artemisia nodded.

Atoosa took the mug and began gulping it down. Slurring, she said, "You're a little shit. After three months you think you're so close to us that you can make me do this?"

"I—"

"I don't care what you were thinking." Atoosa shoved the empty mug back into the Carian's hand.

Artemisia quietly refilled it.

Khshayarsha gave Artemisia heart-melting eyes that seemed to be saying, *Forgive my mother*.

As the empress fell deeper into a stupor, Artemisia wondered what she was saying or whom she was even saying it to. Khshayarsha winked as his mother leaned against his shoulder.

He's seventeen, mature beyond his age, handsome, the heir to the greatest empire the world has ever seen, and HE LOVES HIS MOTHER!

Atoosa took another mug, but slowly her arm went limp. Artemisia had been dreading that moment. She didn't bother to stop mug from spilling its contents onto the floor. Instead she helped Khshayarsha straighten his mother out lengthwise on the couch. Demokedes examined the queen and then turned to the prince. "Your Excellency…"

All the men, save Demokedes, left. Artemisia watched as Artystoneh pulled the gown from the queen. Her servants took the clothing and brought in blankets. A pot of steaming water and a brazier with a red-hot iron were set at the end of the couch. Demokedes took his dagger and set it into the hot water and then placed it on a blanket. He pulled the bandage from the ulcer, exposing a smaller new one.

Servants rolled the queen over to put more blankets under her, and then once she was back in place, they tied her arms and legs down.

"I want to go quickly. I want to finish before she awakens."

Artemisia didn't know if she could keep her emotions at bay.

Demokedes brought her to the empress. "I'm going to cut off the left breast only. I'm going to cut the skin and soft flesh underneath. I must feel my way with the knife. I don't want to cut any muscle, but I won't be able to see it."

He pulled out a length of twine. "I need to you to hold the breast tightly so that I can secure this cord around it. Then during the surgery, you are going to have to hold it in place so that I'm cutting a stable...something firm. You need to pay attention so that you're never in the way. So that I don't cut you."

Artemisia nodded, but she was overwhelmed and wondered if she could remember all he said.

"Take hold of the queen's left breast."

Hands trembling, the Carian princess bumbled around, trying to figure out where to hold it. She didn't know whether to cover the ulcer or the nipple or both. Demokedes moved her hand to the position he wanted. With her hand over both, he said, "Now squeeze."

She did.

He wrapped the cord around the breast and tightened and tightened. It started to turn purple.

Artemisia squirmed. "How could she bear such pain?"

"She gave birth to four sons," Demokedes countered.

"Truly, are these equivalent?" Artemisia was on the verge of vowing to never get pregnant.

"No, you're right, but women have a great capacity for pain."

"I've hit Myron on the cheek with a wooden sword. He didn't even wince. I think men have a great capacity for pain."

Artazostreh retorted, "That's not the same thing!"

When Demokedes finished tying off the breast, he turned to speak to Artazostreh, but she fainted before he said anything. He looked at Artystoneh. "Your Majesty, please attend to your sister at her head. If she should awaken, I want you there to comfort her." He handed her a leather strap. "She can bite on this."

Then he turned to Parmys, "Your Highness, I want you to direct the handmaidens. They're to keep the area clean. When I'm done cutting the breast, I'll need you to bring me the hot iron."

He waited for everyone to take their places. "Let's all take a breath. Good, now exhale." When they had exhaled, he began cutting. The blood flowed immediately. Artemisia wobbled. She turned away, wondering if she was going to make it. The image of Artazostreh's body laying half on the couch, half on the floor was strangely soothing.

Then she looked back at the cut. It was deep, and muscle was visible. It was shaped like a fan but with the texture of steak. Blood trickled through the little troughs.

Atoosa moaned. Everyone turned to her.

"Please don't wake up!" Artemisia whisper-pleaded.

The empress groaned and began to open her eyes. Artemisia began to cry.

Atoosa screamed in agony.

Her sister offered the leather strap.

The queen bit into it and began to thrash under the binds.

"I can't work like this! Handmaidens, lie on the empress! Hold her down—something!"

Even with the queen's thrashing under control, she still twisted her head from side to side.

And then Artemisia noticed that the breast was in her hands. She wobbled and instinctively moved towards the door. Parmys bumped into her to push her away from the brazier. A servant ran up to Artemisia and took the bloody breast.

The young Carian crumpled.

When Artemisia awoke, she jumped up. *My bed*. She ran to Atoosa's room.

Two of Darayavahu's immortals blocked the door. "The emperor has ordered that he not be disturbed."

"The queen?"

"Her majesty lives."

Artemisia went back to the living area and began pacing. She was not sure how long she'd slept and felt no hunger. As she drank the door opened. Artazostreh, Artystoneh, and Iokaste entered. They carried cloth and wool. After sorting out the various patterns, Artazostreh asked, "Do you want to help us make breasts for the empress?"

"Breasts?"

"We're going to make a few little pillows that she can wear when she recovers," Artystoneh answered.

Artemisia found it difficult to give voice to an answer, so she nodded.

"Your hand," Artystoneh said.

Artemisia looked down at her hand and saw dried blood. After washing it, she selected a cloth with an elegant pattern and began sewing it into a ball. The work was a good distraction, despite her lack of skill. Artemisia could not get the image of the severed breast out of her mind.

That night and the next, she could hear moans through the walls. Two days of pacing went by, before Artemisia was permitted to see the empress. When Artemisia entered the room, she saw the empress laying in the arms of Darayavahu. "Come in, Physician Artemisia."

She walked towards the royal couple, bowing her head.

The empress feigned a smile through her grimace.

Darayavahu said, "I'm told that you were quite the champion."

Artemisia didn't know how to respond.

Artystoneh walked in with a mortar filled with the brown paste and a mug of red wine. "I told the emperor how brave you were." The queen handed Artemisia the mortar.

She walked up to the royal couple.

Atoosa sat up with the help of Darayavahu. Drool hung from the corner of her mouth. Artemisia applied the goop to her finger and put it into the empress's mouth. She sucked it off Artemisia's finger. The empress's lips were hot to the touch.

Demokedes came. "Ah, there's my apprentice."

Artemisia detected no sarcasm.

"How are you? Rested?"

"Yes, master," she said.

"Good, because I need your help. The empress needs constant attention, and though the emperor won't leave her side, and her handmaidens are constantly taking care of the blankets and cleaning, I need someone with training to tend to the wound." He opened the bandage.

Artemisia could not believe how horrible it looked. Demokedes pointed at where the skin was pulled together. She was not sure how the wound was held together or how cauterizing it helped. The burn itself must have been as painful as the rest of the surgery.

"So, we need to keep this wound clean. Egyptians are masters at such things. This…" He pulled out a small clay jar from a pocket hanging on his belt. "This salve has properties in it that cleans wounds. I don't know how. I know only that a chief ingredient is honey." He handed the jar to Artemisia. "It's worth more than its weight in gold. We don't get much of it, so use it like this." He took a stuffed cotton bag and applied a stingy quantity of the salve to it. "Put this bran poultice on the wound. Tie it on."

Artemisia managed to whisper, "Yes."

"Why are you upset?"

"I failed her. I passed out."

"Oh, sweetheart." The physician opened his arms and gathered her into them. He kissed the top of Artemisia's head. "You did something few adults could have managed. You helped me, and the surgery was a success; it happened because of you. We're all judging you, and we've concluded that you're brilliant!"

The words sank into Artemisia, and she began crying.

Demokedes held her for some time, but as her emotions began to dissipate, he asked, "Are you ready to get back to work?"

Still filled with emotion, Artemisia nodded.

"I'm worried about giving the empress solid food, so she's drinking Zagros barley beer, Egyptian honey beer, and Armenia wheat beer. If she can't get full, then have the servants boil a Chinese yam and mash it. They can put a little salt and honey on it but no spices." His voice deepened. "Definitely no pepper."

Artemisia nodded.

"She has fever. Keep her head cool. Damp cloths and fanning but the rest of her body should remain warm. Blankets will do."

The empress's condition worsened over the next few days. Artemisia spent every waking hour with her. She wiped the sweat from her brow, applied the Egyptian salve on the bran poultice, and helped change the sheets when the handmaidens needed it.

She slept at the foot of the empress's bed, which was strange, because Darayavahu slept on the floor at the side of the bed. Artemisia could not believe she slept inches from the emperor's feet. She couldn't sleep for half of the first night; her mind raced with all the strange directions that her life had taken.

After a week Ariomardus opened the door and gestured for Artemisia to leave the room. When she walked out, she found Artazostreh in the hallway. "I'm so ashamed."

"Don't be ridiculous, Zoster!"

"I passed out before anything happened."

"No one thinks ill of you."

"But you assisted," Artazostreh countered.

"I did, but I also fainted."

"I've refused every attempt by Demokedes to make contact."

"No, you're being silly." Artemisia knew the shame she felt. "No one thinks what happened was bad, except you. Go see the empress and then Demokedes."

"Come with me," Artazostreh half demanded, half pleaded.

"Yes, of course." Artemisia loved the idea of helping her friend.

In the days that followed, Artazostreh and Artemisia took turns tending the queen.

When it became apparent that the empress was improving, Demokedes approached Artemisia. "Our lessons have come to an end. The empress is making a full recovery and will probably live three more years."

"Three? Our lessons?"

"Three's a lot. When such lesions occur accompanied by such tumors, the disease never truly goes away. This is what the Egyptians discovered. My treatment bought her time." He handed her his sharpened dagger. "You show great promise. You should pursue your studies, but you must do so without me. The emperor has granted me a wish for saving the empress. I've asked that I be allowed to visit my home of Croton."

"Where's Croton?" Artemisia hardly noticed the dagger.

"Italy. I'll be gone for two years, at least."

"I'll keep up my studies and await your return."

Demokedes gave a strange look. Artemisia wondered what the look meant. It made her feel like he was trying to tell her something negative. *Does he mean that he won't take me back when he returns?* She believed he didn't wish to discuss the matter further and so left it as it was.

Two days later, as Demokedes said farewell, Artemisia was overwhelmed by a deep sadness. "I will miss you, master."

"I'll miss you too!" He gave a weak smile as he waved.

By the time the empress needed one visit per day to apply salve, Artemisia and the emperor no longer slept in the queen's room. To Artemisia's surprise Iokaste rarely slept in their room, but Artemisia found the bed rather comfortable.

After training with Myron on a mid-March day, Myron led Artazostreh and Artemisia to the palace livery. There he walked up to three horses and patted their sides. "Hector, Paris, and this is Priam."

"They are named for Trojans," Artemisia observed.

"Indeed."

"I'm surprised the Persians would name horses after Trojans," Artemisia said.

"They didn't. I did."

"Why would you name them?" Artemisia asked.

"Because they are mine." Myron's eyes revealed a flash of pride.

"How did you have money to buy them?" Artemisia was confused.

"That's not your concern. Your concern is learning to ride."

"What!" Artazostreh cried out.

Myron grinned.

Artemisia and Artazostreh hugged each other as they squealed.

"Before we start you must know some things. Pinned-back ears means he's angry, frustrated, or annoyed. Let me know if you see that. A high-pitched neigh is an expression of anger, anxiety, or tension. What you want are low-pitched, soft neighs."

Myron led Artemisia to the side of Priam. "The first touch on a horse should always be on the triangle of its neck. Nowhere else." He took Artemisia's hand and led it to the area between the base of the head and the top of the shoulders.

She liked the warmth and strength as the muscle twitched. The excitement was overwhelming. *Women don't ride horses!*

Then he had Artemisia keep contact with the horse and led her along its length. "When you go around his rear, you need to stay close to him. If he kicks, the closeness will take the power away. If you let a horse flex that leg, he can kill you."

Artemisia felt the growing tension as she neared the rear haunch. They crossed behind Priam's tail and then on to the animal's right side, until they returned to the neck. Myron guided Artemisia's hand to Priam's belly. Then he said, "You need to be able to lift the leg. You'll know that a horse trusts you when he lets you."

He guided her hand down to the top of the leg. "Slowly, gently move your hand further down until right before your reach the hoof. Good. Now gently pinch the tendon."

Artemisia could not believe what she was doing.

"It will make him give you his foot."

The horse complied. He bent his knee and lifted his leg until it came up into Artemisia's hand. She looked at the bottom of Priam's hoof and marveled that the large animal submitted to her.

Myron had Artazostreh do the same steps. Then he gave each girl a brush and had them groom their horses. When they were done, he had them lead the horses around by a rein.

Two days later, Myron had Artemisia stand on the horse's left side, close to his shoulders, facing the hind end. "When you swing…don't swing yet…when you swing your outside leg—your right leg—your goal is to get enough power to get over the horse's back. If you grab the blanket, you will just pull it off. So, you have to take hold of the mane at the bottom with your left hand. Yes, there's where it begins. Now swing up."

When Artemisia first tried, she felt foolish for failing.

"Try again, but kick up so you get momentum."

Artemisia felt a surge of resolve. "I'm going to get up there." She kicked off and swung her leg as hard as she could while holding onto the mane. She was not sure how it would work, but she swung like a door on a hinge and found herself over the horse. She popped down right on the horse's back. "I can't believe it worked."

Being so high up was exhilarating. But then Myron had her dismount.

He did this with Artazostreh and then had the two repeat it again two more times. Artemisia felt Priam's back through the blanket and his ribs on her thighs. She felt it was impossible not to feel intimate to the animal beneath her as she sat holding the reins.

When two days had passed, Myron had Artemisia stand on the horse's left side. He put the headstall into her right hand and the connected bit into her left. "Put your right hand between the ears. Good. Now, while holding the top of the headstall place the thumb of your left hand and index finger inside the horse's mouth."

"This is a violation of the horse's will."

"What?"

"How can I justify jamming my hand into his mouth?" Artemisia felt horror for Priam.

"Horses love their riders, bit and all. They want us as much as we want them. At the center of the relationship is trust. He trusts you."

Artemisia reluctantly pushed her thumb and index finger into Priam's mouth.

"That's it, above the tongue...don't let go of the bit. See how he's opening his mouth? Listen before you do the next part. Be gentle; avoid the teeth. If you hit the teeth, it'll hurt! Guide the bit into the mouth, over the tongue, not under. Go ahead."

Artemisia did as Myron said.

"Good. Now with your right hand, pull the headstall behind the ears and adjust it."

Artemisia used both hands to adjust but then looked at Myron, realizing she didn't know what she was looking for.

"You want to see a little bit of a wrinkle on the lips. Too tight and it will rub. Too loose and it will clank against Priam's teeth."

When she was done adjusting the headstall, Myron wiggled it. "It's good."

Artemisia looked at Priam with wonder. She stared into his big brown round eyes. "You let me put my hand in your mouth. You are this powerful creature, and yet, somehow, I'm your master." She patted his shoulder but felt strange about what she had said. "How can I be master over you? Let's be friends, but that's not true, is it? You'll never ride me."

After Artazostreh was done, Myron had both young women mount up. Then he held the reins of both horses, standing between them, and showed them how to get the animals to walk. Artemisia laughed with joy as she ordered Priam forward. Myron taught them how to stop. "I'm going to get on Hector, and let's ride."

In the days that followed, the two princesses would leave first thing in the morning for the stables. Artemisia lost herself riding.

The last Wednesday of the Persian calendar fell on March 18. The full moon was two days away.

"Do you know what today is?" Artazostreh was excited.

Artemisia shrugged.

"It's Chaharshanbe Suri and the second day of Hamaspathmae-daya!"

"Oh?" Artemisia felt like this was information she was supposed to have.

Artazostreh tilted her head. "You don't celebrate in Caria?"

"No." She said in embarrassment.

"We're going to jump over fire." Artazostreh's was overrun by en-thusiasm, even while Artemisia found herself apprehensive about the idea of it. "It's part of the preparation for Nowruz."

Artemisia shook her head.

"This is the first day of the new year! It'll be so much fun! Chahar-shambe Suri is my favorite holy day."

In the palace garden, several pits were dug and filled with wood and tinder. As the sun went down, the pits were lit. Artazostreh and Artemisia stood by a pit with Darayavahu, Khshayarsha, and five of the Imperial wives.

Artemisia had come to believe that she belonged. In the five months she had been at Royal Court, she had received more love and acceptance than the fourteen years prior.

"Empress of Persia, second wife of Darayavahu, Queen of Queens."

All stared as Atoosa approached.

Artemisia looked at the empress's chest. *Two breasts.* She smiled, and to her delight, the queen smiled back.

Atoosa walked straight to the Carian princess and wrapped her arms around her.

The empress kissed her on the top of her head. "We are going to jump over fire tonight. When we do, we will chant, '*Zardi ye man az to, sorkhi ye to az man.*'"

Artemisia translated the words into Ionian to see if it made more sense. "My yellow is yours; your red is mine?"

"It's our way of getting rid of the weakness of the past year, the yellow, so that we might be infused with renewed strength, redness. When that happens, my relationship with you will also be renewed. And all the things that I said to you will be gone. But I want to atone before that happens. Before those things are burned away by the fire, I want to make things right. I'm sorry for all the unkind things I said to you. Please forgive me."

Artemisia buried herself into Atoosa's gown. She pressed up against the pillow, pretending to be a breast.

"That's the one that you made for me."

Artemisia had never been happier in her life.

Slowly other members of the royal family came to hug Atoosa, but the empress kept her left arm on Artemisia, not letting go. When

Khshayarsha hugged his mother, he ran his fingers through Artemisia's hair. And then when the hug was done, he picked up Artemisia, separating her from his mother. He lifted her high and asked, "Does the shore shape the sea?"

Artemisia looked down at the prince. She was surprised by the question. "Or does the sea shape the shore?"

He pulled her back down until their lips met and kissed her.

Artemisia felt lightheaded. She was giddy with delight. But the moment was gone all too soon. Then the realization of what he had done struck her. *When equals meet, they kiss on the lips. For Khshayarsha to kiss me, before the Imperial Court, while being held aloft...that is an unimaginable promotion.*

When the time came for Atoosa to jump over the fire, Khshayarsha held her right hand and Artemisia held her left. The pit was a skinny oval and the queen jumped at its thinnest. The young men, including Ariomardus and Khshayarsha, leapt the fire at its widest to show off to the girls.

When it was Artemisia's turn, she could not resist. She made sure she walked back to where the boys started and took off. When she reached the edge, she began the chant, "*Zardi ye man az to, sorkhi ye to az man,*" and kicked off with all that she had, landing on the far edge and rolling forward. Several of the boys hooted.

Artazostreh came to Artemisia. "I'm scared. Watch! I'll miss, burn myself, and the boys will laugh!"

"Zoster, if I can make it, you can make it!"

"What if I don't?"

"The boys will laugh at you. If you jump the narrow path, the boys will laugh at you. There's only one way that the boys won't laugh at you."

"Maybe I can try it on the side and see if I can make the distance first."

"Zoster!"

Pressured by Artemisia, Artazostreh took her place at the far end of the pit. *What if she falls into the pit? I'm an idiot for pushing her!* But there was no backing out.

Before Artazostreh began running, Artemisia ran to the spot where the princess would land, positioning herself to receive the princess if necessary. Artazostreh began the chant, ran, and then she leaped.

Artemisia was not sure if everyone around her had actually become silent or if she had just tuned them out, but the leap seemed to last forever. When the princess came down, her right foot slipped. Artemisia grabbed her hand and yanked forward. The princess cried out in surprise and tumbled away from the fire. Artemisia tried to play it off as if she hadn't done anything.

Artazostreh stretched her hand above her head and stood. A cheer rose up from the boys.

Artemisia felt the pulse of victory.

Thick, red fruity wine was passed around by Zoroastrian priests. When a person took a mug, they chanted, "Do good deeds. Say good things. Have good thoughts."

After everyone had jumped, the priests gathered in front of everyone. The high priest, wearing a tall, pointed hat, cried out, "Think of the good we have and the good that we do. The empire is at the sacred frontline of the battle between order and chaos."

Artazostreh turned to Artemisia. "Thanks for the help."

The Carian smiled.

"Do you like our religion?"

"Very much, Zoster." Artemisia wondered if she should not become a Zoroastrian. "The fire jumping is competitive. With drinks in their hands and laughter on their breath, people gossip, joke, and tell stories in the orange torch light. And Ahura-Mazda is an example of the good that you ought to be."

"Isn't that what your religion does?"

"No, none of that. Our Gods don't ask us to do good, to fight chaos, to be truthful, or support order," Artemisia explained. "Our Gods are petty and jealous and revel in punishing mortals. In my religion your goal is to be loyal to the Gods and remembered by the living."

"Remembered?" Artazostreh was puzzled.

"Indeed. Let's say you were good, but no one knew of your deeds." A teenage boy intentionally bumped Artemisia in the elbow. She turned and could not help but smile. He returned the smile, and for a moment Artemisia forgot what she was saying.

Artazostreh shooed the boy away with the flick of her hand. "You were saying?"

"Ah yes, if you do something worth remembering, but no one remembers, then in my religion you will spend the afterlife in Asphodel Meadows. It's a gray and dreary place."

"That seems cruel." Artazostreh was confused. "So, if I save a person's life, but no one knows about, I'll be punished for all eternity?"

"Yeah, and if you piss off the Gods, you go to Tartarus, where you are tortured in the most terrible ways for all of eternity, like Sisyphos, Tantalus, or Chronos."

"Well, that seems reasonable. But what if you do something awful and are remembered?"

"If you do something worth remembering and the Gods aren't angry at you, then regardless of whether it was good or evil, you'll spend eternity in the Plains of Elysium."

"Even if you created suffering and chaos?" Artazostreh thought to clarify.

"If the living still say your name, and the Gods approve of you, then you're spending all eternity in bliss. The Gods approved of Agamemnon, and he was a horrible person, but he's in the Plains of Elysium."

Artazostreh shook her head. "That's very strange. Even if the priesthood discovered that was the true nature of Hades, I'd think that wise rulers would make up a religion that would motivate people to do good."

"Unless, of course, the leaders making up the religion are chaos-creating, jealous, vengeful, and cruel. Then they would make up Gods like themselves, to justify their behavior," Artemisia stated, as if she was an expert on the topic, but in truth it was the first time that she had ever made those observations.

When Nowruz came three days later, Artemisia estimated that the food and partying in Shoosh alone amounted to more than all the partying in all of Caria over the course of a year.

The next morning Artazostreh and Artemisia snuck through the halls until they reached the Great Colonnade Hall. They worked their way past distracted guards who were busy bragging about their conquests.

"I fucked Iokaste last night."

Artemisia put her hand over her mouth.

"What? I fucked her the night before!"

Now frozen in astonishment, she did all that she could not to laugh.

"She let out this cry. It could have moved the Zagros Mountains to tears."

"Oh, tell me about it. That is one sweet creature."

Artemisia looked at Artazostreh, and the two silently giggled and blushed.

They worked their way past the guards, reaching the back of the throne. The Great Colonnade Hall was empty, save the two miscreants. In their possession were two chamber pots, two pillows, a heavy wool blanket, two large mugs of mead, and a bag containing beef jerky and dried mulberries. The throne was cut white marble and massive, but hollow. They slipped into the dark space beneath the seat and arranged everything so that they would be as comfortable as possible.

Artemisia slept but soon voices woke her. Courtiers were speaking too quietly to be understood, but she strained to listen. Then she elbowed Artazostreh, startling her, but clapped a hand over her mouth in time to muffle the cry.

Moments later the booming voice of Artobazanes, the emperor's oldest son, announced, "King of kings, Emperor Darayavahu Achaemenes."

Everyone became quiet as the emperor's leather soles glided toward the throne. When he sat, Artemisia and Artazostreh looked up, though they could see nothing. Various men came to talk about minutia. "This road... That town... Those merchants..." Artemisia's mind was like her belly at a massive Nowruz banquet.

Artobazanes announced, "An audience is requested by Ariabignes, second son of Darayavahu, Spahbed Datis, and Marduniya son of Gorbyas."

After a moment of silence, Darayavahu said, "My son, a spahbed, and my brother-in-law come at the same time! My hand shakes in anticipation."

Ariabignes spoke over laughing courtiers. "Father, I've been talking with Datis and Marduniya about the matter of preparing our western frontier against Hellene aggression. We believe it's a matter of time before Athens attacks Ionia or Thrake."

"If we take an aggressive posture, it will create an aggressive response." Darayavahu's voice caused the courtiers to become quiet.

Artemisia was engaged.

"Father, we propose that we send men and ships to undertake an attack against a Hellenic state to set an example to the rest," Ariabignes said.

"Fear is an excellent tool when ruling, but it can also turn against you." Artemisia could feel the concern oozing down through the stone seat. "Is the situation in the west stable?"

"You brought that Carian princess here to help secure Caria, but as you know it is the Ionians who're the problem." Ariabignes seemed eager. "The tyrants have done a poor job of keeping the Ionians content. Miletos has proven to be difficult for the tyrant Aristagoras to rule. He constantly relies on Artaphernes for help."

Miletos! City of my dreams!

"You're suggesting we attack a polis to make the Ionians obeisant?"

"Yes, Emperor." Ariabignes' voice was decisive.

"I'll consider this. Artaphernes has sent word that Ionians remain incorrigible."

Artemisia was thrilled at the conversation, but Artazostreh fidgeted as much as their tiny space allowed.

"How about your brother-in-law?" the emperor asked.

"My Emperor, if the Ionians don't live well under tyranny, then maybe we should remove tyrants like Aristagoras and replace those governments with democracies. Then if they don't like their policies, they'll only have themselves to blame."

Marduniya's solution to an unruly population is to give them more independence! I wish I knew more about human nature! Is that genius or folly?

"The Carians have much autonomy, and Lygdamis has proven an effective ruler."

Father! Artemisia filled with pride. She bumped Artazostreh to make sure she shared in the moment, but Artemisia couldn't tell what her reaction was. She realized then that she was both proud of him and disliked him. *How can I hold conflicted feelings for him? How does Artazostreh feel about Darayavahu?*

The emperor slapped his thigh, startling Artemisia out of her thoughts. "This has been very good. I'm proud to call you family. I'll consider the matter."

When the footsteps of Ariabignes, Datis, and Marduniya had walked away, Darayavahu asked, "Artobazanes, what you do think of making Ionia into democracies?" The emperor's voice was sweet, like when he talked with Artemisia.

"I don't know, Father. You've a child who misbehaves, so you give the child more freedom?"

"Maybe too much control makes a child act up. Well, it's much to think upon. For now, I go to Atoosa." The emperor stood and walked away.

Artazostreh and Artemisia waited until they could hear no one in the Great Colonnade Hall and then snuck off, leaving behind the pillows and blanket. When they were clear, they went to the garden and dumped their pee.

"Oh God, that was boring!" Artazostreh professed.

"What? I loved it!"

"How? How? It was so tedious!"

"Yes, in the beginning," Artemisia admitted. "But when they started talking about Ionia and Athens? That was incredible!"

"The bridge, the road, the ship, the port, the Hellenes, the Indians, the Bactrians...it was all just a mash of gray." Artazostreh pretended to yawn.

"How can you say that? It'd be my dream to have a role like your father's. Each problem is like a riddle. You have to think until it unpacks itself in your mind."

"I'm just glad that such tedium is left to men."

"Really? You'd rather talk about clothing, clean babies' butts, and gossip about which courtier's sleeping with whom?"

"No, all that's just as boring. I want to learn medicine. Leave politics to men. After all, they'll die because of their mistakes."

"But women also die because of men's mistakes." Artemisia could not relate to Artazostreh. "Medicine? You're still interested?"

"Yes, I talked to Demokedes before he left. He said that I shouldn't let what happened change my dream. He said everything worth doing takes hard work."

"Will you find a new mentor?"

"I will, but what does it matter?"

Artemisia was unaccustomed to Artazostreh expressing hopelessness. "What do you mean?"

"Soon, we'll be married. No prince is going to let me practice." Artazostreh looked at the ground.

Artemisia stared at her friend, studying her, as if from her she might find some hidden truth in the details of her face. "I'm beginning to dread my birthdays. Marriage is some sort of impending doom."

Artazostreh nodded.

"Well anyway, I can't wait for our next time under the throne. Your father's so brilliant and sarcastic!"

"Why don't you go by yourself?"

Artemisia was pretty sure she would never go again with her companion. The prospect of going alone was too scary.

When a week had passed, Artazostreh said, "You haven't gone again, have you?"

"The opportunity hasn't presented itself." That was the lie she had been telling herself. In truth Artemisia was terrified to go alone and had been hoping that Artazostreh would change her mind.

"You've time now." Artazostreh looked at Artemisia even as the latter tried to avoid eye contact. "You're scared!"

"Of course I'm scared!" Artemisia felt ashamed.

"What if I go with you? I won't stay. It's too boring, but I'll take you there."

Despite the help, the day was short and uninteresting.

She went again a few days later, alone. And then again. As each visit progressed, she learned more and more about statecraft and stealth. Soon she could recognize when Darayavahu stretched the truth or when he manipulated the petitioner. Eventually she could tell when the emperor thought the other person was lying or stretching the truth. And the emperor had a way of not giving the petitioner what he wanted but making him leave happy anyway. *I want to learn how to do all that!*

Artemisia decided that politics was more interesting to her than riding, combat, reading, or medicine. The details were much deeper than those in Hecataeus' books, and though, at first, she was bored by the details, after a month had gone by, she found them delicious. She spent much time trying to guess how Darayavahu would solve each problem and was delighted when she got it right.

Every time she snuck in was like the first. She could not shake the fear. *What will happen if they catch me? Would they treat me as a spy?*

In late spring the palace exploded with activity. Everyone from the highest courtier to the lowest maid worked day and night packing.

"What's happening?" Artemisia asked.

"We're going to the summer palace," Artazostreh answered.

"Summer palace?"

Artazostreh smiled. "Shoosh's all but uninhabitable in the summer. We spend the summers in Ecbatana. Here, help me." She handed Artemisia a stack of folded clothing. "We can pack your clothes into my trunk."

Before she knew it, Artemisia found herself in a massive line of people. It stretched from horizon to horizon. In front of them were desert Zagros Mountains.

As the royal procession made its way up the barren trail, Artemisia was stunned by the effort put into it. It was built up or cut out to get rid of some of the up and down. In addition, there were seven villages spaced six miles apart. Each was equipped with large kitchens and a massive flat campground. The people in the villages happily greeted the procession as it arrived. They provided food, beer, and wine.

In the high mountains, where the trees had thickened, Artemisia went off to pee. When she dropped her loincloth, she noticed brown blood on it. She had noticed wetness earlier but had just assumed it was some discharge. *Am I dying? I'm dying.*

When she rejoined the group, she frantically searched for Empress Atoosa as her heart sank into her belly. "Can I speak to you?"

"Yes, of course." The empress put her hand on Artemisia's shoulder.

"I've brown blood in my loincloth."

Atoosa hugged her tightly.

Terror filled Artemisia's heart. "What's wrong with me?"

"You've become a woman. You got your monthly."

"But it's brown."

"That's normal." Atoosa became teary eyed.

"Then why are you crying?" Artemisia's distress was only increasing.

"I think of you as my daughter."

Artemisia found no space to bask in the love. "What does all this mean?"

Still crying, the empress said, "You can have babies now."

"I don't want babies!"

"Not right now." Atoosa's face was filled with kindness. "When you get married. But for now, you've become a woman."

Artemisia's panic turned into despair. "I'm fourteen. I'm not ready to be a woman."

"Why?"

"I've seen what happens to women—marriage. I see little reason to celebrate."

"My dear." Atoosa pulled her close. "There's burden put upon us but more joy. My life's good. I've carved out a large measure of power and comfort. I know Darayavahu loves me. My sister is close to me. I've you and my children. Khshayarsha alone makes every ounce of suffering worthwhile! The air is crisp. These mountains are beautiful. You mustn't dwell on the unpleasant. You must think of the good. It's true that many relationships get off to a bad start. But most marriages get better with time. Women find the strength, and most men are tamed."

"So, our role is to tame men?"

"Yes, to a degree."

"Why don't they tame themselves?" Artemisia was annoyed.

"Look at what they must do: war, rowing, fighting, building, breaking. They need their wildness." Atoosa appeared to be shrouded by a light; patience and compassion emanated from her. "Do you know the story of Gilgamesh?"

"No."

"In it Enkidu, a Wildman, lived with the animals and spoke their languages. He was made by the Goddess Annu from clay and water to fight Gilgamesh. The king had been too harsh with his people, and so the Goddess made Enkidu to balance him out.

"Gilgamesh was informed that Enkidu was freeing animals from the royal traps. To stop this, Gilgamesh sent Shamhat, a sacred whore. She spent six days and seven nights with Enkidu making love to him. Afterwards, when Enkidu went back to the wild, the animals ran from him." Atoosa spoke slowly to emphasize the point. "You see, Shamhat gave Enkidu civilization.

"In despair he returned to her, and she taught him shepherding. Eventually, though, she also tells him of the great city of Uruk. He goes there and challenges Gilgamesh to a wrestling match. Gilgamesh defeats Enkidu, but they become best friends in the process."

"I don't understand."

"Men must challenge each other. But that does not preclude friendship. Women, on the other hand, glue themselves to their families and to their communities. When men see a man, they want to fight. When they see a woman, they don't see a potential rival. Women soften men. In this way we can even glue men to men." Atoosa's voice deepened for emphasis. "They must challenge each other and establish who's the physically and mentally strongest amongst themselves. Even civilized men must do this."

Artemisia looked Atoosa in the eyes. "I want to be Gilgamesh, not Shamhat."

"You might become a Gilgamesh, but not if you deny who you are. There have been women who have possessed the lives of men. Sparetha, Tomyris, and Hatshepsut, Pharaoh of Egypt. The first two are recent.

The latter was a thousand years ago, but it's possible. You're a woman. Embrace that. Learn from it. We have much wisdom. Use the power that it gives you, and only then will you be able to become what you want to be. Do you understand?"

"I'm not sure." Artemisia found herself liking what the empress was saying.

"If I give you the map that Hecataeus has made of the world and carry you up into the air on a griffin, blindfolded, and that griffin drops you off in a random place in the world, you don't know if you are in Libya, Europe, or Asia. Then the map will be of no use to you. To use a map, you must have some idea where you are, first."

Artemisia nodded.

A servant came carrying a box. "These are yours."

Artemisia opened the box. It was filled with finger-shaped vascular material. "What is it?"

"It's an Egyptian invention. They are called tampons. The Royal Court imports them, as many as we can. They'll free you!"

They traveled for thirty-one days before arriving in Ecbatana. Artemisia was happy to have Artazostreh on the trip. They played thought games and chased each other from time to time.

The palace was glorious, though smaller than Shoosh. Artemisia marveled at the gold, colorful dyes and meticulous stonework. Artemisia and Artazostreh spent much of their time riding horses or training with the men and the rest of their time listening to the women and their court gossip. Artemisia missed listening to Darayavahu negotiate. She wanted to, but the throne in Ecbatana wasn't hollow.

Artemisia wanted to read, but she had read Thales and Hecataeus too many times to enjoy another pass at either. Ecbatana was a little warmer than Halikarnassos, but to hear people speak about Shoosh, it sounded like an inferno.

On a hot July day, a priest spoke to the Imperial Harem. He stood before the empresses and princesses. Artemisia tuned him out until he said, "Remember that the devil arose from his stupor, kissed her face, and the pollution called menstruation appeared on her. In this way Ahriman transferred menstruation to Mashyana and all subsequent generations of women. Menses therefore is the periodic sign of women's affliction by evil. As you know, a core principle of our religion is pollution. Your menses is a pollutant that must be contained and kept away from others. You yourself must cleanse to fight against the evil."

Artemisia was furious. She turned to Artazostreh, and the two snuck off. They worked their way into the livery. When it was momentarily empty, they snuck out with Priam and Paris and rode west into the mountains and up a forested valley. When they had traveled for some time, they came upon two buildings surrounded by trees. Above, the mountains were arid and devoid of trees, but the valley was lush. "What's this place?"

Artazostreh dismounted. "A temple." She reached down and picked up two dried up cowpats.

"Zoster, what are you doing?" Artemisia was surprised that her friend would pollute herself by touching dung. But Artazostreh gave no response.

Instead, she crouched low and ran to the closest building. Artemisia tied the two horses to a low-lying branch and ran after her friend.

They scooted against the wall and then glanced in through the unshuttered window. A priest prayed at an altar. They ducked down below the sill and waited.

Artemisia whispered, "What are we doing?"

"I'm sick of being told that I'm a source of pollution." Artazostreh handed Artemisia a dried disc of manure. They heard the door open and close. Both looked up over the sill. "Empty." Artazostreh climbed into the room.

Artemisia followed. They began searching. The young Carian was filled with adrenaline. "Maybe I could help you if you told me what you're looking for."

"Incense."

Artemisia looked down at her cowpat, then squinted. "No!"

"Yes. Here it is." She pointed at a tall barrel and waved Artemisia over.

She looked at the tan powder. It smelled delightful.

Artazostreh grinned and began crumbing the dung into it. She looked at her friend and gestured for her to do the same.

Torn, Artemisia hesitated.

"Look, why am I pollution? Because I'm a girl? Look at my aunt." Artazostreh's whisper was filled with indignation. "What did the priests tell her? She caused her breast ulcers, because she was polluted. From what? Fingernails and farts? Then why don't my farts and fingernails kill me? Demokedes told me that the Egyptians believe that we don't know what causes the breast tumors and ulcers. Either the priests are right, or he is. My aunt lives because of the physician."

Artemisia was surprised. "I can't argue with your logic." She began crumbling the disc into the incense. When they were done, they mixed it in with their hands.

Footsteps. Artemisia realized she couldn't make it to the window. Against the wall was a tapestry. She ran to it and stood up behind it. Artazostreh crammed in next to her. The door opened. Their feet stuck out from under the bulging tapestry. Though they stood still, Artemisia knew that the priest could see their feet if he looked.

She listened for his movements and decided that she would make a break for the window if he got too close. He started to approach. Artemisia and Artazostreh held their breaths.

He stopped and was stationary for a long time. She wondered what he was doing. *How long can we go without breathing?*

Then she heard something being scooped. *The incense!* Artemisia took Artazostreh's trembling hand and squeezed it. The steps started again, but in the wrong direction. Artemisia tensed; she knew it was a matter of time before the priest saw their feet sticking out. He stopped again.

The Carian tried to discern what he was doing. *Is he chewing something? I need to inhale, but now it will be loud because it's been so long!*

"Hello!" Artemisia thought the speaker's voice sounded like Myron. She was baffled. "Is anyone here?" The speaker was clearly not in the same room. The words were not intended for them.

The priest turned around and headed for the door. Artemisia sucked in a large breath and popped her head out from behind the tapestry. She saw the priest in the hall talking to someone. She kept Artazostreh's hand and raced for the window.

But Artazostreh pulled away.

Zoster! Artemisia shouted in her mind. She gestured wildly for the Persian to come.

Instead Artazostreh ran up to the wall. She put her hand under her gown. It took a moment, but she brought out a bloody finger.

"No!" Artemisia whispered.

Artazostreh nodded as she smeared the wall with a bloody "x."

"That's too far," the Carian protested as they again headed for the window.

With a jump and roll, they were on the ground scrambling for their horses. They never galloped so fast.

"I don't think it was too much," Artazostreh shouted, out of breath.

"It made me uncomfortable."

"Well, they can eat dog shit!"

As they reached the outskirts of Ecbatana, Artemisia asked, "Do you think that was Myron?"

"It sure sounded like him," Artazostreh answered.

The Imperial Court was excited. A terrible omen had befallen the empire. The High Priest's message to the emperor was retold by Atoosa. "The sacred incense from the Fire Temple of Vafrejin has begun producing a foul odor. It's clear that Ahriman has polluted the supply and smeared blood on the wall. We must redouble our vigilance against evil!"

Artemisia and Artazostreh smiled at each other. But Artemisia saw that they had been caught by Artystoneh. The Carian liked that Artystoneh might have figured out what they were smiling about. She found herself wanting to brag and wondered if the empress would turn them in.

Before Artemisia knew it, they were traveling back to Shoosh. The idyl summer was over. She decided to resume spying on Darayavahu. She told Artazostreh, "I have to do something to break up the monotony of waiting for the day when I'll be *sentenced to marriage*."

The day before her fifteenth birthday was cold. A frost covered everything. But the space under the emperor was warm enough.

"Emperor Darayavahu, king of kings."

The emperor walked to the throne.

"My Emperor, may I present to you Hecataeus of Miletos."

Oh, Hermes! The author of my second favorite book! The man who, with my father, negotiated the surrender of the Labraundians at the White Pillars. The man whom I wish was my mentor is in the palace!

"Hecataeus of Miletos, I've heard many great things about you. Welcome to Shoosh. I hope that your journey was pleasant."

"Yes, Your Excellency. I've gotten to see more of the world." He cleared his throat. "I can hardly wait to resume my travels."

"I'm told that you have written a book on geography."

"Indeed, Your Excellency. *Periodos ges.* It's about Europe."

"Why have you not written about Asia?"

"It's my current project, Your Highness." Hecataeus' voice filled with enthusiasm. "I'm planning to go all the way to Egypt."

Hurry! I want to read more about the world!

"The empire will support your project," Darayavahu declared.

"If it's to your liking, I should like to stay in Shoosh for a month."

"Yes, of course. You could tutor my sons while you're here."

What about me? How do I ask?

"I'd be honored."

"On a different matter, I want to know what you think of your fellow Milesians."

"Satrap Artaphernes is just and reasonable." Artemisia noted that Hecataeus' voice deepened, as if he were about to say something profound. "Aristagoras, however, has had some trouble as tyrant of Miletos."

"I've an advisor who suggests that I should remove the tyrants and allow the Ionian cities to become democracies."

"Oh." Hecataeus' voice filled with surprise. "I agree with Cleisthenes reforms in Athens. He has liberated the citizens."

Hecataeus, Hecataeus, if the Gods are real, then surely Athena or Hermes sent you here to become my tutor!

The next day as Artemisia sat under the throne, the emperor said, "Send for Artemisia of Caria."

Artemisia of Caria! I'm already here! Do I step out or do I stay? She could no longer feel her heart. It beat so fast. *What do I do?* She looked out the back and tried to assess whether she could sneak away. But Artemisia knew that there was no way out. The columns were too far apart. She might get past Darayavahu, but Ariabignes would see her. If she ran she would be heard. Climbing, crawling, walking—she tried to envision every different escape route.

Maybe I can get Myron to lie for me. He can say we were out riding. But what if someone sees Myron here? What if the palace guards say that they never saw us leave. They'd execute Myron! So, I have to be punished. Which is worse? Ignoring the summons or getting caught under the throne? The throne! Definitely the throne.

The emperor's voice interrupted Artemisia's panic. "Now that I think about it, I want to take a break. Let's clear the hall and come back in an hour. Don't bring the princess just yet." He stood.

The Gods must be real! Artemisia counted the steps of all the men in the room. When they had gone far enough, she slipped out from under the throne. Her heart was still racing. She was half convinced that it was a trick and that the emperor himself was standing, waiting for her to make her move.

No one was there. She got past the guards and worked her way to the harem. But just as she got to the main door, Ariabignes came through it. Artemisia thought about running, hiding, or pretending to be someone else, but it was too late. He locked eyes on her.

For a moment the prince stood staring, confused. But nothing seemed to confuse him more than what was in her hand. She looked down. *My chamber pot! I grabbed it out of habit. What do I do?*

"Artemisia?"

"Yes, Prince?" She filled with horror as she tried to come up with an explanation for why she was holding her pee, why she held material so taboo to the Persians.

"I...I was looking for you."

"I see." She realized that she was trembling. "Well, you found me!" Her voice had too much enthusiasm.

"What's that?" He cocked his head to the side.

"Oh, I'm so embarrassed." She could feel her face turning red. "I can't believe you've seen me with this." She allowed herself to look down and let herself succumb to her fear.

"Whatever, it...no matter. The emperor has summoned you. Go get rid of that and come back. I'll wait for you."

"Yes, Your Highness." Artemisia ran to the uric acid-smelling stairs, where the sewage tunnel was, and dumped the pee.

Ariabignes brought her before the emperor in the hall with its regular fill of courtiers. His robe was yellow, speckled with green and white flowers, and trimmed at the bottom and on the sleeves with a thick deep red trim. "Artemisia of Caria, you have been summoned before me to request a wish."

"A wish, my emperor?"

"It's your birthday. Isn't it our tradition that I grant you a wish on your birthday?"

Birthday? Why does he care? "Your Excellency, my wish is that the widows from White Pillars be freed from bondage."

Chatter erupted.

Darayavahu tugged on his beard. "Alas, you have asked for a wish I cannot grant."

More talk came from the courtiers and some laughter. *Are they mocking me?*

"I've already done it. The widows have been settled here, in the Satrapy of Sousianeh, as free women. I've even given them silver staters to restart their lives."

Artemisia's eyes grew. *He didn't enslave them?*

"You're surprised?"

"Why didn't you enslave them, my emperor?"

"What have they done to me? I'm sad that they had to journey here, torn from their homes."

"Then why bring them here, Your Excellency?"

"I wasn't at the negotiations. I didn't choose this punishment, but once it was done, it served a purpose—fear."

Artemisia nodded. She found herself liking the emperor more than she could have imagined possible. Artemisia could hear someone approaching.

"Because your failed wish was so selfless, I'll give you another."

"Then I want Artazostreh and me to be allowed to travel with Hecataeus to Egypt." The words came out without hesitation.

"I cannot believe what you are asking!" The emperor was dumbfounded.

A person walked into Artemisia's peripheral view, but she resisted the urge to look.

"Your Excellency, I want to go to Egypt with your daughter and Hecataeus."

"I understand what you're asking. I just can't believe it." He sat back in his throne and tugged at his false beard. After what seemed like hours, the emperor asked, "Why would I send my hostage and daughter to Egypt?"

"Does the *why* matter, Your Highness?" Artemisia didn't know what else to say.

"You're both dear to me and such a journey is very risky." Artemisia was surprised by the tenderness in the emperor's voice.

"It'll be part of our education, Your Highness."

"You are both princesses. What need of you for such an education? Isn't it enough that I indulge you with medicine, combat, and horse riding?"

"May I ask why you indulge us at all?"

Courtiers gasped and talked excitedly.

Darayavahu raised his hand to quiet them. Then he pulled at the left end of his mustache but said nothing. The man in her peripheral stepped towards the emperor. It was Khshayarsha. When he reached the throne, he quietly turned back.

Artemisia felt his gaze fall upon her. She glanced at him, but quickly looked away. As usual, a sense of humble confidence was draped over him. *He's only four years older than me, but look at how powerful he is!* "Master, perhaps you are sending us, because I'm fulfilling your wish?" Artemisia finally declared.

The emperor stared at her for a long moment. She had tried to be humble in that statement but could not discern if it was taken that way or as arrogance. His eyes looked concerned or maybe stern, but that was all she could get. "How so?" he finally asked.

"It seems to me that you are indulging me for a reason. I cannot for the life of me understand what it is, but your majesty is the king of kings. Who am I to question it?"

He glanced at Khshayarsha. The prince gave a half nod. The emperor raised his hand and then waved it several times.

Artemisia left confused.

Hecataeus, two attendants, three soldiers assigned to him, Artemisia, Artazostreh, Iokaste, Myron, and two female warriors, Nijara and Vadhut, assigned to Artemisia and Artazostreh departed for Egypt in late

February. They traveled by horse south, then turned west along the Persian Gulf before entering Mesopotamia. After three weeks they came to a great walled city. Artemisia was left breathless—*Babylon!*

The walls were faded blue and yellow, covered in lions, and decorated with massive Lebanese cedar gates. Several tall buildings rose higher than the walls, hinting at the grandeur of the city on the other side. Around the walls Artemisia saw a shantytown bigger than any city in Caria. As they walked along the garbage-strewn road towards the massive gate, Artemisia felt as though it was built for Titans. Once they were in the city she was surprised by the noise. The smell of vinegar, dirt, sewage, rotting garbage, and cooked bread invaded her nostrils.

Her mouth hung open as she marveled at the crowded streets surrounded by straight tall buildings. It took one hour to reach its center. A massive palace sprawled to their left. They looked into a canal from stone walls built to keep the mighty Euphrates from flooding the city.

"I could never have envisioned such a place correctly." Hecataeus looked around. Pleasure and curiosity filled his face. "To truly understand Babylon, one must visit. If this is halfway across the city, it must have one hundred gates and two hundred thousand denizens."

Artemisia could not adequately comprehend two hundred thousand people, and she thought that one hundred gates might be too many. But she agreed that the city was massive.

"Look," Hecataeus said, pointing north. "That's where Kurosh the Great came in, when he captured this city!" There, the Euphrates entered the city through massive iron bars.

The next day they crossed the bridge over the Euphrates and exited the western gate. Artemisia was sad to leave but eager to see more of the world.

Eventually they arrived at Halab. It had massive walls and, like Babylon, many gates, but was a quarter the size. In the middle of the city, they found a hill with a ruined temple on top. Artemisia walked up to a man sitting on the rocks. "Excuse me, can you tell me about these ruins?"

"This Temple of Hadad."

"Hadad?" Artemisia had never heard of the God.

"Storm God."

"I see. Thank you." Artemisia turned to Myron, Artazostreh, and Iokaste. "Imagine that. A God who once had such a massive temple, but now it's in ruins and he's forgotten."

"That's all the more remarkable," Artazostreh said, "because the Persian Empire funds the reconstruction and maintenance of temples."

"You mean if Hadad had worshippers, they could get your father to rebuild their temple?"

"Yes, my grandfather made that the law."

"I thought that Zoroastrians believe that there's only one God?" Artemisia was confused.

"Yes."

Artemisia looked at the ruins. "But, Zoster, if you pay for the temple of another God aren't you encouraging others to believe in something you believe to be false?"

"I suppose so." Artazostreh wore of a look of confusion. "Maybe it's meant to say, 'We honor your beliefs, even if we disagree with them.'"

Artemisia was stunned. "I can't imagine any Dorian saying that."

After leaving Halab, they traveled to the Mediterranean, boarded a ship, and sailed south. Artemisia felt like she could dedicate her life to exploring the world.

After ten days of travel by sea, they came upon a line in the land. Behind them was desert. In from of them was a lush wet green landscape. Artemisia could not believe the suddenness of the transition from desolation to swamp. "Egypt!" Soon they reached the mouth of the Nile and were rowing up it. Swallows shot through the air. Kingfishers dove into the water. Eventually the swampy wilderness gave way to drained fields dotted in young bright green crops, farmers, egrets, and ibis. The birds and farmers were dressed in white uniforms, tasked by some ancient authority to work the land.

Suddenly the shore exploded into violence. A great beast thrashed. Artemisia stared trying to discern what was happening. "A crocodile!" Artazostreh and Artemisia smiled at each other as they both pointed.

"A bird got careless!" the captain explained.

On the fourteenth day in Egypt, Hecataeus stared out of the starboard bow. Artemisia tried to make out what he was looking at. Then she saw it. Beyond the expanse of green was a beige plateau stretching along the western horizon. On the top, towering above all else, was a massive granite triangular mountain. It was far away, and yet it was obvious to Artemisia that it was on a Godly scale.

"Is that a ziggurat?" Artazostreh asked.

How can she not know of pyramids? "It's a pyramid. That's the largest thing ever built. It's two thousand years old."

"What? How can something be so old?"

"The Hellenes and Persians are new nations." Artemisia could hardly contain her excitement. "The Egyptians are ancient. Captain, how far away is that?"

"Twenty miles."

"How can I see something so far away?"

"It's large and on that plateau."

Artemisia only rarely took her eyes from the pyramid, which was soon joined by a second one.

A river forked off starboard. "What river is this?"

"The Nile," the captain declared. "It splits in two here."

"I think there is a third smaller pyramid to the right!" Artazostreh shouted.

"Yes," the captain agreed.

They reached a second fork in the river, this time on their port. "What river is that?"

"That's the canal that connects the Nile to the Red Sea. If a person wanted, they could travel that way to get to Shoosh."

"How long would such a trip take?"

"Eighty-five days."

They pulled ashore not a moment too soon. Artemisia was ready to jump into the Nile and brave the crocodiles. After they unloaded the horses, Hecataeus paid off the rest of the ship's fare, and they set off towards the west. In every village children ran up to them shouting questions in the language of the Pharaohs. Artemisia didn't know how to answer and so would replay with random one-word answers: "Caria!" or "Artemisia!"

When they had reached the base of the plateau, Artemisia looked up and tried to gauge the size of the pyramid. An Egyptian in his thirties with two boys approached on horse. They had black curly hair like Persians and Greeks, but their skin was darker, features more rugged, and their eyes were rounder.

The man seemed interested in their party but approached slowly, at an angle, as if to say, *I would like to make contact, but only if you want.* When the two groups reached each other, the Egyptian spoke in Persian. "I'm Horemheb, a guide."

"I'm Hecataeus of Miletos. We were hoping to tour this place in the morning."

"Come, I'll show you a great place to camp. Tomorrow, if you like, we can guide you."

Hecataeus nodded.

Horemheb led them to a place at the base of the plateau. From the campsite they could see two of the massive pyramids and three small ones in front of them. To the left was a massive head sticking up over the plateau; it wore a hebset and a long, braided beard.

Artemisia wondered what sort of people could build mountains of granite and statues on such scale. The head alone was larger than any statue she had ever seen. She looked at Artazostreh to share her enthusiasm.

Artazostreh looked around, her mouth open. "How could people have done this? Gods must have done it."

Artemisia nodded.

"I feel as though we've come here to be humbled," Artazostreh added.

Horemheb pointed to a nearby mudbrick home. "That's my place. If you need anything, come get me. Otherwise, we will be back in the morning with breakfast—eggs, bread, and onions."

That evening Artemisia huddled next to Artazostreh with the fire between them and the pyramids on the other side. The moon shone brightly on the pyramids, and the crackling glow of the fire gave off eerie light.

In the morning Artemisia hardly ate. A woman announced herself as "Horemheb's wife, Roti."

After everyone was done eating, Roti mounted a horse and said, "When you are ready, follow me."

"But I thought Horemheb would take us on the tour." Hecataeus' voice filled with disappointment.

"He does tours, sometimes."

"I don't understand." Hecataeus seemed baffled.

"He's knowledgeable enough." Roti shrugged.

Artemisia understood Hecataeus' confusion. She too had been expecting that Horemheb would guide them. But she was thrilled by the idea of a female guide.

"Shall we start?" Roti asked.

Slowly the group made its way up a causeway bisecting the cliff and reached the base of the massive pyramid. "This is the Pyramid of Khufu," Roti began. "It's the largest pyramid. It was built 2,200 years ago with volunteer workers. Khufu intended for the pyramid to be a devise for all his people to defeat death."

"Do you mean because their fame would be so great?" Artemisia asked.

Roti seemed confused. "No, it's a machine that takes us to the afterlife."

"Truly?" Artemisia was excited. "Does it work?"

"I believe so. Inside, there's a room that cannot be accessed. It was built sealed in. That room contains the most important pieces of the machine."

"Can we go to it?"

"No. I mean it was built closed off. Only a tiny few of us retain the knowledge of its existence, but none of us know where it is."

As they got closer, Artemisia realized she could not fully comprehend the size of the pyramid. "Can we go inside?"

"We can!" Roti answered. They left the horses with Roti's son on the north side. She handed out unlit troches, and then they climbed a roughhewn staircase. "This was made by thieves."

Artemisia saw what appeared to be a blocked-off entrance and then to the right of that, a cave. They went into the cave, where Roti took the time to light the five torches. "We have to move through the pyramid before the torches run out."

They walked through a left-curving cave until they reached a hall-way with stairs leading down and a ramp leading up. "There is a false tomb down there, but we don't have time to go to it before the torches are finished." They climbed up.

Artemisia realized that the torchlight didn't reach the ceiling. "How high is this room?"

"Tall. It's difficult to know why this room is so tall."

They climbed a ramp high into the pyramid. Roti's voice penetrated the darkness. "You are going to have to crawl on all fours to get through from here."

Soon Artemisia was in an undecorated room. There were two small holes in the sides and an empty sarcophagus with a smashed lid. She ran to it, hoping to see the Pharaoh. "He's not here!"

"Yes, this is where Khufu was laid to begin the journey to the after-life, but thieves broke in and stole his body."

"How horrible! But to think that we are in the middle of a pyramid and that such a thing could be built! How much money did it cost?"

"There was no money back then. We didn't have horses either. Egyptians built all of this with their backs, without slavery, and by no other incentive than to make their communities great!"

Artemisia was stunned. *How can that be? What does this mean about my people? We have no human-made mountains? What do we ever do solely for the benefit of our community? If I ever become queen, I'm going to change that!*

The next morning, they settled their debt to Roti and said their farewells before heading off towards Memphis. From there they took a felucca up the Nile to Waset. As they reached the ancient capital, Artemisia cried out, "Can it be that there is a place even more remarkable than the pyramids and Memphis!"

They went straight to a massive temple complex. Leading from the dock to the gate was an avenue lined by ram-headed sphinxes. Artemi-sia calculated that the outer wall was over half a mile long. As they entered the compound she saw that there was a massive temple within. "We're like bugs!" Artemisia said to Myron and Artazostreh.

They walked through the pylons into a large courtyard. Several priests walked with shaved heads and one wore a long, flowing leopard skin. Two turned and walked towards their group. "Welcome to Waset."

"Thank you," replied Hecataeus.

"Where are you from?"

"Ionia," he answered.

Artazostreh added, "I am Persian."

"I'm from Caria," Artemisia said.

"Welcome. What brings you to Egypt?"

"We're travelers who seek to know the world," Hecataeus said.

"Egypt's the mother of the universe."

"I don't think that there's one amongst us who'd dispute that," Artemisia agreed.

The priest took them to a place where the walls were painted in vibrant red, blue, yellow, black, and green. Above their heads was a partially collapsed roof. She intended to ask about its age, but Hecataeus controlled the conversation.

Artemisia tuned him out and began studying the images of the Gods on her own. Between them were hieroglyphs that she wanted translated. "Are these instructions or prayers?" She got no answer and so tried to discern their meanings from their appearance. Finally, she turned back toward Hecataeus and the priest, hoping to find a way to break Hecataeus' continuous chattering.

"That's complicated. Erechtheus the king of Athens had a daughter, Creusa. She mated with Apollo and gave birth to Ion. However, she didn't want the child and so abandoned him. Apollo had the child saved. Then the Oracle of Delphi told Xuthus, King of the Peloponnesus and son of Hellen, that the next child he came across would be his."

"Helen of Troy?"

"No, Hellen the son of Deucalion. He's the man whom Hellenes are named after."

"Indeed, I'd misunderstood. I thought that Hellenes were from Helen of Troy."

"No, she's a woman. Well, anyway, Xuthus found Ion and thus adopted him..."

Artemisia rolled her eyes. *Did we come all the way to Egypt so that you could go on and on about the Hellenes?* Normally such a story would have kept her attention, but at that moment, she wanted to know about Egypt. *How could anyone care about the Aegean when standing in this temple! It's like the ant telling me his life story.* She went back to staring at the walls, looking for clues.

Another priest walked up to her. "You appear to have a question?"

"I'm looking at something incredible. This winged Goddess, who is she?"

"Ise, the Goddess of the throne, mother of Heru, and guide to resurrection."

"I see." Artemisia grabbed her nose. "The Persian God Ahura-Mazda is regularly depicted with outstretched wings, just like these. He's the God of order, truth, and light. But when Ahura-Mazda is portrayed as winged, he is said to be khvarenah, 'splendor.' In that state it's said that He reflects the divinely inspired empowerment of emperors."

"How do you know all of that?" Artazostreh asked.

Artemisia blushed. "Your father!"

The priest looked puzzled. "Ise wears a throne on her head and is considered the representation of Pharaoh's power. It never occurred to me that there was a connection to Ahura-Mazda."

At that moment, Artemisia was drawn back into Hecataeus' conversation by the priest's question. "Isn't Apollo a God?"

"Indeed, we've several Gods in our lineage. If you go back before Erechtheus you get to Minos and he was the son of Zeus and Europa. And Europa was the granddaughter of Poseidon and Libya. And Libya was the granddaughter of Zeus. On my mother's side I'm descended from Cadmus and the Goddess Harmonia through Polydorus."

Artemisia would have returned to ignoring Hecataeus if it were not for the look on the Egyptian's face. He appeared as a lion about to pounce.

"In fact, if you go back the other way Libya and Poseidon were the grandparents of Aegyptus, who is great-great-grandfather of Danaë." Hecataeus seemed unaware of his audience's reaction to his words. "She mated with Zeus to make Perseus the father of the Persians."

"Your list took you back to the God Apollo in sixteen generations?"

"Yes, sixteen," Hecataeus confirmed.

"You think you have so many Gods in your ancestry and *so* recently?"

"Yes, I see no reason to disbelieve our history."

"Let me show you something." The priest led them through a large section of the temple into a massive room. Artemisia estimated that it was two hundred feet wide by 350 feet deep. It had massive sixty-foot columns.

"This is like the Great Colonnade Hall!" Artazostreh called out.

"Only much bigger!" Artemisia replied.

"Ah, you mean in Shoosh? We built that," the priest said.

Artemisia tried to make sense of his sentence. "We?"

"Egyptians. The Persians employed Egyptian engineers. Shoosh is 185 square feet. It has thirty-six columns. This hall has 144 columns, four times as many, and twice the area. But the columns are all the same height."

Artemisia was astonished. She could not believe that the Apadana Palace was not the largest hall in the world. "When was this built?"

"One thousand years ago."

"One thousand years ago?" Iokaste was in awe. She looked at her mistress and then her face softened.

When they reached the back, the priest led them through two more decorated rooms until they were in a large well-lit room filled with statues. "This is the inner sanctum. Few people in the world have seen this. Your ancestry takes you back sixteen generations to a God. These statues each represent a generation. Not a single one of these statues is a God."

Hecataeus stood open-mouthed. "How many statues are these?"

"Three hundred forty-five."

"Three hundred forty-five?"

"Yes."

"Each is a generation?" Hecataeus' voice became quiet.

"Yes."

"You have 345 generations here?"

"Yes." The priest wore a calm but certain face.

"Not a single God amongst them?"

"No, not a single God."

Hecataeus looked at Artemisia with bewilderment, as if to say, All that I believed is now in doubt.

She felt a deep satisfaction at his humbling and the utter destruction of their false history. "It's as if a layer of itchy, sunburnt skin has finally flaked off."

Artemisia and her people returned to Shoosh eight days before her sixteenth birthday.

Hecataeus stood in the middle of his companions.

"Daughter, light of my eye, how much of the Persian Empire have you seen?"

"Father, we've gone to the end of Egypt, the Satrapy of Aithiopia, as we call it. They call it Nubia. I've seen and learned more in these past few months than all the days of my life prior. I can't thank you enough for sending me."

Darayavahu smiled. "Hecataeus, what of your experience?"

"King of Kings, I'm humbled." Hecataeus was almost whispering as if revealing a secret. "The things we've seen are bewildering—"

"I went to Egypt the first time as soldier with the army of Emperor Cambyse II in twenty-six years ago," Darayavahu interrupted. "When I became emperor three years later…" He raised a hand. "Bah! Revolts everywhere. The empire was unraveling! I fought here and there and there for two years, and then I returned to Egypt and put down the rebel Petubastis III. Can you believe that was twenty-one years ago? I'm sure little has changed, but you've seen things that I didn't. Tell me the details."

Hecataeus gave a summary of the expedition.

Artemisia was frustrated listening to the historian. *He left out too much! And bragged too much!*

"You'll write a book?"

"Yes, I've organized most of my notes already."

"I want a copy for the Imperial Library," Darayavahu declared.

"Of course, Your Highness."

Then the emperor turned to Artemisia. "What's your impression of Egypt and the land between?"

Finally! "Your Majesty, I can't comprehend what I've seen. Persians and Hellenes measure time in decades. Egyptians measure time in millennia. Persians build lovely palaces that command empires using Egyptian engineers. Egyptians build monuments to the Gods that command the cosmos. There was a place far in the south, fourteen days up from Waset, in Aithiopia: The Temple of Ramesses, beloved of Amun. In front of it are four statues of Ramses II sitting on a throne. Each faces the east to receive the rising sun. Each is sixty-five feet tall.

"So great is Egypt that such a monument was built 750 years ago and on such a scale that though it is buried to its knees, it towers above everything outside of Egypt. The only wonders outside of Egypt that compare are this palace, its sister in Ecbatana, the city of Babylon, the ziggurats of Sousianeh, and the Hanging Gardens of Nineveh."

Darayavahu opened his mouth. Artemisia stopped speaking. "You're right to view Egypt that way. Cambyse II took Egypt, and I retook it, not because Egypt was weak, but because Egypt was vulnerable. I've spent much money developing Egypt and intend for my successors to remain Pharaoh of Egypt, not because doing so makes us powerful, but because Egypt frightens me. Either Persia or Egypt will rule the world. If we rule Egypt, then Persia rules the world."

Artemisia thought the logic infallible.

The emperor turned to the historian. "Hecataeus, I've decided to grant you a wish."

"I should like to have Artemisia's notes."

"What!" Artemisia cried out. "You're stealing my notes! You said it without hesitation, as if you were preparing for such an opportunity!" She stared at the emperor, wondering if he would give her an out.

"It'll make my book better, Your Majesty."

The emperor took hold of his long beard. "I'll grant it."

Darayavahu turned to Artemisia. "It's your sixteenth birthday. As is my custom, I grant you a wish."

Artemisia pounced. "King of Kings, I request that you order Hecataeus to swear an oath of allegiance to me."

Hecataeus snapped his head to look at her. She could see it in her peripheral vision. Several courtiers gasped. Darayavahu slapped his thigh. Khshayarsha and Artazostreh laughed out loud. And Iokaste cried out, "Oh Zeus!"

Artemisia resisted the urge to look around or to reveal any emotion.

"Again, you've been granted a wish for anything in my realm. You could've asked to become the Queen of Amyrgioi or to take possession of the thirty-five-foot-tall statue you saw in Memphis, but instead you ask that I make Hecataeus your servant."

"Your Highness, if you had wanted me to become the Queen of Amyrgioi, then you'd have crowned me already. And though my heart desires some great monument in Egypt, I dare not challenge their Gods. I'm not asking for Hecataeus' servitude. I can't imagine how reducing a man, such as this, to servitude could serve anything but evil. Yet if Hecataeus will own my notes, my ideas, and make them part of his book, then I should get something in return. I don't think it's any serious risk for him. I'm most likely going to spend the rest of my days in this court, removed from Aegean politics. Even if I return, he will be in the Satrapy of Lydia, and I'll be in Caria. This is almost certainly a symbolic gesture."

"So be it!" the emperor proclaimed. Hecataeus opened his mouth to protest, but Darayavahu raised a hand. "Hecataeus of Miletos, kneel before Artemisia."

The historian wore a look of shock and humiliation, but he obliged. He turned his back on the emperor to kneel but hesitated, waiting for a courtier to clarify whether it was one or both knees. With the flash of a single finger from Khshayarsha, Hecataeus knelt before the sixteen-year-old.

The prince stepped up to the two and said, "I, Hecataeus of Miletos."

"I, Hecataeus of Miletos."

"Swear before Ahura-Mazda, the King of Kings, the Prince of Persia, the Court of Shoosh, and the God Apollo, my fealty to Artemisia of Caria, Princess of the Carians, in all matters lawful, good, and in compliance with the will of the Emperor and his Prince."

When the oath was said, Khshayarsha added, "Arise, Hecataeus of Miletos."

Later that evening Artazostreh retold the story to Artystoneh and Atoosa, laughing hard the whole time.

When two months had passed, Artemisia watched Hecataeus leave. Though she had humbled him before the Imperial Court, she was still angry that he stole her notes.

In April Ariabignes, Datis, and Marduniya reappeared before the emperor. Artemisia was in her hiding place. "I've sent the men and ships that Artaphernes requested."

Ariabignes spoke, "Father, I've reconsidered the matter, and there's still time to retract your orders. Fast horses could reach them. I fear that we'll provoke the Hellenes."

"Have you navigated east?"

"I think that we've made a mistake," Ariabignes' voice faltered.

"You've advocated for this course of action for two years. Now that I've finally accepted, you'd have me send fast horses to stop them?"

"Why throw stones at the hornet nest?"

"You're like a bride before her wedding. I'm not retracting the orders." An awkward silence followed. "Aristagoras will lead the men against Naxos as planned. But before we adjourn, there's one more issue. Marduniya, you'll marry Artazostreh."

Artemisia wanted to jump out and plead with the emperor. She wanted to run and warn her friend, but instead she froze. *I have to breathe. Breathe. They're not asking her. It's like she's not a person.*

She's a thing to be given away. A thing like me.

The meeting continued, but Artemisia heard nothing. It was all she could do to keep herself confined to that small space beneath the emperor's butt.

"I'm to be married to Marduniya!"

"Yes."

"I hate that guy. I feel nothing for him."

Artemisia wrapped her arms around Artazostreh.

"Why don't I get a say?"

"We should run away," Artemisia said. "Myron would come with us. He'd do anything for us."

"And become what?"

"We could join the first group of goat herders we find. If they have handsome men, that is. Why not? We would be freer than we are as princesses!"

"Oh, Artemisia. Why couldn't you have been a man? You could marry me."

Artemisia was struck by implications. "But if I was a man, then you would not now love me. How'd I be any different from Marduniya?"

"You mean if you were a man, you wouldn't be who you are?"

Artemisia shook her head. "I don't think so."

The two cried until they fell asleep.

Artemisia and Iokaste walked to the dining area. They saw Marduniya with two members of his entourage. He approached. "Artemisia, I'm to wed Artazostreh."

Artemisia stood, mouth open. She was not surprised, of course, but she didn't know how to react. Was she supposed to feign surprise and be sad or feign surprise and pretend to have joy? Or was she supposed to reveal her true emotions? Her indecision settled on a look of confusion.

"I've come up with the best imaginable wedding present—you."

"Me?"

"Indeed, the two of you are inseparable."

"I—"

"I want Artazostreh to be happy."

For a moment Artemisia's heart lightened. "Happiness is good."

"I'm going to ask the emperor for you."

"For what?"

"To make you my second wife." With that he left.

Artemisia stood in terror for a long moment. Then slowly she looked at Iokaste, hoping she had an answer, but all the handmaiden managed was a frown.

Before the wedding Iokaste came to Artemisia with a beautiful Egyptian linen gown. It was white and elegant. "Try this on."

"I could never fit in something you own."

"I got it for you."

Artemisia undressed and pulled the gown over her head. It was thin and felt cool on her skin. She looked down and declared, "I love it!"

"Good, you have your gown for the wedding."

"Gown to be married in?" Artemisia's heart raced, thinking perhaps Iokaste knew that Marduniya had gotten the emperor to give her to him.

"No, silly! Well, not as far as I know."

That evening, when she walked into the hall, several men glared at her. She was surprised but shrugged it off. She approached Artazostreh, and on the way three more men glared at her. She looked herself up and down to see if maybe something was wrong but found nothing.

When she reached the wedding couple, Marduniya gave her the same look. It was too much. Artemisia turned to ask Iokaste what was happening. When she did, she made eye contact with Ariabignes. He too gave her that look. She was no longer sure it was a glare. It was something else. It made her feel vulnerable, dirty, and exposed. She imagined it was the look that a leopard gave a deer.

She liked Ariabignes but felt betrayed. She saw herself through his eyes, no longer deserving care, but rather something to be consumed.

Artemisia fled back to the harem's quarters. She could hear feet behind her but resisted looking back. Once in her room, she shut the door. It opened as she landed on the bed. A gentle hand lay on her back. It caressed her while she lay in the bed. Artemisia rolled over to see who it was. To her surprise it was Iokaste.

Artemisia sat up. "Why are you here?"

"I wanted to talk you through this."

"Since when do you care?" Artemisia hissed.

"I don't know," Iokaste said, breaking eye contact.

"I never meant to make you too feel powerless," Artemisia said.

"I know." She looked relieved, as if a weight had been lifted off. "But I intended to make you feel powerless."

"What?" Artemisia felt more betrayal. "Vengeance?"

"No, you're a woman and don't know it."

"I thought that happened when I got my period. Everyone keeps telling me."

"Ah, but now your breasts are coming in."

Artemisia looked down. There they were. She had noticed soreness from time to time, but hadn't paid attention. She realized that they were bigger than she remembered. Nothing like Iokaste's, but much more than a month prior. "So why did those men glare at me? What have I done?"

"Those were not glares. That was leering."

"Leering?" Artemisia was confused.

"The gown I gave you, it brings out the nipples."

Artemisia looked down again and saw that her almond color nipples were clearly visible through the material. She looked back up at Iokaste, hurt writ across her face.

"You were a fawn until this evening, frolicking in a forest filled with wolves. When you didn't shout at Marduniya and his foolish harem offer, you made me realize that it was time to wake you up!"

"Shout at him? What good would that do?"

"Nothing." Iokaste turned her head in contempt. "He'd have laughed at you, but at least then I'd have known that you had the appropriate amount of fear. That pig was offering to turn you into his rape slave and you acted like he had suggested rabbit for dinner."

"But even Ariabignes gave me that look?" Artemisia was confused.

"Why not? He has a penis."

"Isn't it reasonable that I stay with Artazostreh?" Artemisia was trying to sort out her emotions.

Iokaste's eyes blazed. "You saw the look he just gave you. He's hoping to turn you into his play thing. He's a rapist as sure as vultures eat the dead."

"How do you know?" Artemisia was incredulous.

Iokaste raised her eyebrow and puckered her lips to say, *I know, dummy*.

"Oh, Athena! He raped you! No! What about Zoster?"

Iokaste thinned her lips.

"What about Zoster!" Artemisia insisted.

"She won't enjoy tonight nor many nights after."

"Why? Why? I must tell Darayavahu that he has just given his daughter to a cruel man!" Artemisia filled with despair.

"He knows. It's life. I mean odds are good that neither one of us will end up any better. If we get back to Caria, we'll be married off to secure an alliance. Peasant girls look at us with large, dreamy eyes. They're fools. We're born to be pleasure slaves for powerful men. Our fathers offer us to those powerful men for advantage. So, every day that you're not subject to that is a day you stole for yourself."

Artemisia tried to take it all in. "I thought that you wanted to get married."

"I did, but I've learned too much about the world to be so dreamy about it now." Iokaste continued, "Your goal is to save yourself. Now that you know what's at stake, you've got a chance. Make an appeal to Darayavahu. He has reason to believe that you'll be of use to him still."

"What if he doesn't?"

"Khshayarsha." Iokaste had calmed down.

"Wait, what about Khshayarsha?"

"Oh, you don't know." Iokaste grinned. "So, when he looks at you it is pure delight. You could walk up to him right now, nipples and all, and his feelings towards you would only grow."

Artemisia folded her arms over her chest.

"You'd never need to do that with Khshayarsha. He'd look, and he'd lust, but it'd be the kind you want. That sort of man does not turn that lust into power and rage. He's not powerless and eager to feel power. He's the sort of man who delights in women and really likes them. And he loves you."

"How do you know?" Artemisia could not believe the wisdom Iokaste possessed.

"I know men. I know the looks they give. He would marry you if you asked him."

"I thought that he was supposed to marry Amestris and Vashti?"

"He'll be the next emperor." Iokaste looked Artemisia in the eyes. "You could easily become his third wife."

"It's so much to think about. I wish I were the man marrying a bevy of women." Artemisia felt powerless. "Did this lesson need to be so hard? Couldn't you have just taken me aside and explained it?"

"You would've thought I was a fool, misleading you from ignorance or as a prank."

Artemisia looked down.

"Now you know why the Persian elites veil themselves."

Artemisia felt like a cloud, floating without the ability to direct her course. She decided to trust Iokaste.

Artemisia changed into a thick, brown baggy gown. The two made it back to the wedding just as it ended, just in time to see Artazostreh crying. Artemisia felt sick. Marduniya led the bride out of the room by her elbow. As she walked past she gave Artemisia a pleading look, and Artemisia spit right on Marduniya's silk robe. She regretted it immediately, but he didn't seem to notice and Artemisia was grateful.

Wedged under the throne, Artemisia heard Marduniya's voice utter the dreaded words, "I'd like to take Artemisia as a second wife."

"She's my hostage, to use as leverage against Lygdamis. And then he'll want to use her to cement an alliance."

"I'm your nephew, your brother-in-law, and now I'm your son-in-law. Marrying her to me would cement his relationship to us."

"I'll consider it."

Artemisia could not stop herself; she vomited.

The king stood.

He heard it! He walked off the throne. *I could run, but where to?* Artemisia stayed still, looking out the back of the throne.

The emperor walked into view. *Maybe he won't investigate.*

He squatted. The two locked eyes.

Darayavahu straightened and walked back to the throne. "There's nothing back there. It must've been a cat spitting up."

Marduniya's voice was incredulous. "Your Highness?"

"You know what? I'm done for the day. God go with you." When the last of the courtiers left, Darayavahu said, "You can come out now."

Artemisia wiped her mouth and crawled out. She trembled as she came around the throne and bowed her head. When she looked up she could see a smile between the long-braided beard and the mustache. The steps of two imperial guards walking up behind her momentarily took her attention, but she fought off the urge to turn around.

Darayavahu waved them off. "You're braver than any man I've ever seen, save one."

Artemisia expected to be punished, not complimented. Blurry-eyed, she looked at the emperor.

He stood and when he reached her he wrapped his arms around her. Then he took her by the elbow and walked down the massive line of columns. "You've been there for weeks. What do you think of how I run this empire?"

"My emperor, you're brilliant beyond my understanding. I can't wait to hear your next session."

"The matter of my daughter and Marduniya, however, isn't to your liking?"

"No, Your Majesty." Artemisia dared not lie to him; she knew from all those hours of listening that he could tell when someone was lying to him. "You need to secure Marduniya's loyalty."

"But you're not satisfied with that?"

"No, Your Majesty. Zoster was...*is* a ray of pure light. My hand-maiden was raped by Marduniya, and she says that he's cruel. Why would you give your daughter to such a man?"

Darayavahu stopped walking. Artemisia saw tears well up in his eyes. "You see me as all-powerful, but I'm weak. I've a massive empire that stretches from India to Thrace and from Egypt to Amyrgioi. You'd think that would make me like a God. But it makes me a slave to one thousand masters. I'm hostage to their whims, lusts, and petty ambitions. How many people have died because of rebellious foolishness? I put down three rebellions when I became emperor and I'm keen to avoid more. I know it will be hard, but with time Artazostreh will tame Marduniya."

Tame men! That's what Atoosa said. Artemisia wasn't satisfied, but didn't know how to push back.

Darayavahu looked Artemisia in the eyes. "What should I do in the west?"

"I'm sixteen, Your Highness. What do I know of the world?"

"You believe age matters more than it does because you don't understand the depth of human ignorance. You have a unique way of seeing the world and you've seen more of it than anyone outside of merchants and soldiers."

"Ionians are a proud people. The Milesians are the smartest people on Earth. Only Egypt is even in competition."

"Truly is Miletos so wise?"

"It created a new way of seeing the world—philosophy. And they've already produced five philosophers. Emperor, even Homer is from Ionia or maybe Aeolia! I'd keep Miletos in the Empire for that reason alone."

"How?"

"I wouldn't attack Naxos. I think it would be better to give up on the tyrants and turn Ionia into democracies."

"That's Marduniya's recommendation."

Artemisia nodded.

"What sort of inquiry is philosophy?"

"It's the pursuit of wisdom for the sake of wisdom. It relies upon a methodology that rejects prejudice and explanations that rely upon the Gods. Never has any place sustained such a system of inquiry. Curiosity in most cultures is anathema, but amongst the Milesians it's a virtue."

"I see." Darayavahu absentmindedly rubbed her back. "That's why you're so fascinating to me. You're only a sixteen-year-old girl with no formal learning and yet you've successfully turned yourself into the person whom you wish to be."

Artemisia frowned.

"Why the disapproval?"

"If I can't choose my destiny, how can I make myself into the person I wish to become?"

"When did you learn how to read?" The emperor grinned.

"When I was eight."

"Who taught you?"

"I taught myself." Artemisia said with pride.

"Did your father support this?"

"No, of course not," she said with indignation.

"Yet you did it anyway." Darayavahu folded his arms.

"So, I must fight to make my future?" Artemisia copied the gesture.

The emperor leaned against a column and slid down it until he reached the ground. He gestured for Artemisia to do likewise. "I must fight. You must fight. Artazostreh must fight. I'm hoping that her time with you influenced her."

"So, you aren't sending me with Marduniya?"

"How did you come to that conclusion?"

"Your Majesty would've said, 'I'm hoping that you'll continue to influence her.' And you might have added, 'In fact, you could struggle together.'"

"*Aha.* How many people would've caught that?"

"You. I've heard you catch everyone. People give clues to their deception. You're the master at finding them."

The emperor grew a look of contempt. "I wouldn't waste you on Marduniya. If my daughter's insufficient to secure his loyalty, then you won't make a difference. You're still of use to me; I'll not spend you like silver to a rich man."

"Silver?" Artemisia did not mean to say it aloud. She was upset at being compared to silver instead of gold.

"You are gold in my eyes. It was just a phrase."

In truth I should be upset that the emperor acknowledged that I'm little more than a part of his treasury. "So, what are you going to do with me?"

"I don't know. For the next two days, I want you to stay in your man's quarters with your handmaiden and the women soldiers I sent with you to Egypt."

"What about Artazostreh?"

"She's the ward of Marduniya." The emperor grimaced as if he had been pierced by a spear.

Artemisia was happy to see the pain emerge on his face. *Maybe he really had no choice!*

Darayavahu led Artemisia to Myron's quarters. He held her hand the whole way. It felt natural to her, but she could not help thinking about how little power she had over her own destiny. *This man decides my fate without asking.*

Myron startled when he saw the emperor, but recovered quickly and scrambled to his hands and knees. Darayavahu left without ceremony.

Myron's bachelor apartment was crowded with three times as many residents as intended, but Artemisia loved the gathering. He and the two warrioresses, Nijara and Vadhut, told stories about their time as soldiers.

The next morning, they watched as Marduniya, his men, and Artazostreh set off to north. She ran after them. "Zoster, I love you!"

Artazostreh looked down from her horse. Her face was filled with sadness and her cheeks were red. She reached down with a hand and put it on Artemisia's cheek. "I'm going try to use my influence to protect you. My father will listen to me more."

Artemisia could not believe how broken her heart was. She didn't want her friend to ride away. A part of her wanted to charge Marduniya and kill him. She calculated her odds and then looked back at Myron. He stood straight, emotionless, solid, and ready. "I'll never forget you, Zoster. You'll always be in my heart!"

Artazostreh managed a smile as she withdrew her hand. "And I you."

Artemisia would have fallen into despair were it not for the strange living situation. Her four companions spent every minute crammed together telling jokes and stories. She wondered if Myron liked having four women in such small quarters, but he made no fuss. As the evening wore on and after getting a little drunk, he suddenly became somber. "I've got a secret I can't keep anymore."

"Well, tell it!" Artemisia demanded.

"I swear by Apollo that my mother, Milesia of Caria, was Thales' lover. He died on top of her, moments after conceiving me."

At first all stared blankly at Myron, trying to discern the punch line.

"I don't get it," Artemisia declared.

"Get what?"

"Your joke."

"It's not a joke," Myron said dryly.

"You named your mother Milesia. What are the odds that your mother was named 'Woman of Miletos' and had sex with Thales of Miletos? It just seems like too much of a coincidence."

"The sex wasn't in Miletos. He died in Olympia. They had gone to watch the games. He was seventy-eight, and she was thirty-eight. He'd given up on children and she didn't expect to get pregnant. Apparently, he overexerted himself during the day and then finished himself off during the night."

All became silent. The extra details made the story believable. "How old are you?"

"Forty-six."

"That fits," Artemisia declared as she looked at everyone else.

Just then the door burst open. Myron's legs were moving before Artemisia fully understood what was happening. He grabbed two swords. He threw one towards her. She caught it as Myron raised his still scabbarded blade to fend off an attack.

Artemisia unsheathed her weapon in time to see Nijara bloodied and laying on the ground. Laying next to her was Iokaste. Hovering over them were four assailants. Vadhut was in distress but holding her ground. Myron swung at an assailant, but the enemy parried. Then Myron punched him hard with a surprise left hook. The man fell back.

For a moment Artemisia hesitated, but the fear of shame overcame the fear of injury. With a scream she charged the men around Vadhut. She had seen men such as these; they were from the northeast of the empire. *Amyrgioi?* She swung at the closest one. He parried. But she was undeterred and swung again, this time cutting his arm.

But before Artemisia could swing again, Iokaste reached up with a dagger and cut his calf. He began squealing and dropped to his knees.

Another attacker looked down to see what had happened to his friend. Myron struck. His sword pierced his opponent's chest on the right. The wounded man turned towards Myron, terror filling his face. This proved too much for the remaining two intruders. They pulled back and ran out the door, disappearing into the darkness.

Artemisia dropped her sword and bent down to Nijara. She had a deep gash in her thigh.

"Iokaste cut a piece of bedsheet." Artemisia gestured to Vadhut. She knelt beside them as they straightened out the leg. Artemisia took the length of sheet and wrapped it around the wound. "Pull this firmly, but not tight. I need you to hold it, because it's not meant to cut off the blood. Demokedes was adamant about that."

Artemisia went to see the condition of her two would-be captors. She looked the first in the eyes. "I want you to understand that blood is filling your lung. I don't know how to fight that. You're going to drown."

The assailant nodded.

She tied two bandages around the other assailant.

Myron asked, "Who sent you?"

"I no know. Pay good. We no expect fight girl."

Myron closed the door. Vadhut and Iokaste joined him. Then the door burst open. The emperor's voice came through it. "Is the room secure?"

"Yes, my emperor," Myron called back.

The emperor squeezed in. "What happened here?"

After he was told, he again asked the wounded Amyrgians why they had attacked. They added that they were to bring Artemisia to a village to the east. Darayavahu had the men removed. He looked at Artemisia and declared, "We leave in the morning."

"I'm too excited to ever sleep again." She packed her things and then lay in bed, reliving her first combat over and over again.

As the massive royal court assembled, Artemisia and her entourage were peeled off and sent south. At Shoosh's southern gate, they joined the emperor.

"Aren't we going to Ecbatana?" Artemisia whispered to Myron.

He shrugged.

The smaller fragment of the Imperial Court made its way south. Artemisia wondered if they were going to Egypt, but on the second day, they turned east instead of west. To make conversation Artemisia turned to Myron. "Is it true?"

"Is what true, mistress?"

"You are Thales' son."

"I've told you what I was told." Myron seemed sincere.

"That would make you half Carian and half Phoenician."

"Oh?"

"Thales was from a powerful Phoenician family that lived in Miletos." Artemisia loved to share what she knew. "His parents were Examyas and Cleobulina. They were descendants of the first hero, Prince Cadmus. And he's the grandson of Poseidon and great-great-grandson of Zeus."

"I'm the descendant of a philosopher, royalty, two gods, and the first hero? It's a good day." Myron grinned large.

Artemisia chuckled. "Yeah, but after Egypt we know the truth about those godly lineages!"

Myron laughed. "Oh well, a philosopher anyway."

Ariabignes approached. "My father has asked me to swear you to secrecy."

"Secrecy?"

"We're going to Persia's secret capital—the Parsa Palace. We'll only stay there a couple weeks, but he wants to inspect it. No one on Earth is to know of its existence." Artemisia and her people took oaths of secrecy.

It took three weeks to arrive. A massive palatial complex sat on a raised plain at the base of a desert mountain. The air filled with the clicking sound of masons cutting rocks. Laborers stopped as the emperor approached. *Egyptians!* When the emperor came close, they knelt.

Artemisia toured with the emperor. Everything was decorated with a lotus, the symbol of Egypt. The scenes were brilliantly carved—men in national costume, in lines holding gifts or each other's hands, heading to the enthroned emperor, Darayavahu.

"Ionians! Lydians! Lycians! Look there! Carians are leading a bull!" She followed the procession of nations up the stairs. "Such power and wealth!"

The next day Khshayarsha showed up to train with Myron, Vadhut, and Artemisia. The four put out as much as they could give. It was obvious that Khshayarsha's exertion was intended as a display of his physical prowess for Artemisia's benefit, and the attention made her blush.

While sparring with Myron, Artemisia stumbled, and Khshayarsha caught her from behind. She looked up backwards at him, and though it was awkward, she enjoyed gazing into his eyes.

That evening Artemisia imagined marrying the prince. She was his third wife but fancied that her role would be like Artystoneh—the emperor's true love. Suddenly she felt as though she were being watched. She looked up from her feet to see a woman standing in the doorway. Artemisia wondered how long she had been there and was grateful she had kept her thoughts silent. "Mistress, how can I help you?"

"You don't know who I am, do you?"

"I know that you're a daughter of Lord Utana, but I don't know which one."

"I'm Amestris." She paused to let it set in.

Artemisia knew that Amestris had hoped to get a reaction out of her and so made every effort to leave her face blank. "You're Khshayarsha's betrothed. It's nice to meet you." *How strange that our names are so similar!*

"I'm betrothed." Amestris paused. "Not you."

Artemisia nodded, though she felt anger boiling in her heart.

"Do you know why?"

"No, mistress, I don't," Artemisia said through her teeth.

"Because of my father. He was the one who realized that Gaumata was pretending to buy Bardiya."

Artemisia could not believe that the words could be spoken with a straight face. *Surely it was Atoosa who discovered the imposter, but I suppose she's a woman, so credit must go to a man!*

"My father's the reason that the pretender was removed from the imperial throne. My father's the reason Darayavahu is emperor." Artemisia noticed that Amestris was shaking. "My point, you little fly, is that I'll squash you. It's bad enough Khshayarsha's going to marry that Jewess, Vashti. I'm not going to suffer a third wife." She walked right up to Artemisia. "You'd better take steps to help Khshayarsha hate you, or there'll be a little accident." She started to leave, then turned around to add, "You think you're a princess? You're nothing more than a hostage."

With that she left.

Artemisia was breathless. She felt the urge to scream, cry, run away, and fight all at once. She wanted to chase after Amestris and slap her across the face and bite her arm. She wanted to strangle her. "You might win here, but you'll never achieve all that I will!" Artemisia screamed at the door. "I'll outshine you like the sun outshines the moon!"

"How can I make a man hate me?"

Iokaste looked up at the ceiling, as if to discover the answer there. "There are different kinds of men. But in your case, I don't think you can."

"What do you mean?"

"The reason that men would like you…well, there's nothing that you can do to make that go away."

"Really?" Artemisia was frustrated.

"Really."

"So, my likability is my body?"

"I don't think that you'll find happiness in life."

Artemisia was annoyed. "Why?"

"You think too much. The way you frame your life makes everything seem bad. When a man makes love to me, I feel whole. But you don't look at anything so simply. Everything's unfair. Nothing in the universe is fair! Do you know what's worse than submitting to a man's will?"

Artemisia shook her head.

"Loneliness. The terror of being unwanted and empty. Men for all their flaws will give you attention, and you can live some of your life through them."

"I don't want to live my life through someone else! What does that even mean?"

"You know how you spend all that time with Myron learning how to fight?" Iokaste asked.

"Yeah."

"Well, all of that training, what's it for?"

"To learn to fight?" Artemisia asked, as if Iokaste were an idiot.

"You'll never be a man." Iokaste's voice was monotone. "You are wasting your time. No matter how good you get, a man with a quarter as much skill will use his strength against you and—"

"You're an idiot! I saw the Amazon at Miletos! I have two Amazons in my service! You cut that soldier with your dagger! And I managed to slash his arm!"

"You're a princess. You'll never serve in combat. Your role is to make babies and give pleasure for the king who beds you."

"Atoosa and Artystoneh are powerful and influential! What I want isn't so outrageous."

Iokaste shrugged.

"Tell me how to make a man hate you," Artemisia demanded.

"You can't. All they want from you, you can't deny them."

"So, if I tell a man 'no,' he will take me anyway."

"Maybe. It's up to the man. Who is it?" Iokaste was annoyed.

"Khshayarsha!"

"Oh, Amestris paid you a visit!" Iokaste nodded. "Zeus, that *is* a problem!"

"Why?"

"A man like that cannot be fooled. He'll know. You can't talk to him. He might take it out on Amestris, and then your problem with her will grow. If you ignore him, he will think you're playing hard to get. He will probably just play back. If you overplayed your interest, that would turn most men away, but I think Khshayarsha is the type of man who knows what he wants. He'd probably just respond by being extra loving."

"What do I do!"

"I don't know!"

When Khshayarsha showed up for training a few days later, Artemisia tried to avoid interacting, but she found it difficult and confusing. She realized she *was* interested in Khshayarsha, and she feared how Amestris would react. The princess constantly looked around to see if Amestris was somewhere watching.

The next day Artemisia was summoned before the emperor. Upon being told, her heart filled with fear. "Amestris has talked the emperor into executing me!"

"Oh Zeus, you're so crazy!" Iokaste pulled Artemisia close to her.

"Don't be so worried."

"Why's he summoning me?"

"The emperor likes you. He tolerates you sneaking into the throne room and hiding under his throne."

"You know about that?"

Iokaste smiled and looked ahead as they walked through the corridors.

Artemisia rested her head on her handmaiden's arm. "How do you know so much?"

"Men love to talk, especially if you make love to them. My power is to submit. When I do they tell me all they know. I have information. Information is the most valuable commodity on Earth."

After Artemisia bowed, the emperor's voice was stern and serious. "Princess Artemisia of Caria, I have grave news."

The Carian felt weak.

"Your brother, Pissindelis, has drowned. Your father has requested that you return at once. I've granted his request. You'll leave Parsa tomorrow. As a parting gift, I grant you one last wish."

"If it pleases your highness, I'll keep Vadhut and Nijara in my service."

Iokaste groaned and then whispered, "You're such an idiot!"

Darayavahu again looked surprised as he nodded.

That evening Atoosa gave Artemisia a gold brooch of a lion's head roaring. The mane was made with eleven golden stems linking twelve discs. "It's elegance is unmatched, Your Majesty! How can you part with something so beautiful?"

"I'm losing you. The pain of that is much greater than some silly piece of gold." Atoosa pinned the brooch to Artemisia's crimson peplos.

Artystoneh and Parmys stepped up with an earring each. They were gold, blue, and red discs featuring seven Ahura-Mazda figures, fringed with twenty-eight little lotus flowers. They replaced Artemisia's earrings and stepped back. "Beautiful!"

"If you see Artazostreh, give her my love." Artystoneh's voice cracked.

All the women burst into tears.

In the morning as they gathered their belongings by the horses, Khshayarsha arrived. He led a dark red bay with perfect black stockings and a saddle. The stallion pranced as if to announce, *Surely you'll agree that I'm the most beautiful horse in the world!* Khshayarsha brought the animal straight to Artemisia and gave her the reins. "His name is Simurgh. He likes galloping."

Artemisia's eyes teared up.

Khshayarsha hugged her for a long moment and then left.

She looked up and saw Darayavahu staring from the top of the wall. She felt fatherly love from him. Emptiness filled her heart. "This has become my home. The Imperial Court, my family. How can I part with them?"

"Who knows, mistress. You may return to this place," Myron said.

Artemisia tried to find her voice. "I'll probably never see Atoosa, Darayavahu, Artazostreh, or Khshayarsha again."

Book II · The Oak Throne

The journey back to the border of Caria took eighty-eight days. They turned off the Royal Road, while still in Greater Phrygia, southwest towards the Colossae Mountain. The peak was massive and still topped in snow. At the Meander River, they forded into Caria and began to climb towards the Tabae Pass. When they reached the top of the pass, Artemisia declared, "There's such boundless beauty in the world!"

They came down from the pass to the town of Tabae. It was embraced by snowcaps to the north and east, hills to the south, and an expansive plain to the west. There they ate chickpeas, chestnuts, olives, dried sea bream, and onions. Artemisia looked at her companions and with food in her mouth declared, "Carian food! I've missed it! Truth be told, I'm happy to be home."

From Tabae they traveled through the Idrian Pass. Her father's words rang in her head. "Whoever controls the Pass of Idria controls Caria's interior!"

It took two days to reach Chrysaoris. "This is the birthplace of Caria, Idria." Artemisia felt nostalgic. "Though it is said that Chrysaoris was the first city founded by Lycians, it is here that the Carian warlords forged the alliance that founded Caria. That's what I want to dedicate my life to."

"You will be a great queen of Caria, mistress," Myron said.

The next day they reached Labraunda. At first Artemisia looked at the place with suspicion. She thought of the Battle of the White Pillars. But as she looked upon its buildings and denizens, her heart softened.

It took another day to reach Mylasa, the capital of Caria. The gate was open and welcoming. Artemisia stood before the walls and looked at the two banners hanging. One was black and yellow and displayed a ram's head facing the curly-haired head of a young man. The other had two red bulls on a white background charging each other. "Father is still Satrap of Caria." Artemisia smiled at her companions.

They traveled straight to the palace. When she looked at it, she declared, "Everything in Caria is small. After Memphis, Shoosh, Ecbatana, Halab, and Babylon, Mylasa seemed like a village." They traveled to Tripolyn Avenue and turned left, towards Mylasa Mountain. A closed gate blocked the way.

A guard approached. "Who seeks entry into the Royal Palace?"

Myron's voice was grand and official. "Princess Artemisia of Caria."

The guard bowed. Slowly, with much complaining, the gate opened. Artemisia and her four attendants rode in. After delivering the horses at the stables, they walked to the Great Hall. Artemisia took in the smells. This had been home for one-third of her childhood. *How alien this palace feels now.*

They walked through the outer buildings. They were adjacent to the main hall, and though they served as rooms for storage, living, sleeping, and dining, they also served as passageways to adjacent rooms. "After hallways in Persia, walking through rooms to get to other rooms seems so barbaric." When Artemisia reached the Great Hall, her eyes had to adjust from sunlight streaming in from the numerous windows set towards the top of the twenty-foot walls. "This hall is one-third the area and one-third the height. There is a sort of symmetry is our smallness," Artemisia whispered in Persian to her companions.

When she could see again, she began walking towards the two marble thrones at the front. One was white, and the other was the famous blood red marble from Iasos. Eight of the columns were white, and eight were blood red. Her somber father sat in the red throne, clad in white. King Myrtis sat on the white throne, also in white. The white and red were all so austere that the gray produced by shadows was a welcome break to Artemisia's eyes. She had become accustomed to the vibrant colors in Persia, Babylonia, and Egypt.

A courtier standing next to the throne declared, "Princess Artemisia of Caria, Your Majesty."

"Look how you have grown." King Lygdamis remained sitting, while the other king remained silent.

"I've aged three years and three months since last you saw me, Father."

"Now you call me 'father.' You've become a woman."

Artemisia was not pleased by her promotion. She realized she must not have hidden her expression well, as her father's brow furrowed.

"I'm pleased to see you. I didn't think the emperor would honor my request." Lygdamis waited for a reply, but when he got none, he went on. "You're a gift from the Gods. Which ones? Well, with your brother's drowning…you're my only heir."

What does that mean?

"I'll teach you all that I know."

"Are you saying I'll inherit the throne of Halikarnassos and the title of Satrap of Caria?"

"Yes, of course, briefly at least. Why else would I send for you?"

"I've learned that when kings tell their daughters they've become 'women,' it's because they plan to marry them off to men they hate so that they can be raped until they are fat with unwanted babies."

The hall became quiet. Neither guards nor courtiers, nor Artemisia's entourage, breathed. The king stood. He walked slowly towards Artemisia, putting his hands behind his back. Then he walked behind her, forcing her entourage to back away. Her hairs stood on end as she felt his warm breath on the back of her head. *Will he hit me?*

"Artemisia, we can do this as a king ordering his subject, as a father ordering his daughter," he walked to her right, "or we can do this as two allies with the same goal."

She turned her head, openmouthed, but nothing came out.

"You're surprised."

"I don't know what you want."

Lygdamis' voice was steady. "I want to teach you, but even while I do, let's start looking for a husband."

"Oh, then I did misunderstand." Her face filled with annoyance.

"What did you misunderstand?"

"You said 'allies.' If we were allies, then we'd talk about my marriage."

"There's nothing to talk about." Lygdamis was firm. "You must marry. Forget that a king must be a man. Or that a satrap must be a king. You must marry for the same reason that a prince must marry. A marriage will solidify an alliance. Alliances are what give you power. Marriage gives heirs. Heirs are trained to replace the previous monarchs, giving stability to the kingdom and the satrapy over the generations.

"There are fourteen kingdoms in Caria, divided between four factions. We represent one of those kingdoms and one of those factions. Your marriage will tie us to another kingdom and another faction. It's how we bind the fourteen kingdoms into one satrapy. Otherwise the satrap would not have the power to rule. A weak king will make a weak satrap. A weak satrap will be overthrown."

Artemisia's annoyance built back up, but she resisted speaking.

"If this is to work, you must speak. We must talk this out. I want you as a partner. It'll work better. The Kingdom of Lydia conquered Caria. Kurosh the Great carved us out, liberating us. That was forty-seven years ago. Do you know how many satraps we have had in that time?"

"What does that have to do with me?"

"Nine." Lygdamis seemed to ignore her question. "The first satrap was Adusius. I'm the ninth. In between Adusius and me were seven satraps. None lasted for more than two years. And three lasted less than half a year. Together the seven ruled for just six years! Adusius ruled for twenty-one, and I've ruled for twenty. The instability of 'The Seven' was terrible for Caria. But when I became satrap, I brought order! I'm

Eunomia's son—stability manifests as a man!"

Lygdamis chewed on his lower lip, waiting for his daughter to speak. When she didn't, he went on. "Before me, we warred against each other incessantly. We're so eager to shed each other's blood that even while we were ruled by the Lydians and the Hittites, we found every excuse to field an army. You saw what the Labraundians did three years ago! That's how Carians are. We are Carians, Dorians, Phoenicians, Lycians, and Ionians all on the same land trying to share it and live together. Each nation makes us stronger in their own way. Each nation pulls us apart. But even when we were just Carians we killed one another."

Lygdamis looked his daughter in the eyes. "When Kurosh reached the walls of Sardes, the two warring factions of Caria asked him for assistance. But Kurosh was building siege equipment and preparing to reduce Sardes. He sent Adusius. The Persian spahbed didn't conquer us. He tricked us into a peace deal that lasted while he ruled us. But when he died, it all fell apart. It took six years for me to restore order. I don't want there to be six years of civil war when I die. You're the glue that will prevent that. That's what this has to do with you."

Artemisia absorbed the words and found no way to argue against her father.

"I've built something here, something stable." He turned away and looked at the sky through a window. "The thought of it going away just because I'm going to die is the worst terror. But to complicate our situation, Persia has just lost the battle of Naxos."

"What?" Artemisia was drawn back to those conversations between Ariabignes and Darayavahu.

"Apparently the Naxians were warned. They had prepared defenses, and after a four-month siege, Aristagoras ran out of money. He's returning, even as we speak."

"Ariabignes was right about changing his mind!"

"What?"

"One of Darayavahu's sons had advocated for the attack against Naxos but changed his mind, but it was too late anyway."

"This'll come at a cost. I'm sure Athens will see this as weakness in the empire. In this time of uncertainty, I'm asking you, my only living child, to work with me."

Artemisia was convinced. "I need assurances, Father. I don't want to be crushed. I want to be my own person."

"How about this? While I train you, we'll start looking for a husband, but you'll have final say in who he is."

"I'll agree to that, if we also agree that I'll not be married until I'm eighteen."

"You'll turn eighteen in sixteen months." Lygdamis took some time to think.

Artemisia held her breath.

"I accept, but we start interviewing for your husband during the Boule in ten months, and I want the wedding by the following Boule."

"Agreed!" Artemisia found herself surprised that she was happy about her prospects.

"Though I mourn the loss of your brother, maybe this is Apollo's will. Maybe he wants you, because you're brilliant. He was a lovely boy but lacked ability. With your brother, I needed to find a brilliant queen and hope that he'd listen to her. With you, we can pick a good king, and you can be his advisor."

Artemisia felt uneasy with her father's tone. *To reduce his memory—*

"Ah, I made you uncomfortable. Good. Our first lesson: no sentiment. We must see all tragedy as opportunity." He gave a weak grin. "Go rest. We'll get you and your people set up in the royal chambers. Let's begin in the morning after we eat."

Lygdamis turned to King Myrtis and nodded.

After breakfast they met in the living chambers. A red tapestry with two charging bulls proudly displayed Lygdamis' presence. Several wooden chairs were arranged around goat skin rugs. Servants brought out amphorae of wine, trays of bread, and fat purple and green olives.

Artemisia sipped and greedily ate the salty, bitter fruit.

"There are ten hereditary kingdoms, one electoral monarchy, two democracies, and an aristocracy in Caria. These are divided into four factions: Mylasa, Kalynda, Xanthos, and Leleges, ours. The aristocracy and two democracies are of no use to us. The democracies have no head of state, merely an elected ambassador, and though the aristocracy has an elected archon, he, like the ambassadors, only serves a one-year term. And we're in the Leleges League with Aphrodisias, one of the democracies.

"For purposes of finding a mate, ideally you'd marry someone from the Mylasa League, either the Kingdom of Knidos or the Kingdom of Mylasa. A Leleges-Mylasa alliance would make a powerful voting bloc—twenty-six out of forty-seven votes. Everything you presented would pass."

"Father, I find all this talk of marriage very strange." A ball of dis-affection was rising from Artemisia's bowels, and she was unsure she could fight it. "We've established that I'm cementing an alliance, but is there no way to frame this information without constantly talking about marriage as if it were like choosing a stallion for your broodmare?"

"I don't see how." Lygdamis waited for Artemisia to react.

She stared at her food for a while, then bit a piece of bread and nod-ded.

"The other two leagues are the Xanthos and the Kalynda. They are fierce rivals. Each is determined to get the advantage over the other. King Kandaules of Kalynda has already asked me for your hand for his son, Damasithymos."

Artemisia felt like she was floating. Talk of marriage and alliances was how she spent the rest of the summer, and these were the least pleasant months of her life. She daydreamed of running away, marrying Khshayarsha, and even Marduniya. *It doesn't seem like I'll end up with a husband I like anyway, so why not? At least I'd be with Zoster!*

At the start of October, they moved their court to Halikarnassos. Seeing Royal Island again for the first time in almost four years had an emotional effect on Artemisia. The smell of the sea and the shape of the walls made her feel at home, much more than Mylasa. Her father's voice echoed in her mind, *He who controls Royal Island owns the coast of Caria!*

"What happened to my mother?"

"She was a beautiful Cretan. The most beautiful woman I've ever seen!"

"Father, I know, I know, and you married her, though it meant sacrificing an alliance-marriage."

"And I've paid for it ever since." Lygdamis squinted at Artemisia. "It's why the Leleges League is so weak, but you won't make the same mistake."

"And yet, you brag about being the son of the Goddess Eunomia because you are the state of order manifest as a man."

"It's true, but it's been difficult. Too many compromises. I'm not really the leader of anything. I'm more like the facilitator of transactions my power is very limited."

That's what Darayavahu said! "I really want to know how my mother died. I've no real memory of her. Some vague images but I'm not sure that those are even of her."

Lygdamis became somber.

"Sentiment! No, Father. Remember? There's no place for sentiment." Tears welled up in her father's eyes, but she continued anyway. "All tragedy should be regarded as an opportunity. Why didn't you remarry? Why not cement an alliance!"

"I thought about it." A tear ran down Lygdamis' cheek. "But I couldn't bear to."

"Why? Were you that in love? Is such a thing possible?" Artemisia was incredulous.

"Yes!" her father shouted as he stood.

Artemisia was surprised. "You broke all the rules, but I must obey!"

Lygdamis straightened out his white himation and then sat. "You were eight months old. Laodike was the light of my life. She was in Mylasa when the uprising against my rule began. The fighting was in the city as someone had opened the gates during the night. We fought from house to house and I killed the rebel leader. But his son struck me in the groin. The wound was very bad and might have killed me were it not for my physician. Though I was out of the fight, we defeated the rebels.

"They laid me down in the palace. I heard Laodike's voice. She said, 'Love.' I turned to look at her. Her eyes were locked on mine but glazed over. I asked what's wrong, but she only repeated, 'Love.'" Lygdamis wiped more tears. "I said, 'I love you,' and took her hand. She managed a grin, and then her face relaxed and she drew no more breath."

Artemisia went to her father and hugged him from behind.

"She died when the rebels tried to take you and her hostage. She fought to defend you. My guards got there in time to rescue you, but it was too late for her." He turned his head towards Artemisia. "My injury took away my manhood. It was as if the Gods wanted to punish me for marrying Laodike. They were so thorough that they took away an option of another marriage or more children. Even if I could put my heart back together, I'm of no use to any woman."

Artemisia wanted to talk, to make her father feel better, but she was too overwhelmed by the guilt of making him cry. *To see a man so powerful reduced to tears. How can I have inflicted such pain on him?*

Artemisia spent her days learning from her guards and her father, walking the grounds, and looking out over the Gulf of Kerameikos. She celebrated her seventeenth birthday cold and missing life in the Imperial Court. The Royal Palace of Halikarnassos was comfortable but austere and quiet. And worst of all there was not Artazostreh to get in trouble with and share her secrets.

In late March a ship arrived in the harbor. Artemisia watched it come into the Grand Harbor and pull ashore on the west coast of Royal Island.

As the men disembarked, Lygdamis walked out, his himation fluttering, his arms wide open. The wind brought a feint "King Kandaules of Kalynda, welcome to Halikarnassos!"

"They're here too soon," Artemisia whined. "Father said the Boule!"

"Artemisia, the Boule starts in a month," Iokaste countered.

"In a month and a half!"

The two men were followed by a third as they walked to the castle, arm in arm.

"Mistress, we ought to get ready."

Artemisia nodded. "Do you think that man behind them is the prince?"

"It seems likely."

"He seems pleasant enough."

"Yes, mistress." Iokaste's voice revealed her approval.

Artemisia, bathed, bejeweled, and perfumed, glided towards her mother's oak throne in a new crimson peplos. When she was seated, a courtier opened the door. In strode the two men she had seen from the wall. "King Kandaules of Kalynda and Prince Damasithymos of Kalynda!"

They stopped fifteen feet away and bowed.

Four courtiers carried in two large wooden chairs and set them on the ground behind the two Kalyndian guests. Damasithymos tried to make eye contact with Artemisia, but she decided that she was going to avoid it and instead stared at her father.

"I hope your journey wasn't too hard."

"March trips by sea are always challenging. The air is cold, and the seas are choppy, but we wanted to be the first to welcome Artemisia back to Caria."

The two men stared at Artemisia. It felt like their eyes were burning through her linen peplos. And she was not at all convinced that her cotton undergarment could withhold under such conditions.

"We're most honored," Lygdamis declared.

"It must be nice to be home, Princess?" Kandaules' voice was measured and soothing.

"It is. Caria is very dear to me." Artemisia made eye contact briefly with both men.

"How long were you in the Imperial Court?" Kandaules went on.

"Three years and three months."

"We are pleased to have you back."

"I... Well, I'm... My heart has been in Caria all this time." She was not sure what she was supposed to say and felt dumb for repeating herself.

"You must be very proud of your father. He has completed twenty-one years as satrap and has been a brilliant ruler."

"Indeed, I am."

"I'm sure that Damasithymos will find you most acceptable. You are pleasing to the eye and ear, and seem demure and thoughtful, but I would like to straighten the Meander River. A marriage between Halikarnassos and Kalynda would create a very powerful alliance. We'd be only one vote short of a majority. An absence from another faction, or a well-placed bribe, and we could control the Boule."

Artemisia nodded, though she hated having her marriage constantly put in terms of a transaction.

The satrap suddenly stood, causing the Kalyndians to scramble to their feet and the courtiers to scatter. Artemisia let out a laugh as she slowly stood. All turned to her to discover the joke, but after finding none, Lygdamis spoke. "My people have prepared a meal for us. Let's retire to the dining hall."

Lygdamis walked up to Kandaules and took him by the elbow. Artemisia walked behind them, next to Damasithymos, watching her feet. As the two fathers spoke in soft voices, Artemisia scrambled for something to say but was at a loss.

Damasithymos was medium height and well-built. He had a strong chin but pouty eyes. He wore a proud expression as he began to speak. "What was Persia like?"

"Oh, I... I think trying to explain it could never do it justice. Well, I assume that you mean Sousianeh. In truth I have never been to Persia proper." That was not true, of course. Parsa was in the heart of Persia, but Artemisia took her oath of secrecy seriously.

"Oh, is the capital not in Persia?"

"No, they have two capitals." Again, she lied and found herself thinking, *Three capitals!* "Shoosh in Sousianeh in the south for the winter and the other is Ecbatana in Media in the north for the summer."

"Two capitals, like the satrapy!"

"In our case it's because of history. Mylasa is the capital of Caria, but my father, the King of Halikarnassos, is the satrap. But in Persia it's to mitigate the weather. It got chilly on occasion in Shoosh and a little hot in Ecbatana, but overall the summers and winters were mild because of the move."

"What would we do to avoid the worst of the seasons?"

"Aphrodisias in the summer. No, wait, Tabae in the summer and Halikarnassos in the winter." The two chuckled.

When they sat down at the table, Damasithymos leaned over and asked, "What was the strangest thing you saw in Sousianeh or Media?"

"Ooh, that is an interesting question." She took a long time, thinking through Atoosa and her surgery, the emperor and his wish granting, the ritual washing—

"Do they really drink after making a ruling and then vote again? Then if the decision does not pass drunk, they don't do it?"

"I never saw that. But farting, that was the strangest thing. Persians will hold in burps and farts in public. The shame is so great, I was on more than one occasion in terrible pain and waited for the first opportunity to escape!"

"Dionysus!" Damasithymos burst into laughter. "I've never heard a girl talk about farting and burping." Tears streamed down his face.

Artemisia blushed and looked up at the two kings. They were smiling big at their children. This caused Artemisia to blush harder.

"You've got character!" Damasithymos could barely speak through the convulsive laughter. "I can picture you in pain buckled over. A group of Persian courtiers asking you, 'Are you okay, Princess? Can I get you something?'"

Servants entered the dining chamber. They were dressed in fine cotton chitons. They carried trays of baked fish, stacked boiled red crabs, bread, onions and olives, and cheese.

Artemisia lifted a small red crab and said, "This is what I missed most!"

During the dinner Kandaules and Lygdamis chattered away, but Artemisia and Damasithymos paced their conversation. "The throne that I was sitting in, that was my mother's," she said as she pulled tiny bits of meat from a crab.

"Ah, I see. And your mother passed away many years ago?"

"Yes, she died when I was eight months old." Seeking to change the subject, she went on about the throne. "Well, it's made of kermes oak, which is the very tree that the kermes insect lives on. Its shell is ground up to make crimson dye, the dye used to color my peplos."

"How do you know all this!" His tone revealed that he was impressed.

"I don't know really." Artemisia felt self-conscious. "I've read four books and remember almost everything someone tells me."

"Four books! That's amazing!" He stared at her for a moment, as if he were taking apart her words, and then he said, "Tell me the most incredible thing that you saw."

"In truth there was so much I saw that I don't know how to pick."

"Tell it all!"

Artemisia was shocked at Damasithymos' attention. She had been back in Caria for seven months, and no one had asked her about her time in the Imperial Court, not even her father. "All? Let's see… The pyramids of Giza, that was something! They're basically three man-made granite mountains."

"You went to Egypt!" Damasithymos was baffled.

"Yes."

"Oh, I had no idea. I thought that you were a hostage in Persia, but

I come to find out you were never in Persia, but you *did* go to Egypt."

"Yes, I traveled there with Hecataeus."

"The Polemarch of Miletos?"

"The very one." Artemisia could not contain her pride.

"Where else have you been?" Damasithymos was excited.

"Nineveh. We saw the Hanging Gardens on the way back. Truly spectacular! It's a garden that you would imagine gods would make. The plants…most I'd ever seen before, but even with all their grandeur and the grandeur of the pyramids, I don't think those were the most amazing things."

"What? You must tell me!"

Artemisia thought of all the times she had been ignored. She had Artazostreh and Myron to share her thoughts, but Iokaste and Hecataeus mostly ignored her. She was tempted to tell Damasithymos that the most incredible part of the trip was her friend Zoster. Instead she said, "The Persians have the very impressive Imperial Palaces. Splendors to behold! The Great Colonnade Hall is half the size of this castle."

"What! Truly?"

"Yes, our Grand Hall is not grand compared to the one in Shoosh. We have sixteen columns twenty feet tall. They had thirty-six, sixty feet tall!"

"What!" He took a sip of wine. "Yet you say it as if that too isn't the most incredible."

"You're right." *And you're listening to my tone!* "There were two massive cities, Babylon and Memphis. The former is two hundred thousand people. How big is Caria?"

"Maybe the same size?"

"Can you imagine so many people in a single city?"

"No!" Damasithymos seemed to be truly enjoying their conversation.

"It was humbling. So much of what I am is Carian, and then to see the world and see how small Caria is…" Artemisia opened her thumb and forefinger apart and then brought them close and closer together.

"But as they say, love is greater than truth!"

Damasithymos smiled.

"Anyway, Memphis isn't as large. Maybe it's fifty thousand today, but that's because only a fraction of the city is still inhabited. You can see the ancient footprint. It was once a rival for Babylon. And it has a community of Carians! Did you know that?"

"I had no idea."

"There are so many Carians there that they have their own neighborhood—Caromemphis—and they still speak Carian. They even still write with Carian letters, though they write them from right to left. At first, I was confused. I said out loud, 'Who's writing gibberish in Carian?' A Carian heard me and then had me read it backwards!" Artemisia looked at her audience of one and savored the attention.

"Anyway, in Memphis there was this massive statue, thirty-five feet tall! It was of a pharaoh standing. Only the Great Sphinx and some statues in Upper Egypt were taller!"

"So, these aren't the most amazing things you saw either?"

Someone who listens to me! "No, they aren't! There are three temples that occupy my mind. I saw forty, including a unique one in Palestine. It was built for the Jews, on a massive man-made mesa, by Egyptians engineers with Persian gold. But in truth there were three in Egypt that are indescribable."

"Oh, that's not fair. You have to at least try!"

Artemisia described the Temple of Amenhotep III, the Temple of Ramses, beloved by Amun, and Waset as best as she could. It was obvious to her that Damasithymos hung on her every word. *A man who's interested in the world and who listens! That's rare!*

"What did you think of Damasithymos?"

"He was very charming and a great listener."

"I think that he'd be a good match. And from a political standpoint, he brings a lot to Halikarnassos. During my private interview with him, he gave all the right answers and he's trainable."

Artemisia could not believe how much emotion she had tied up in Damasithymos. She walked around thinking about him. He partially replaced Khshayarsha in her heart, and it made her feel disloyal. *Is love so fleeting, exciting, and frightening for everyone?*

In April a second suitor came. His name was Terpander of Telmessos. He was also handsome, more than Damasithymos, though not as handsome as Khshayarsha. Terpander was Lycian and spoke Ionian with a charming accent.

"I'm named after Terpander of Lesbos."

"I don't know who that is."

"He was a musician. I'll be right back." Terpander abruptly left Artemisia, while their fathers talked in the corner. They lit a fire in the hearth and stayed warm on the unusually cold April day.

When Terpander returned he had a seven-string lyre. He plucked it and smiled, then began to play. The room became silent, save the melody. The music was simple, but elegant. When he was done, everyone clapped.

"Another," Artemisia requested.

Terpander nodded and this time sang:

Under the fig tree,
We did meet
Your curls were long
My heart beat strong
When our eye met
I lost all regret
Until the day
I lost my way…

"What did you think of Terpander?"

"He's a lovely musician and pleasant to look at."

"But?"

"But he isn't smart. I'll hire him to play for me in my court when I'm queen, but I don't think he would make a good satrap."

"Agreed."

The next day Kharax of Kaunos visited. This caused Artemisia some alarm. "Why are all my suitors coming from southeast Caria?"

"It's close to Halikarnassos, and they're rivals," Lygdamis answered. "Though, it should be said that Kaunos and Telmessos are allies."

After some awkward time in silence seated on a couch, Artemisia spoke, "How was your trip?"

"Good," Kharax said.

"Is it true that there is a pass that connects the Kalbys River with the Marsyas River?" Artemisia already knew the answer—the Idrian Pass. She was trying to start a conversation and thought that the strategic importance of Kaunos might be a good starting place.

"Yes."

Oh, dear Athena, give this man the ability to talk! The evening wore on without the Goddess granting Artemisia her wish. Conversation-killing, one-word answers were all she got.

Mnaseas of Myndos was a lanky man with a large hooked nose.

Artemisia found his short stature a little off-putting at first.

"You've been to Egypt?" Artemisia's mouth fell open.

"I have. And India, too."

"India!" Artemisia jumped out of her oak throne.

"Indeed. I went to Egypt on a trading mission to India. My father took some chances on the olive oil and loaded up his ships. We came back with cotton, linen, and steel!"

"Oh, Hermes! You're like Thales!" *I've found someone whom I can relate to! Perhaps if we were married, we could travel together.* "You must tell me about India."

"We went as far as Tambapanni."

Artemisia shook her head to let him know she did not know where that was.

"Past the southern tip. We were 1,500 miles past the furthest edge of the Persian Empire!" Mnaseas cleared his throat. He was clearly proud of his travels.

"Incredible! To have been so far!"

"That's where we got the steel ingots. They have forges which are powered by the monsoon winds."

"What?!"

"The winds create a fire so hot that the iron can be made into steel."

"I can't believe what you are telling me." Artemisia tried to imagine the forges.

"It's true. I saw it myself."

"Tell me what else you saw."

And so, it was that the two carried on sharing tales of their travels.

"What did you think about Mnaseas?" Lygdamis asked.

"He's brilliant. I think we'd get along magnificently! He'd make a good satrap." Artemisia felt suddenly defeated. *I'm not going to be satrap, and it hurts.*

"There's a problem, of course. Myndos is a minor ally with Kalynda. I suspect that Kandaules won't approve of Mnaseas marrying you over

Damasithymos. If we go that direction, we'd separate Myndos from the Kalyndian League to add it to the Leleges League. They're rich, but it wouldn't be a strong move. They'd increase our vote in the Boule from eleven to fourteen, but we'd be far from the twenty-four we need."

"I see. Does that mean we shouldn't consider it?"

"Not necessarily." Lygdamis waved a servant over. The man brought a piece of papyrus and a small bowl. Another man behind him had a small black block and a reed. They put the block into the bowl with some water. Lygdamis took the reed and rubbed it on the block, making ink. Then he wrote "Damasithymos," though it took two inkings. He tore off the corner of the papyrus and then wrote "Mnaseas" and then tore it off. He put them into a small leather pouch. "This can be the list of potential princes."

Artemisia nodded.

Lobon arrived with his father, Lycophron from Labraunda, on a mid-April afternoon. As Iokaste helped Artemisia into her crimson peplos, the latter said, "Let's take care not to let our lips loose on language with the letter lambda in large measure, lest the Labraundians be led to believe us ill-bred."

Iokaste chuckled. "You aren't hating this process as much as I'd expected."

"I'm filled with anxiety. I can't get it out of my mind that we're interviewing so that a man will have the right to sow himself into me."

Iokaste shrugged. "Half of the world is made up of farmers and the other half farms."

"You see my protests and confusion as a rejection of being a woman. I don't dislike who I am nor my body. I'm protesting the notion I must accept a man is going to dominate me. I want a partner, not a master. But having said that, this is all so strange to me because I have a say. I'd assumed that father would pick someone and that would be the end of that."

"Some men are like that."

"Like what?" Artemisia was confused.

"Partners, but I suspect that they're rare. My father is the manliest man I've ever met. He's gruff, his voice is gravely, he has pockmarks on his cheek, he wears his hair long, and he has a beard, but when it comes to my mother, he allows her to rule more than he does. She makes two decisions for his one."

"Why are they rare?"

"What do the Athenians say? 'The strong do what they can, and the weak suffer what they must.' Most people are in love with power and convinced that they understand the world better than anyone else! Such people will take what little they get and twist it. Even a weak man has power over a woman. He can make himself feel less powerless by making someone else lose their power completely."

Ah, there it is! Cruelty comes from weakness!

There was a knock on the door. Iokaste called, "One moment." She folded down the top of the crimson peplos and then called out, "Come in."

Lygdamis walked in, smiling. "Lobon and his father, Lycophron from Labraunda, are waiting for us." He smiled as he offered his elbow to his daughter.

Artemisia was stunned by the beauty of the man before her. *More handsome than any man I've ever seen. His face, his body, his style… Wow!*

Artemisia found herself nervous and looking down, even when she talked. She was surprised at herself. She didn't know how to look at the man. It didn't help that he was so confident and measured in his speech.

At dinner Lobon asked, "Do you know about the Battle of the White Pillars?"

"Very little. I was thirteen when it happened." She left off the part that she was there and saw it.

"I was the commander of Labraundian forces when we took it from Aphrodisias."

Artemisia's face filled with surprise. "You look to be thirty!"

"I'm thirty-one. I was twenty-six at the time. The fight was terrible.

I led men over the wall in a poorly defended part of the town and then took the men through the city, towards the southern gate. The Labraundian army was on the other side. If we could get it open, then we would win. We fought for an hour over that gate, but finally, I personally operated the winch and got it open. I was injured in the fight and so didn't fight in the defense, but I am the one who took it."

Interesting that you would brag about your role in a rebellion against my father.

"Before the Milesians showed up, we thought we had a chance," Lobon went on.

"How was it that you were such a young man and in charge?"

"My father was wounded. So, I took command." Lobon clapped his hands, startling all save Artemisia, who saw what he was about to do. "It was glorious. I look forward to commanding men again."

"Incredible!" Artemisia could not contain her enthusiasm, despite her unease at the betrayal of her father. *Perhaps he's right to brag, but it's a little off-putting.*

"I liked him, Father, even though he was a rebel." Artemisia wrote "Lobon" on the papyrus and tore the piece off.

As she reached for the bag, Lygdamis took the bag.

"Why? He's a brilliant tactician and charming and beautiful. I'm very attracted to him, and it seems to me that having a warrior for a king would be an asset."

"I agree. But that boy is no military genius," Lygdamis said.

"But the White Pillars?"

"He was there. He commanded a unit of Labraundians. But he wasn't in command of the Labraundians, nor did he come up with any plan or open the gate!"

"He lied! But why did he think that he could get away with it?"

"It was his cousin, Leon. Leon died in the battle. The two were similar in appearance, though they were ten years apart. Lobon, Leon." Lygdamis shrugged. "I don't know. It was four years ago. Maybe he thought I wouldn't recognize him."

Iokaste nodded.

"Men exaggerate, stretch the truth," Lygdamis went on. "Men brag. Most of us are cowards but wish we were heroes. Perhaps he really thinks he could have been as brilliant as Leon if he had had the opportunity."

"What a horrid thing to do!" Artemisia felt betrayal for Leon. "He compromised his own cousin's immortality."

Lygdamis shrugged. "Don't be mad at Lobon."

"Why not?"

The satrap took the papyrus piece from Artemisia's hand. "He's not bad, just misguided. He probably thought that what he did was harmless."

"Well, if I shouldn't be mad at him, shouldn't we consider him?"

"No, a man like that's likely to make many mistakes trying to support his mountain of lies. Worse yet, he'll always want someone to blame. You don't want to be that person."

Two days later, Hecataeus arrived by ship. Artemisia hastily dressed. "Father has accelerated all these interviews by a month or two!" She tried to be patient but found that she was too eager. She ran through the halls followed by Iokaste and her three bodyguards.

Breathless, Iokaste called after her. "Mistress, Miletos isn't in Caria. Hecataeus didn't bring a suitor!"

Artemisia stopped and looked at her handmaiden and then turned and ran into him in the hall.

Hecataeus smiled large when he saw her but was caught off guard by her hug.

The anger she felt towards him for stealing her notes washed away. "I missed you."

Hecataeus grabbed her by her shoulders and gently pushed her back. He looked her up and down. "Look at how you've grown. You're a beautiful woman!"

Artemisia blushed.

The historian turned towards the man standing next to him.

Another handsome man! Who knew there were so many in the world!
He wore his chiton in the Ionic style, with sleeves. His black hair was
long, curly, and oiled. His chin was chiseled and his nose hooked like
an eagle's. But his eyes, his brown eyes cut through all they gazed at.
Artemisia was sure he saw straight through to her soul and therefore
knew her immediate attraction to him.

"Princess Artemisia of Caria, this is my nephew, Melanthios of Miletos."

Artemisia was so lost in Melanthios that she almost failed to respond
to his bow with her own. Hecataeus, grinning, offered his elbow and
escorted her to the Grand Hall.

When everyone was seated, a courtier declared, "Hecataeus, son of
Hegesander, and his nephew, Melanthios of Miletos."

The two men walked to the heavy wooden chairs and bowed their
head to Lygdamis before sitting.

"You arrived just in time. We were about to leave for Mylasa."

Hecataeus nodded. "We're most pleased that you'll allow us to attend the Boule."

"Your words will carry much weight." Lygdamis seemed very serious.

"If you wish for us to take you—" Hecataeus started to offer.

"I appreciate the offer, but my rowers need to stretch their muscles."
Lygdamis stood. "Please, let's retire to the dining area."

As the food and drink were served, Melanthios turned to Artemisia.
"My uncle has told me much about you."

"How do you know each other?" Lygdamis gestured to Hecataeus
and his daughter.

"Your Highness, we met each other in Shoosh," Hecataeus said.

"Why don't I know this?" Lygdamis was surprised.

"Father, you've never once asked me about my time in Shoosh."
Artemisia was happy for the opportunity to point out how little interest

he had shown her.

Lygdamis seemed stunned by this revelation. "I haven't?" His tone asked, *Could I really have failed in this way?* "How strange."

"I'm sure that you have been so overwhelmed, Lygdamis." Melanthios sympathized with the oversight, but hearing someone call her father "Lygdamis" was jarring. Artemisia put her hand over her mouth and watched her father's eyes grow.

Melanthios appeared not to notice his transgression and turned back to the princess. "I understand you traveled to Babylonia, Syria, and Egypt with my uncle."

"What!" Lygdamis stood. "You've seen those countries? With Hecataeus?"

"Father, I've talked about such travels to Damasithymos and Mnaseas in front of you, in this very room."

"I was talking to their fathers."

"Again, you never asked me. I wanted to tell you."

Lygdamis appeared to be hurt. "Why didn't you?"

"All our lessons—Carian geography, Carian traditions, how critical the Idrian Pass is, the importance of Mylasa for the satrapy, how to expand trade with Miletos—"

"We get the idea, Princess." Lygdamis was obviously flustered. "Tell us about your travels with Hecataeus."

She began with the massive and endless expanse of farmland in Mesopotamia. When she finished with the return to Shoosh, Melanthios clapped. "That was a brilliant story. So well told that I thought that I was with you. I could see the temples and gardens, and pyramids and ziggurats in my mind."

"Really, did you like it?"

"Oh, very much. My uncle told me some of this, but he left out so much." Melanthios' smile was heartwarming. "Have you been to Miletos?"

"No," Artemisia frowned. "I dream of seeing the city. I've read everything that I could from your uncle, Thales, Anaximander,

Anaximenes, and Cadmus."

"Oh," Melanthios groaned as he looked up.

What was that look! Is he bored with my reading list? Or... is that a look of pleasure? Hoping it was the latter she asked, "What's the matter?"

"I've never heard anyone say that they have read everything from those men."

"Is that a bad thing?"

"No." Melanthios smiled big, his eyes gleaming. "No, it's just I can't believe that you exist!"

Artemisia felt her face burning. She looked away, half closing her eyes, and took in the moment, her heart beating hard. "Have you read much from these men?"

"I, too, have read everything available."

That night Artemisia paced in her room. *I refuse to be frightened by sex. Why am I so scared of all of this?* She stopped. *I can't marry Melanthios. There's nothing to lose with him.* And then she wondered if she had not just contrived an excuse for going to Melanthios. She steeled herself. *I'm doing this!* She rolled out of the window and into the courtyard. Artemisia walked from window to window, trying to figure out which room Melanthios was in. When she was confident of which, she climbed into the room. She heard breathing and wished that she had an oil lamp. "Melanthios?"

She could hear movement on a bed.

"Melanthios?"

"I am."

She stepped softly until she reached the bed and then slowly lifted the sheet.

"Artemisia?"

"Yes." She slid into the bed. The hairs on her body stood as she nuzzled up against the Ionian. She felt like she was floating. Then she touched his cheek, lightly pressing her lips against it. Her thumb found his lower lip. Caressing it, she kissed her way towards his mouth.

As Melanthios started to press up against her, she gently pushed back.

He gave up his advance, and she resumed kissing him on the cheek. With a sigh and dizziness, their lips touched.

She pushed against his open mouth, licking and tasting Melanthios. She moved her tongue onto his. She could not believe how intense the experience was. The pleasure seared itself into her mind. As their tongues mingled, she lost herself into him. Slowly, she rolled him onto his back, laying in him. He was hard and strong and warm. She noticed the wetness of her lips, the ache in her groin, the hot breath escaping his nose.

Will he let me go, if I get up?

She was not sure how long they kissed, but she resolved to pull away and leave. As if backing away from a wild animal, she eased herself off him, slowly. She withdrew her tongue and then her mouth, got a foot off the bed and then the other. He made no gesture for her to stay. He made no attempt to keep her, and she realized how irresistible his inaction was. Every nerve in her body wanted to jump back into the bed. *He's letting me go! Now I don't know if I can leave.*

Her body was betraying her mind. *A man who would let me go is a man I want to keep.* But her will prevailed and she made it to the window and out and then ran through the garden. In a moment, breathless, she was back in her bed, too wound up to sleep.

Oh the Gods, that kiss! She sank into the bed as she reimagined the feelings. *And he let me be in charge!*

Before she knew it, Iokaste opened the door. "Wake up, Princess."

After breakfast Artemisia boarded her father's ship, *The Morning Red.* Her father had named the ship after her mother passed away. She never understood the name until that moment. The sun had reddened the morning sky, but it was also a play on words. The Ionian for morning *proinos* was similar to a Carian word for mourning *proimas.* As she stood there, she realized that her father had done it on purpose. The ship was a memorial to her mother. *How much did he love her?*

As they set sail, she found that she could not get the previous night's mischief out of her mind. She stared at Melanthios' ship for hours.

Iokaste stood next to her. "When are you getting married?"

"What?"

"You shouldn't stare."

"What?" Artemisia tried to make sense of Iokaste's words.

"By now he has looked this way six times. He has seen you staring each time."

"Why is that bad?"

Iokaste didn't answer.

"If you won't answer that, then why won't you marry?"

"I can marry after you do," Iokaste said.

"Has my father ordered you to wait?" Artemisia knew the answer.

"No, I've decided to wait until I know where you'll be queen."

"You've decided to wait…when you don't have to? Does that mean that you want to remain my handmaiden? I thought you hated me?"

Iokaste walked away.

"Do you know the thing in the world I hate most? I hate it when people ignore me! I'm not stupid—you are!" Artemisia took her handmaiden's advice and avoided looking towards Melanthios' ship.

Later as they were passing Caryanda and Madnasa on their starboard, Iokaste came back. "No man wants his prey to surrender too quickly."

"What do you mean?" Artemisia decided to ignore what had been said earlier.

"Men are hunters. They love the chase. There's enormous pleasure in desiring something but not as much in possessing it. And of course, women can't stand men who need them."

"So, I should make myself difficult to catch."

"Not too difficult and not too easy. A man must seem a little uninterested, and a woman must pretend to not want to be caught."

"What? How are those not the same exact thing? And why's that good?"

"I just told you why. We love desiring a thing, but once you have such a thing you can no longer desire to have it."

"I don't understand."

"Thales' book?"

"*Water Is Best*." Artemisia was sure Iokaste knew the title.

"When you didn't have it, how much did you want it?"

"So much that I stole it and risked my father's wrath."

"When you got it, did you still want it?" Iokaste's voice was confident.

"Yes."

"Did you want to steal it?"

"No, I had it." Artemisia was starting to let down her guard.

"So, did the desire to have the book diminish?"

"Oh Pothos! I think I see."

"Now that you have read it, has your desire diminished more?"

"Yes…" Artemisia was shocked at this revelation.

"Would you give me that book?"

"Sure."

"That's not what I meant. Would you give that book away to a stranger and lose it forever?"

"My heart says 'no' but my mind says 'why not?' And I don't know why!"

"If your father had given you the book, instead of you stealing it, would you love the book as much?"

"I don't know."

"Yes, you do! You earned that book when you stole it!"

"I don't think it would be as important to me," Artemisia confessed.

"Something that comes without work, we don't love." Iokaste had the look of an artisan having just crafted her best work yet. "Something that we earned through sweat, fear, and pain we'll love for all eternity, even when our desire for it diminishes."

"You're brilliant! I didn't know you could be so thoughtful."

"Don't get me wrong. I don't care about how the universe was made, what it's made of, and how many Carians live in Memphis, but people, especially men, that's something I'm happy to spend time on."

Artemisia thought for a moment. "Wait, you didn't explain the difference between not wanting to be caught and seeming not needy."

"Women fear men who need them too much. We want a man who can take care of us when we are vulnerable. But usually it's women who do the caregiving. We want to have a man who knows how to defeat a rapist, runs down a thief, holds us when our parent dies, fixes a chair when it breaks, moves the chair when it is in the wrong place, or disciplines a child when it gets out of control. But a needy man will want us to do those things. A needy man is a man who wants to replace his mother."

"I can see all of that, but if the man is chasing us…I mean, isn't that impossible to differentiate from neediness?"

"It is hard, so sometimes it's important to see if we can get him to quit. If he quits and is willing to walk away, then he is exactly what we want." Iokaste locked eyes on Artemisia. "A man wants to hunt. We're their prey, but if the hunt is too easy, if there's no challenge, then there's no sense of having earned the quarry. No attachment, no sense of achievement, and therefore no respect."

"But I've seen you make yourself available fast!"

"Ah, I'm not looking for a mate. I'm looking for some fun. If a woman makes herself available, she can get sex, but she should know that that man won't want you afterwards."

"I'm still not convinced that I see the difference. I think that when I don't want a man to be too eager, it's because I also want to earn him. And when he does not want to be caught too quickly, maybe it is also because he is afraid of someone who is too needy."

Iokaste mulled that over. "You might be right."

Artemisia could not believe that she was admitting it.

Then Iokaste blurted out, "I enjoyed this conversation, but I still think you don't know your place."

"Why does that matter to you so much? Why wouldn't you be happy for me if I don't end up submitting to the will of a man? I know you care, because of what you did when Marduniya was after me."

"Because if you failed, then your suffering would be like mine. I'd feel like you and I had something in common, something to bind us—"

"But you realize that I just might get away with this!"

Iokaste was stunned. "I hate that you're so much luckier than me! Yeah, it infuriates me! Khshayarsha paid you all that attention! Why?"

"I don't know!"

"Because you're so brilliant." Iokaste was nearly shouting.

"What do you mean?"

"You were a hostage of some unimportant part of the empire. The Imperial Court doesn't need to worry about Caria. Shoosh doesn't have a shortage of beautiful women. Khshayarsha can have anyone in the universe that he wants, but you got his attention. Not because you're pretty, but because you're audacious, brilliant, and unusual. I could've never turned the head of a man like that."

"Oh, Iokaste—"

"Dog shit! Shut up! I'm putting all of that aside, but on the condition that you and I finally resolve to be friends. True friends. We'll tell each other everything we know and say everything like it is."

Artemisia nodded.

"No, I want you to swear on Artemis."

"I swear by the Goddess Artemis, Great Mother of Nature, with her twenty-four breasts-eggs-testicle things. Now you swear."

When they ran aground on the Casolabian beach, Artemisia was slow to go to the gunwale. She stared at the numerous ships and their banners. It was a banquet of Apollo heads, griffins, a horned Pan, fig leaves, winged women, lions, four-pointed stars, quails, goats, rams, bulls, Pegasos, and ketos. When she reached the gunwale, she found Melanthios waiting for her. He smiled. Artemisia could feel her ears redden. This in turn caused his smile to deepen. He reached up in a gesture for her to jump.

Artemisia jumped before she thought it through. Effortlessly, Melanthios caught her by the hips, but instead of letting her down, he pushed her back up into the air.

Exhilarating!

The two walked, side by side, towards the town. In front of them, Hecataeus walked with his arm hooked in Lygdamis' arm. A thunder from the planks announced the arrival of horses on the beach. A marine brought Simurgh to Artemisia and then dropped to all fours. She pulled her stallion forward and, when she was clear of the generous marine, mounted.

"You have a saddle?" Melanthios asked.

"Yes, it was given to me by the Khshayarsha."

"Incredible. I've never seen one before! You've seen and done so much. I can't believe that the crown prince would give you anything, let alone a saddle."

"It came with the horse."

Melanthios' mouth fell open.

Artemisia enjoyed that. "These earrings and this brooch are from the empresses." She nodded her head towards Vadhut and Nijara. "They're gifts from the emperor." She was dying to add, *And your uncle—also a gift from the emperor.*

"I've a dream for Miletos." Melanthios was clearly self-conscious.

"Oh, tell me!"

"I want to restore the ancient Sanctuary of Apollo of Delphinios and at the same time build an Agora at the southern end of the Harbor of Lions. Like the one you have in Halikarnassos." Melanthios looked her in the eyes. "And then, behind the Delphinion, I want to build a philosophy school."

"A philosophy school?"

"Yes, a gymnasium where philosophers and their students could freely meet. Thales had no such place. He walked the streets of Miletos with his students following. In fact, his pay came by his students buying him food and letting him spend the night at their homes. I want to put rooms in the school with a kitchen and have the city pay for a cooking staff. Even the students would be able to eat there."

Artemisia stared at the Ionian. "That you've thought this through and care about philosophy is remarkable to me."

Melanthios' look made Artemisia feel respected and liked. She was thrilled.

He asked, "If you could only do one thing in Caria, what would it be?"

"Expand the size of the fleet." Artemisia grinned.

"Brilliant! You would increase trade, influence, and make Caria more valuable to the empire." Melanthios nodded. "You really love Caria?"

"It's my home." Artemisia didn't know how much to share but decided to go ahead. "I could've stayed in Shoosh when my father asked for my return."

"Oh?"

"The emperor gave me a parting wish, anything. I could've said 'I wish to remain at the Imperial Court' or even 'I wish to be wed to your son.'" She felt immediately strange telling Melanthios that. And then she saw an unmistakable look of jealousy. *He really likes me.* "But Caria's my destiny."

Melanthios nodded.

I could lose myself in this man. Why aren't you Carian!

In Mylasa they proceeded straight to the palace, where they were greeted by King Myrtis and his son Bion. As the greetings were conducted, Prince Bion said, "Welcome, Princess Artemisia. Who's your friend?"

"How do you know my name?" Artemisia asked.

"A woman, with a saddle, that horse, those earrings, and that brooch? Surely such a creature would have to be the Princess of Halikarnassos. You're more beautiful than I imagined. Indeed, your stallion's superior to that of Melanthios'." Bion wore a strange grin. "When you were approaching, I thought that he was riding a dog."

Artemisia found herself feeling defensive for Melanthios and found Bion's manner to be indecorous.

The banners from Casolaba's beech were duplicated at the palace, but with several additions, including a scorpion, Artemis, a horse, Aphrodite, a labrys, and Zeus. When everyone was settled, Lygdamis took Artemisia by the elbow and took her to the large hall with the red and white marble pillars.

King Myrtis approached, his arms open. He kissed Lygdamis on one cheek and then held him by the shoulders. "You bring honor to our hall, Satrap of Caria, King of Halikarnassos."

"Your welcome brings honor to the satrapy, King of Mylasa. Your open palace, our ancient capital, makes the satrapy one." Lygdamis nodded to a priest.

The priest turned to two more. They began to shake two sistrums and swung an incense burner. The jingling made a holy sound, and the smell of the sweetgum incense was intoxicating. The senior priest said a long prayer to Zeus. Artemisia wondered if it was wise to leave out Athena and Apollo but suspected that none of it really mattered.

When the prayer was over, Lygdamis declared, "May the Boule begin."

Applause erupted from the forty-seven Bouleutai and their attendants.

When the Boule had calmed down, Lygdamis declared, "Our friend Hecataeus of Miletos has come to ask that we join Aristagoras against Naxos. I'll let him present his case."

"Thank you, exalted Satrap." Hecataeus stood. "Thank you, Bouleutai of Caria. Aristagoras' defeat at Naxos represents a problem for all of the western Persian Empire. First, we appear weak, weak in the eyes of Shoosh and weak in the eyes of Athens. Though I'm Ionian and have a familial affinity to Athens, I—"

"Athens!" mocked a member of the Boule.

Artemisia did not see who shouted.

"I'm a practical man. Our future is with Shoosh and not Athens."

"Athens!" came the mocking again.

This time Artemisia saw the man. "King Lycophron of Labraunda, why do you mock our guest?" She clapped her hand over her mouth, horrified that she had spoken up.

Lycophron stood. "Satrap, fellow kings, ambassadors, I've information that makes this Ionian's words worthless."

Artemisia was stunned. *Are Labraundians naturally rebellious or just their king?*

"An army of Athenians and Eretreans have landed in Ionia. They're marching with Ionia towards Sardes. They are led by Charopinus of Persia, Hermophantus of Miletos, and Eualkides of Eretrea."

"What!" Hecataeus shouted. He turned to Lygdamis. "Forgive the outburst, Satrap. I was sent to gather men and money for another attack against Naxos. Now I see that Aristagoras has sent me here to get me away from Miletos. He knew that I'd oppose any such action. If you'll allow, we should return to Miletos to try and talk sense into my people."

Lygdamis nodded, and with that the two Milesians left.

Artemisia felt empty. *More time with Melanthios would have been nice. Another kiss at least!*

The Boule burst into commotion. It took much time before the hall returned to order.

"King Nicander," Lygdamis called out.

A tall man stood and, using a loud voice, declared, "I object to how our guest was treated by King Lycophron. I propose that we censure King Lycophron."

Shouting erupted, again. Soon men were standing up and waving their open hands at each other. Often, they would get so close that Artemisia was sure they would hit each other. She felt like it was a choreographed dance. Each dancer would execute his move and get closer than the previous but without making contact.

Lygdamis stood and shouted, "Order! Order! Order!" But when none came, he signaled the commander of the guard. The commander ran, waving his hand to men by the door. In an instant, guards poured in and began to wedge themselves between the shouting Bouleutai. After some time, the members of the Boule calmed down again.

"This is a difficult situation, but we must be better than our circumstances. I'm going to adjourn the Boule. You'll leave by faction. The guards will escort you to your section of the palace, and each faction will remain separated for the day. Tomorrow we will reconvene when our minds have had some time to think. Xanthos, you'll go first."

As a child how many times had I begged my father to take me to the Boule? Now that I'm here and see what it is, I'm left to wonder how Caria makes it from day to day.

That evening Artemisia followed her father and Dibikom, the representative of the Aphrodisian democracy, who paced back and forth. Occasionally they would say something, but then they'd return to sipping wine and aimlessly walking.

"It's like following the Meander River," Artemisia whispered to Iokaste.

"Did you say something?" Lygdamis shot eyes towards Artemisia.

"No, Father."

"Why don't you call me 'Papas' anymore?"

"What did you call your father?"

"'Tata,'" Lygdamis said.

"Why didn't you raise me saying 'Tata'?"

"My father was Carian. He chose it. The dominant language in Halikarnassos is Ionian. I don't know why. It just worked out that way." He rubbed his chin. "Tell me what you think about the rebellion."

Artemisia couldn't believe she was being consulted. "We can't fight Persia. Their might is almost limitless. But forget that. If there's a righteous cause, we're duty bound to fight for it, even if it means losing. What's the cause here?"

"Honestly I don't know." Lygdamis allowed his face to wear his confusion. "Aristagoras, the Persian tyrant of Miletos, went to Naxos last year to capture that island. He met a prepared city. Someone told them of the impending attack! Not knowing what else to do, he set up a siege. After four months he ran out of funds and returned to Ionia. Now his brother's leading a force of Athenians, Eretreans, and Ionians towards Sardes."

"Is Aristagoras motivated by good?"

"He's a Persian in rebellion alongside Hellenes against the Persian Empire. But I don't know why."

"I suspect that Hecataeus knew something," Artemisia said. "We should've made him tell us more."

"They've taken fast horses to Latmos. They'll get to Miletos tonight."

"Really?"

"Latmos is a day's hard ride, but they each took two extra horses."

"What's the goal in marching on Sardes, Papas?" She grinned as she gave in to her father's request.

Lygdamis returned the smile. "I don't know. Even if he captures Sardes, it's not like Darayavahu can ignore this."

"What's our best interest?"

"If we join the rebellion and it fails, we'll be destroyed. If we fail to join the rebellion and it succeeds, we'll be destroyed."

"But what does success look like?" Artemisia was confused about how such a rebellion could succeed.

"I can't imagine that he believes he can capture Shoosh, so I can't imagine what success could look like."

"Many of the men in the Boule seem to want to join him," Artemisia added.

"And then there's that!" Lygdamis looked up at the ceiling. "What if we don't join but then have a rebellion of our own?"

"This is a riddle unlike any I've heard! I wish I could see a clever solution." *I could prove myself. It's a chance to show that I'm satrap material.*

"I'm going to push for neutrality tomorrow." Lygdamis appeared forlorn. "We have to buy time to think!"

The Boule convened in the morning. Artemisia sat in the oaken throne next to the blood throne. "As for the rebellion, I propose we take a position of neutrality for as long as we can. This way those of us inclined to loyalty to Persia can get along with those of us not inclined to fight against Ionia. In any good compromise, no one should walk away with a smile." Lygdamis looked at the Boule and then gestured. "Xenocrates of Loryma."

"I'm sure that I speak for the Kalyndian League when I say that fighting Hellenes is a most odious proposition. Even this neutrality that you have proposed would be hard. I'm sure we'll need something to compensate to keep out of the fight."

"Lycophron of Labraunda?"

"I agree with Xenocrates. This situation's intolerable. However, we've an unresolved dispute with Aphrodisias. Perhaps if that were resolved, we could accept neutrality."

"That dispute was resolved four years ago at the Siege of the White Pillars!" Artemisia called out.

Lycophron scowled. "Satrap, these out..." A smile slowly grew.

What sort of human can change their emotions like that?

"It was resolved." Lycophron changed his demeanor. "You are correct, Princess." Lycophron yielded the floor with a wave of the hand.

Everyone treats me with deference because they know I have a say in who'll marry me. But now I know why I sit in the Oaken Throne. I'm both the side of beef on display in the butcher's shop and the honey used to pacify the tantrum-prone children.

"Karkinos of Casolaba."

"It seems premature to take up a position on the rebellion. We don't even know if they're going to attack Sardes. Perhaps Artaphernes and the rebels will come to an understanding, and all this talk will've been for naught. Perhaps Artaphernes will destroy them, and all of this will be wasted. We need more information!"

He's counseling, not even declaring neutrality!

"We haven't heard from the Xanthian League, though I commanded that they start the Boule. King Kboktis of Kaunos, would you like to add something?"

"I'm inclined to wait. It seems too early to act. Casolaba is correct: we need more information. If the Ionians and their allies take Sardes and can keep it, I might be inclined to reconsider, but for now we'll vote for neutrality."

Artemisia was confused. *It seems obvious that there were three proposals: neutrality, rebellion, and inaction. Somehow Kboktis has managed to declare support for neutrality* and *inaction. How can men with such sloppy minds be kings?*

"I'm prepared to ask for the vote, if no one else is inclined to speak," Lygdamis announced.

King Myrtis stood from his throne. "I urge inaction."

Artemisia stared at her father to see if he caught the different proposals.

"If no one else will speak, then let us vote. All those for maintaining our neutrality remain seated. Those for joining the rebellion stand to the right, and those for assisting Persia stand to the left."

Even my father has misunderstood what has been proposed! She looked to Myrtis to see if he would clarify, but the king didn't.

Lygdamis waited for the delegates to stop moving. Then he began counting. "Three for assisting the Persians. Eight for joining the rebellion. Thirty-six for neutrality."

Artemisia noticed that six of the eight votes for rebellion came from the Kalynda League, but its leaders, Lycophron, Kandaules, and Xenocrates, along with their sons, remained seated. *Incredible! Look how they manipulate and maneuver! They proposed rebellion but voted for neutrality. Is it to avoid alienating my father for purposes of marrying me?*

"It is decided then. Let us take stock of the situation and reconvene tomorrow."

Later that evening Iokaste and Artemisia sat sipping wine in their room. "Everything is so contrived, so deliberate," Artemisia said. "It's all about getting the other side to make a mistake and then taking advantage."

"And yet for some reason, you dream of being party to it." Iokaste rolled her eyes.

"I do. I can't explain it."

When the Boule was in its third day, Artemisia was visited by Prince Parydik of Loryma.

"Did you hear the one about the Aphrodisian and the donkey?"

"No."

"A donkey asks an Aphrodisian, 'What are you?' 'A Carian. What are you?' 'A horse.' Get it?"

"No."

"The Aphrodisian thinks he's a Carian, and the donkey thinks he's a horse."

"I don't get it."

"The donkey's not a horse, just like the Aphrodisian isn't a Carian."

"But Aphrodisians are Carians. We're Dorian and Phoenician settlers."

"Not really, right? They call themselves Leleges."

"But that's just a different word for Carian." Artemisia was having trouble concealing her annoyance. *How ironic that you are saying all of this in Ionian!*

"Right, but they're so backwards," Parydik went on.

"Oh, I see." She didn't and didn't wish to, either.

"Seriously, I'm not sure about these Ionians."

"What do you mean?"

"Do they think that they can defeat Persia?" Parydik's smile vanished.

"Satrap Artaphernes is likely to defeat them."

"More like slaughter them," Parydik said, not fully believing his words. "I think we should go to war with Athens and crush them! Persia's our future, and I want to be in on the plunder! Ionians are traitors.

I'd start by sacking Latmos and Miletos."

Artemisia was sure that his hostility to Ionia was an act. She looked around nervously. "I thought that your faction was for joining the rebellion?"

"But don't you love Persia?"

Artemisia stood. "I can hear my father calling."

"I didn't hear anything."

"I have amazing hearing."

The business of the Boule had become mundane, but Artemisia liked it. It was the same sort of political work that Darayavahu's Court dealt with.

After three more days, Bion of Mylasa arrived for his interview. Artemisia sat next to him, fidgeting with her peplos.

"That large dog that Melanthios rode in on! Right? *Ruff, ruff*!"

"I don't think his horse was that small."

"But compared to yours or mine? Imagine if you married him. You could never ride your horses together in public. It'd be too humiliating for him." Bion smirked.

"He's from Miletos. I'm to marry a Carian."

"Princess, what do you do for fun?"

"Read and train."

Bion squinted. "What training?"

"Combat." She hoped he would find this off-putting.

"Combat?"

"Sword and horse riding."

"Are you any good?"

"For a girl." She found herself wanting Bion gone.

He chuckled. "I've some skill in sword and riding. We should test wits. Do you know the joke about the Aphrodisian and the donkey?"

"A horse."

"Ah-ha! Yes? Let's see, how about... How many Athenians does it take to row a pentekonter?"

"Fifty?"

"Six thousand, five hundred, and fifty! Fifty to row, five hundred to propose rowing, and six thousand to vote on it!"

Artemisia faked laughing, even though she found it clever. She was surprised that Bion knew anything about the Athenian government.

"I recently put a statue to Apollo in our gardens."

Artemisia faked laughing again.

"No, really, I did. I can show you if you like."

"Oh, I see. Sure." Artemisia hoped that would give her an opportunity to escape.

"It'll be dark soon." Bion backtracked. "Maybe tomorrow."

"Sure." *Why not! Whatever* you *want!*

"So, will you give up riding and sword play when you marry?"

"Why would I do that?"

"I mean, it doesn't seem appropriate for a queen to do such things." Bion's voice had become fully condescending.

"Oh my, I forgot. I have to attend to my medicine." She stood abruptly.

"I'll wait for you."

"Oh no, I wish I could. It's too embarrassing. I take it, and it makes me fart really loudly, with a terrible odor."

Bion frowned with disgust.

Artemisia couldn't help but grin.

That night she fantasized about a life with Melanthios, until she fell asleep. In her imagination they divided the year up with four months each in Halikarnassos, Mylasa, and Miletos. He was Polemarch, replacing his uncle. She helped him run the gymnasium. Hours were spent talking philosophy and policy, and she conjured up three young children crawling all over him.

But then she got stuck. *Who sits in the Oak Throne? Who sits in the Blood Throne? Maybe because I'm the Carian, it must be me!*

"Number eight!" Artemisia was beside herself.

"This is it." Lygdamis tried to console her. "But you'll like this one. He's smart."

At least he's figured out that I like them smart!

"King Nicander of Knidos!"

Ah, the one who wanted to censure Lobon's father, Lycophron!

A tall man in his thirties, with long, oily curls, walked into the room. He was confident, and when he saw Artemisia, he smiled large. Artemisia was stunned by his height. When he reached her, he bent at the hips and bowed low. He turned to Lygdamis and bent down to kiss him on the cheek.

"I had no idea your daughter would become so beautiful." He turned back to Artemisia, who began to blush. "I saw you last when you were six, I think."

Artemisia tried to remember him but couldn't.

"I've heard much about your intellect. You travel, read books, train with sword, and ride horse."

"Yes!" Artemisia was astonished that Nicander cared enough to find out about her. She hesitated and then added, "I also studied under the physician Demokedes."

"What?" Nicander turned to Lygdamis and then back again as he reached for his seat and sat. "Demokedes of Croton?"

"Indeed, Your Highness."

"He's in Croton now."

"What? He was supposed to return to Shoosh."

Nicander nodded. "He escaped and has stayed in Croton."

"How do you know of him?" Artemisia was surprised.

"I, too, am a physician. Demokedes is famous in our profession. You had a brilliant teacher."

"You're a physician?" Artemisia's mind was overrun. *Four: Damasithymos the Listener, Mnaseas the Traveler, Melanthios the Kisser, and now Nicander the Physician. How do I make such a decision? Especially since the one I want isn't an option!*

"I am." Nicander leaned in. "What were you taught? Demokedes is fast to cut."

"I've done a surgery! It was a mastectomy."

"What!" shouted Lygdamis. "You cut a woman's breast off! Have you been in combat, too?"

"There was an attempt to kidnap me in Shoosh, and I fought. I managed to strike my attacker in the arm." Artemisia found herself wanting to brag.

Her father stared at her, sizing her up. "You've been in combat?"

"I swung a sword twice at a kidnapper. He successfully parried my blade the first time, but I cut him the second time. Iokaste slashed his calf open."

"Persia gave you an education that I could never have hoped to give Pissindelis," Lygdamis declared. "What other training have you had?"

How ironic that you sent your daughter! "I spent months of my time lying beneath Darayavahu's throne, listening to the daily work of the Imperial Court."

"Remarkable!" Nicander's smile remained. "So, what have you read?" When she had answered, he asked about her travels. When she told her story, he asked, "Which do you prefer, the blood red marble or the white marble?"

"Oh, blood red for sure! It's stunning."

"You're a remarkable creature!" Artemisia found the look Nicander gave her father at once flattering but also alienating. It was the sort of look that a person might give after seeing a lovely sculpture, wanting to share the moment with a fellow admirer. It made Artemisia feel too much like a thing. "This has been a splendid evening. I realize that all of this is rushed. You must make a decision for which you have no experience, and you have too little information. I'm a widower with a six-year-old daughter. I was seventeen once, and I can't imagine how you make this decision. I'm sure that you have met several worthy men. So, let me leave you with some thoughts.

"First, most advice is dog shit. This is probably no exception.

Second, there's no right answer. Each of us has flaws, and each will have strengths. I'm prone to a terrible mood once or twice per year. If you pick me, life won't be perfect. Third, your mind and heart will pull you in two directions. Listen to both. Don't let one rule over the other. And fourth, don't worry about breaking hearts. You must choose for yourself."

Artemisia was surprised at Nicander's humility. "I'm without words for such advice."

"You don't need my advice. I just wanted you to know what I'm thinking. Should you pick me, I'll say 'yes.' I can't imagine a dull moment with you."

With that he stood. He bowed to the king. And then as Artemisia stood, he placed a soft, lingering kiss on her cheek. She shivered.

That night Artemisia wept in bed for an hour. The door opened. "Mistress, *enough*." Iokaste's voice was soft but commanding. She sat on the edge of the bed.

"What am I supposed to do?"

"Pick one."

"I don't know them well enough." Her voice was filled with distress.

"You'll make the best decision you can."

"What if the one I pick tricked me?"

"That's life. Isn't that possible with every decision we make?" Iokaste put a soothing hand on Artemisia's back.

"Whom would you pick?"

"I'm glad I don't have to!"

"Whom!"

"Nicander, I think. Or Melanthios. It would be one of those two. Damasithymos is lovely and Mnaseas was, too, but Melanthios and Nicander were my favorites. But you don't have to decide now. You have until your eighteenth birthday. However, you can't cry for that many months! You'll die."

Iokaste crawled into the bed. She rubbed the princess's back until she slept.

The next day Artemisia asked Nijara and Vadhut. They picked Damasithymos and Nicander, respectively. When she approached Myron, he said, "I don't know which one you should choose but rather whom not to—Damasithymos."

"Really? Why?"

Myron shrugged indicating that he did not know why. But then his eyes grew as if he understood her face to be saying, *I cannot base my opinion on a shrug.* "I can't tell you really. I just know it. I feel it the same way I know when a man is going to swing right instead of low. Maybe he shows it in his eyes, but I don't know, exactly. Damasithymos reminds me of those men who are so perfect, so clean, but... well they aren't good and you find out too late."

"If you say 'no,' then he's off the list."

Artemisia attended the Boule as they debated spending money to fix a stretch of road on the Idrian Pass. The Labraundians objected, saying that the pass belonged to them and no money could be spent on it until it was returned to them; however, they were outvoted.

The Boule also voted to build a new ship for the satrapy. It would be under Lygdamis' command but belong to everyone. Each of the four factions was to provide eighteen rowers, two marines, and a sailor. Lygdamis would provide the officers.

Artemisia found herself trying to avoid contact with the suitors. Damasithymos and Nicander seemed to intuit this and obliged, but the other six took every opportunity to make eye contact. Artemisia hated the attention. Parydik and Bion, on occasion, leered at her. Parydik even stuck his tongue out. Kharax's eyes were sad and eternally pleading. She wanted to scream at those three in particular. Terpander, Lobon, and Mnaseas were not as annoying; however, Artemisia was in no mood.

In mid-June, as Artemisia had been getting increasingly nervous, she found a surprise outside their living quarters. It was a sword. Carved on the blade, on one side, was the front quarter of Pegasos and script: ΛΛＢＹＡＣＱＮＢ *pikartmi*, "Luminous Artemis." On the other side, it said, ＹＯＱ ΛΛＡＣＡΓＡＹＣＡ *not parabanda*, "Brought forth victory."

"What does Pegasos' front quarter mean?" Artemisia asked. No one answered. "Who brought this?" she asked.

Myron shrugged. "I didn't see anyone."

"Your guess?"

Iokaste said, "Nicander."

Myron said, "Mnaseas."

"It's beautiful." She hefted it. "It feels balanced."

Myron gestured with an open hand.

She handed it to him, and he swung it. "Very high quality steel, amazing balance, brilliant craftsmanship. This might be the best sword I've ever held."

"I love it. It was someone who believes in me. He's the person I want to marry!"

The Boule was interrupted by a scout. He walked in out of breath. "Speak," Lygdamis commanded.

"Your Highness, I'm Thuxra and have come from the Sardes!"

"What news do you bring?"

"Satrap Artaphernes fled. Not only did the rebels capture Sardes, they plundered it and then burned it!"

"What! Why?" Artemisia stood up. She surprised herself with the outburst. "I'm sorry." She bowed her head and sat back down.

Shouting exploded. Lygdamis stood and waved his arms. "Order! Order! Order!"

No order came until Lycophron managed to quiet the members of the Kalyndian faction. "I've consulted the Oracle of Apollo in Didyma. I asked whether we should enter an alliance with the Ionians. The Oracle declared, 'If it's black, then you go. If the end is white, you should stay.' It seems to me that fire has most certainly blackened that city!"

More shouting ensued. Lygdamis nodded to his guard commander. When the guards had positioned themselves in the hall, the Bouleutai became silent again.

"I call on Nicander to speak."

"When the Oracle speaks, sometimes its gives flawed advice." He waved his hand to stop Lycophron from interrupting. "Ash is white. And how do you know that 'go' means to rebel? And how do you know that the 'end' means Sardes?"

Lygdamis looked around. "King Karkinos of Casolaba?"

"Any decision we make involves risk. Not deciding, however, results in certain defeat. Not joining the Ionians would mean punishment if they prevail. Not joining the Persians will mean the same. If we join one side, then at least we have a chance of avoiding defeat. I propose that we first vote on whether to remain neutral or to join a side. And then if we vote to join a side, we vote for which one."

"Oh, that's interesting! If you were for joining the Persians, you might vote to remain neutral, in order to avoid the risk of this Boule voting to join the Ionians," Lygdamis observed.

Papas! Don't explain it to them! Use their stupidity against them!

"Where do you fall, Satrap?" King Myrtis asked.

"I believe in the empire. Persia has brought us liberation, prosperity, and peace. We'd be fools to jeopardize that! Our history under Lydian rule, and before that the Hittites, was one of constant strife, fighting each other and our conquerors on every opportunity. Surely Persia is better?"

"I've no love for Ionians," King Kandaules started but then stopped to ask for permission to speak. When Lygdamis nodded, he started again. "But we speak their language and share much of their culture. We have a kinship with them—"

Artemisia found herself feeling disdain for Kandaules.

Dibikom interrupted. "I feel more kinship with Lydians than Ionians. The latter just burned down Lydia's greatest city! To Tartarus with Ionians!"

More shouting ensued. Lygdamis had his guard clear the hall.

The civil war my father has kept suppressed is like a black cloud on the horizon.

That night Artemisia came up with a solution. I'll sleep with each of the remaining three men twice! Since sex isn't pleasant in the beginning, the first three times will be to get past that. Then I'll have at least some idea of who's the better lover.

When she had broken into Nicander's room, the king awoke. "Who's there?"

"Artemisia."

He got out of the bed and strode to her, enveloping her in a warm embrace. Then he picked her up and carried her to his bed.

Panic started to set in. *This is going to happen!* They held each other for some time. This did much to calm Artemisia. Mustering all her courage, she attempted to kiss him. He kissed her back. She liked the kiss; it was tender. After they had kissed for some time, Artemisia lay on top of Nicander and began rubbing against him.

He broke off the kiss. "No, I want to wait until we know each other better."

Artemisia jumped out of the bed with the speed of a person having just found a scorpion on her pillow. Her pride was stung. She wasn't sure what to do. *What does this mean? Is he attracted to me?* She scrambled out the window hot, annoyed, and ashamed.

Once out, she decided to try Damasithymos' room. Artemisia spent an hour squatting, waiting for an opportunity to get passed his guards, but none came. *Why's he so heavily guarded in the palace?*

Not sure what to do with herself, she decided to walk towards Mnaseas just to get a sense of her feelings. She was no longer sure she wanted to do anything. The possibility of another rejection drained most of her desire. As she snuck through a living area, she was forced to turn by a group of men entering the room. She ducked into the room that opened to Nicander's room.

In the darkness she heard his door open and then voices. A woman was whispering to Nicander. He let the woman in and closed the door. *What was that? Is he going to sleep with another woman?* Artemisia's mind ran away with the thought. *To Hades with all these shiteaters!* Her pride smarting, she decided to go back to her bed.

The next day, the Bouleutai met in small groups. Artemisia watched from afar as they struck deals, compromised, schemed, and plotted. Lygdamis approached her as she stared at a group of men in the garden. "Look at them, Papas."

"Politics is a messy affair."

"Why do men do such things?"

"They want power." Lygdamis nodded.

"Why?" Artemisia asked.

"Some men lust after it as surely as they lust after women."

"And others?"

"They do it out of fear," Lygdamis said. "They worry what would happen if someone else did it." Lygdamis put his hand on Artemisia's shoulder. "In truth most do it because they were born to it."

"Born to it?"

"Yes, even a man like me. Though I wasn't born a prince, I had enough on my side that becoming a king was possible."

"What do you mean?"

"I couldn't have become a king were it not for the combination of a powerful family, a loyal combat force, some talent, and a good education."

"I see." Artemisia considered her own opportunities. "So, what would it take to make me into such a man?"

"You can't be such a man. The best that you can be is an excellent queen. You can be the satrap's best advisor. You'll make policy through him. When he's ruled by emotion or missing information, you can balance him out. You're brilliant beyond imagination. My seventeen-year-old daughter's a scholar, physician, world traveler, statesman, swordsman, and horseman."

"Why did you send me to Shoosh instead of Pissindelis?"

"Isn't that obvious?" Lygdamis' left eye squinted.

"Because I couldn't inherit the throne?"

"Yes."

"Is it also because you didn't love me as much?" Artemisia looked off to the distance. "You could bear to miss me, but you couldn't part with Pissindelis."

"That's not what was in my heart, no."

"But you could bear to part with me."

"My decision was political and not sentimental." Lygdamis was frustrated.

"What if it was?"

"Why does it matter?" Lygdamis raised his voice.

"I don't know, but it does!" Artemisia insisted.

"It broke my heart to send you, but I couldn't show it. I knew that I had to send you, but I didn't want to. But who cares what I wanted? A fool focuses on what he wants when he has no choices." Lygdamis squirmed. "Can we talk about your marriage?"

Her father's answer was good enough. "I dreamed last night that Artemis and Apollo stood next to each other. In unison the two said, 'Nicander.'"

"What does that mean?"

"I understood that as them saying that I should marry Nicander," Artemisia said.

"Is he your choice?"

She wanted to ask about the woman visiting Nicander but knew that to do so would be to expose her own attempt at sex. Instead she said, "I'm leaning his way."

But when some days had passed, she asked Iokaste, "What does it mean that Nicander had a woman visit him?"

Iokaste's face filled with a look of betrayal.

"I don't feel betrayed."

The handmaiden nodded.

"What if I offered myself to him and he said he wanted to wait to get to know me and then he brought a woman to his chambers to have sex?"

"Oh my, that's messy. I can't know what's in his heart. Maybe he was feeling overwhelmed by your approach and slept with the woman to get rid of the desire."

"You mean, I stirred him up, but then he was so dedicated to waiting, he had sex with the other woman?"

"Yes."

"That seems…like dog shit. So, what if I did stir him up?"

"We both know that the rules for men don't apply to women."

The vote in the Boule took place in the middle of August. Shouting ensued, a few punches were thrown, and the guards came in to restore order. Lygdamis proposed a vote between staying neutral and joining the Ionians. He had successfully reasoned that to join Persia would result in a civil war in Caria.

The pro-Persia elements allowed his suggestion to pass. Nonetheless, he had a look of horror as the voters headed toward their perspective sides. Kalynda voted as a bloc this time, all for revolt. The Leleges League voted for remaining neutral, bringing the total to eleven for neutrality and twelve for rebellion.

It was up to the Xanthian and Mylasa Leagues, but they were divided. Nicander voted for neutrality and Karkinos for revolt, and Kboktis voted for neutrality and Iarjas voted for revolt. By the time the votes settled out, Xanthos was five for and four against, bringing the total to seventeen to fifteen. Mylasa came down nine against and six for. The Boule had by a vote of twenty-four to twenty-three voted to remain neutral.

"I'm pleased with the result and endorse it, but I'm horrified by the deep divisions it reveals. I want everyone to swear loyalty to the ruling of the Boule so that we might avert civil war."

Even if we don't rebel against Persia, Father might not be able to avert a civil war in Caria. Artemisia wanted to discover a solution. Between agonizing about whom to marry and the impending crisis, she remained in a heightened state of anxiety and lost sleep and weight.

In late September, soon after returning to the court on Royal Island in Halikarnassos, the messenger named Thuxra arrived.

"Your Highness, Artaphernes rallied Persians in the weeks after Sardes was burned. When he was ready, he moved on the ruined city. As the Persians approached, the rebels fled. However, the Persians were mostly horse archers and pursued them faster than they could withdraw. The rebels were forced to fight just outside Ephesos.

"Their morale was ruined by the speed of the Persian pursuit. Though they put up a fight, they were ultimately no match. The Eretrean general Eualkides was killed in the battle, and the Ionians fled to their cities. The Athenians and Eretreans have left Ionia."

"Unbelievable! We were almost part of that disaster." Lygdamis' face filled with relief. "Caution wins the day! Why risk so much for so little? Fools! What fools the Ionians and Kalyndians are! Fools!"

Artemisia didn't know when she had seen her father so happy. "Papas, you're vindicated! You saved Caria!" She wanted to say more but feared that if she said too much, it would diminish the meaning of the compliment.

The days that followed seemed lighter than normal. The view from Royal Island was more beautiful. Artemisia was certain it was going to be Nicander, but she would not have to choose until her eighteenth birthday, so the only people she told were her four attendants.

Iokaste wasted no time and began courting the Knidos proxenos in

Halikarnassos. He was a short, strongly built Dorian, with a permanent scowl. Artemisia especially liked his condescending attitude.

On her eighteenth birthday, January 26, the representative of Knidos arrived before Artemisia, scowl and all. She wore her finest white chiton, Zoroastrian earrings, and lion brooch, and her Artemis-horse sword was scabbarded on her lap.

As the proxenos approached, Artemisia noticed how powerful she felt and liked it. After the representative genuflected, she commanded, "Arise," and involuntarily smiled as he did. "I've made my choice—Nicander."

"Thank you, Your Highness." With that the proxenos backed out of the room.

With Knidos only a half day's journey, Nicander arrived that evening.

Lygdamis interrupted the festive dinner. "It's Carian law that when a monarch rules two kingdoms, he give up one kingdom to a relative or a vote by his people."

"Isn't it also Carian tradition for the queen to go to the man's kingdom?" Nicander asked.

Artemisia was stunned. She looked to her father to see his reaction.

"I'm sure Knidos is lovely, but is that something you really want? Halikarnassos is five times larger and wealthier."

"You're correct."

"You're influence as King of Halikarnassos would be ten times greater."

"There can be no doubt," Nicander yielded.

"And yet you're not saying you agree that you should switch to my kingdom?" Lygdamis appeared baffled.

"I can't tell you the part of my arm that hurts," Nicander said, "only that somewhere I'm in pain."

What does that even mean! Demokedes had spoken of patients who complain about a pain but could not say exactly where it hurt.

"Well, there's the other matter—faction alliance." Lygdamis

seemed eager to explore this new development.

"I'm sure that King Myrtis will be upset you chose me over Bion." Nicander was confident. "Myrtis is faction leader. He's not likely to give that up."

"So, the best that would come of this is the division of the Mylasa League," Artemisia interjected.

Nicander turned to her. "I can't imagine that Caryanda and Madnasa would ever side with Halikarnassos. The rivalry is too bitter. Casolaba as well. But we might be able to bring Alinda with us."

"So, we will go from eleven votes to thirteen or fifteen?" She went on.

"Yes," Nicander answered.

"You can see why I'm bringing all of this up then?" Lygdamis said.

"Because a marriage to Damasithymos would be better?" Nicander wiped his mouth.

"Indeed, and so here you are saying you won't move to Halikarnassos, and I'm wondering why we are doing this." Lygdamis was perplexed. "I've no heirs, save Artemisia. You have relatives whom you could—"

"You could select someone unrelated to replace you," Nicander interrupted.

"You're my friend of how many years? I want it to be you." Lygdamis was clearly disappointed.

Nicander looked down at his plate of piled lamb bones.

Artemisia remembered that night when Nicander refused to make love to her. Maybe he sent me away because he is not attracted to me. Maybe he just wants the marriage for political purposes. *Why does he keep rejecting me? None of this makes sense.* "Wait!" In a flash she had an insight. "I get why you don't want to move to Halikarnassos."

Startled, everyone turned to her.

"I can see it in your eyes. You are the King of Knidos. There you would remain king. But if you come to Royal Island, you fear you would become the Prince of Halikarnassos. If I go there, I'll have no power, but here, here I will always be a powerful queen. Your power would come from me. You'd be obliged to listen to me."

Nicander looked up.

Lygdamis titled his head as he squinted. "You'd choose to rule a kingdom one-fifth as powerful and stay the subordinate in a faction because you fear my daughter?"

Nicander squirmed in his seat.

"Papas, I've changed my mind. I could never marry a man who feared me. It would be inappropriate." Artemisia stood up and walked out. When she was clear of the dining area, she ran to her room. She dove on a couch and curled up into the fetal position.

"What's wrong with me! Why's all of this happening? I've submitted to marrying, to subordination. Why are things still a mess?"

"Mnaseas is my second choice."

"Not Damasithymos?" her father pleaded.

"I get what is at stake politically, but I think you overestimate Aphrodisias' loyalty to Halikarnassos. If we align with Kalynda, we will surely lose that alliance. Our faction will break. Aphrodisias will turn to Mylasa or Xanthos, increasing their voting power. The Kalynda League would increase to eighteen." Artemisia dared not express her real reason for rejecting Damasithymos—Myron.

"You make a good point."

"For me what's at stake is my life. Damasithymos is my third choice, but I suspect that Mnaseas will make me happier. He'll probably appoint his younger brother as king and take Myndos out of the Kalyndian League, decreasing their votes to nine and increasing ours to fourteen."

"It leaves Mylasa only one faction away from ruling the Boule."

Artemisia nodded.

It was February 13 when the proxenos of Myndos was brought before Artemisia. Because of the proximity of Myndos, Mnaseas could have arrived the same day, but he didn't.

Artemisia was surprised. She paced until her knees hurt. In the morning there was still no sign of him. "I'm cursed."

"Mistress, there could be many explanations!" Iokaste's face was filled with distress. "He might be traveling. You shouldn't see things that are out of your sight."

"Except, if he was traveling, surely his people could send a ship to tell us. How long does it take to travel eighteen miles?"

By the next day, Artemisia had decided that the answer was *no*. "Father, I'm down to Damasithymos, but I want to wait for the Boule."

"That's in a month and a half."

"It'll give me time to sort this out in my mind, and I want to look at him one more time without him knowing my intentions."

When they ran aground, on the Casolaba beach, Artemisia noticed that the seven ships on the beach were all Kalyndian. Two flew the banner of Kalynda, three Myndos, and two Loryma. *Damasithymos, Mnaseas, and Parydik are already here…with the entire Kalyndian navy.* The sailors with a compliment of marines sat around fires. There was nothing unusual about it, but Artemisia was nervous. *It must be the whole wedding thing.*

When they had unloaded and took three steps forwards, the Kalyndian sailors stood. *All of them at once.* Artemisia turned towards them. They ran, forming into ranks, weapons drawn. Artemisia shouted, "Ambush!"

Vadhut, Nijara, and Myron moved in front of Artemisia. She pulled her sword and stood readying herself for the charge. The Halikarnassians turned in time to draw their weapons, but it was too late to form ranks.

The sound of battle rang out along the beach. Artemisia looked at Simurgh and then her father. To the north were small farms, to the east Casolaba, and to the south marsh. *Outnumbered seven to one, and with my father's men in disarray, defeat is certain.* She mounted Simurgh and rode to the king. "We have to make for the city!"

"You go. I'll delay them!"

She spurred her horse forward and looked back. Iokaste, Myron, and Vadhut were behind her. But Nijara had stayed with her father. *No time for sentiment!*

They didn't gallop far before horsemen appeared between them and Casolaba. Artemisia turned Simurgh towards the marsh. Once in it the horse had to jump and jump. But he sank into the mud. Artemisia realized that he might be able to swim in the deeper parts of the marsh.

"We can't go on like this, mistress!" Myron shouted. "The horses'll never make it."

"We can cross the lagoon." She pointed. "It's deep enough for the horses to swim over there."

"That's a half mile, mistress!" Myron's voice filled with distress.

"What should we do?"

"We have to turn and try to ride past those horsemen!"

They turned back, Myron leading, and charged straight towards their pursuers. As they got close, Myron turned a hard right, skirting the marsh, but it wasn't enough. The horsemen were going to catch them.

They reached a stream, and Myron led them through the thick brush into the water and then took an arrow in the back. He turned and charged the horsemen. Artemisia followed her guard with her eyes, even as Simurgh charged away. She wanted to scream, *No don't!* She wanted to take out the arrow.

Another arrow struck Myron. This time in the chest, then one in the side. His horse was slowing down. "What man stays mounted after three arrows!" Myron suddenly spurred the stallion forward to the right. A startled man raised his sword, but it was too late. Myron swung out. Artemisia could not fathom the power in his arm. The sword struck the pursuer in the pectoral muscle. She could hear ribs breaking as the man grew a look of surprised agony. The sword took off his arm at the top of the bicep as it passed through muscle and bone.

But a horseman on the other side of Myron drove a javelin past his shield and into his chest. Myron and the horse took a hard left. He wobbled as the horse stopped and then fell off and onto the hard ground with a groan and became still.

Artemisia spurred Simurgh on. She felt as if part of her had died.

Vadhut turned to face the Kalyndians. She fired arrows into three assailants, but six were already past her.

Iokaste turned her horse back towards those men.

"Io!" Artemisia shouted.

The maneuver was brilliant. Iokaste cut off the paths of four of them and collided with the last one. Both riders were thrown. "*Io!*" Artemisia wanted to turn back around, but her mind knew that Iokaste's only chance was for her to escape and then pay a ransom. Artemisia wanted to cry. She wanted to scream, but there was no time. She still had two pursuers she had to get away from.

Then she recognized one of the two pursuers—Lobon.

She knew that Simurgh's haunches were bleeding, but there was no time for compassion and she dug her spurs in deeper. The animal obeyed with a snort. Soon they were in a small patch of farmland. Beyond that was a hill covered in dry briery brush. Artemisia aimed for the hill. She was tired and heartbroken, but she knew if she could get away, back to Halikarnassos, then she could pay ransoms, or maybe Caria would rally around her, and she could fight the rebels. But she also knew that she could not gallop Simurgh for twenty-three miles.

When she reached the hill, she looked back and saw that Lobon's companion had dismounted and had given his horse to Lobon. With the ability to change horses, Lobon could ride a more rested animal as he chased Artemisia. *There's no chance of escape now. I have to fight.* She drew the Pegasos sword and turned down the slope.

Artemisia charged Lobon's right side. She figured he would not attack with his sword and wouldn't be able to use his shield. *He'll parry or duck. At that point I'll smash Simurgh into Lobon's mount, and he'll be thrown off balance.*

Just as they reached each other, the princess swung high as hard as she could. What came next surprised Artemisia. Lobon did lower his head but not to duck. He leaped from his horse and wrapped his arms around her.

I should have swung low!

She came off her saddle, the full force of their weight crashing down on Lobon's right arm. She heard a snap and then the two bounced into the air. Lobon didn't let go of her. They rolled together for ten feet over branches and rocks before coming to a stop.

Cut and bruised, Lobon wore the look of a crazed man. Artemisia tried to pull away, but he held on as if his life depended on it.

She managed to scoot back but couldn't get free. His right arm was bloody. She hit it as hard as she could with her left. He cried out as he pulled himself up. Bone was protruding. Or maybe it was a branch or rock sunk into his flesh. It didn't matter. She struck again. The pain on his face was matched only by Atoosa's after the surgery. She knew that she could defeat Lobon with more such attacks, but by then he had managed to get to his knees. He struck her hard in the face with a left. Dizzy and disoriented, she struck him in the shoulder a third time, but another left on the cheek laid her out.

She awoke tied on Simurgh's saddle, belly down. Artemisia turned her head in the direction they were walking. Lobon led both horses on foot. He held the reins by his left hand. *I can defeat him if I can get to his right shoulder.*

As she wiggled in the saddle, Lobon spoke, "You are one tough bitch."

"Why've you done this?"

"How many months have you taunted us?" Lobon spit blood. "Dangling your pussy in front of us, your power over us. And then you picked Mnaseas! You almost broke the Kalyndian League!"

"How?"

"Most people at this point would plead for mercy. But not you. You want to know why?" He looked back at her, revealing a large gash on his cheek. "Your offer to Mnaseas…he had two choices. Take you up on it or stay loyal to the Kalyndian League. He chose the latter, but we still had a problem. Who should marry you? He was the best candidate, but none of the rest of us were happy with that. So, we came up with a simple, better plan. The Kalyndian prince who captured you would marry you."

Artemisia's mind caught fire. "Not you!"

"If you had stayed on the beach, you'd have ended up with Mnaseas, Damasithymos, or Parydik. But instead you came to me, the one Kalyndian prince without ships! It's as if Pan himself arranged our marriage." He leaned forward. "Ah, look there, my men. Anyway, so why not me?"

"You lied to me!" Artemisia was panicking.

"Oh, did I?"

"The White Pillars."

"Ah, yes. So, I did." He looked back at her. "I know what you're thinking. You'll use your charm to talk the other men into turning on me. I want you to know this is a signed contract. We traded collateral. Hostage lives are at stake. Mothers and sisters would die. There is a truth as solid as a broken bone—we're getting married!"

"I won't agree." Artemisia's mind scrambled for ways to make a deal.

"You will."

"Why would I do that?" *I need time. Wait for a mistake. The emperor said, "Everyone eventually makes a mistake."*

"No, you have to marry me. I get that you don't care about the Kalyndian women whose lives depend on this, but your people. I'll execute them, and then I'll kill you. Like I said, lives are at stake."

Someday you'll make a mistake. Then I'll kill you. Artemisia sighed hard and nodded her acquiescence. She could feel her heart hardening.

More men arrived. They picked her up and set her into a cart. A moment later Artemisia heard a snap and Lobon cry out. "She broke your arm!" She didn't recognize the voice. "It's like marrying a leopard."

"She's one tough bitch." Pain infected Lobon's voice.

The road was painfully bumpy. Not just to her body but also her heart. She imagined her father dying on the beach. *It happened so fast. Father and I had reconciled. I'd have liked more time with him. I'm broken.*

Then she remembered Myron laying on the ground. *He was pure love. Losing him is too painful. I've lost everything.*

When they got to Mylasa, King Kandaules stared at her. "You've a choice to make." He gestured to his men. They brought over Vadhut and Iokaste. "These are yours, yes?" It was a rhetorical question. "I'll spare them both. In fact, I'll give them to you as your handmaidens if you go into that palace on your own and say you'll marry Lobon. Do you understand me?"

Artemisia tried to think; she tried to clear her mind.

"This hesitating is making me mad." He pointed to a soldier, who cut Vadhut in the bicep. "I'm going to have pieces of her cut off and fed to my dogs if you keep thinking."

"I'll do it. I'll do whatever you want." Artemisia felt relief as she surrendered. It surprised her. *Surrender brings relief.* "I accept my fate." She wanted to try out the words. It was a test, but it produced a nod from Kandaules, and she assumed that was good. "My father?"

"He's on the beach."

She knew that was no answer but also knew that it didn't matter what he said.

"We need to get you cleaned up and into a new peplos, Princess. You made a mess of this one."

They moved into a farmer's hut. Iokaste silently tended to Artemisia's cuts and helped wash them with water and a sponge. King Kandaules walked in. He looked her up and down. "I wouldn't mind a turn with you, but alas you belong to Lobon."

Iokaste brought Artemisia her torn crimson gown, but Kandaules waved her off.

"No, I'll keep looking. I'm going to let you keep your jewelry." He tossed her a white gown, but it fell onto the dirt floor.

Artemisia gazed at it.

"Do you feel powerless?"

Artemisia gave no reply, but she did.

"Is it shame that fills your heart?"

Still only silence. *Not shame so much as hatred. I'll kill you, too, when I get the chance.*

"I don't blame you. You could've had my son."

"Master, why don't you give me to your son?" Artemisia hoped to split the Kalyndians. *Anything that would set them against each other.*

"Ah, see, there you go. That's the Artemisia that we know."

"I've already submitted to your will." Artemisia realized that her heart was swinging from resignation to determination. *Is this what happens to people who suffer such catastrophic losses?*

"See, we had to figure out a solution to our dilemma. This was the one we came up with. If I tried to alter the agreement..." He clapped his hands together and made a high-pitched "wiiiiish" sound as he raised one hand up high. "Too many people would die. I'm not interested."

Artemisia was not sure what the gesture meant exactly, but she suspected it meant something akin to *massacre*.

They went straight to the palace in Mylasa. In the Great Hall, King Kandaules ordered Artemisia to the blood red throne. When she sat, King Myrtis demanded, "What's the meaning of this?"

"I've most regrettable news," Kandaules said. "Satrap Lygdamis has suffered a terrible accident. Artemisia is now the Queen of Halikarnassos and the Satrap of Caria."

The words were like a dagger through her heart. She knew that they had killed her father, but hearing it brought in more grief. *Papas, I wish I told you I love you.*

"We're retrieving his body now. In the meantime, the queen has expressed to me her eagerness to marry Prince Lobon."

"Is this true?" Myrtis looked at Artemisia with suspicious eyes.

She managed a nod.

"For something like this, I need to hear it."

"Yes." Artemisia's heart could bear no more. Tears began to stream.

"Tears of joy, in such a sad moment!" Kandaules' voice boomed throughout the hall. "Such courage, such courage. Bravo!"

"I won't sanction a wedding until I see the satrap's body." Myrtis' voice was firm.

"So be it, but get the priests ready, because the wedding will be to-night."

Kandaules indicated that Artemisia was to follow.

She found it difficult to put one foot in front of the other.

That evening Lygdamis' body arrived. Men unceremoniously dropped him on a table. Artemisia stood and went to him. "Say your farewell, Princess," Kandaules ordered. She stared at the torn body but felt nothing. She knew she should feel something. *Something is broken in me. Is it that my impending rape occupies my heart, or has so much happened all at once that I've nothing left to take? Father, we let our guard down. We should have seen this coming. I took too long. Stubborn!*

Later that evening Artemisia was wed to Lobon before the nobles and kings of Caria. She was numb. During the ceremony Kings Myrtis and Karkinos never looked her way, and she noticed that Nicander, Mnaseas, and Dibikom were absent. Afterwards Lobon was proclaimed King of Halikarnassos and Satrap of Caria.

Artemisia was led by Lobon and two of his men to his room. He opened the door and gestured for her to go in. She noticed that a man walked behind her. "Do I need Agamemnon here to help, or can we do this just husband and wife?"

Artemisia looked at the guard. He was nearly as big as Myron. Without a weapon she could offer no resistance. But in that moment, she understood something about Lobon. *He doesn't let pride get in the way of relying on someone.* "No, my lord, we don't need help."

Agamemnon closed the door behind him, and Lobon approached.

He looked Artemisia up and down. "I like the peplos. It suits you."

She gave no answer.

He reached out to stroke the side of her face, but she instinctively turned away.

"See, that's unfriendly. No husband wants an unfriendly wife."

She turned her face towards Lobon.

"No, I want more than that. On your knees."

Artemisia hesitated.

Lobon put his hand on her shoulder and began to push down. "Knees."

She bent until she was on her knees.

"Say, 'I'm sorry, master.'"

"I'm sorry, master." The shame welled up in her throat, and she feared she might gag.

"See, that's not so bad." His right hand shot out fast. She might have been able to evade it, if she were not on her knees, trying to avoid making Lobon angrier. He caught a fist full of hair and pulled towards him. Artemisia winced as she stood and came to him.

When she reached him, he pushed her hard to the side, using her hair to guide her. She realized that he had meant to push her onto the bed.

What more can you do to me that you've not already done? But she knew that raping her as a virgin was going to be hard. This was not practice with a wooden sword.

She crumpled onto the bed but could feel her groin tense up in anticipation of the violation. Lobon didn't let go. He landed on top of her. She closed her eyes. *Should I plead with him? I know it hurts the first time. Will he respond to that? Should I remain silent and save my dignity? Do I give into pride and fight him knowing that I can't win, that he will hurt me more? How many countless women have been in this position?*

She remembered Myron's lifeless body filled with arrows. Then Lygdamis' battered body lying on a table in the Boule, his himation torn, and bowels exposed. Her cold, calculating mind gave into the grief, and a whimper escaped.

"Oh, I'm not that horrible," Lobon said as he slithered onto her. He put all his weight on her, pinning her to the bed.

Her stomach turned at the overwhelming sense of helplessness. She tensed more and pulled her head to the side, forgetting the fist full of hair in her attacker's hand. She felt a chunk tear.

He pulled hard against what he seemed to perceive as an act of defiance. "I'll break you."

Her neck bent as far as it could, and she let out a sob, not from the threat but from the stinging in the side of her head. *If I could go back just a few weeks, to before I picked Nicander. I could've just chosen Damasithymos. But I have to have everything my way.* She felt him reaching down to the bottom of her peplos. *It's a lovely gown. I probably make a lovely bride, except for all the sobbing. Maybe I can pretend he is someone else.*

As her thigh came uncovered, she let out a scream. Panic filled her heart. "Not you! I didn't pick you!" She tried to pull out from under him. Melanthios' handsome face came to her. Then Khshayarsha's. "I should've stayed in Shoosh!"

Lobon let go of her hair and slapped her across the cheek. Her face turned to the side. He jammed a knee between her thighs and pressed hard. She realized then how tightly she had pressed her legs together. *Am I going to resist?* She knew the question was meaningless. *Artemisia is going to resist, because she has no other way of being.*

The pain in her thigh was tolerable, but his knee made progress. Lobon brought his head close to hers. She brought hers up fast, surprising both of them. The collision sounded like two rocks colliding. He came out of the bed, grabbing his forehead.

Artemisia was dazed. She saw green stars and found herself disoriented.

Lobon used her inaction to undress. She looked at his naked body through the stars. He grabbed her legs and pulled them off the edge of the bed. He pried both knees apart, shoving them to the side. He walked into the gap, licking his hand. "I'm going to teach you a lesson, bitch-face!"

Artemisia mouthed the words, before she could stop herself, "You *koprophagos*, shit eater, *metrokoites*, motherfucker, go to the crows!"

Lobon punched her in the face and then really hurt her.

The next day at the Boule, Artemisia stood beside Lobon. Her face was flush, her groin was sore, and she felt sick in the stomach as the courtier announced, "Satrap Lobon, King of Halikarnassos, and Queen Artemisia."

Lobon wasted no time. "Our first order of business is to vote to join the rebellion."

"Are you mad?" Nicander shouted. "Didn't you hear what happened at Ephesos? The rebellion's over!"

"It's well known that you are a coward, Nicander. The Persians haven't captured Miletos, nor Ephesos, nor any of the Ionians' cities. The rebellion's still going."

"But the Athenians and Eretreans have left the country."

"So, someone needs to come to the aid of Ionia. Thrake has joined the fight, and now we will!"

"I can't believe that the Boule will vote for rebellion," Nicander said. "It was a close vote last time, but now after Ephesos—"

"Let's find out."

When all had committed, save Xanthos, it was twenty for rebellion to eighteen against. Artemisia watched, holding her breath as Xanthos committed. "Alabanda's two votes against. Telmessos three votes for. Kaunos four votes for!"

"We are joining the Ionians in rebellion against Persia!" King Lobon announced.

What did the Kalyndian League offer Xanthos?

"We need a polemarch. I propose Kboktis of Kaunos."

And she got her answer. They voted with no discussion, and Kboktis won by the same twenty-seven votes. *The Kalyndian League struck a deal with Kaunos and Telmessos before murdering my father! I'm not only a means of taking over the satrapy. I'm also their means of taking Caria into the rebellion. They had to kill my father.*

That night Lobon had Artemisia stripped by Agamemnon. He ordered Agamemnon to hold Artemisia down. She stared at the ceiling, dreading what was coming. "I've taken Caria into rebellion," Lobon bragged as he lay down on her. "Soon we will be killing Persian dogs."

Artemisia's legs were apart. She could not stop what happened next, but all the muscles in her body tensed anyway. She felt ill as he forced himself into her, not just for the pain and hatred filling her heart, but for the shame at what the emperor would say. As her body rocked back and forth, and the dividing pain split her in half, she imagined Darayavahu receiving his messenger. *Why has Artemisia let me down like this?*

It was too much. Artemisia turned her head and heaved.

Lobon stood up. "Bitchface! You will get used to this." He leaned in and slapped her. "Clean her up, Agamemnon, and put her in her cell for the night. Then bring me the tall, skinny maid. The one that cries."

A week later Artemisia found herself sitting in a cart with the Carian army, heading northeast. They went to Labraunda, where they stayed for two months.

Iokaste and Vadhut approached Artemisia in a private moment. "Is the sex any better?" Iokaste asked.

"No, rape is rape."

"If you submit and accept him, it won't be as horrible."

"I want it to be horrible."

"Then we must look for a way out," Vadhut declared.

"There's only one way." Artemisia was matter-of-fact.

"I count four, mistress." Iokaste frowned. "Suicide, escape, accepting the marriage, and killing him."

"There's only one. The first three allow Lobon to keep the Blood Throne of Caria and the White Throne of Halikarnassos. I'll never let that happen."

"Be careful of revenge, mistress." Vadhut interjected. "It can poison the soul."

"No revenge." Artemisia felt little emotion as she said it. "None needed. I don't want to kill him for some misguided sense of balance. I must liberate Caria from tyranny and..." Artemisia felt her heart break a little more than she wanted. "We need to make things right with Persia. My whole life I have wanted to rule Caria in my own right. Now my wants matter no longer—this is a matter of duty!"

"We can steal a dagger and—" Vadhut was interrupted.

"He only allows me to approach him naked, and that pig Agamemnon is usually there to help him." Artemisia felt a scowl emerge on her face, "When he mounts me, he pins my hands down. I'm not even allowed to use a pillow. Let's keep thinking about it."

In early June the Carian army moved into Aphrodisias territory. The democracy had declared itself in a state of rebellion against the rest of Caria and in alliance with Persia, but offered no resistance.

"The White Pillars!" Artemisia exclaimed when the army stopped.

"Won't it be ironic, dear?" Lobon gloated. "Your father defeated my father here, and now I'll defeat the Persians on the very same spot with you as my queen. That'll make my lie a little less dishonest, don't you think?"

During the war council, Artemisia listened. The Kilikian king had sent his son Pixodoros to advise the Carians. He said, "Since Lygdamis tore down the walls five years ago, we should fight with the Marsyas River to our backs."

My father made this place undefendable, and now you will defend it against the mighty Persian army. That's the real irony, dear husband.

"Why would we do that? Shouldn't we make the Persians fight their way across the river instead?" Polemarch Kboktis asked.

Pixodoros seemed genuinely puzzled by the question. "No, we should eliminate the possibility of retreat so that your men fight harder."

Kboktis turned to Lobon. "I want the river between us and the Persians."

"Agreed."

It took three days for the Persian army to arrive. They numbered in the thousands. Artemisia estimated it to be three times the size of the Carians.

"My queen, that's Daurises in command. Do you know him?" Lobon asked.

"No, I don't."

"What good are you to me anyway?" He shoved the side of her head.

The Persians made no attempt to parley. Instead they began to cross the river.

Artemisia noticed a large nest at the top of one of the white pillars. "I hadn't noticed that before. Eagle? Something large."

"Lesser spotted an eagle or maybe a golden eagle," Vadhut responded, to Artemisia's surprise.

The splashing of the Persian soldiers in the Marsyas River drew Artemisia's attention back to the battle. Horse archers still in the river stopped. They pulled back and let go of a large volley. Volleys of arrows landed on elevated shields and had a withering effect on the Carian rebels.

Artemisia felt tortured watching but felt certain that a defeat could serve her purposes.

The cries of battle rang out along the valley. Artemisia watched with disdain as Lobon led a counterattack. And then another. The Persians pushed hard, fell back. It became clear, however, that the Carians simply didn't have the numbers to sustain a prolonged battle against such a large host.

But the Carians rallied and drove the enemy back into the river. The hot day was beginning to cool. Artemisia looked around. All the women from the baggage train stood on carts and watched intently as their men killed and died. At dinnertime several mothers gathered the children around the fire and had them pass out bowls of stew. Artemisia could taste the hint of lamb. It was warm and calming.

Lobon led another charge. Again, the Carians rallied, but it was obvious to Artemisia they were on the verge of collapse.

Several soldiers arrived. "We're withdrawing!" The baggage train began to move, but Artemisia lingered in the back to watch as long as she could. Soon she saw units peel off and head south towards the baggage train.

As the sun set, the horsemen arrived. "We are heading for the Idrian Pass!"

When they had traveled half the night, the first Carian infantry units reached them. King Lycophron was in command. "This baggage train is too slow. You must get off the carts, take the horses, and travel as quickly as you can back to Labraunda. Queen Artemisia, you'll travel with me."

They crossed the pass over the Carian Mountains. Traveling as fast as they could, it took three days to reach Labraunda. Retreating Carians arrived in intervals. Artemisia watched, eagerly hoping Lobon was amongst the dead, but soon he came sitting on her saddle, mounted on Simurgh.

When Lobon reached Artemisia, he brought her to the Grand Hall of Labraunda. They each sat in oak thrones.

"We suffered terrible losses," Mnaseas declared.

"Whom amongst the kings?" Lobon asked.

"Only King Myrtis of Mylasa is dead, but is anyone here unwounded?" Damasithymos asked.

How ironic that the only king who died voted 'no.'

"What've we done?" Mnaseas asked.

You idiot! You could've married me. Right now, my father would be teaching you to be satrap. We might've even been happy together.

"Maybe we should leave?" Mnaseas went on.

"Leave?" Lobon asked.

"To Sicily or Calabria or Lucania. Far from here. Far from Persia!"

"You want to abandon Caria!" Lobon screamed.

"You want to stay and be defeated again?" Mnaseas was startled. "The Persians will be here in two days! We'll be dead in three days."

"You're a fool, Mnaseas!"

"Your Majesty," Damasithymos broke in. "I think we should discuss this."

"You too?"

"We lost five thousand men at the White Pillars. That was a catastrophe. I'd be surprised if we killed two thousand."

Artemisia found herself shaking her head. She stopped the instant she noticed.

"That's because we had to leave our wounded behind."

"And the baggage train!" Mnaseas shouted.

"It doesn't matter how we lost those men. We lost them!" Damasithymos declared.

"I'm not abandoning my home! Maybe we should've done what the Kilikian representative had suggested. How hard were your men fighting, Damasithymos?"

"Hard enough that half are dead."

"Bion, what's your opinion? You represent the Mylasa League," Artemisia asked, knowing Lobon would probably punish her. He gave no reaction.

"Your Majesties, we should surrender and beg for good terms," Bion replied.

Never. I need you to stay in the field.

"And risk execution? Is everyone here a coward?" Lobon's face turned red.

Artemisia was surprised at how angry he had gotten. *He'll drive a wedge in his own alliance.*

"Son, you go too far," King Lycophron said. "These are good men, not cowards. They fought bravely at the White Pillars. We just didn't have the numbers."

"What are you saying, Tata? Should we abandon Caria?"

"No. You're the Satrap of Caria, and I'll fight to the death to defend it for you, but we need to have a thorough conversation about our options. That's our way. And without impugning anyone's honor. Even Mylasa, which voted against this rebellion, was there and suffered such great losses."

Lobon looked down. He drew a deep breath and then let it out slowly. He straightened and adjusted his chiton. "You are correct, Father. I was carried away with emotion." He turned to the kings and nobles and bowed his head towards them. "You're the bravest. We fought a host three times our number and held them for five hours."

Artemisia was stunned by the display of contrition. *Was that sincere? Or did he see that he was making a mistake?*

"What sort of options do we have?" Lobon humbly asked.

"If we stay, I fear our men will suffer from low morale." Kboktis scratched his chin. "That was a terrible bruising. Between our numbers and morale, I vote we retreat."

"You're polemarch. Your vote carries much weight." Lobon looked at the floor. "I want to sleep on it. Our scouts say that the Persians will get here in two days. We must give our men a day to rest, anyway. Let's talk more in the morning."

That evening Artemisia gave no active resistance. Lobon began to rape her as usual but left the bed before he finished. Artemisia was surprised. She sat up. *Rage, contrition, and now what's this?*

In the morning Artemisia went to a window. Labraunda was nestled in the forest in a rocky, dry area. *"It controls a strategic pass linking Mylasa to Chrysaoris and Alinda."* Her father's lesson came to her.

As the sun reached its high point in the sky, horns blared from the south. "Persians?" From the second floor, Artemisia saw the Ionian banners. *Reinforcements. Lobon's lucky!* Before long she recognized Hecataeus and Melanthios. Her heart warmed and broke all at once.

She ran down to the Grand Hall. It seemed like forever before the

Ionians came in. Hecataeus walked in with Lobon at his side and Melanthios trailing. Hecataeus walked up to Artemisia. "Queen Artemisia, it's so good to see you."

"I thought you and Melanthios opposed the rebellion." *Please kill Lobon and take me to be your bride, Melanthios!* Artemisia screamed in her mind.

"Oh, we do, but I'm Polemarch of Miletos, and Melanthios is prytaneis. It is our duty to serve our polis, even when it clashes with our personal beliefs."

His statement was jarring. She was not sure where she fell in relationship to that understanding of duty. "Is Tyrant Aristagoras not the polemarch?"

"No, Your Majesty. He deposed the tyrants of Ionia and replaced them with democracies. Now he's in Thrake expanding the rebellion."

Lobon impatiently leaned in. "We must begin the war council."

Melanthios revealed no emotion, neither tenderness nor contempt nor heartbreak. *Has he cooled off towards me or is he a good actor? I want to scream! I want to shout my affection! I want to beg you to fight for me! But I must play it cool. I must wait for my opportunity. For now, Melanthios, I will return to you an emotionless face, though I have died ten times since I set eyes upon you.*

"Dearest kings and nobles of Caria, Ionia is here to fight the Persians!" Melanthios' voice was commanding. A roar rose up from the hall. "Let's see to the defenses!" Another roar rose up.

In an instant the men were pouring out of the hall. The long debate that Artemisia had been anticipating evaporated with two sentences from Melanthios.

Oh, to have had such a man at my side!

By noon the next day the Persians arrived. Again, their army was in greater numbers. But again, the rebels formed into ranks.

The Persian advance was made all the louder as they clacked swords against shields and shouted Zoroastrian blessings. Artemisia shuddered;

she knew what was coming. *If Daurises captures Lobon today, he will be executed, and I will be sent to Darayavahu to tell what has transpired here. He'll believe me and forgive me for my part. But he'll see me as a powerless woman and will never let me rule anything. If I'm lucky I would be allowed to become Khshayarsha's third wife.*

Victory for me must be shaped differently. I must put my mind to doing what I failed to do with Father! This riddle will be partially solved today. All that I know is that I can't afford for either side to win outright, and somehow, I must leverage myself into a position where I'm influencing outcomes!

As the collision of the two armies rang out, Artemisia startled, and birds exploded out of the trees. Men fell on both sides in large numbers. Artemisia turned to Iokaste. "Why do they do this?"

"Fight?"

"Yes. Look at that! It's pure madness," Artemisia said. "Remember that day? I was so eager to see, to understand battle. I look on, and I still don't understand. They're cutting each other to pieces. For what?"

"Honor, glory, power, women, gold, land, the Gods, the Plains of Elysium—"

"Don't women want such things?"

"No, mistress," Iokaste said. "I want warmth in the winter, shade in the summer, fatty food in the spring, grapes in the fall, and a man filling me with love all year round."

"I've failed you. You're still unmarried." Artemisia looked down.

"Of all times to bring that up!" Iokaste shrugged. "It doesn't matter anyway. I've been sexually active for six years. At first, I thought that I was mistress of the moons. But now I suspect I'm just sterile. I should've gotten pregnant by now."

"Oh, you could adopt."

"Or I could help you raise your children." Iokaste winked.

"What! How do you know?" Artemisia was surprised.

"I'm your handmaiden, mistress."

"I only just missed my period."

"It'll be a joy, pure delight to hold your baby." Iokaste beamed.

Artemisia softened. She imagined herself with a child.

"Mistress, you'll love him or her, regardless of how it was made."

Artemisia believed it. "This child will be mine. Lobon's nothing."

Just then Artemisia saw Melanthios lead men against a vulnerable spot in the Persian lines. Suddenly the Persian line buckled. Melanthios drove the men hard and deep towards the Persian rear. But Artemisia saw the danger.

She ran down the stairs to the polemarch of Caria. "Kboktis! The Milesians on the right flank have created a deep salient in the Persian line. However, if the Persians conduct a pincer movement, they could cut Melanthios and his men off."

Kboktis looked at Artemisia skeptically.

"Look for yourself! You can see from the palace balcony."

But the polemarch didn't go look. Instead he ordered men to reinforce the base of the bulge just as the Persians attacked that spot. When Artemisia reached the balcony, she could see it was all Melanthios could do to keep his salient from being destroyed. Slowly the Milesians were pushed back.

For hours the two armies clashed. Then Lycophron showed up. His arm was in a sling. "Your Majesty, you and your handmaidens must come with me."

"Where are we going?"

"We're running again." Lycophron's voice was tempered.

"Is it over?" Artemisia asked.

"It will be. Kboktis is breaking off the engagement." Lycophron gestured with his hand for Artemisia go with him.

The women mounted up and soon were trotting south. The king began to wobble. Artemisia wondered what was happening. Then he fell off his horse. The angled way his head hit the ground could have been enough to kill him, but the queen dismounted to be sure. "He's dead but not from the fall." She examined a wound on the inside of his thigh. "He bled to death."

Lycophron's aid was somber. "My orders are to escort you south."

"Where're we going?"

"Mylasa."

"Mylasa will fall too," Artemisia said matter-of-factly. "I hope Lobon survives." And she meant it.

The army arrived in Mylasa well after sunset. The kings and nobles poured into the Great Hall. "We have suffered another terrible defeat," Lobon said. "I need options."

"First I want to point out that we've lost your father and Kboktis," Mnaseas said. "I want to acknowledge the men on their way to Elysium and the heroics of the Milesians. No force took heavier losses and sent more Persians to Tartarus!"

A moment of silence set in. Artemisia saw Lobon's tears. *He has a heart?*

"We cannot defend Mylasa," Xenocrates declared. "We must retreat."

"We don't have time to bury the dead or say our farewells," Bion lamented. "But the enemy host will reach us tomorrow if we don't flee before first light."

"Where would we go?" Mnaseas asked.

"Halikarnassos?" Kharax, son of Kboktis, suggested.

"I'm told that I'm here today because Kboktis sent men to reinforce my salient into the Persian lines," Melanthios declared. "I'm also told that that maneuver was suggested to him by Artemisia."

All eyes turned towards her. *Is this my opportunity?*

"We'd have been completely overrun had Melanthios not successfully conducted that salient and then managed to extract his men," Mnaseas added. "It both disrupted their lines and bought us precious time. We owe the queen a debt of gratitude."

Artemisia scrambled for the right thing to say.

"Since Melanthios and Mnaseas have so eloquently attributed a portion of our survival to the queen," Hecataeus said, "we shouldn't just
honor her but seek to deepen the source of this well of wisdom."

Lobon nodded. "Very well, let's hear it. What would you do?"

Hecataeus! You gave me my in! "I'd run to the Pedasos Mountains.
Gather stray Ionian and Carian forces over the following months. The
Persians will want to secure the important Carian cities, and they will
take their time doing so. We use that time to prepare and train. When
everything's in place, we send out a raiding party. They'll feel the need
to retaliate and chase our raiders into the Pedasos Mountains. Only
we'll have prepared an ambush for them in the pass."

"You just came up with that?" Lobon asked.

*Look at how humbled Lobon is. My rapist listens to me. For him this
is personal. For me this is politics.* "No, Your Majesty, after the disaster
at the White Pillars."

"Why didn't you give your idea then?" Lobon asked.

"I'm a woman. It's not my place."

"Indeed, but you were a woman when you gave your idea to the
polemarch at Labraunda."

Artemisia shrugged, not wanting to admit that she had listened to
Iokaste's lesson and didn't want to seem too needy. She wanted to appear uninterested. She wanted them to come to her.

Lobon squinted, as if to discern some hidden writing on Artemisia's
forehead. "How long do you think it'll take?"

"I'd think we could attack in spring of next year."

The council talked, worked out the details, and concluded by agree-
ing to Artemisia's plan, thirty-one to ten.

*I betrayed Caria by keeping my plan from them. Now I've betrayed
Persia by giving them my plan. I've made pacts with Thanatos, the God
of Death, and Eris, Goddess of Chaos, so that I can position myself to
take back what's mine! If there's an Ahura-Mazda, could he forgive
me?*

After three hours of sleep, the army abandoned Mylasa and raced south. It took two days to get into the Pedasos Mountains. On the third day, they found a deep, forested canyon with a thin, flowing stream beside a mountain village that overlooked the Kerameikos Gulf. They sent scouts to watch for the Persians and retrieve the rest of scattered forces of Caria and Ionia.

That first night in a tent, laying by the babbling stream, Lobon turned towards Artemisia. "What would it take for you to stop hating me?"

"I'm glad that you knew not to ask about love!" *I can't imagine not hating you, but I'm not motivated by my hatred.* "You must surrender to me."

"Surrender?"

"Give yourself over to me. Declare in public that you've remorse for what you've done and that you're returning my status as queen and satrap and annulling our marriage because it was made without my consent."

"You're already queen. I never took that from you."

"I'm not a queen. I'm your rape toy." Artemisia tried to contain the venom.

"What if I stop raping you?" Lobon's face reminded her of her brother when he pleaded with her father.

She shook her head, though she knew Lobon could not see her.

"Well?"

"It'd be a start." Artemisia laughed inside.

"But it wouldn't be enough?"

"No, but I'd hate you less."

"To get rid of the hate, I'd have to surrender to you." Lobon was skeptical.

"Yes, completely and unconditionally." *What could you possibly do to repair my torn pride? Bring back my father, Nijara, and Myron? No amount of groveling could make that right.*

"But then you could execute me."

"Yes, I could, but if you surrendered I'd be inclined to show mercy.

Imagine how magnanimous that would make me seem. My first act as satrap—pardon my tormentor. That might be enough to heal the wound between Labraunda and Halikarnassos."

"But would I still be king?" His voice had a hint of whining in it.

"Of Labraunda, but since our marriage would be annulled, you'd lose Halikarnassos."

"What does that mean?"

"Well, with your father dead, you're the heir to Labraunda."

"I mean of Halikarnassos." His voice became high-pitched.

"Well, I'd look for a husband. You could interview for it."

"What are my chances?"

"Not as low as you think." Artemisia tried to imagine another round of interviews. Instead of handsome young men, her mind conjured up only empty chairs in an empty hall.

"Really?"

"You've shown yourself to be brave, audacious, and even open to criticism. Those are all rare features. But who are your competitors? Bion? Mnaseas?"

"And Damasithymos. He surely is high in your esteem," Lobon admitted.

"He is. It'd probably boil down to you two," she lied.

"Why would I take the chance on winning you back?"

"What was the question you asked?"

"Why would I take a chance on you picking me, when I already have you?" Lobon was confident he knew the answer.

"No, the original question. 'What would it take for you to not hate me?'" Artemisia reminded him.

"Why would you stop hating me because I freed you?"

"All men and women wish to possess some measure of dignity." Artemisia wondered if he would surrender. "If you let me freely choose, then I'd be inclined to forgive you for all that you've done."

"And would it be replaced by indifference?"

"No, that is hard for me to imagine. You murdered my father and two of my friends. And you have raped me for three months. Indifference is impossible."

"Then what emotion would you have for me?" His voice remained whiny.

"I'm not sure. It's one of those things which I don't think a person can truly understand, maybe even after it's transpired."

That night Lobon didn't force himself on Artemisia.

How interesting that he's even talking to me. I didn't expect that.

Lobon stopped raping Artemisia, and they started sleeping in separate tents. *What fool thinks that stopping torture would be enough to change my heart?*

In mid-September Artemisia approached Lobon. "I'm pregnant."

He froze.

"Yes, from one of the times you raped me."

Lobon seemed unable to understand. "How long?"

"Two months."

He burst into tears. She pulled back in surprise. He fell to both knees. "I'm sorry. I am so sorry. I don't know why I was so cruel to you."

Artemisia felt a hint of sympathy for Lobon. "Why were you cruel to me?"

"I don't know."

"Really, was it something you just did?" She was baffled.

Lobon hesitated. "I guess."

"Did you enjoy it?"

Again, Lobon took a while before answering. "Yes, very much."

Artemisia felt rage boil up from her bowels. "It brought you pleasure to cause me pain? Forget the pain. Pain can be exhilarating." Her voice got raspy as she talked through her teeth. "You crushed my soul and humiliated me. You poured shame into me like a man dumps his chamber pot into a stream. I had dreams." She paused and gauged his attentiveness. "Do you know what I imagined?"

He shook his head.

"I fantasized that I'd lose my virginity to the man of my choice. He'd be kind. It'd hurt, but I'd know that he was doing all he could to make it bearable, because he was my friend, my partner. And..." She realized that his moment of regret had caused her to lower her guard. She decided to stop sharing.

"I'd like to hear the 'And.'" Lobon's voice filled with kindness.

"I'll tell you the rest. All you have to do is annul our marriage and abdicate."

Lobon looked at the ground. Artemisia walked off, her resolve unshaken.

Life in the canyon was lovely. Vadhut and Iokaste attended to Artemisia as her belly grew. Lobon had a house built and they moved into it. "Just in time, too. I don't think I could have survived colder weather!"

In October, Iokaste came to Artemisia. "My period's two weeks overdue!"

"What! Io! This is such great news! Who's the father?"

"I don't know!" The women burst into laughter.

On Artemisia's nineteenth birthday, Iokaste sat in a chair in the cabin Lobon had built for the queen. They sipped a sour wine. Vadhut mustered the deepest voice she could conjure. "Artemisia of Caria."

"Approach, young princess." Iokaste's voice was also deepened. "You have turned nineteen. As king of kings, I, Darayavahu, grant you a wish. You may have anything—my son, my horse, my crown, Egypt, all of it, whatever you desire!"

"Your Excellency." Artemisia was stern. "I want your earwax."

The three women burst into laughter.

Lobon left to find recruits, for all of February and half of March. When he returned he continued trying to be kind to Artemisia, but she mostly ignored him.

"Mistress, Lobon has become bearable," Vadhut noticed.

Artemisia shrugged.

"You're not going to give him a chance?" she asked.

"No." Artemisia waddled toward Hecataeus' tent.

"Your Majesty, should you be walking about in the cold like this?"

"It's good for me," she insisted. "Hecataeus, can I have a moment with you?"

"Yes."

Melanthios left.

"Is your oath still good?"

"It is."

"But you're in rebellion against the man who made you swear it." Artemisia reminded him as she scanned his face for hints of insincerity.

"I'm in a reluctant rebellion. I'm honor bound to my polis, but none of that matters: I swore before Apollo."

"But now you know he's not your ancestor!"

"Regardless he's still my principle deity. I dare not break an oath sworn before Him. If you like, I'll renew the oath of allegiance."

"That won't be necessary. I need three things from you." Artemisia's voice became stern.

"Does that make us even?" Hecataeus asked.

"No. You swore an 'oath of loyalty,' not an 'oath of three favors.'"

"I see." Hecataeus seemed resigned.

"I'm glad that you do. Well, are you going to do them?"

"Yes. What are they?"

"First, I want you to propose that I be made the polemarch of Caria. They haven't appointed one since Kboktis' death. I can execute my strategy as I see fit and that would give us a fighting chance."

"Agreed."

"Next, I need you to send word to Dibikom, Prytaneis of Aphrodisias." Artemisia still watched his eyes for clues of his commitment. "Tell him to go Mylasa immediately. I need them to move there before twelve days are out. Send your man by fast horse. I want them at the southern gate to the city."

"But Aphrodisias is in revolt against Caria! What makes you think he'll come?"

"Tell him that I'm requesting it."

"Won't that alert the enemy of our plans?" Hecataeus was confused.

"If Dibikom betrays us, it will make the Persians believe we plan to attack Mylasa. They will still come up here to dig us out, but my instinct is that he won't. He was loyal to my father. I'm hoping that loyalty extends to me."

"Very well."

"And I want you to stay in with us until we make contact with him."

"After we win here, we must get back to Miletos to defend it against the Persians." Hecataeus seemed worried.

"After I get your help in this, there won't be a need to rush."

"Why not?"

"I plan to utterly destroy the Persian army in Caria."

Artemisia sat in the birthing chair sweating. Her groans did some to ease the pain, but she was in trouble and she knew it.

After a quarter of a day of labor, Artemisia's feet soaked in a puddle of sweat. She was in pain, angry about her powerlessness, and exhausted.

"Drink," the midwife insisted, while Iokaste tipped a cup to Artemisia's lips.

Artemisia felt the urge to push and responded, but nothing came of it. Earlier her bowels had emptied, and she was embarrassed, but that was the closest she had gotten to delivering the baby. The contractions were intense, but it was the urge to push that was the problem.

The midwife inserted her fingers into Artemisia's vagina. The strange intimacy of the action was canceled by the discomfort and frustration of the situation.

"Your cervix needs to open up more, but the last three times that I've measured, it has begun closing up."

Artemisia felt panic set in. "What does that mean?"

"It means that you need to push only after I tell you to. It's too early. You're battering the baby's head into your cervix, and it's swelling."

"I can't resist the urge."

Just then the door opened, and Lobon could be seen outside. Artemisia felt the hatred hotter than she had in months. She would have killed him if he were close enough, and the intensity of the feeling surprised the queen. Vadhut came in and closed the door.

"Your Majesty, you must obey me. I've seen this before! It's dangerous! I need you to let go," the midwife said. "Relinquish command to me, even if only temporarily. Order me to take command, whatever you have to do to save yourself and this baby."

"I order you to get this baby out of me!" Artemisia's voice was a shrill scream. She shocked herself.

"Artemisia, give her the power," Iokaste said. "I'm right here with you. I'll defend you."

It was jarring hearing Iokaste call her Artemisia. *Why does being called by my name feel so strange? This is about powerlessness! If I surrender to this midwife, what do I have left to control?* "I order you to take command. I completely surrender to you."

"Vadhut, take her other hand," the midwife commanded. "Artemisia, when the next impulse to push comes, fight it. Don't give in. Squeeze the hands of Iokaste and Vadhut instead."

Artemisia nodded. When the urge came, she fought it. Her back arched a bit from the power she put into holding the urge.

"Good."

Vadhut wiped the sweat from the queen's brow with her free hand.

Artemisia got into the rhythm of listening to the midwife, resisting her urges, and focusing on her breathing between the contractions, but she was tired and didn't know how much longer she could go. Her mind wrapped itself around random memories. Egypt, Shoosh, the Pegasos sword *now in someone else's possession*, the sunsets in Ecbatana, and Artazostreh's beautiful face.

The midwife probed her more. "Artemisia, all your hard work is paying off. The baby's head is in position, and you are opened up. Now on the next urge, push."

It came with a contraction, and Artemisia happily surrendered to it. The discomfort of the contraction was mitigated by the pushing sensation.

"Good. Every time the urge comes…"

Artemisia pushed and pushed. "I like working." She groaned. She felt like another quarter day had passed since she surrendered, but once the pushing had started, she found relief.

"The head's crowning."

The crowning came with an intense burning. Artemisia wanted someone to throw water on her groin. She tried to lift up, as if she could retreat from the source of the burning, but she was too tired to move her large body.

"Keep pushing. Not long now."

Artemisia marveled at the abuse her body had endured. The tearing pain, the burning pain, the muscle pain, the soreness from her legs where they met the seatless birthing chair, and the pain in her back all mingled in with the strength of a soul. "This is life—pure, raw life. I'm coming apart to make a new separate person."

No one responded, so she was not sure if they understood her.

Crying, who? Me? A baby?

"Your Majesty." The midwife's voice was soothing and lilting. "You've given birth to a healthy, strong-willed baby boy."

A moment later she passed the placenta. She could see the midwife but couldn't focus. Vadhut and Iokaste helped Artemisia stand and led her to the bed. They laid her down. And then put the baby on her chest. He immediately tried to latch onto the nipple. With the coaching of the midwife, Artemisia and the baby managed what seemed to be a second Heraclean task—breastfeeding.

"I'm naming you Pissindelis, for your uncle. I'm going to make the world right for you."

On a warm day in the middle of spring, Artemisia sent King Mnaseas to lead the raiding party against Mylasa. With Pissindelis attached to her breast, she watched as they left. "What's good about this?"

"What, mistress?" Vadhut asked.

"Motherhood!"

"I don't understand." The Amazon turned handmaiden cocked her head.

"I haven't slept in a month. My nipple feels like it's going to fall off—in fact, a piece has! Breastfeeding is the hardest thing I've ever learned. This creature takes, takes, and takes…"

"But his smile! Mistress, his smile!"

"That smile!" Artemisia slapped her chest.

As if on cue, Pissindelis gave them a heart-melting smile.

When Mnaseas returned he went to Artemisia's mountain home. "Polemarch, I've struck the hornets' nest. They're behind my men and will arrive tomorrow."

Artemisia convened the war council.

"I know we've already voted on the matter, but it causes me concern that we've let this woman be polemarch," Bion said.

"Duly noted," Lobon replied. "Yet here we are. We voted for the polemarch's plan and soon the enemy will be upon us. This is no time to change plans."

Look at that shiteater. He defends me to the war council in hopes he can win me over! You had your chance. I offered you surrender. It's too late now.

"Agreed," Xenocrates added. "To change polemarch now would only lead to confusion. No one understands her plan better. I, for one, am ready for this to be resolved one way or another. Pedasos!"

The kings shouted, "Pedasos!" The men replied in kind.

"We've trained for this moment. The queen has deployed us throughout the pass. We've drawn hundreds of reinforcements and rehearsed what we're supposed to do." Lobon looked at each king. "Let's resolve to take back what's ours or die as Carians!"

The kings roared. The men replied.

Fearing that the Persians might approach during the night, Artemisia convinced Lobon to deploy the various units. They slept in the three side valleys that merged with the main pass.

In the northwest was Lobon and Bion: all of Xanthos and Mylasa and one-quarter of the Kalynda. In the central eastern valley, she put Xenocrates with half of the Kalyndians. In the southwest valley, she deployed the rest of Kalyndians under Kandaules and the Ionians under Hecataeus, save the Milesians and Melanthios. Artemisia kept them with her at the top of the hill formed by the pass, the northwest valley, and the southwest valley. From the wooded top she could see the pass and all three side valleys.

"Satrap, I want my horses." Artemisia's voice was confident.

"Simurgh?" Lobon was skeptical.

"Yes."

"Why would I give him to you?" He looked her in the eyes.

"I need to be able to move quickly. You can't have me as polemarch and without a mount. Vadhut's my bodyguard. I need Priam for her."

Lobon gave in reluctantly.

Once everyone was deployed to her satisfaction, she put Simurgh and Priam on the back side of the hill with the Milesians. She found a tree she could climb and slept beneath it next to Vadhut, Iokaste, and Pissindelis.

Early in the morning, Mnaseas' raiders ran through the pass and came into view. Artemisia tensed. "There they are! Look how fast they are running! The enemy must be right behind them."

The Persians were. The pass was too wooded to bother with horse archers, and so they harried the Myndosians with javelins. The line of Persians came and came and came. Artemisia climbed the tree and looked down each valley.

It took nearly an hour for the Persians to get into place. They were stretched over two and a half miles of winding mountain road. It was then that she heard the southwest valley blow its horn. The Carians in the other two valleys charged. Their roars bounced off the hills, making three asynchronous echoes. Artemisia climbed down from the tree and walked to Melanthios. "Prytaneis, give Vadhut and me each a sword."

"You are going to fight?" Melanthios was surprised.

"Yes."

He nodded to a man who brought two swords. "It will be a while, but just in case an opportunity avails itself, keep the men ready."

"Won't they see us?"

"Not only are you my reserve, Prytaneis, but you are also their distraction." She looked down into the central valley. The battle was ferocious, but Artemisia managed her emotions. *This is my moment.* "Melanthios, under no circumstances are you to move from here." Vadhut following, she rode Simurgh south along the mountain ridge. The southern end was partially cleared of trees before the battle, to allow Artemisia to observe the southernmost tip of the ambush.

Iokaste sat, large and beautiful. She held Pissindelis. Artemisia dismounted and breastfed her baby. For twenty minutes she took turns making eye contact with the boy, watching the battle below, and looking out at the calming Kerameikos Gulf, visible beyond the mountains. When she was done, she handed the child to Iokaste.

Artemisia reassessed the battle. There were a group of Persians trapped between Mnaseas' men and Kandaules' men. Kandaules led the Kalyndians up the pass. There the fight was intense, and the Persians appeared to be in disarray. But Artemisia was annoyed. Kandaules had agreed that he would merely hold the Persians and not fight his way north. That would allow them to be drawn downhill and pool up. "But not if the idiot pushes them back up the hill!" She passed her baby back to her handmaiden. "Bring me Pissindelis in two hours."

Artemisia rode to the Milesians. There she could see that the central force under Xenocrates was fully engaged trying to cut the Persians in two. They waited and watched for over an hour.

Melanthios came to Artemisia. "My men are eager and anxious to join the fight."

"Are they exhausted?"

"Of course not." Melanthios was confused by the question.

"Those Persians are going to be a mess in two hours." Artemisia studied the fighting.

"You want us to wait two more hours?"

"I want you to listen to the polemarch." Artemisia glared at Melanthios.

He replied with a look of hurt surprise.

As the battle raged, the Milesians and Artemisia began to pace. "We must be patient. I haven't stayed our hands for nothing. There are thousands of Persians down there. Daurises has kept a reserve force to face us. But his patience will end. He'll rotate some of his exhausted men with the reserve. When he does we'll go."

Iokaste arrived with Pissindelis. Artemisia eagerly opened her gown and let the baby latch on and felt an instant relief from the pressure. Moments later, as the sun reached its highest point, Daurises rotated his reserve into action and replaced them with an exhausted force.

"Men, ranks!" Artemisia handed Pissindelis back to Iokaste and mounted Simurgh. The Milesians wasted no time. When Daurises had completed the exchange, Artemisia shouted, "Charge!"

Leading by horse, Artemisia, Vadhut, Melanthios, and six Milesians worked their way down the hill. The men behind them were roaring. The exhausted Persians crammed into formation along the narrow road.

Just as they got close, Artemisia shouted, "Thanatos and Eris!" Her nine cavalrymen blasted between the trees and into the ranks of Persians. Artemisia swung, taking opportunity shots as Simurgh plowed through the enemy.

The first blow landed hard on a man's head. She heard the crack as his skull broke, sending a vibration through the hilt. The soldier fell straight down. A bloodied Persian raised his spear against Simurgh but was bashed by Vadhut's steed. An exhausted Persian tried to hold his position as Simurgh knocked down his comrade, but the man could barely swing his sword. Artemisia parried and then struck down hard, knocking the weapon from his hand.

A terrible crash came from behind. Artemisia turned to see the Milesians rushing the Persians she had passed. She turned Simurgh around and charged back through their ranks. The Persians were sent into disarray. Artemisia rode up to Melanthios. "I want to lead the Milesians south, down the road! We can connect with Xenocrates! Then I want to hunt Daurises!"

Melanthios nodded, and the Milesians turned south. Artemisia's arms were already sore. She realized she was tiring fast and fell back as the battle raged in front of her.

"Xenocrates!" Melanthios shouted.

Artemisia looked in the direction to the Lorymians fighting their way towards her. Soon they connected. Xenocrates, Parydik, and three horsemen rode to Artemisia, Melanthios, and Vadhut.

Xenocrates began. "We have punched a large hole in the Persian center! But they managed to fight their way into the central valley. My men are doing all they can to push them back out of the valley."

Artemisia took in what the Lorymian said. "Have you seen Daurises?"

"He's in the center."

Melanthios asked, "What if instead of trying to push that force back into the pass, we tried to cut it off from the rest of the Persian army? That way, at least, they can't expand or develop their position."

"You mean attack across the road to make a Carian salient that's the size of the mouth of the central valley?" Xenocrates sought to clarify.

"Yes."

Artemisia liked what they proposed. "And we could try to locate Daurises in the process."

"I only have four horsemen left, including myself," Xenocrates said.

"We have nine," Melanthios said.

"Let's combine the thirteen horsemen and put them in reserve." Artemisia ordered. "We'll keep us on the ready to create shock when the opportunity is right."

Artemisia watched as the Kalyndians and Milesians formed up and fought their way across the road. The Persians tried to swing their force out so that their line was turned rather than cut. The maneuver slowed the Carian and Ionian advance, but an hour later Artemisia had cut off the Persians in the central valley.

The Carian-Ionian line, however, was thin. Artemisia feared that the Persians might realize this and counterattack. "What if we created a salient like Melanthios did at Labraunda? We could aim our tip directly at Daurises."

"We're so thin, it'd be extremely dangerous, Polemarch," Xenocrates cautioned.

"But the queen's proposal has merit," Melanthios countered. "They'll believe that we're trying to cut them in half. Their natural response will be to defend, not attack."

Xenocrates pointed. "What if we take those men there and send them up the valley. They could come back down on the other side of our salient."

"Divide our forces?" Artemisia's voice was high from surprise, and it made her self-conscious.

"We're thin, and I'm proposing thinning us out more, but having that flanking force might plunge them into chaos," Xenocrates offered.

"Dangerous." Artemisia shook her head but wasn't ready to rule it out.

"A trapped army is unlikely to allocate more men to anything but fighting their way out," Melanthios attempted to reassure. "They'll put everything they have in the north and south."

"Two to one," Artemisia said. "So be it. Send the men up the valley, and we'll make a salient towards Daurises."

Artemisia didn't feel very rested, but she knew she had to prove herself. As the salient pushed deeper into the wooded valley, Artemisia could hear fighting from behind the Persians. "It's either an echo or the flankers. *Charge!*"

In an instant the thirteen horses lurched forward. They hit a group of horse archers fighting with swords and javelins. "Oreios and his Oxylos, and his wife Hamadryas, I give thanks for the trees that negate their arrows!"

A horse archer, wielding a javelin, stabbed at Artemisia, but she ducked as she veered Simurgh right. Then she saw Daurises.

He rode a mount as proud as Simurgh and wore bronze scale armor. His helmet was decorated with brightly colored plumes, and his small round red and white shield was decorated with a scorpion.

Look at that armor! A woman, without armor, is about to charge a trained cavalry general covered in bronze scales. I must be touched by the Goddess Lyssa!

Artemisia rode past two Persians to reach the general. He looked Artemisia up and down and then charged. She counter-charged. A branch surprised her in the head. The blow was disorienting and Simurgh turned a hard right. She found herself charging up the mountain, away from the general, into a thick patch of trees.

Annoyed, she turned Simurgh around and rode back down. By then Daurises had engaged Xenocrates. The two men clashed swords. As Artemisia drew near, the spahbed pulled back, allowing two horse archers to engage with Xenocrates. When he was clear of the Lorymian, the Persian turned towards Artemisia and began another charge. Her breast hurt, swollen with milk. They bounced relentlessly, but she was determined. Myron's voice came to her, *Watch your enemy's eyes. Don't watch his arms. The eyes show you where he is going. Hands can be used to deceive!*

She interpreted his next move as a spear throw at her chest. Knowing she couldn't duck, and fearing another branch to the head, she prepared to block with her sword. She caught the javelin with the edge, and it shot up as she turned her head to the left. The tip caught her cheek, slicing it open as it flew past.

Artemisia tossed her sword and caught it backwards. She aimed for Daurises' shoulder, bringing her fist down as hard as she could manage. The tip smashed the bronze scales over the clavicle. Her forward momentum drove the blade between them and deep into Daurises. However, she misjudged and didn't let go in time. The two were pulled out of their saddles and crashed onto the rocky forest floor.

Gasping for air, with the wind knocked out of her and a sharp pain in her back, Artemisia tried to stand. Daurises rolled over and got onto all fours. She tried to walk but stumbled and landed on Daurises' back. She pulled his helmet with her left hand and with the other grabbed the hilt sticking out of the top of the man's chest.

She pushed but could not move it deeper. She pulled but could not get it to come out. Fumbling, she found a rock and used it to bash him in the face. He groaned. She hit him again; blood covered her hand. Then she reached under and smashed the pommel of her sword, sinking it deeper. And again.

Daurises' left arm gave way, and he collapsed under her. The clopping of hooves caused her to spin around. A Persian horse archer was closing in on her with a javelin. She watched his eyes and then gambled that he would not throw towards the spahbed. She rolled off and propped him up on his side. The Persian rode past.

Again, she grabbed the hilt. This time she braced her feet against the general's shoulders and pulled as hard as she could. The sword came slowly free, scraping against bone as it did. The taste of blood filled her mouth, and she realized that she could suck in air through the slit in her cheek.

She looked for Persians in the area. When she realized she was safe, she held Daurises' head by the helmet. He reached up with his hand, trying to grab her. She slid the sword under his throat. "I'm sorry, Spahbed."

"I'm—"

She didn't let him finish and cut his throat. His arm fell to the side, and he gurgled as he convulsed. A moment later he was completely still. She severed his head with two more cuts. In pain everywhere and still wobbly, she managed to stand. She grabbed the general's sword and scorpion-decorated shield. She slid Daurises' sword under Simurgh's saddle. She knew it would cause Simurgh discomfort, but she also realized no one was likely to look there. Then mounting her stallion, she held up the spahbed's head in one hand and his shield in the other. In Imperial Court Persian, she shouted, "Daurises is dead! Surrender and you will be spared."

Persian morale collapsed as Artemisia rode with the spahbed's head. Just over twelve hundred prisoners surrendered; nine hundred were wounded.

Satrap Lobon called a war council. As Vadhut sewed Artemisia's cheek, a Kalyndian soldier came to take the sword Melanthios had lent Artemisia. She gave no resistance. When another went for the shield, she grabbed it. *Let me keep it, bitchface!*

Lobon shook his head. He stepped up to her and raised her hand. "The queen!"

The men roared.

Artemisia could not fight the pride in her veins, even as she clutched the shield.

"Your plan worked beyond all expectations!" Lobon declared.

Your expectations; it met mine!

"We've killed thousands of Persians today, and though our losses are high, as you promised, we have utterly wiped out the enemy." The king tried to look Artemisia in the eyes. She looked at his, reluctantly. "You've redeemed the White Pillars and Labraunda. Our victory's so great, we haven't lost any kings today, though I believe that all of us are wounded." He looked around as if to provide evidence.

"I'd like to invoke Eleos, the Goddess of Forgiveness, and implore you to take her into your heart." Lobon added. "I've wronged you and don't know how to redeem myself."

Artemisia was surprised at the public contrition Lobon displayed, but she didn't hesitate. She stood, letting the shield hang by her side. *I don't forgive you.* "I forgive you." *How could I, you fool! You didn't surrender.*

"There." He opened his arms wide for a hug.

Artemisia walked slowly to accept the hug, never letting go of the shield. *If I pretend that I want this, perhaps it'll never occur to them that there's something I want more under Simurgh's saddle.*

That evening she hid Daurises' sword in her saddlebag as she took off his saddle. "He let me keep you to soften my heart," she whispered as she combed her steed.

The next day the work of stripping the equipment and burying the dead began. She took Vadhut and Pissindelis to visit the Persian prisoners. A group of them stood as the queen approached. "Men of Persia, I'm in need of your help."

"How do you speak the Persian of the Imperial Court?" a surprised soldier asked.

"I used to be a ward of Emperor Darayavahu."

"There's no amount of help that can save you and Caria now!" a second soldier said.

"I serve Persia. Help me, help Persia."

The Persians scrutinized the queen. "I doubt that we're in a position to help you," the first soldier said.

"What's your name?" Artemisia asked as she approached him.

"Ravant."

"Ravant, you and your men are exactly in that position," she said. "I'm going to have you strip the dead and prepare them for burial."

"We're slaves of Caria. What choice do we have?" Ravant asked.

"I want you to rearm yourselves secretly."

The second Persian stepped forward. "Why?"

"I need men who'll fight for me."

"We're exhausted and demoralized," he protested.

"We've been defeated in a manner that the Persian army is

unaccustomed to," Ravant added. "I doubt many of my people are going to take up arms. Who are you?"

"I'm Queen Artemisia, the rightful Satrap of Caria, but my father was murdered, and my throne stolen. I'm going to lead a revolt against the pretender and return Caria to Persia."

Ravant's eyes narrowed. "I know you. I was in Shoosh, in the Royal Palace five years ago. You were the Hellenic princess! The emperor gave you a wish. You were so confident." Ravant turned to the men standing near him. "You wouldn't believe what she asked for. What were you? Thirteen?" A tear ran down his cheek. "She asked that the emperor order our beloved Empress Atoosa to have a surgery that saved her life." Ravant genuflected. "You have one immortal. I swear my fealty to you, as Ahura-Mazda is my witness."

In an instant a group of Persians joined Ravant on a knee.

"No, no, get up. Don't bring attention to us." She waved her hands, gesturing for them to stand. "Get the weapons from the dead and injured and hide them. Put them somewhere that you can get to quickly, even if it means arming with daggers."

"We'll do it," Ravant said.

"Wait," said a third Persian. "I saw this woman yesterday. She is the woman who killed Spahbed Daurises."

"Is this true?" Ravant asked.

"It is," Artemisia admitted.

"You don't deny it?" Ravant seemed skeptical.

"No. I also came up with the plan that destroyed your army. I'm riddled with shame and remorse, but it was what I had to do."

"Why?" Ravant grimaced at Artemisia.

"I've told you. I must free Caria from my rapist and return it to the Persian Empire."

"But if Daurises had won, it would've been returned to Persia." Ravant was clearly confused.

"As a conquered land, without me as satrap. Those were two wrongs that I couldn't allow. Serve me, and we'll put things right. I'm going to return Caria to order."

"You were honest with me, and I've already sworn my oath to you before Ahura-Mazda and these men. I serve Your Highness," Ravant declared.

Artemisia stared at the third Persian. He frowned and walked off.

"Hecataeus," Artemisia said, "it's going to take us a long time to get all of the dead and wounded taken care of. Perhaps we can enlist the Persian prisoners?"

"Brilliant idea."

Artemisia watched as the Ionians guarded the Persian prisoners who worked the corpses. They were careful, but she saw that on occasion one of them would hide a dagger.

So terrible were the losses that it took ten days to tend to the wounded, strip the dead, and bury them. And it took another day to load the wagons and horses.

Artemisia led Simurgh as the army slowly worked its way north. It took two days to reach the base of the Mylasa Plateau. As they set up camp, Artemisia noticed a horseman on the northern horizon. He watched for a moment and then rode off.

The next day Artemisia kissed Pissindelis on the top of the head. She gave him to Iokaste and then kissed the woman, large with eight months of pregnancy. They rode in a cart with several wounded men. She put Daurises' scorpion shield on her back and mounted Simurgh.

Artemisia took stock of the kings and princes. Damasithymos rode in the rear. In the front, from left to right, were the four Kalyndian kings: Mnaseas, Lobon, Kandaules, and, Xenocrates. They raved proudly about their exploits. Artemisia rode behind them listening. *You take too much credit!*

"How's the—" Vadhut was cut off by Artemisia's hand.

She did not want to risk losing her focus, but Artemisia knew the question and so was compelled to stick the tip of her tongue into the gash through her cheek. It stung and tasted like iron.

After the road turned towards the north, the Mylasa Plateau reclined on their left, the farm filled Plain of Mylasa lay on their right, and Mount Mylasa stood in front of them. Slightly to the right of the mountain, Artemisia saw the city's southern wall. She squinted and made out a group of men in formation in front of it. Her heart jumped. *Dibikom came! The kings haven't noticed! Either they're drunk on our victory or they think that those men are Persians.*

When they reached three thousand feet, Kandaules raised a closed fist. The whole army stopped. The kings looked at the Aphrodisians. They studied them, as if they could discern Dibikom's intentions. Kandaules looked at Lobon and then back to the Aphrodisians. "It looks like all of Dibikom's army's here."

"My men," Artemisia whispered.

"Mistress?" Vadhut whispered back.

Artemisia gave no reply. She reached into her saddle bag and grabbed the hilt of Daurises' sword. *Now ends my pact with Thanatos and Eris! Don't move, husband. Don't move, Kandaules. I spring upon you like an Anatolian leopard pouncing two fallow deer.*

She laid Daurises' sword in her lap and put Simurgh into a gallop. As she pulled near the two men, she raised Daurises' sword. Kandaules glanced at her and then back to the Aphrodisians. She swung it two-handed, as hard as she could, aiming the tip towards Lobon's neck. It made contact, cutting deep, nicking bone, and passing through the muscle and skin. The sensation that vibrated through the blade was thrilling.

Lobon grabbed the side of his neck as one might do when stung by a mosquito.

Artemisia kept the sword in full swing, rolling over her wrists so that the blade pointed backwards. Kandaules turned again to look at her, just in time for the blade to sink into his throat. It plunged until it passed through bone. She spurred Simurgh forward, pulling the sword out.

Kandaules slumped forward and fell off his mount, gasping as he crashed into the road. Artemisia shouted, "I forgive you too, shiteater!"

When she was twenty feet away, she turned Simurgh around. Lobon was still mounted. He held the side of his neck with such strength that his knuckles turned white. His neck was bent at an odd angle. His eyes were closed, as if he could concentrate hard enough to keep his life from pouring out from between his fingers.

Artemisia raised her bloody sword high. "I *am* the Satrap of Caria and the Queen of Halikarnassos. If you dispute this come fight me!"

A roar rose up from the Aphrodisians as they began running towards Artemisia. A moment later a second-roar came from the middle of the Carian army; the Persian prisoners had toppled over a cart and were tossing weapons to each other. Vadhut began to form them into ranks.

"Hecataeus and Melanthios!" Artemisia shouted.

Both men turned to their men and ordered them into ranks.

"Men of Halikarnassos, I've avenged your king! Fight for me!"

A roar rose up from the Halikarnassians.

Mnaseas and Xenocrates turned to each other and then back to Artemisia.

The minutes grew long, but that gave the Aphrodisians time to arrive.

Lobon opened his eyes. They pleaded with Artemisia as he started to open his mouth. She wondered what he would say, but no voice come. Instead he fell to the right, crashing into the road, his head bent at a peculiar angle. Xenocrates stared for a long moment at the two dead kings. Then he looked at Mnaseas, again. The King of Loryma dismounted. He walked ten feet, drew his sword, dropped to a knee, and pointed the hilt towards Artemisia.

Mnaseas mimicked his comrade. Then Kharax, Parydik, and Bion followed suit. Only Damasithymos hesitated. But soon he grew a look of resignation. The prince whom Artemisia had just turned into king rode to a spot next to Mnaseas and genuflected. The Aphrodisians, Persians, Ionians, and Halikarnassians roared, "Artemisia!"

Book III · The Blood Throne

Artemisia rode up to the Halikarnassians. From her saddle she looked at each man. "Am I your queen?"

The men dropped to a knee and bowed their heads. The highest ranked amongst them, a powerful Carian named Saroljats, shouted. "By Zeus, we are the Queen's army!"

The men shouted, "By Zeus we *are* the Queen's army."

She rode to the Persians. "You've served me here today, but I want you to serve me for all eternity."

Ravant looked up at the queen. "We're your slaves to do with as you please."

"No, Ravant, I serve Persia. When you took up weapons to fight for me, you returned Caria to Persia. You may join up with Artaphernes if you wish. However, I want those of you willing to serve me to stay." Of the 314 unwounded Persians, 144 chose to stay. The rest formed into a line and after farewells headed north.

Ravant shouted, "Take a knee!" In unison the 141 men and three women did so. "By Faravahar we swear to serve Artemisia for all entirety," they called out together.

To her surprise the Persian who had objected to her killing of Daurises was one of the men kneeling. Artemisia rode up to him. "You stayed."

"A warrior wants a commander to be calm, brilliant, and lucky. To serve such a commander is the greatest reward."

Artemisia felt like her heart would explode. *If my father could see me now!* The pain in her breasts had been replaced by an overwhelming sense of accomplishment. She smiled as she surveyed her soldiers. "How can it be that the Gods love me so much that they have made me your servant? I'm truly under Tyche's good graces."

Artemisia turned to Hecataeus and Melanthios. "Go to Miletos. Talk your people into ending this revolt."

"I'll try, Satrap." Hecataeus bowed his head.

Melanthios smiled as he reined his horse around in a circle. "You are truly luminescent!"

Artemisia blushed.

He then put his men into column and led them north.

She shouted to Bion, "Come with me!"

The two, plus Vadhut, galloped to the Aphrodisians. When she reached Dibikom, she shouted, "Prytaneis, you came!"

"Your father was my friend. When he was murdered, we went into rebellion. When Hecataeus' man came to us and told us of your request, we marched here as fast as we could. You've avenged your father and restored order. Now you're our friend."

Artemisia dismounted and walked up to the Aphrodisian army. The army behind her followed. The gray-haired archon bowed. Artemisia returned the bow. Still bowed, she reached out her arms. Dibikom took them in his hand, easily wrapping them. *Being with men is like riding a horse, a massive animal. He could buck you off and then step on you. I've offered Dibikom this gesture of trust. With the flick of his wrist, I would be his slave. How can I trust any man?*

Together they returned to Mylasa's southern gate. She looked at the closed gate and up at the wall. There was a Persian officer looking back. "I'm Queen Artemisia, the Satrap of Caria."

The officer gave no reply.

"I've killed the pretender and ended the rebellion. Now I need my capital."

"Where's Daurises?" the Persian asked.

"He died in battle," Artemisia said.

"How do I know that you are telling the truth? Maybe this is a rebel trick."

Artemisia turned to Vadhut. "Bring Ravant. Let him testify."

When Ravant arrived he shouted, "You saw the satrap kill the pretender on the road. Let her in so that she might return Caria to order."

Artemisia added, "Retain control of the walls." She turned to King Bion. "The king will accept that."

"What happened to the rest of the Persian army?"

"We're all that's left." Ravant hung his head. "The Carians destroyed our army and killed Daurises in battle. But Artemisia avenged Daurises by ending the rebellion."

Artemisia felt waves of guilt and relief wash over her.

"I'm now the ranking officer then!" the officer on the wall shouted.

"You are," Ravant acknowledged.

"Will the remainder join me?"

"No, sir. Those remaining are sworn to Artemisia. The rest returned to Sardes."

The officer sighed hard, and then the gate groaned open.

As Artemisia, her men, the Mylasians, and the kings walked into the city, she made a point of keeping Dibikom next to her. They headed straight to the palace. Mylasians lined the streets or stood on balconies to watch the procession.

Once inside the palace, the satrap walked straight to the blood red marble throne. She leaned her scorpion shield up against the side and sat. Iokaste waddled over with Pissindelis in her arms. Artemisia pulled out a breast. Several men turned, but she made a point of not acknowledging their discomfort. *Or was it a sign of respect?*

Bion walked up to the white throne. He hesitated and then nervously sat. For several minutes Artemisia cooed to Pissindelis as he suckled loudly. Then she moved him to the left. The room remained otherwise silent.

When she was done, Iokaste took the child and sat on the oak throne. *As if she's my queen! I love it.* She rubbed the itchy scab and stitches on her cheek. Then she looked at the white peplos that Lobon had given her. It was stained in Daurises' blood and the blood from her cheek. A thin spray of Kandaules' blood was bright across the top of her right shoulder. She looked at her left shoulder. Lobon's blood was red and damp. She grinned. "It's truly the blood throne now!"

The corpses of Lobon and Kandaules were brought into the Boule and dropped unceremoniously on two tables brought in for the occasion. Artemisia glanced at them and then took in the Halikarnassian, Aphrodisian, and Persian lined hall. The perspective from the blood throne was different somehow. The kings of Caria sat waiting, and the three Bouleutai priests stood, motionless.

Artemisia nodded to Bion.

He didn't hesitate. "You bring honor to our hall, Satrap of Caria and Ki...Queen of Halikarnassos."

"Your welcome brings honor to the satrapy, King of Mylasa. Your open palace, our ancient capital makes the satrapy one." Artemisia nodded to the priests.

The high priest turned to the other two. They raised two sistrums and the incense burner. The jingling sounded like a metallic rain, and the smell of the burning sweetgum was intoxicating. The senior priest said a long prayer to Zeus.

When he was done, Artemisia said, "I want a prayer to Apollo, Athena, and Artemis. Surely this council would benefit from some harmony, wisdom, and virginity." Several men laughed, but Artemisia successfully fought off a smile.

The priest took the matter seriously and said three quick prayers. When it was done, Artemisia declared, "May the Boule begin. The first order of business is *who* has my Pegasos sword?"

When no one replied, she added, "On one side it says, *pikartmi*, 'Luminous Artemis,' and on the other side it says, *not parabanda*, 'Brought forth victory.' I want it back."

Xenocrates stood. "I retrieved it from Lobon, Your Highness. I didn't realize that it was yours."

Artemisia gestured for him to step forward. Ravant received the sword and offered it to Artemisia. She unsheathed it and laid it in her lap and remembered with a shock. *Melanthios! He said, "You are truly luminescent!"* She chewed on the compliment and quietly sighed. "Melanthios." *He gave me the sword.*

She straightened her back and declared, "I want to discuss rehabilitating Caria. That requires not merely repairing the damage and training of a new generation of warriors, but it also requires us to get right with our own people and the Imperial Court. I'm going to dispatch men to both Satrap Artaphernes and to the emperor to announce the end of the rebellion.

"Second, this was the second time that Labraunda revolted in six years, and now it has no ruler. I'm reducing that kingdom by taking the Idrian Country and adding it to Halikarnassos. In this way the dispute with Aphrodisias is resolved, and reparations for the death of my father are made.

"In addition, I'm appointing Trielis to the throne of the Labraunda. He's both my cousin and a cousin of Lycophron, and therefore will be acceptable to all. Finally, he has told me that he is removing Labraunda from the Kalyndian League and bringing it into the Leleges League.

"And fourth, I've sent for Nicander and Karkinos. I propose that we wait until they arrive to conduct any further business. How do you vote on these matters?"

The measures passed without objection.

Artemisia sheathed the sword and left for her father's quarters in the palace.

When five days had passed, Xenocrates was summoned to Artemisia's quarters. He came with an attendant and sat on a padded chair.

"You'll support me?"

"Yes, Your Highness."

"I've killed your friends." Artemisia examined his face for emotion.

"I did count both Kandaules and Lobon amongst my friends."

"You've no desire for revenge."

"Why should I?" Xenocrates appeared to be telling the truth.

"They were your friends."

"You didn't bring me here to find out if I was plotting vengeance. If you thought I was, you'd have killed me by now. It's also obvious you didn't bring me here to form an alliance. Taking Labraunda away from us has left the Kalyndian League with only eight votes. You or Mylasa need only ally with each other or Xanthos to pass a resolution, but allying with us isn't enough to get anything done. Moreover, I'm the weakest king in all of Caria. I've no other delegates, just one vote. One vote isn't enough to make a difference in anything."

"That's why I've brought you here, your calculating mind. I've thought about what I should do to the Kalyndian League. Your weakness isn't useful to me."

Xenocrates raised an eyebrow.

"I'm going to propose we add a delegate to Loryma today."

Xenocrates sat back, his mouth open. "You're...I don't know what you are. Athena incarnate? Giving me an extra vote doesn't do much for me, but it resurrects my faction. The extra vote brings the total in the Boule to forty-eight. Currently if you or Mylasa ally with Xanthos, you would have the twenty-four votes necessary to pass a law. But with the extra delegate, the new minimum becomes twenty-five."

"Yes." Artemisia smiled.

"The only way Mylasa could pass something without the Leleges League's consent would be if it could get both of the other factions to agree. We'll vote for the extra delegate because we would become important again. Xanthos will vote against it, because it will dramatically cut their influence. So, you need to get Mylasa to vote for it."

Artemisia's smile grew.

"Oh Zeus! I'm going to talk Mylasa into it." He slapped his thigh. "I'll present this as my idea; as a way to prevent a Leleges-Xanthos alliance from passing a law without Mylasa's consent. They will see it as a way to curry favor with us, while limiting your power!" Xenocrates shook his head. "I'm glad you didn't kill me. I want to see how this turns out!"

At the Boule, Artemisia feigned reluctance to vote for Xenocrates' resolution to add a delegate to Loryma. But when the votes were counted, only the Xanthian League voted against it. The Boule voted to spend money to repair the walls at Labraunda. Afterwards Artemisia called the Boule to an early end and took her Halikaranssian and Persian soldiers to Aphrodisias with Dibikom and his army.

"I'm happy for the company, Your Majesty, but it isn't necessary," Dibikom said.

"I've been to Tabae but never Aphrodisias itself. I want to see more of Caria." Artemisia said.

On the sixth day, while in the Idrian Pass, Artemisia was returning from relieving herself when she saw a deer. She followed it with her eyes through the trees. It was a buck with a tall, slender rack, only it was not a buck at all. It turned its head and had the face of a woman. Artemisia was confused. She followed. It weaved through the trees like a wild animal: graceful, quiet, and sure-footed but on two legs and no faster than Artemisia. *Is this a sort of deer-centaur?*

Artemisia broke a branch. The creature looked straight at the queen and fled. The satrap gave chase, jumping dead trees and rocks. Her milk-laden breast banged against her chest, but she pushed past the pain. She rounded a large boulder and stopped cold in her tracks. She was in a perfect circle of trees, around a patch of thick moss. In the middle was a woman wearing antlers and dressed in a deer hide. Artemisia was struck by her beauty. "Are you a nymph?"

The woman smiled.

"A dryad?"

She tilted her head, still smiling.

"A God? Are you Artemis?"

"You're funny," the woman said. "I'm Qyris, and you're Satrap Artemisia."

"You already know that I've taken back the satrapy?"

"And I saw how you did it, too!"

Artemisia turned her head, as if to get a better angle on understanding. "How?"

"I like to keep up with what happens in my Caria." Qyris approached. "I watched as you gathered and trained your army in the Pedasos Mountains. Then I followed you to Mylasa and watched you kill those kings." The strange deer-clad woman reached Artemisia. "I'm grateful for the opportunity to meet you."

"You're so beautiful and fast. You're what I would imagine Artemis to be. One of her sacred animals is the deer."

Qyris stroked Artemisia's cheek. The queen took a step back. Qyris closed her eyes, as if to savor the touch. The satrap was surprised at how beloved it made her feel. "Do you live in the woods? Alone?"

"I'm more alone than you but only just barely. You must go back to your people. They're looking for you." Qyris grew a mischievous grin. "But I want to give you a piece of wisdom first. You mustn't believe in yourself. Those men you hate—they believed in themselves. What you did at Pedasos Pass and then in front of Mylasa... Unbelievable! You are like Hippolyta. But in the end, even Hippolyta was bested by Heracles."

With that the nymph turned and ran.

Aphrodisias was more beautiful than Artemisia imagined. They went straight to the Temple of Aphrodite and gazed upon a life-size statue.

"Aphrodite is fully clad," she said to Iokaste, who could barely walk. "She's dressed like Artemis of Ephesos, only without the twenty-four breasts-eggs-testicles things hanging from her chest!"

Iokaste glared at Artemis. "I'm about to give birth, but you *had* to go on a trip, so you could compare the Goddess of fucking to the Goddess of not fucking!"

Artemisia burst out a laugh and then tried to contain it.

"What I want to know is why we never make statues of a pregnant woman." Iokaste went on. "I bet we'd have a lot less sex if they did. Just a massive round creature with a puffy face and big, sagging tits!"

Artemisia struggled to not laugh in the sacred place. She wanted to ask Iokaste to stop but was enjoying her dry humor too much.

"I had to become the servant of an Amazon, who traipses around between battles. 'Oh, let's see, no kings to kill today. I know, wouldn't it be nice to see another part of Caria? Let me just drag this three hundred-pound girl along!'" Iokaste managed to keep an annoyed face during her rant.

A priestess walked in and glared at Iokaste. Artemisia wondered what Iokaste would do in response and was surprised. Water appeared on the floor. "Am I peeing?" Iokaste asked as she looked down.

"Your water has broken," the priestess said.

Expecting the priestess to throw them out, Artemisia opened her mouth to say, *We'll be going*, but the priestess took Iokaste by the arm. Artemisia followed them into an inner chamber. There a priestess and priest leaped up. "Boil water. We're going to need blankets."

"We could leave," Artemisia offered.

"Nonsense! A baby in the temple! What a blessing!" The priestess declared.

Iokaste's labor took half a day. Artemisia wiped the sweat from her brow and held her hand. Iokaste named her daughter Aphrodisia.

When they returned to Halikarnassos, much of Artemisia's time was spent attending to Pissindelis and helping Iokaste with Aphrodisia. Otherwise she spent hours hearing disputes between competing interests or broken contracts and spent minutes solving them. On occasion she suspected that the disputes were concocted so that the two parties would have an excuse to meet her. At first it was flattering.

The fall set in, then winter, and before she knew it, her twentieth birthday had arrived with news from Thuxra.

"Aristagoras died four months ago fighting in Thrake."

"Incredible!" Artemisia slapped her hands together loudly. "Surely the rebellion will crumble now."

Thuxra nodded.

"This is great news. Go get food."

That April Artemisia traveled to Mylasa by land with three hundred Persians and Halikarnassians. During the Boule of 495 BC, Artemisia focused all her attention on trade, including commissioning another trireme for Caria. The resolution barely passed, but the victory was savory. That fall she took frequent ship rides and explored the coast and islands near Halikarnassos with Pissindelis, Iokaste, and Aphrodisia.

In April 494 BC, the Boule began with Mylasa and Xanthos trying to pass a resolution that Leleges and Kalynda opposed. Artemisia smiled at Xenocrates when the measure failed by only one vote.

In mid-May Thuxra burst into the hall. He walked fast to the satrap and bowed low and whispered, "The Persians have landed at Casolaba."

Artemisia filled with anxiety. *Darayavahu might not have accepted our surrender.* She stood, resolved to face whatever consequence awaited her. "I'm adjourning the Boule today. There's a Persian army at Casolaba." The Casolabian delegates stood in alarm. "I'm going to go to try to clean up your mess." She turned to Ravant, Vadhut, and Saroljats. "You three, with me."

King Karkinos approached. "Satrap, I must go as well. It's my kingdom."

They took the poorly maintained wooded road that sat in a gorge between Mount Mylasa and the Mylasa Plateau. Once they were out of the gorge, they saw the Persian army stretched out in the farmland of Casolaba. As they approached, the Persian spahbed peeled off a dozen men and rode out to meet them.

"I'm Spahbed Datis."

"I know you," Artemisia blurted out.

"Yes, Your Highness. I was at the Imperial Court when you were there."

"Seeing you takes me back to those days of innocence!"

Datis smiled. "The emperor had received word of what transpired here. He sends his condolences for the loss of your father."

Artemisia nodded.

"He also expresses great pride in your achievements, and the emperor requests your assistance in putting down the rebellion."

Artemisia had hoped Datis would say, *And he absolves you of all that transpired.* "The rebellion continues?" She was shocked.

"Haven't you heard?"

"No."

"Ionia won't voluntarily return to the empire." Datis was clearly annoyed.

Artemisia put her hand on her forehead. "What are Hecataeus and Melanthios doing? Are you sure?"

"When Aristagoras died we sent a delegation to the Milesians. They refused us."

Artemisia felt sick in her stomach. *Oh, Melanthios!*

"We're going to start by retaking Miletos," Datis declared. "Hopefully taking the capital will end the rebellion."

The satrap looked around uncomfortably. "I agree. It has to be done."

The Persian army stayed behind, but Datis and an entourage of three hundred men returned with Artemisia to the Boule. "Kings and delegates, Spahbed Datis has been sent by the emperor to put down the rebellion. We're called upon to join that force. I believe we should make haste and dispatch all our ships. Including the trireme my father commissioned, our fleet numbers twenty-three ships."

Nicander stood to be recognized. "I've few resources and am not eager to risk my only ship. Isn't it enough that we already lost so much?"

Xenocrates stood. Artemisia nodded to him. "This council's aware of your tendency towards cowardice. Loryma is poor and small, but it'll contribute both ships!"

Karkinos stood. "The Kingdom of Casolaba offers its four ships!"

Artemisia raised a hand. "I'm hearing no debate on the matter. If there's none, I propose we vote to have all of Caria commit to this action."

Forty-four voted to join the expedition against Miletos. Four votes from Knidos and Alabanda were against. "We go to war against the city of Thales! I'm adjourning the Boule. Bring your armies to Euromos and your fleets to Casolaba!"

Artemisia put Saroljats in command of her army, and she set off for Casolaba to take command of her fleet. When they arrived, Artemisia was utterly dumbfounded by what she saw. "Ships and more ships! Vadhut, there must be five hundred ships here!"

"Maybe more, Your Majesty!"

"Phoenicians, Egyptians, Kilikians, Cypriots, and now Carians. This is surely the greatest navy in human history!"

When eight days had passed, all the ships had arrived, save Knidos'.

"How far is Knidos, Satrap?" Datis wore a look of irritation.

"Sixty miles. Even if he didn't have everything he needed and went back to get something, he could have gotten back here in four days without effort."

"What do you recommend?" Datis asked.

"We should leave without Nicander and let me deal with him when we get back." Artemisia hesitated and then asked, "Are we going to have to fight all of Ionia?"

"They've refused surrender. I hope that conquering Miletos will get the rest to quit," Datis added.

"What if we could divide Ionia?

"How?" Datis asked.

"Where are the tyrants?" Artemisia thought she had an answer.

"They're with me, but I don't have much confidence. Aristagoras overthrew them, because they were so hated."

"Why did you bring them?"

"I was going to restore some of them." Datis hesitated.

"But?" Artemisia asked.

"If they were so hated, then..."

"What if we sent the tyrants now to try and talk their people out of the war?" Artemisia posed.

"You think that some might?" Datis was skeptical.

"Yes."

Datis nodded his head. "Even if we turn just one polis."

"Indeed, even just one." Artemisia agreed.

Artemisia walked up to Xenocrates. He was lean and appeared to be in his mid-thirties. His rugged exterior seemed permanently austere. "Are your men ready?" she asked.

He turned to his crews. "To Miletos!" They gave a deafening roar. "Yes, Satrap."

"I want you to be my second."

Xenocrates smiled. "Not Bion or Karkinos? They think it'll be one of them."

"No, I want you. I don't have much confidence in either one."

"I'm honored, Satrap." Xenocrates' eyes revealed a hint of pride.

They set off a day after the tyrants were dispatched. Artemisia hoped to run into Nicander as they left Iassicus Gulf, but it didn't happen. The navy traveled for seven hours before nearing the island of Lade. It was early afternoon. A hot, southerly breeze pushed the Persian fleet. Blocking the way around Lade Island was the Ionian navy.

Artemisia had hoped that the bewildering size of the Persian fleet would scare the Ionians, but they didn't budge. She turned to the trierarch of the *Morning Red*. "What do you think, Godamos—350 ships?"

"Yes, Your Majesty, against our 598."

"So many Ionian ships!" Artemisia examined the banners of the ships and saw that they were from the west to the east: Samos, Lesbos, Phocaea, Erythraea, Chios, Teos, Myos, Priene, and Miletos.

"Thank you, Thalassa, Goddess of the Sea, that I don't have to battle the Milesians. At least if Melanthios dies in this battle, it won't be by my hands!" The thought of him dead left her momentarily breathless.

The Carians charged the Samians at full speed. The southerly wind filled the Carian sails. However, the Samian ships turned and fled north. Artemisia walked over to the trierarch. "Godamos, what are they doing?"

"I don't know, Your Majesty." Godamos squinted. "Forty-nine of the sixty Samian ships have turned."

"Could this be a trap? We go after the eleven ships and then the forty-nine come back and crush us between them?"

"Could be."

"What should we do?" Artemisia felt uncertain.

"If the Samians are indeed running, we should let the Egyptians on our right fight the remaining ships," Godamos said. "Then we sail past them and swing hard to starboard. In this way we will end up in the rear of the rebel fleet."

"If it's a trap?"

"Then we hold this position like an anchor to await the Samian return."

"If we do this flanking maneuver, it will be devastating to the rebel fleet?" Artemisia asked.

"Very." Godamos nearly grinned.

"If we're attacked in a trap, then we'll be destroyed?"

"It'll be bad," Godamos answered.

"How far must the Samians go before we'd no longer be able to see their ships?"

"From mast top to mast top we can see about seven miles." Godamos tugged at his gray beard. "That's about an hour of rowing."

"If they go out that far but it's a trap, would we have enough time to disengage?"

"Yes, Your Majesty."

"Then I want us to wait for three-quarters of an hour and then flank them."

Godamos bowed and began shouting orders at the signaler.

The collision between the massive Egyptian fleet, the remaining Samians, Lesbians, and Phocaeans sounded like a mountain falling into the sea. The shouting vibrated from the water, into the hull, and through Artemisia's bones.

Twenty minutes into the fight, Xenocrates brought his ship close to the *Morning Red*. He gestured to encourage Artemisia to attack.

"What do you think, Godamos?"

"I think that those Samians are fleeing. If we strike now, we'll cause chaos in the rebel lines."

Artemisia gave the order. She wasn't sure which beat harder, her heart or the drums. The *Morning Red* led the charge. Artemisia felt like they were flying. She looked up with pride at her new Pegasos and goat banner.

They made the hard turn starboard, losing most of their wind, and came up along the aft of Samian and Lesbian ships. With full speed the Carian fleet began ramming. The *Morning Red* turned into a rebel ship. The enemy's aft smashed to pieces. Their crew was forced to divide to fight the Egyptians at their bow and the crew of the *Morning Red* at their aft.

Swords clashed. Artemisia was eager to join the fight but couldn't find a gap between her marines. When three Lesbians broke through, she raised her scorpion shield and the Pegasos sword and greeted the first with a parry. The warrior looked fierce. Artemisia was frightened, but she knew not to let her fear overwhelm her. *Fear makes you fight harder.* That was what Myron taught her. *Let it flow, but don't let it take over. Don't focus on what might happen, but rather what you want to happen.*

Artemisia backed up to give the man space and let him charge again. This time instead of parrying, she stepped to the right. As he swung hard, she hit him with her shield and ran behind him. Before he could turn, she plunged her blade into his ribs.

Vadhut ran to her back and parried the attack of another Lesbian. As they clashed Godamos ordered the *Morning Red* to row backwards. The sound of the breaking wood pulling apart and scraping was ominous. Artemisia saw the rebel ship tipping. Realizing the extent of their defeat, the remaining enemy crew surrendered.

Once the *Morning Red* was clear, Godamos ordered it forward at an angle. Just as the ship reached maximum speed, it crashed into another Lesbian ship. The vulnerable ship broke with a ceremonial *cak'cah*.

Artemisia was sickened. "So much waste!"

Again, enemy on that ship divided their forces and tried to fight both the Egyptians on their prow and the Carians on their starboard, but again Godamos ordered the ship to pull back.

The remaining Lesbian ships began to pull away. Artemisia counted them and came up with forty-five. "The rebels are losing their heart!" She turned to Godamos. "Can we capture ships?"

"Yes, Your Majesty…" His voice trailed off as he watched the enemy ships attempt to extract themselves. "There, those ships there." He pointed at a cluster of fifteen. "They're close enough."

"Let's go after them!"

The trierarch ran to the gunwale. A signaler waved a banner in a frantic manner. Artemisia wondered how anyone could understand what he was signaling.

Wearing a big smile, Xenocrates waved to her. The gesture made her feel powerful and liked.

The drums got faster. Soon the twenty-two ships of the Carian fleet were rowing, sails catching wind, on a course to intercept. One of the Lesbian ships pulled away from the pack, but as the minutes burned,

Artemisia could see that her fleet catching the rebels, the *Morning Red*, was in the lead.

Godamos managed to force the frontmost ship to turn to avoid colliding. The turn to starboard forced the ships behind it to turn as well. *Godamos is using the enemy against themselves.*

It wasn't long before they had no more space to maneuver. Artemisia couldn't believe it, but Godamos had caused the enemy ships to box themselves in. As the hulls neared, the rowers of both ships were at risk of fowling their oars, but Godamos was unmoved. Only after the first oars hit did he turn the ship. "Bring in all starboard oars!"

Artemisia marveled at his calm. The rowers pulled them in with a *zhunk* and bang. The ship lurched to the right and into the Lesbian ship. Artemisia could see the desperation in their eyes. After the first oars on the Lesbian ship were sheared off, the crew reluctantly withdrew the remainder. Marines exchanged arrow fire as Artemisia raised her shield.

On the second volley an arrow sank into the scorpion shield. It stopped in front of Artemisia's right eye. Adrenalin surged through her veins. As the ships dragged across each other, the vibration shot through the deck and through her bones. Marines from the *Morning Red* threw grappling hooks. Lesbian marines swung their swords at the ropes, but it was too late. Carian marines leaped onto their ship.

Artemisia drew her sword and ran to the gunwale, Vadhut by her side. They looked at each other and jumped. Just as they landed on the deck of the Lesbian ship, it rocked back and forth, knocking both women down hard. Bruised, Artemisia scrambled to her feet and looked aft. A second Lesbian ship had collided with the one they had boarded.

Just then a Lesbian thrust a spear at her. She smashed it as hard as she could to the left with her shield. But it slashed her shoulder. She spun in a circle so that she was inside his spearhead. The marine was surprised and pulled the spear back to try again. It was too late. Artemisia closed the distance; the best he could do was side swipe her with the shaft, bruising her hip. She stabbed him in the chest, dropping the

Lesbian to his knees.

Behind him was an officer. The man was ready. His knees were bent, his sword out, but then Vadhut showed up on Artemisia's flank. Despair replaced the determination his face originally held. He dropped his sword and genuflected. The rest of the ship surrendered a moment later. Artemisia looked around and realized that she stood on a wooden island. She waved her sword in the officer's face. "Who are you?"

"I'm Polemarch of the Lesbians."

"I'm inclined towards mercy. Tell your men to surrender."

"Why's a woman telling me to surrender?" Isarion shouted.

"I'm Queen Artemisia, Satrap of Caria."

"I won't surrender to a woman."

"You just did!" Artemisia was baffled by Isarion's reaction.

"I won't surrender my fleet."

"Your men will die needlessly." Artemisia looked around. She saw another man of rank in custody. She waved for him to be brought to her. "Who are you?"

"I'm Hippomenes, archon of this cohort of ships."

"Hippomenes, are you ready to surrender to me?"

Isarion began to speak. "Bring me a man to—"

Artemisia thrust her sword into his throat. "What use are you to me?" She turned back to Hippomenes. "Are you ready to surrender?"

"We surrender." He nodded enthusiastically.

As her marines secured the Lesbian ships, Artemisia tried to assess the situation. Xenocrates walked up to her. His clothes were blood splattered.

"Your Majesty, the battle appears to be down to the Milesians and Chians. The Egyptians are past us and flanking the remaining rebel ships."

"Godamos, can we peel off some ships from this mess and rejoin the battle?"

"Yes, Your Majesty. I'll get you some ships."

"Xenocrates, get as many marines you can."

When they were done, three ships were ready: the *Morning Red*, Xenocrates' ship, and Karkinos' ship, though Karkinos was too wounded to command it. They headed straight toward the remaining Milesian ships. By the time they reached them, nine ships were in flight, and as many were already fighting the Egyptians. Two had turned towards the approaching Carian ships.

"Men who turn towards death for a lost cause are the sort of men I want serving me!" Artemisia pronounced.

Godamos shouted orders as the marines readied their bows. He maneuvered the three Carian ships so that the *Morning Red* would take the middle. When they reached each other, there was no room for the oars.

"Remember, boys, we're trying to capture!" Artemisia shouted.

"Oars in! Marines, fire!" Godamos shouted.

Instinctively they raised her shield before the other side's arrows reached them. The sound of arrows bouncing off the shield and sticking into the decks was followed up by the scraping of hulls. Shouting and clanging metal rang out.

"These Milesians know they cannot win!" Artemisia charged into the fight, Vadhut at her side. The two women fought until they reached Xenocrates. "Where's the archon?"

"There." Xenocrates pointed with his sword.

Artemisia charged him, screaming at the top of her lungs. She imagined herself to be Hippolyte and so did the Milesian archon. He threw up his arms in self-preservation.

Once on the shore, Xenocrates and Godamos were brought before Artemisia. "Your Majesty," Xenocrates began, "we lost three ships. Of our 2,862 men, 235 died and 424 men have suffered serious injuries."

Godamos added, "We've captured twelve Lesbian ships and two Milesian ships, including 983 men."

Artemisia nodded just before Vadhut applied the cauterizing dagger to her shoulder. Artemisia screamed from the pain and was glad she didn't see the red-hot iron until after it was applied. She sat covered in sweat and shaking from the pain.

Hippomenes, the Lesbian archon, and Milesian arrived while she sat.

"Your Excellency." Hippomenes bowed.

Artemisia looked at both men. "I'm Satrap Artemisia of Caria, the Queen of Halikarnassos."

"We heard Your Majesty is a woman," the Milesian said, as if to confirm that his skepticism had finally been put to rest.

"I'm willing to free all your people, if you serve me after the Ionian Revolt ends."

"What are the conditions?" Hippomenes asked.

"I've no hatred for Ionians." Artemisia tried to seem austere. "It's my hope that when the revolt is over, we will restore the familial bonds between us. And that you and your men will join me in Halikarnassos."

"Many have joined our ranks," Xenocrates said.

Artemisia stared at the walls of Miletos. "The city of Thales." She turned back to her advisors. "We should mine the walls."

"I think that spot there is vulnerable." Xenocrates pointed to an area not far from the Sacred Gate. "We can build trenches and tunnels to get there, but it will take a week, at least."

When a week had passed, Artemisia stood next to her people as her men hauled out dirt.

Dust rose up from a section of the wall. Men scrambled to get into columns. Rumbling shook the ground. The satrap raised her right hand. She glanced at the Carian army. A thick cloud of dust rose up from where the wall had been. Artemisia swung her hand forward as she lowered it. The whole Carian army ran forward. The satrap felt as if she were a boat at the top of swell being carried towards a rocky shore. She doubted any order could turn the men back. A sense of powerlessness washed over her. *I wonder how much control I really have.*

She started to fall behind as the army ran past her, but as they reached the roiling dust, they slowed. Proceeding cautiously through the gray cloud, Artemisia caught up.

Xenocrates leaned towards her. "I fear they'll counter-attack in all this, and we won't see them."

They climbed over a wall segment and stepped on broken rocks, until they reached the top of the pile. *The city of my dreams: the city of Thales, Anaximenes, Anaximander, Cadmus, and Hecataeus. I'm finally here but as a conqueror, and Hecataeus and Melanthios are de-fending the city against me.*

Milesians began a counter-charge towards the breach. Artemisia readied her sword, her knees bent, and she took in a deep, gritty breath. A spearman neared her, but Ravant moved to intercept him. He was followed by a swordsman. Artemisia met his thrust with a parry but stumbled over a rock. The misstep was dangerous, and her instinct was to fight against it, but Myron's training set in: *Worry about what you can affect and ignore what you can't. Turn every bad situation into an opportunity.*

Artemisia realized that her Milesian opponent was as surprised by the stumble as she was. Instead of fighting it, she moved through it, ducking down and then thrusting the tip of the blade up. It found the soft underside of the Ionian's chin. She was sure he would have cried out if he could have but wasted no sentiment on the dead man. She thrust her blade into the side of the spearman fighting Ravant.

Artemisia maneuvered to the left and engaged another Milesian swordsman. Milesians and Carians were intermingled, and she realized that she was in a particularly thinly populated section of the enemy.

Artemisia turned back. She gathered a group of Lorymians and Hal-ikarnassians. Running, she led them through the thinly defended area. A moment later they were in the city. Before them were homes and businesses. Milesian soldiers came at them from the left and right, des-perate to close the hole, but in insufficient numbers. It was too late.

Vadhut caught up to Artemisia. Her gown was torn, and her right breast hung exposed before all. Artemisia was drawn back to that day at the top of the olive tree, watching her father fight through the breach at White Pillars. "We are Amazons!" she shouted. Vadhut turned and smiled.

With so many of her men between her and the Milesians, Artemisia sheathed the Pegasos sword and bent, catching her breath. She looked in front of her at the businesses and homes. A butcher, a bronzesmith, a wool dealer. *If this is like Halikarnassos...*

Artemisia grabbed twenty-three men and ran with them through the stores. They ran into a courtyard and then through the back doors of more businesses, emerging finally into the empty street, save the panicked children scurrying in every direction. They ran past two blocks. She looked left. There before her was the gate. Hundreds of Milesians stood ready for the Persians to come through. She froze for a moment. *If they see us, we're dead!* Vadhut nudged Artemisia.

They crossed the street unnoticed and then ran through the empty streets and made the first left turn. When they had gone the length of two blocks, they reached the wall. Artemisia looked around; then she took her men left again. Before her was the object of her heart's desires—the gatehouse. No guards stood in front of the door.

She pulled on the door; it was locked. She ordered the two men with axes to smash the door at its hinges. The compromised door collapsed, revealing two Milesians trying to block the stairs. They shouted for help, but Artemisia and her men pushed against them with shields and stabbed at their feet.

Soon they had reached the pulley room. Only four Milesians were there to defend it. As Artemisia stepped towards them, they threw down their weapons. The Carians began to turn the wheel, and the gate started to creak open.

The satrap took twenty men and ran back into the street. She retraced her path, but she only went one block this time. She and her men looked right and saw the backs of the Milesians fighting to keep the Persians out of the slowly opening gate. Artemisia looked each one in the eyes. "This is going to be rough."

"We're ready, Satrap!" a soldier declared.

She turned right and led her men against the Milesian rear. The surprise was thorough. Artemisia struck a man in the back, and he crumpled in screaming pain. Milesians turned around. She clashed swords when a spearman struck her in the thigh. The pain shot up through her body. Vadhut slashed the spearman in the side of the head. He dropped the spear and fell to his knees, clutching his head.

Artemisia grabbed the shaft and pulled hard. The pain was pure. She felt a strange sense of relief as the pressure in her thigh was released. With an arm around Vadhut, the satrap limped to the wall. Her bodyguard wrapped a tight bandage around the wound and then took up a defensive position in front of the satrap.

Half of her twenty men were already wounded or dead, but just then the Milesians broke. They moved suddenly as if a wave on the sea. Carians ran to the wall to avoid being trampled. The Milesians ran past them. It felt like some great Godly force had been released.

When they were two blocks away, they rallied and took up a new position in the street. A moment later Persians ran past. Artemisia regrouped her men. Two men reached down to pick her up, when she said, "Wait, take me there." She pointed at a wounded Milesian.

The man leaned his head against the wall. She looked down at him; he looked up at her. *"Melanthios!"* Tears filled her eyes. "Set me down." She scooted next to him. "Where are you hurt?"

He pulled open his tunic, revealing a deep wound in his abdomen. "Is that really you, Artemisia?"

"Oh Gods, Melanthios, it's bad. Yes, it's me." she stroked the side of his face. Artemisia wanted to stand but resisted. She wanted to run away, as if somehow that would make the wound vanish. Despair overtook her as the reality of the wound set in.

"I was worried I had conjured you up." Melanthios' voice pulled her back. "I think I'm losing a lot of blood."

"I'm going to fix you. Vadhut, get me cloth."

"We both know that's not possible." Melanthios' eyes were filled with adoration.

Tears streamed down her face. "I studied under Demokedes. I can heal you."

Somehow Melanthios' face conveyed love and skepticism all at once.

She took a piece of chiton handed to her. "We have to stop the bleeding."

"Even if you stop the bleeding, we both know that's not what's going to kill me. This wound goes all the way through." He readjusted. "I've a few minutes left. Let me spend them with you, the only woman I've ever loved."

"You love me?" The pain in her heart became overwhelming.

"You are luminescent."

"You gave me that sword." Artemisia tried to see him through her tears.

"I thought you'd need it to fend off your suitors. It's Indian steel, you know."

"Why didn't you tell me?"

Melanthios managed a grin. "You didn't need another panting dog chasing, sniffing your ass. We couldn't marry."

"Oh, Melanthios. I can marry you, now. I'm satrap! I can do anything I want!"

"Then marry me!" The dullness in his eyes vanished.

Artemisia turned to Vadhut. "Say a prayer to marry us."

As Vadhut invoked an Avestan prayer, Artemisia wrapped her arms around her groom. He smiled and leaned his head on her. After a minute she nodded to Vadhut, who finished by saying in Persian, "By Ahura-Mazda and Apollo, you are married."

"Thank you, Your Majesty." Melanthios' voice was faint. "So, does that mean that I'm king now?"

Artemisia could barely contain the grief. She still wanted to run, but she could not bear the idea of abandoning her groom. "Yes, my love, you're King Melanthios."

"I'm the happiest man in the world."

Artemisia nodded, feeling some strange sense of joy rise like a bubble in boiling water.

"We'd have had lovely children," Melanthios said. "I think we could've taught them philosophy and raised them to be kind queens and kings."

"Why didn't Miletos surrender?"

"We're a democracy. The people voted to keep fighting."

"Can you issue a surrender?"

"Hecataeus can. He's still polemarch."

Satisfied that Melanthios had not been a fool, Artemisia ordered, "Tell me more about our marriage."

"The love making will go on for hours. We'd take a ship to the islands and bring the children and let them play. You'd be a just queen and satrap, and I'd be your friend and advisor." He exhaled but did not inhale.

"Melanthios, I love you." She hugged him hard and then closed his eyes. Artemisia stood. "I want my husband buried in Halikarnassos." She pointed to two soldiers. They nodded and picked him up. "Get his sword, too. Let's finish this foolishness."

They gathered at the Temple of Athena, to the northwest of the Sacred Gate. Artemisia's eyes were heavy and bloodshot. She sat between Spahbed Datis and the Egyptian spahbed. To the right of the Egyptian were the Phoenician, Kilikian, and Cypriot commanders. To the left of Datis was Satrap Artaphernes, the emperor's brother. In front of them, next to the statue of Athena, was Hecataeus. He was pale and splattered with blood.

Artemisia sighed hard. She gathered her strength and resolved to show no more emotion.

"Satrap Artaphernes, if I might." The sixty-year-old Hecataeus waited for the Persian to give his permission. After receiving a nod, he went on, "My people were wrong, but we've suffered terrible losses. Most of the men are dead. We lost so many men in Ephesos, then Labraunda, the Battle of Lade, and now here in our foolish attempt to hold the city. We've lost tens of thousands of men.

"Our Ionian allies abandoned us after Lade. The bitter taste of our defeat will make a future alliance between Miletos and the rest of Ionia unlikely. I can't imagine we'll ever revolt against Persia again.

"Moreover, sending the tyrants and using them to convince the majority of the Samian and Lesbian fleets to withdraw at Lade was brilliant! Your name will be recalled for all eternity. I realize that you still must deal with Thrake, but for us the rebellion is over. I say all of this because I believe that mercy would serve Persia. It would send a message to all Hellenes that Persia is mighty, but just."

"Hecataeus, son of Hegesander, your plea is well considered." Artaphernes pulled his legs up and under him. "Queen Artemisia, as the Carian commander, I wish to hear what you have to say."

She was surprised that she was called upon at all, let alone so soon, and she noticed that he didn't use the title of satrap. "Master, I agree that a display of mercy to Miletos would be a good. After all, the city is the greatest city in Ionia."

"No, I want to discuss Caria."

"Master?" They were both satraps, but to pretend they were equals was foolish.

"We've discussed the surrender of Miletos, but we've never discussed the surrender of Caria."

What! I thought this was resolved! Betrayal filled her heart as she shot her eyes at Datis. "I'll of course ask for mercy—"

"There's the destruction of Daurises and his army. The emperor wants redress."

"Satrap, Caria has already returned to the empire. We fought a naval battle and stormed Miletos. It seems inappropriate that we should be punished considering the losses we took and the important role we played. I'm the one who flanked the enemy at Lade and the one who opened the gates at Miletos. And I'm the person who executed Lobon. Isn't our fealty already established?"

Artaphernes dropped his feet to the floor and scooted to the edge of the step he sat on. "When the Athenians, Eretreans, and Ionians burned Sardes, we lost gold and homes. Then we lost men and gold while putting down this rebellion. Then the Carians rose up, and we lost a general and his army. How do we make things right?"

Artemisia was confused. *Is the satrap asking for me to punish Caria or Athens, Eretrea or Ionia?* She hesitated, then looked down at her feet before starting to speak. "So that Caria might rebel, my father was murdered, and I was forced into an unwanted marriage and raped."

Artaphernes interrupted. "We believe that it was you who planned the ambush at Pedasos and that you personally slew Daurises."

"Yes, both are true." Artemisia looked up.

"So, you were a rebel."

"A slave has no choice over her destiny." The Carian satrap made eye contact with the Lydian satrap.

"You didn't have to give them such good advice."

She wanted to cry out, *Datis told us we were forgiven!* But she knew such a plea would have the opposite effect. "Ah, but I did. I'm loyal to Persia, but if I let the rebellion be destroyed by Daurises, then Caria would've been crushed by Persia. Caria would've never accepted such treatment and would still be in rebellion. The only way to end the revolt was to give Caria a way to believe that it had voluntarily returned to Persia. The only way for that to happen was for me to become satrap."

Artemisia's heart raced as she continued. "If Daurises had crushed Caria, he'd never have given me the satrapy. He'd have thought me a weak woman, and he'd have been correct. He might've taken the satrapy for himself, thinking himself to be Adusius, but he'd have been wrong. If he lasted a year, it would've been only through the intercession of a God.

"Even if he had appointed me, my people would've seen me as an illegitimate tool of the Persian Empire. I'd have lasted no longer than he. The power to rule doesn't come from the office. It comes from the power that you bring to the office. The only way for me to regain the satrapy was to earn it. Pedasos gave me that opportunity. I did so in a way that hurt Persia in the short term, but in the long term I've helped Persia.

"The six satraps who followed Adusius were forced from power. My father stabilized the satrapy because he earned his legitimacy as I have. Now the satrapy fears and admires me.

"No other Carian has my understanding of the world. And no other Carian is as loyal to Persia. I'm not merely the rightful heir, I'm the only one who can give Caria and Persia what they both need. If I was cruel, it was cruelty in war. And why should I have chosen Daurises over me? I chose me."

Artemisia gauged her audience. She realized her argument had not yet succeeded. "Truth be told, the Persians wouldn't have been wiped out at Pedasos if Daurises had shown caution. He was arrogant and reckless, as I knew he'd be. His recklessness gave me the opportunity to kill him, arm myself, slay Lobon, and earn my legitimacy." Pride for what she had achieved infected Artemisia's voice.

"It would be your right to plunder our countries, slaughter our men, castrate our sons, and enslave our women and daughters. But any cruelty towards Caria would reignite the rebellion in Ionia and Caria. For Persia's sake, you must find a way to pardon Caria, Ionia, and me."

Artaphernes' eyes had grown large. "My brother said that if you were truthful, it would prove your fealty. The emperor's orders were, 'If she tells the truth, she is of us.' Satrap Artemisia of Caria, you are of us." Artaphernes took a moment to let it set in, then he added, "What would you do with the Ionians?"

Artemisia looked at Hecataeus. *I have the responsibility to punish my friend.* "Forgive Ionia, all of it. End your campaign against them now. The prosperity of Ionia serves Persia. Your forgiveness will allow them to return to production, trade, and taxes. Mercy will be the measure of your success, and it will ease the bitterness of defeat for a proud people."

He nodded. "Indeed, but I must punish Ionia, even if only symbolically, so that Hellenes don't come away believing that such behavior is without consequence, and my brother will expect some form of redress."

Artemisia thought for a moment.

"Master?" Hecataeus again waited for a nod, which came instantly. "I would like to suggest a just surrender."

The Persian turned to the Milesian and nodded to him.

"We have some gold—"

"We can just plunder that." Artaphernes was outwardly annoyed.

Artemisia remembered the punishment that her father had proposed for Labraunda at the Siege of the White Pillars. "The Milesians have lost so many men that many women will be forced into poverty or servitude. I propose that you take from Miletos a number of women and children to Shoosh as a tribute."

"As your father suggested, eight years ago." Artaphernes smiled.

"It will appear as punishment." Artemisia carefully repositioned her leg so as not to restart the pain from the spear wound. "But it won't be punishment, since such women are facing destitution in any case. But I would add another punishment. Today I was reminded of Miletos' past, as told by Homer. According to the poet, this is the city of Amphimachus, son of Nomion, and his brother Nastes, who led the Carians as allies of Troy in that war.

"A quick glance at our geography, and one can readily see that's true. I would do two more things to Ionia. First, give Caria back all lands south of the Meander River and the southern shore of the Gulf of Latmos. Second, separate Ionia from Lydia into its own satrapy. That way they can have some sense of autonomy."

"And what would you do with the land Caria receives?"

"I would keep its current divisions: Myos, Miletos, Latmos, and Didyma. I would let them all chose their governments, save Miletos. Carians will be sent here to help repopulate this city. They will elect a king for a ten-year term. The Carian settlers will vote for my candidate, Iokaste, and with help from Hecataeus, some Ionians will as well."

"Will they accept a Carian to rule them?"

Artemisia shrugged. "They'll know it's me and that my woman is my representative. But Hecataeus will be elected to serve as eponymous archon. In that way they'll believe that they're still in large measure their own rulers. In addition, I've captured fourteen ships. We're taking seven. We'll give the remaining seven to the four Ionian provinces as a gesture of goodwill."

"Hecataeus, these are your people. What do you think of the satrap's proposal?"

He looked around and made eye contact with all the leaders in the room. Then he locked his eyes on Artemisia. She wondered if he would hold to his oath. "I agree with the satrap. She's wise, and I support her."

After some time Artaphernes spoke. "I've heard your words and concluded that Artemisia's plan is the best. I'm going to leave a number of Milesian women in Miletos, equal to twice the number of men. The rest will be composed only of widows and will be taken as tribute with their children to Shoosh."

Artaphernes looked to Artemisia and Hecataeus to gauge their reaction. The Persian seemed satisfied and so continued. "Artemisia, I'm returning to you Carian lands from Ionia, and I'll create an Ionian satrapy." Artaphernes clapped his hands together and declared, "So be it!" He stood. The room stood with him.

I've made my mark on the world! If I died tomorrow, I'll be remembered for all eternity as a just and powerful woman.

When Artemisia reached her temporary residence in Miletos, she found Iokaste with Pissindelis and Aphrodisias. "I heard about Melanthios. I'm so sorry." Iokaste hesitated before asking, "Will you now marry Mnaseas or Damasithymos?"

"Both were part of the conspiracy to murder my father…. And, I'm uninterested in giving my offices away to a man. But I've news for you." Artemisia grew a wry grin.

"Oh?"

"I've made you Queen of Miletos."

Iokaste stopped in her tracks. Her eyes locked on the satrap.

"It's a ten-year term." Artemisia continued to grin. "You'll have Hecataeus as eponymous archon to assist you."

"Why would you do that?"

"Because I need someone loyal to me to rule Miletos."

"I won't know what I'm doing!" Iokaste's voice was filled with a mixture of skepticism and pleasure.

"We'll talk about all the decisions." Artemisia added, "You'll be elected. I'm going to interfere on your behalf, and Hecataeus will endorse you."

"Oh Zeus! You're insane! That birthday wish…when you had Darayavahu make Hecataeus swear an oath of allegiance. Now, here in this moment, that strange thing that you did has come back. It's like a seed that you planted has turned into a massive tree. And now you've made me queen of Miletos! What sort of being are you?"

"You can finally marry. Find a good Milesian man——"

"And make him king!" Iokaste's enthusiasm washed away. "But wait, Princess…" Iokaste blushed. "Satrap."

Artemisia smiled. It was funny to think that Iokaste still thought of her as a princess.

"When will I see you? This feels like exile."

"You hate me anyway. What difference will it make?"

"Ah, yes. I'd forgotten."

Artemisia bit into a delicate piece of lamb. The juices burst in her mouth. She turned to Hecataeus. "Why did Aristagoras rebel? This has been a disaster for everyone."

Hecataeus chewed for a moment and gave her a questioning look.

"Yes, why did Aristagoras rebel?" She asked again.

"He rebelled because of his failure at Naxos." Hecataeus' face was filled with sadness. "He rebelled to avoid being fired for incompetence."

Artemisia shook her head. "What sort of fool acts in such a way? I accept that as his reason, but why did Ionia follow him? And then why did they continue after his death? After Lade!"

"He offered them independence but not at first. At first, he merely carved them out of the Satrapy of Lydia. He overthrew the tyrants and created democracies, causing the tyrants to flee. Then Ionians worried that Persia would restore the tyrants." The historian looked up at the ceiling. "Somehow and for some reason, Aristagoras secured the help of the Eretreans and Athenians. Then Ionians believed they could prevail."

"I don't understand. Did the Ionians want to rebel?" Artemisia was annoyed.

"The Ionians were encouraged to follow Aristagoras because of the Athenians." Hecataeus looked at the wall.

"You have not explained why Miletos refused to quit the field."

Hecataeus chewed on the question for a while. "I don't know. I begged. I pleaded. I tried everything I could. They refused to stop."

"Baffling." Artemisia could not understand it. "So how do we ensure that this was the last rebellion?"

"I'm unsure, Your Majesty." Hecataeus was somber.

When they had finally reorganized the ship crews, affected the repairs, and loaded, Artemisia stood next to the box containing Melanthios. She was dressed in black peplos and kept one hand on the wood and the other on the hilt of the Pegasos sword.

I'm returning as a hero and to bury my love. The ceremony was somber. A drum, a priestess, and a sistrum were all she employed.

Artemisia looked at slate ledgers marked with white chalk. A figure walked into her peripheral. The satrap ignored the person for a long moment. Finally, she looked up to see a young teenager. "Ah, you must be Dryo. I apologize. I was deep in thought." She stood and walked to Dryo. "These moments when Pissindelis sleeps give me a chance to have a thought." When she reached Dryo, she put her arms around her. "Your home is here in Halikarnassos?"

"It is, Your Excellency." The young woman avoided eye contact. "Queen Iokaste told me that you are looking for a new handmaiden."

"How old are you?"

"Thirteen, Your Majesty."

"Well, you have come to the right place," Artemisia confirmed. "I need help with Pissindelis, but I want to be clear. Your aunt suffered. Her life was put on hold for mine. I don't want to do that to you."

"Yes, Your—."

"This isn't going to work if you keep calling me by those titles." Artemisia remembered her first day in Shoosh. "When we are in the presence of others call me, by my title. Otherwise…

"May I call you 'mistress?'"

"Yes!" Artemisia looked her in the eyes, "It has been my experience that people say things they don't mean and agree to things they don't believe will happen. I'm sincere. I want you to believe it."

"Yes, mistress."

Artemisia wasn't convinced but decided to move on.

Artemisia stood at the prow of the *Morning Red*. She watched the town of Knidos as a ship set sail.

"How did you know King Nicander would run, Your Majesty?" Godamos asked.

"A feeling."

Six of the queen's ships converged on the Knidosian ship from six directions. The Knidosian trireme turned hard to port and towards the *Morning Red*. "Why turn at all?" Artemisia wondered aloud. "All directions lead to one of my ships."

As they neared, Artemisia noticed a fishing vessel leaving Knidos. The *Morning Red* successfully sideswiped the fleeing ship. Marines boarded the surrendering Knidosian ship. But after a search, Nicander was not found. Artemisia split the marines and sailors in half and swapped them with half of the Knidosian crew.

"Godamos, pursue the fishing boat."

The fishing boat was quick to surrender.

Artemisia boarded it with eight marines. She approached a young fisherman, and without saying anything, he nodded towards a net on the deck. Two marines lifted the net, revealing Nicander laying on his side.

"King Nicander, so good to see you." The marines escorted him onto the *Morning Red*. "Still a coward, I see."

They proceeded to Knidos, entering the western harbor. Artemisia led them straight to the agora. Knidos had a massive temple in the center and stretched into the surrounding hills, which reclined between two harbors. "It is as if Poseidon himself designed the land to host a port city. I love it. Nicander, you'll have to show me around."

The king looked surprised.

Soon a crowd gathered. When it was large, Artemisia raised a hand. "Some of you'll be surprised to find out that I'd chosen Nicander to be my husband. But he refused me." She drew her sword. "Can you imagine the outrage in my heart!"

The crowd gasped.

Artemisia sheathed the weapon. "Aw, it's nothing! Besides, what kind of person wants to be in a relationship with someone who doesn't want them?!" She smiled and put her right hand on Nicander's back. "Do you know why he didn't choose me?"

The crowd shook their heads.

"Because of how beautiful this city is! And now that I'm here, I can see why, but that's not why I'm here." Artemisia waved her hand to keep them silent. "The Boule voted for war on Miletos. Alinda and Knidos voted 'no.' That isn't a problem. Vote 'no' if you like. But the resolution that passed ordered Nicander to provide one ship and 130 men. He failed to do so. That's a problem. The authority of the Boule is sacred. Alinda sent us the soldiers. Knidos didn't. Can you imagine how that makes me feel?"

The crowd mumbled.

"I'm inclined towards mercy, because Nicander surrendered without a single death. Here's what I propose. I'll let you decide the fate of your king. I'll give you two options. Either you can fine him on my behalf; the fee will be one silver stater per man who failed to show up at Miletos and a gold stater for the absent king, which works out to fourteen gold staters from his coffers.

"Or you can decide that Nicander is no longer fit to be king. In which case you can remove him from office and replace his government with whatever form of government you like. But this means you assume responsibility for your polis. As a result, I'd want twenty-eight gold staters from you.

"Regardless of which option you chose, because Nicander was the king of Knidos when he misbehaved, as a penalty, Knidos must forgive Halikarnassos for its indiscretion in the Triopian Games and advocate that it be allowed to renew its membership in the Doric Hexapolis." Artemisia raised her hands to silence the crowd. "Take a knee." The entire crowd did so. "We, the people of Knidos, forgive Halikarnassos for its indiscretion in the Triopian Games and vow to advocate for its rightful place in the Doric Hexapolis."

The crowd repeated.

"Arise! Now vote for the fate of your king."

"Your Majesty," a woman from the crowd shouted. "Before we vote, might we have time to discuss the fate of our polis?"

"So be it. I'll wait until the sun is halfway below the horizon. In the meantime, someone must volunteer to show me your lovely polis."

Another woman shouted. "Your Excellency, can the women vote?"

Artemisia put her finger to her lips and then said in Doric, "We're the descendants of Dorians and not Ionians. We speak Ionian, but that's a convenience. In Sparta, unlike in Athens, women may be seen in public. They serve on councils. They can vote, get divorced and retain custody over their children, and can remarry. Spartan women are educated and are trained in war. Though we have strayed much from such traditions, maybe we're being untrue to our heritage. The women may vote!"

More women emerged from the buildings. When the discussion was over and the voters separated, Artemisia saw that those who favored retaining the king had slightly more men than women, and those who favored removing the king were equal. *Interesting that there is not much difference in judgement by gender.*

When the votes were counted, there were three more votes for retaining the monarchy. Artemisia looked at Nicander. "King Nicander, that was close!" She shook her head for emphasis. "I'll consider the matter ended when I receive the fourteen gold staters."

He sent a man to retrieve the money.

On the journey back to Halikarnassos, Vadhut asked, "Why didn't you remove him? Why let the Knidosians vote? Why'd you make it more expensive to remove him?"

"I know him. I'm ambivalent about removing a known element. He's a coward and selfish, but predictably so. I've reduced him in front of his people, and now he's my little bitch." Artemisia made a high-pitched bark.

The kings arrived in Mylasa for the Boule, in late spring of 493 BC. Artemisia brought half her army and proceeded by land as a precaution.

After getting settled, Iokaste came to Artemisia's quarters. "Your Majesty, I feel like Persephone returning from Hades."

"Io, you are older than me. You raised me. You're Demeter!"

Iokaste shrugged as they embraced.

The Boule might have started off normally if it were not for the looming presence of the satrap. Queen Iokaste and the Milesian delegates sat with the Halikarnassians, Labraundians, and Aphrodisians. Artemisia sat in the blood throne with Bion in the white throne. Dryo sat behind Artemisia with Pissindelis.

After several weeks they voted to send more Carian families to Miletos, to send Miletos more money to repair its walls, and to build another ship for the Carian navy. But then Thuxra appeared. He stood before all and declared, "Spahbed Marduniya has authorized Artemisia of Caria to undertake for the advancement of Caria and the Persian Empire, the reconquest of the breakaway island of Kos."

Marduniya! Where is he? Is Artazostreh with him? How I'd love to see her again! Artemisia could barely contain her excitement. "I'm sure this measure will pass, but in the meantime, we'd like to extend an invitation to the spahbed."

"I'll convey your invitation, Your Excellency."

The vote was forty-four to eighteen in favor of the Kos expedition. The Boule agreed to send thirty of their fifty-three ships.

Artemisia was thrilled at all the banners. Her heart filled with pride at what she had achieved. *What would Father think of me?*

When the expedition had traveled eight of the eleven miles to Kos, fast-moving black clouds came in. The sky was suddenly menacing. At first Artemisia thought it was a thunderstorm, but soon she realized she had never seen anything like it before. She turned to Godamos. "Trierarch?"

"Your Majesty, I recommend we return to Halikarnassos."

Artemisia had never heard so much emotion from him. "What is it?"

"This isn't Aiolos with some storm. This is Hekatonkheires with a storm coiled up like a snake!"

"Give the order!" Artemisia went cold from the fear in Godamos' voice.

As the fleet turned around, Artemisia stood on the aft, studying the black clouds.

Godamos said, "Watch them."

"They appear to be heading north," Artemisia declared.

"Yes, yet the storm is heading this way. I believe it's traveling in this direction at twice our speed. The northward wind appears to be traveling at three times that speed."

"What does that mean for us?"

"We'll be about three miles away from Halikarnassos when the storm reaches us."

"I don't understand how it can be traveling north at sixty knots and heading east, towards us, at twenty knots!"

"This is why I'm saying this storm is coiled up like a snake." Godamos looked Artemisia in the eyes, as if to confirm that she understood. "A spiral turning in on itself is the only shape that I can imagine it having. Ouroboros? It's a mystery."

"What can we do?"

"We are doing it, Your Highness." Godamos sounded resolved.

"But you said that the storm will overtake us when we are three miles away from the shore."

"Maybe two, Your Majesty."

"What if we turn north?"

"It's true that the distance to the shore is shorter, but we will also sacrifice moving away from the storm. It will catch us sooner, and we'll be the same distance from safety. My hope is that if we delay long enough, it will lose power or change course."

"I accept your judgement, trierarch." Artemisia steeled herself.

The anticipation was overwhelming, but as it reached them,

Artemisia wondered if they could survive such an encounter. They pulled up the sails. The waves were terrifyingly high. The *Morning Red* was lifted high and rode down a massive swell. Artemisia felt like she was riding a horse galloping down a steep slope. She looked out to see the fleet scattered. Some ships were in troughs, others on crests, and the rest somewhere in between. The clouds began to let loose and sideways rain joined the waves.

Godamos turned the ship this way and that to avoid the worst of the waves, but the storm seemed little interested in his goals.

Artemisia saw the ship from Knidos. *I wonder what that coward is feeling now?* Soon she realized it was on a collision course. She slid towards the trierarch and pointed.

A moment later the Knidosian ship was gone. A massive wave rose up between them, and the *Morning Red* slipped down the slope. Artemisia watched as Godamos turned the ship into the wave. This had the disconcerting effect of making the ship list towards starboard. Artemisia sat hard on a bench to avoid sliding. The rower on it didn't turn to look at his company. His face was filled with terror.

Artemisia felt like the ship could roll. Then suddenly it lurched to starboard and with great speed raced towards the trough. She looked back and saw that the crest was breaking towards them. The crest was cupped like a Titan's hand rising out of the sea. Her ship sat on the palm as the finger bent down, pointing towards their head.

The wave crashed into the aft of the ship. Artemisia watched with horror as rowers were disappearing behind a wall of water. She grabbed the bench hard. Water flowed down the deck, crashing with a sound like thunder. It relented, and the ship rose up. The bail boys, marines, and sailor did all they could to bail water.

Heavy with water the ship slowed, but they were still afloat. Nicander's ship appeared suddenly, as if emerging from the wave. They were slightly in front and to the port side, and they still appeared destined to collide. Artemisia was unsure what could be done and watched nervously. The *Morning Red* began to tip down again as it rose on a new swell.

The two ships grew closer. The swell moved faster than them, raising them higher and higher. She guessed that they were fifty feet up when the Knidosian ship was in front of them. Godamos did everything he could to steer the *Morning Red* away but to no avail. A terrible crushing sound shot through the wood and into Artemisia's bones. She held on as tightly as she could, but it was not tight enough. As she came free of the bench, the satrap accepted her fate.

She crashed into two rowers on Nicander's ship. They scrambled to their feet as the Knidosian ship cracked in two. Artemisia fell onto the bench, banging her head. She stood but slipped and slid under a bench. Instinctively she touched the lump on her head and then tried to scramble to her feet. Only as the ship's two halves moved away from each other, the ship began to rotate up and to the port. Soon she was standing, her chest against the deck and her back against the bench.

Panic set in. Artemisia knew if the ship continued to rotate, she would be wedged and under water with the ship on top of her. As she panicked she looked around. An oar slid towards her. She grabbed it and put it at the top of the bench and then pulled herself up. By the time that she was out from the bench, the ship was leaning over.

She had seconds to act. Artemisia grabbed the heavy oar and jumped, using it to shove off the deck. The ship caught her in the back of the legs, dragging her down. She struggled to swim up. In a moment of clarity, she pushed down against the oar again. It shoved her out of the water. The overturned hull floated on her left. She tried to climb it, but it was slippery and at a steep angle. Then she saw Vadhut and two rowers on top. They reached out with another oar. Artemisia grabbed it and pulled herself up.

She looked towards the trough and saw the *Morning Red*. Several rowers swam after it. Rowers in the aft helped pull them onboard. But Artemisia knew she and her companions were too far away. They would never make it. Artemisia and Vadhut huddled with the two rowers.

She spotted a man in the water. Artemisia called to him, but he gave no reply. It was Nicander holding on to a bit of debris. She took the oar from Vadhut and reached out toward the king. He reached up and then changed his mind.

"Take it!" she shouted.

"Too many people on the upside-down hull will cause it to sink."

"You'll get cold and die! Climb up!"

"My whole life I've been afraid. I feared all the fearless men: my father, my uncle, my cousins—men who ran into battle. Then you came along, and my fear increased. You were worse than any fearless man. You were a fearless *woman*. I left you to those Kalyndian dogs, because I was afraid. I don't want to be afraid anymore."

"Take this oar. Don't be afraid."

"That hull you are on is afloat, because the ballast fell out," Nicander shouted over the roar of the storm. "There's a pocket of air in its place. You four are lucky and light. I'll add too much weight. And climbing the hull might be enough to tip the ship and let out the air. I can die here knowing that I've saved you. I can die knowing that in my last moments I wasn't a coward."

"Nicander, I forgive you for all of it. Please. There is no need to die."

"I admire you." He went under.

"Nicander! Nicander!"

Artemisia tried to stand, but Vadhut grabbed her arm and held her tightly. "No, Your Majesty, you might tip the hull!"

Artemisia fell back onto her haunches. She looked around and saw the king holding onto a floating plank.

She sat and watched as the swells rose and fell and the King of Knidos slowly lost consciousness in the cold water. She debated jumping in after him, but then she saw Xenocrates' ship. It was tossed about like a leaf in the wind but was heading towards them. "Even if they can see us, they can't steer!" She gave the oar to the two rowers and pointed. "Row that way."

"That will increase the likelihood of a collision."

"Now!"

"Did you see the surviving ships?" Damasithymos paused to allow his audience to answer for themselves. "They were everywhere but the Grand Harbor. I saw a fishing boat on a roof near the Agora, and one was on Mylasa Avenue, near Mylasa Gate. The wind destroyed several homes and most roofs."

Artemisia shifted on the blood throne. Pissindelis squirmed on her lap.

"We lost fourteen ships, and sixteen were damaged!" Damasithymos thumped his chest. "We lost 1,963 men, including two kings! Karkinos of Casolaba and Nicander of Knidos!" He bowed his head for dramatic effect. "This is a sign of Zeus' displeasure. Zeus himself unleashed Hekatonkheires upon us! I propose that the Boule vote to remove Artemisia from the satrapy and to remove her title as queen!"

Where's this coming from! Artemisia didn't think that her son could grasp what was at stake, as a two-year-old, but she knew he would absorb the displeasure in the king's words. *I wouldn't marry you, so this is your revenge?* She nodded to Xenocrates, who stood.

"I interpret what happened differently! If Zeus had wanted the satrap dead, then why not kill her outright? Why send my ship to save her? 'Send' is what happened. We didn't control where we went. We couldn't have deliberately rescued her. In fact, the *Morning Red* and my ship suffered very little damage. Maybe the storm was to punish Caria but clearly not the satrap. If anything, it was to punish us for the rebellion and Knidos' cowardice."

"Surely letting a woman rule is foolishness!" Damasithymos shouted. "They're less capable and ruled by passions!"

"And yet the compeer from the Kalyndian League is demonstrating that he's carried away by his passions!" Xenocrates went on. "Under the satrap's rule, we've avoided punishment from Persia, she has shown us mercy, returned to Caria the land that Ionia took from us, negotiated mercy for Ionia, increased the size of the Carian fleet, and improved the condition of all of Caria."

"And yet we've lost fourteen ships out of fifty-three!" Damasithymos hissed. "That's more than one-quarter of our fleet. How can you ignore such an obvious sign!"

"I'd like to present my trierarch to testify on the matter." Xenocrates turned to Artemisia.

She nodded.

"Of course, you'll let him present his evidence."

"I'll allow your trierarch to testify as well." Artemisia did all that she could to keep her voice free of emotion.

"I've no desire. I'd like to bring in a cleric who's trained in reading of such matters!" Damasithymos declared.

"I'll agree to that." Artemisia suspected this was a trap, but to say "no" would weaken her legitimacy. "In the meantime, let's hear from Xenocrates' trierarch."

The trierarch stood next to Xenocrates and cleared his throat. "I'm Trierarch Hippodamos. I've been in one such storm before."

"When?" Artemisia asked.

"Twenty-one years ago."

"So, this was not unique?" She wanted to clarify.

"There've been ten such storms in fifty years." Hippodamos looked at the kings.

"Indeed, but we were lucky, Your Majesty."

"We were?" Xenocrates asked.

"Artemisia bought us time by sailing east." Hippodamos turned to his king. "By making the storm chase us, it hit us after it had already started to weaken. If we'd been hit earlier, we'd have lost more ships."

"So, Artemisia may have saved our lives?" Xenocrates asked.

"Indeed, Your Highness. Even the way she moved that half-sunk piece of the Knidosian ship. We struck it head on, but our ships are designed to do that. Had it hit us in the side, it might have disabled us or worse."

"Thank you, Hippodamos," Xenocrates said.

"Queen Artemisia." Damasithymos continued to ignore her title of satrap. "I'd like to suggest a solution before we proceed."

She nodded her approval.

"The Gods haven't seen fit to destroy us outright. But why taunt them? Why not marry one of the men in this chamber? It would be a fitting and just solution."

Artemisia gave no response.

"In that case I'd like for the Boule to travel to the Didymaion."

I'd thought he'd ask the Priest of Didyma! But the priest is here. He must want us to go to the Oracle of Didyma. "Let it be done. But before we recess, I want to announce that I'm giving up one of Halikarnassos' ships to Knidos to honor the bravery of King Nicander. Let us adjourn the Boule for four days. We'll reconvene at the Didymaion."

On the trip to Didyma, Artemisia rode beside Xenocrates. "Why did you save me?"

"What do you mean?" Xenocrates seemed genuinely confused by the question.

"When you rescued me during the storm."

"What? And anger Apollo, Artemis, and Athena! I might as well have jumped into the sea myself."

"You don't strike me as an actual believer," she said.

Xenocrates shrugged.

"So, why'd you save me?"

"Why'd you save me?" Xenocrates stared at her. "After you killed Lobon, no one would've said anything if you executed me."

"I cannot say for sure. I had a feeling…" She stared at the Lorymian. "Fine then, why not force me into marriage?"

"What and have my neck slashed?" Xenocrates looked genuinely alarmed.

Artemisia pulled ahead and stayed there until the evening. When they set up camp, she put her tent next to Xenocrates', and after the king retired, she snuck into his tent. "I won't leave until you explain yourself to me."

Xenocrates lit an oil lamp. He set it down carefully and sat up. The light from the lamp exaggerated the age of his face. *He's handsome and rugged. I can't explain why I like him. Or even why I spared him.*

"I saw what you did at Pedasos and on the road to Mylasa." Xenocrates was somber. "I knew then that I'd follow you to the ends of the world."

"But now you're standing up to Damasithymos. It threatens to break the Kalyndian league!"

Xenocrates nodded.

"Why! You must tell me why you saved me and why you're standing up for me!" Artemisia knew it was unwise to be so loud, but passion overwhelmed her.

Xenocrates took her face with both hands and pulled her to him.

She was surprised, but she did not resist.

Though he pulled with strength, he stopped when their lips were a finger's width apart.

Artemisia hesitated. Her mind spun. After an awkward moment, his hot breath on her lips, incredulously she asked, "What are you doing?"

He let go and backed up. "I was going to show you."

"Then why are you pulling away?"

"I wanted to give you the ability to come to me and thought that…" He grabbed her again.

She liked his desire, confusion, and strength.

He pulled her to him, and this time he kissed her. The kiss was gentle. Xenocrates seemed to be savoring her.

Her skin tingled. Artemisia felt like she was floating off the ground as the king slowly gathered her up against him. Soon she was in his lap, stroking the side of his face, never breaking the kiss, melting slowly into him.

She didn't know how long they kissed, when she whispered, "I like you."

He put his arms around her, enveloping her, and warming her. She felt safe and appreciated. Xenocrates had her trust. She moved her hand down his tunic and lifted it over his head. His naked chest bore three large scars. She explored each with her lips.

Artemisia stood straight before the oracle, a tall, pale, slender woman with sallow eyes. Her long, curly hair branched off in every direction. Her shoulders slouched and her back hunched. The oracle walked around the satrap, sizing her up. "What fool called for the Satrap of Caria to stand before me?"

Damasithymos stepped forward and opened his mouth.

He is a fool, and he answers to "fool!"

"Don't speak!" The oracle shouted, waving her hand at him. "Don't approach! Go stand with your comrades. This is a sacred space. Do *not* anger Apollo! You think I'm some three-trihemitartemorion seer! You can't just come here with the Boule and look through the lies of your lies. I'm the Oracle of Apollo! I see the future! Your profane concerns aren't worth my time!" She turned her back on the Boule.

Artemisia was stunned. She had assumed that Damasithymos had some arrangement with the Ionians and that they were working together to undermine her authority. But she realized that Damasithymos had no plan. *He may be a true believer, and she might be as well!* She dropped to both knees. "I, Artemisia, Satrap of Caria, Queen of Halikarnassos, beseech you, o wise Oracle of Apollo, to forgive my Boule. To forgive all its members for any transgression."

"You'd bring such petty matters before me?" The Oracle spun around, her eyes ablaze with outrage.

"Oracle, voice of Apollo, the God of harmony, I beseech you." Artemisia bowed her head. "We've been visited by the Goddess Eris and the God Hekatonkheires. We seek to recover from such ill fortune."

The Oracle hissed, and then she started to shake. Her eyes rolled back, and the trembling increased. "I am Apollo. I speak through this vessel. I am the harmony which can find the inner side of the ear through four storms, and a friend long lost brings dreams of a burning city built of clay and stone ashes covering your hands, though you don't know how the grit got between your teeth, and you'll surely let the fish escape."

Artemisia could find nothing to latch onto.

"You'll drown at sea. Never will you through marriage tame your Delphyne." The Oracle suddenly became still.

"What does all of this mean, Oracle?" Artemisia asked.

The Oracle turned and started walking away.

Damasithymos asked, "Do you mean that I'll never drown but will tame someone in marriage? Or do you mean that I'll drown, never taming someone?"

The Oracle turned right and left through a side door.

"Of course, you would think that message was for you," Kharax of Kaunos declared. "This message could've been for any of us, maybe all of us."

What can anyone do with that? I've no idea what that all means, well, except for the last part. That shiteater will drown, because he'll never tame me.

"You invoke the Spartans, but they don't allow women to serve as king!" In Mylasa Damasithymos turned to the Boule. "Artemisia is the King of Halikarnassos and the Satrap of Caria. These are both transgressions, which the Gods won't tolerate. The Oracle even referred to Artemisia as Delphyne, the monster slain by Apollo!"

Xenocrates stood. "Delphyne also means womb. For all you know, she meant that you intend to marry Artemisia and that you'll drown trying to tame her."

Before that moment Artemisia had never noticed that the monster slain by Apollo had the name "womb." She had heard the words but never put it together. *How much contempt for women did our forefathers have when they made up our stories? Only a man would name a monster "womb!"*

Kharax stood. "Your insistence on dethroning Artemisia comes from your realization that you'll never marry her. Your dreams of power and the satrapy are gone. You're so far from Artemisia in quality, that it would be the equivalent of Artemis herself coming down from Mount Olympus and marrying a donkey!"

"You say this because you were never a contender."

"It's true that I didn't make it far. But unlike you, I understood. I've married and hold out no hope that she'll change her mind. That you think you can bully Artemisia into marriage is proof that you're mad."

Several of Artemisia's allies chuckled. Xenocrates shouted, "Bravo!"

Artemisia looked at Queen Iokaste. The two locked eyes, and Iokaste smiled big. Artemisia wanted to laugh but contained it.

"Apollo slew Delphyne," Damasithymos began again, "and took from her the possession of Delphi and put in her place the Oracle. King Kroisos of Lydia tested the oracles and concluded that none were more accurate than the one at Delphi. Clearly the Oracle of Didyma invoked the Delphian Oracle for a reason!"

"You make the best arguments!" Artemisia laughed. "Kroisos listened to the Oracle at Delphi which told him, 'If you cross the river, a great empire will be destroyed.' He crossed the Halys River, and it turned out that it was his empire which was destroyed, by Kurosh the Great, the very same man who sent Adusius to take Caria!"

"He misread the Oracle. It's still obviously correct!"

"So, the only way we know the meaning of the Oracle is with hindsight?" Artemisia wanted to shout, *You idiot!* But contained it. "We can't know the meaning before? What good is any oracle, then?"

"We aren't dumb men." Damasithymos' resolve seemed to strengthen. "Together we can figure it out."

"Do you even remember the first part?" Kharax asked.

"No, it was too much."

"I do." Terpander pulled out his lyre, strummed it, and then sang.

> *I am Apollo.*
> *I speak through this vessel.*
> *Vague advice followed in three ways*
> *will yield to those who listen to both!*
> *I am the harmony which can find the inner side*
> *of the ear through two storms*
> *and a friend long lost brings dreams*
> *of a burning city built of clay*
> *and stone*
> *ashes covering your hands*
> *though you don't know how the grit got between your teeth*
> *and you'll surely let the fish escape.*
> *You'll drown at sea*
> *never*
> *will you through marriage tame your Delphyne.*

Xenocrates clapped. "Bravo! The lyre-king understands the Oracle. Tell us what it means!"

Terpander looked around, surprised. Artemisia suspected he was surprised that he was the center of attention. Finally, he spoke. "I don't know what it means."

"How will you vote?" Iokaste shouted.

"I'll vote for Artemisia."

"There! The one person in the room who was truly paying attention to the Oracle has intuited that it means we should keep things as they are." Xenocrates oozed sarcasm.

"Fools! I demand a vote!" Damasithymos was bright red.

Artemisia stood. "I should leave so that you can vote your con-
science."

"No, Your Majesty," Damasithymos said. "Stay so that you might
understand how many of us oppose your rule."

Artemisia stood and left anyway.

Later as Artemisia lay in his arms, Xenocrates said, "The Kalyndian
League was divided, of course: seven for removing you and my two
votes against. The Ionian League had the same division. Damasithymos
received six more votes from the Mylasa League, but that was where
his support ended. The final vote was twenty to forty-two. So sure was
he of his position that he stood and shouted, 'The Bouleutai are fools!
The satrap must marry or abdicate. We must demand it, but this body
isn't made of men!' With that he stormed out of the room."

In the days before the winter solstice, Thuxra arrived. "I'm sent by Spahbed Marduniya to inform you of his successful arrival in Ionia."

Artazostreh!

"He has overthrown the tyrants in the Satrapy of Ionia and replaced them with democracies. The spahbed is wondering what has become of the expedition against the island of Kos."

"Our fleet was struck by a tempest, and we lost one-quarter of our navy—two kings, fourteen ships, and two thousand men."

Bitter shame filled her knowing that Marduniya would be told of her disaster.

During the Boule of 492 BC, Thuxra came back. "Spahbed Marduniya sends his condolences for your losses. He's crossing the sea to return Thrake to the Persian Empire. He requests five ships from Caria join his fleet."

Artemisia was disappointed that Marduniya had gone to Europe already. She had hoped she could see Artazostreh.

The Boule debate started with Damasithymos. "I believe that all five ships should come from Halikarnassos and that the satrap herself should lead the expedition."

Artemisia wanted to go but knew that she could not leave Caria without Damasithymos.

Iokaste stood. "Last year, you wanted her removed. Suddenly you have confidence in her!"

"She serves the Persians! She should do their bidding!"

"I'll do it." Mnaseas stood. "I'll take one ship from each faction."

Artemisia spoke. "I would like to relieve the Ionian faction of its burden by having Miletos and Halikarnassos each provide a ship." She hoped the gesture would placate the Ionians.

The measure passed forty-seven to fifteen.

Artemisia sent out criers to announce a contest: "The Satrap of Caria invites all to submit a play for her approval. All approved plays will receive a number of silver staters according to the satrap's pleasure. The best performance will win a goat."

In 492 BC the satrap created a new trade deal with Egypt that involved Miletos and Halikarnassos. She was bursting with pride for making the deal and for showing the Egyptian delegation the Royal Castle. She told them of her trip to Egypt, and though she did not know them, she felt like she was telling a long-lost friend of her rise to power.

She and Xenocrates had gotten into a pattern of getting together once per month for four or five days. She was comfortable with their arrangement. In fact, she said to her handmaiden, "Dryo, I didn't know if I could ever be happy again."

"Mistress, happiness is how you look at your life."

"I suppose that's true."

However, Xenocrates surprised her as spring went into bloom. "I don't understand why you're abdicating?" Panic set in.

"I've already abdicated," Xenocrates clarified. "I did it because I don't like traveling in the winter."

"I don't understand." Artemisia felt betrayed.

"To be with you some of the time requires me to travel back and forth. I can't be both the King of Loryma and the consort to the satrap."

"But you—"

"I want nothing from you." Xenocrates had an air of calm about him. "I don't expect to become the king. You end this anytime you like. If you tell me to leave right now, I will, with no ill feelings. I'm unconditionally loyal to you. My son will make a decent king, and my legacy will live on through you and him."

Artemisia felt a little flattered and suffocated. The dominant emotion she had was one of being pressured into committing to their relationship. A mixture of guilt and dread washed over her, nearly wiping out most other feelings.

"Give me something to ease your burden." It was obvious that Xenocrates could sense her discomfort. "Make me Polemarch of Halikarnassos or how about advisor to the satrap? I've my own wealth and will live off that."

"When the Boule wasn't in session, we saw each other five days per month. Now I'll see you every day," Artemisia said.

"I hear the discomfort in your voice. You have no obligation to see me at all."

"Your sacrifice would be a waste, if I didn't let you into my life more!"

"No waste. That was my choice. How you react to it is your choice." Xenocrates bowed and backed out of the room.

And yet what man would do such a thing for a woman? Is he in love with me? I like him, but I don't want to be bound by marriage. Nor do I want more than the occasional love making. It's too soon!

Is this about trust? I thought I could trust, but maybe I can't. I wish Io were here! Dryo's too naive about the world!

Three plays were submitted, and Artemisia approved all three. The agora hosted a play per day. The first was about Apollo granting Cassandra the power of prophecy but preventing anyone from believing her. She was forced to watch as Troy was burned. The second play was about Medea and the days after Jason leaves her for a new wife. Medea murders the bride by poisoning her dress. Then the Corinthians kill her children in an act of vengeance. Jason and Medea each lament that they lost all whom they loved, in chorus at opposite ends of the stage. The third play was about Herakles capturing the city of Oechalia. Artemisia was surprised at how much screaming the actors managed.

Artemisia gave the goat to the play about Medea and Jason. Though the lines were stiff, and the acting was weak, she hoped that she had started a tradition.

Two months transpired without Artemisia initiating contact with Xenocrates. She dreaded seeing him. What if it's like Iokaste says—we must earn the other person? He comes to me without struggle, without a demand. But I can't help what's in my heart. I don't want him anymore, though it pains me. Thinking of him leaves me filled with anxiety.

Xenocrates came to her at the end of the two months. "I'm leaving for Miletos. I can't help you here, but maybe I can help you there."

"I see." Artemisia was filled with relief but didn't want to seem happy. "I think that'd be great."

"I want to assure you that I thought that I'd make your life better."

"I'm—"

"Please, Your Highness, spare me my dignity. The distance that you have created feels inconsistent with what I believed about us. I can't make sense of it, but the heart's like the leopard in the mountains. It goes where it pleases."

That fall, at the end of a play about Herakles capturing Hippolyta's girdle, Thuxra arrived. "Satrap Artemisia, Spahbed Marduniya sends grave tidings. He has lost his fleet in a freak storm in the northern Aegean. In addition, he has suffered a wound in a battle. Despite securing Thrake and Macedonia, he has decided to flee Europe for fear that his army would be cut off."

"How many survivors from the fleet?"

"None, Your Majesty. The wreckage has washed up on shore with thousands of bodies."

"King Mnaseas?"

"None, Your Excellency."

"The traveler," she whispered. "I considered marrying him."

Thuxra nodded, as if he understood what she meant.

Artemisia was disgusted by her emotions. She felt a great sadness in the loss of Mnaseas and all those men. But she also took pleasure in knowing that Marduniya had been humiliated. And perhaps he'll die of his wounds!

The Boule of 491 BC commenced with the marriage of Iokaste and Xenocrates, presided over by the Priest of Didyma. Artemisia was overcome with jealousy. I didn't want him, but now I do? It's like I'm some foolish woman in some Athenian drama!

Despite all the emotions bubbling to the surface, she said nothing. Instead she gave the newlywed couple a life-sized marble statue of Apollo she had commissioned for her palace. It was not yet completed, but she promised to send it once it was. King Parydik stood next to his father, and Artemisia stood as witness for Iokaste. Though it was difficult, she found a core of genuine joy for the couple.

Xenocrates replaced a delegate from Miletos with some fuss, but made it clear that he was not replacing Iokaste. "We're a dual monarchy in Miletos, equal in power, until Iokaste's ten-year term is concluded."

When the Boule commenced, it didn't take long before it descended into chaos. Timanthes, the Priest of Didyma, stood. "It is the belief of Milesians that the Persians plan to attack Athens. The Ionian League will oppose any support for Persian's campaigns. We'll defy any orders that send our men, ships, or resources."

"With the sinking of our five ships and the death of yet another king, the Gods have demonstrated their continued displeasure with the satrap!" Damasithymos didn't miss the opportunity. "Under her leadership we've lost nineteen ships. We had fifty-three. Now we have thirty-five. How much more of this abuse will the Boule tolerate?"

"And yet," Xenocrates interrupted, "we still have nine more ships than what we had when she became satrap!"

Recriminations erupted. Artemisia knew she had lost the Boule for the day. She looked over at Iokaste and saw that she was rocking her seat. She doesn't like the responsibility I've heaped upon her. I'd thought that by year three, she'd have learned to like it. At least she has a handsome lover.

Before Artemisia left for the Boule of 490 BC, Thuxra arrived. "Marduniya has been relieved of command. Spahbed Datis orders you conquer Kos and neighboring islands in preparation for his campaign against Greece. Emperor Darayavahu has ordered the Hellenes to surrender. All save Sparta and Athens have."

"Neighboring islands?"

"Kalymnos, Nisyros, and anything else you feel like you can get a hold of," Thuxra said, "but then you are to proceed to Naxos and join the fleet there."

"Our expedition will be a punitive one against Athens for their burning of Sardes and their participation in the Ionian Revolt?" Artemisia was surprised. "But our goal is to conquer the remainder of Greece and bring it into the empire?"

"Yes."

"This is going to be hard to sell."

At the Boule, Damasithymos led the opposition. "You carry two swords." Damasithymos asked, "Why two swords? Your shield bears a scorpion, yet your banner is Pegasos and a goat. Which is it? Scorpion or goat? Persian or Carian? Woman or man?".

"Oh, most clever King Damasithymos." Artemisia was genuinely impressed with the king's layers. "My banner displays Pegasos and a goat. Pegasos is powerful and free, and well we sacrifice goats to the Goddess Artemis." You no doubt believe the winged-horse is for my sword. But you don't know that my father called me Pegasos. The goat is because I want to bring plays to Halikarnassos, but I know if I told you those things you'd mock me as jealous men mock each other!

She hesitated for a moment. "Is it true that Kaunos is minting coins with a Gorgon on one side and a Harpy on the other?"

Damasithymos grinned. "The royal artist thought it was a lovely representation of our religion."

Hmm, evil female monsters! I am flattered that you think so much of me that you would feature me on your coins!

"Your shields and swords?" The King of Kaunos pressed Artemisia.

"Prizes for my role at Pedasos. There, my glory eclipsed every man in this room. I keep Daurises' shield and his sword to remind you of that. And the second sword was given to me by Melanthios. I—"

"A man you killed!"

"I killed him?" Artemisia stood. "What are you talking about! Your foolish rebellion killed him."

The room became quiet.

"Did I make Ionia rebel against Persia?" she asked.

"No, but the Gods punished him for serving you!" Damasithymos frowned.

"He fought against me?" Artemisia was baffled by the logic failure. "If anything, the Gods punished him for serving your insane rebellion."

The room remained quiet.

"But I married him." Artemisia's heart was filled with fury. "Isn't that what you wanted? For me to marry?" She managed to soften her voice. "If I married you, would you desist in your attacks against me?"

Damasithymos thought about the question.

Interesting. Is he thinking that maybe I'm sincerely offering? Finally, she could take no more silence. "I'm proposing another fleet of twenty-seven ships."

"At least this time you are risking fewer ships!" Damasithymos shouted.

"If I were a man, would you dare talk to me like this?"

"I talk to you, because you don't know your place!"

"I know my place, King Damasithymos. It's here in the blood throne."

"Yes, if you married me, it would end our problems," Damasithymos confessed.

"Surely, then we must endeavor to marry quickly. Where's Timanthes, the Priest of Didyma?" Artemisia allowed her voice to flow with contempt.

Laughter erupted from the Boule.

"See what you've done to us?" Damasithymos asked.

"I see that you waste our time. We could've presented an argument for and one against this expedition by now. Instead we listen to how you wish you were fucking me! You talk about me and my womb, like I'm your toy. Considering that I'm a widow twice, you'd better hope that we never marry."

"You killed both!"

Artemisia stood. She put her hand on the hilt of the Pegasos sword and glided halfway to Damasithymos, before anyone had a chance to react. "Accuse me of killing Melanthios again."

Damasithymos squirmed in his chair.

All were uncomfortable.

Kharax started to move his hand towards Artemisia in a gesture designed to calm her, when Xenocrates stood. "I propose that we censure King Damasithymos for abusing the satrap and disrespecting this body. He should be silenced for the rest of the day."

The vote was conducted as Artemisia sat back on the blood throne. It passed forty-three to eighteen, as she didn't vote.

"Now," Xenocrates went on. "I propose to give onto Artemisia the honorific 'Hero of Caria, Beloved of the Gods.'"

Artemisia shot him a surprised look. "What are you doing?"

"That's a matter for the priesthood to decide," Timanthes said.

"I would rather not return to Didyma for another prophecy," Artemisia declared. "I'm still trying to figure out if I'll be tamed or if Damasithymos will be drowned."

More laughter erupted.

Xenocrates added, "Very well. I'll modify my proposal to declare Artemisia only a 'Champion of Caria.'"

The proposal was carried thirty-one to thirty because Artemisia again didn't vote. However, despite its passing, she hated that the margin was so narrow. It's embarrassing, and I suspect it's done more harm than good.

The vote to attack Kos passed thirty-nine to twenty-three.

Artemisia kissed Pissindelis. "Mama, where are you going?"

"We're taking over some islands and then we're going to a country on the other side of the sea. You must listen to Dryo."

"Is Zeus going to send a storm to kill you?"

"I don't know."

"Are you going to drown, ena?"

"No, mnos, your mother doesn't like drowning." She ran her fingers through his curls.

"Neither do I. Why don't I have a father?"

"He died because he was mean to women." Artemisia made her voice stern.

"Was he mean to you, ena?" Pissindelis' eye grew wide.

"He was unkind. You must always be kind to women." She kissed him on the top of the forehead and boarded the *Morning Red*.

Big, thick black clouds! Artemisia shuddered.

It began raining. Artemisia filled with panic, but she forced herself to appear calm. She leaned in close to Godamos and whispered, "Are we going to go through this again?"

"I've been studying these clouds and am unconcerned, Your Majesty." The warmth of Godamos' smile gave her much calm.

An hour later the rain stopped, and the sky cleared. They reached Telos after eight hours and it fell without a fight.

When they arrived at Nisyros, Artemisia was surprised to see that the island was a large mountain jutting out of the sea. It had no good harbors. The two fishing villages in the north were abandoned.

When the Carians went ashore they found food on tables. "They fled!" Artemisia took direct command of the marines. "Their fishing boats are here, so they are still on the island. Let's go find them!" She spread her 1,300 marines out from the northwest corner to the northeast corner of the island, three miles in length.

Soon Artemisia found herself climbing the steep mountain in the center of the island. The view was stunning. It reminded her of her days when she was pregnant with Pissindelis high in the Pedasos Mountains. She could see the island of Kos and four small islands in between.

The north side towards the top was green. When she had almost reached the peak, Artemisia found a lovely little plateau and she instantly imagined a small cottage. It was cool, relatively lush.

She looked over the top of the peak into a deep, wide crater. On the north end was an area divided into several small farms dotted with the occasional tree. To the south were two small craters within the large one. Steam rose from one of two small holes in the ground. On the south rim of the outer crater was a village. It was composed of several stone buildings stacked on top of each other. The agora in the middle had an ornate mosaic floor and a little temple to the side.

The villagers looked up at Artemisia and her people. She ordered the marines to regroup in the north end of the large outer crater. As they slowly walked to that area, a group of Nisyrosians arrived. They were led by a woman. "I'm Thalia, Priestess of Hephaistos and representative of Nisyros. You're Artemisia, Queen of Halikarnassos and the Satrap of Caria. Why've you invaded Nisyros?"

"Your island, all the islands from Telos to Leros, now belong to the Satrapy of Caria."

A rumble rolled from south to north, shaking the ground. Alarmed, everyone looked towards the smaller, steaming crater. An instant later a column of steam shot into the air. All cried out in surprise. Then a large white cloud exploded up from the hole. The column was smashed by the violent blast of steam raising behind it. A moment later Artemisia and her people heard an explosion. The ground shook with such force that half the people fell while the other half fought to keep their balance. This was punctuated by a blast of hot wet air that rolled over the villagers and marines, knocking over several more people. Finally, hot droplets of water fell like rain. Artemisia and Thalia were left standing, wincing from the hot precipitation.

The priestess turned to Artemisia and knelt on both knees. "Hephaistos has spoken. We accept you as our queen."

"Thalia, you'll be the delegate representing Telos and Nisyros in the Boule. The Kingdom of Halikarnassos welcomes you and your people." Artemisia wondered if in fact there was a God called Hephaistos.

They spent the night sprawled along the northern slope. Artemisia slept in the little green grove on the plateau near the peak.

In the morning they set off for Kos. As they neared the eastern shore, they could hear a horn blaring. The Kosians were scrambling to form up on the beach. Artemisia turned to Godamos. "Trierarch, if we land and fight from the water—"

"It'll be difficult, Your Majesty. I propose rowing along the coast, landing, and then approaching on foot."

She then divided the fleet into two battle groups of eleven. She appointed Xenocrates to command the northern group and took command of the southern group. Artemisia was careful to put two Ionian ships and three Milesian ships in the north and three Ionian and two Milesian ships in the south, and then ordered the two groups to land north and south of the town.

Kos had no wall, but its small harbor was well protected from both the elements and direct attack. Artemisia watched as the Kosians tried to react to her deployment. Suddenly all of the Kosians turned south. She had expected them to divide into two groups, but they didn't. Upon seeing this Xenocrates ordered his forces to shore.

Artemisia waited until they secured the town of Kos and were turning south towards her before she proceeded towards the shore. Then she saw the Kosians raise a white flag. Artemisia leaped from the *Morning Red* with Vadhut, Godamos, and Ravant by her side. She splashed in the knee-deep waves towards the shore.

A powerful man, in his late twenties, approached. His face was rugged and stern. The bottom of his chiton was caught on his zoster, exposing his whole muscular thigh and yielding a glimpse of his penis. Artemisia found this disarming.

"I'm King Tauron. I wish to surrender."

"How about we dispense with long negotiations. You accept the sovereignty of the Satrapy of Caria, take up membership in the Boule, and become a member of the Leleges League?"

"I understand that some places get extra delegates."

"Yes."

"I want two extra—"

"One."

Tauron reached out his arm. Artemisia grasped it. He leaned in close and kissed her on the cheek to show his subordination in the Persian way. Tauron joined Artemisia's fleet with his two Kosian triremes.

She found herself immediately attracted to him.

Kalymnos and Leros fell without a fight. She gave them a delegate in the Boule after annexing them. She hoped that the five quick victories would bolster the morale of her men. After a vote, Kalymnos agreed to send its trireme with Artemisia. She had thirty ships, the number she left with in 493 BC. *This will weaken Damasithymos' criticism.* But when she saw him, he scowled.

Two days after leaving Leros, they reached the island of Naxos. Artemisia didn't know what to expect, but she was surprised to see that the city was burned. The nearby temple was also burned. People in the ruins scattered as the Carian fleet approached.

A Phoenician ship in the harbor headed towards the Carians. When it reached Artemisia, Thuxra boarded. "The fleet is on the way to Euboea to punish Eretrea. We should head there in the morning."

They sailed hard for the next two days, arriving in the evening of the second day. The fleet was massive. Artemisia suspected that it was greater by half than the six hundred ships brought to bear at the Battle of Lade, though one-third were transports.

Upon arriving, Artemisia and her entourage walked between camp-fires until they found Datis' tent. "Ah, Satrap Artemisia, you made it."

"Sorry we're late."

"Not at all. We haven't yet captured Eretrea." He grinned.

"We took the islands from Telos to Leros without a fight."

"Very good. We attacked Lindos but failed to take it. The Naxians abandoned their city, so we burned it. Eretrea has allowed us to put their town under siege. This is the fifth day. We have stormed the walls twice, with losses on both sides, but to no avail."

On the seventh day, shouting erupted. Men ran every direction. Artemisia called the Carians to get into ranks. Then she saw that an Eretrean gate was open. Persians were fighting to keep it open, and Eretreans were struggling to close it.

Artemisia turned towards her men. "For the burning of Sardes!"

The Carians ran towards the gate. Artemisia fell behind. Xenocrates and the Milesians arrived first. When Artemisia reached her men, she was forced to wait. Soon Artaphernes, the son of the emperor's brother of the same name, arrived with more unarmored Persian reinforcements.

The Eretreans around the gate broke. Carians and Persians poured in. Artemisia ran through and regrouped on the other side. She looked to Tauron. He was stunning. She found herself momentarily distracted. "Let's cut our way to the harbor!" *I want you!*

Soon they were running through the streets. Before them, a group of Eretreans were formed into a desperate line, and Artemisia shouted, "Surrender!"

But they didn't.

She drew her sword and charged, Vadhut and Tauron to her right and Ravant and Saroljats to her left. The first man she encountered swung hard at her head. She ducked and brought her sword towards his face. He tried to withdraw and stumbled onto his back. Artemisia leaped over him and struck a soldier fighting Vadhut in the shoulder.

The Eretreans had enough and began to surrender before Artemisia could swing her blade again. The rest of the day was spent rounding them up and plundering the city. Then Datis ordered the city set on fire. "Vengeance is such a waste!" she mumbled.

Three days later the fleet moved south through the South Euboean Gulf towards the Aegean. After half a day's journey they landed on the Attican coast at a plain surrounded by mountains in three directions.

When they were ashore and setting up camp Artemisia said to Vadhut, "We're in Attica—the country of Athens! To be so close!"

"Truly, mistress!"

In the morning, as they were taking their camps down, to Artemisia's surprise, the Athenians showed up. They blocked the two valleys leading away from the beach. "We never intended to go that way, but they know that. They're here to make leaving impossible."

"How's that, mistress?" Vadhut asked.

"Once we start loading our men onto the ships, they'll attack."

Datis ordered a war council. "If we try to withdraw, they'll wait until we are half loaded and attack. If we attack, they will use the terrain against us. I want ideas."

Artaphernes spoke up. "We outnumber them. We could charge. The horse archers will make their lives difficult."

Datis frowned. "They are eleven thousand armored infantry and archers with the terrain on their side. We are twenty-five thousand light infantry—two-thirds are archers, with one thousand horse archers. We didn't come here for a fight. That son of a dog, Miltiades." He pointed towards the hills covered with thousands of Athenians. "He anticipated where we were going to land! How did he know?"

Artemisia had never encountered such a difficult problem before.

"I want a plan that gets us back on our ships and Athens!" Datis said.

"If we move towards the ships, they'll attack us," a Hellene named Hippias said, restating the problem.

"Yes." Datis was annoyed. "Give me a solution. In the meantime, let's take the opportunity to rest and refit."

Over the coming days, Artemisia tried to come up with a plan, but try as she might, nothing came to her.

On the fourth night Vadhut entered Artemisia's tent. "King Tauron is here to discuss the situation with Your Majesty."

Artemisia was surprised. "Let him in."

Tauron sat on the opposite end of the tent. "Satrap, what if we deployed our weakest men in front, archers behind them, and then loaded the best soldiers first. If the Athenians attack, the weaker units would conduct a delaying action, while the archers softened the enemy up."

"Datis has considered this."

Tauron nodded. "That's all I had."

Artemisia crawled on all fours to Tauron. As she reached him, she stroked his cheek. His eyes grew large. She studied his face. It was unusual, handsome. He had a pointed chin, thick black eyebrows, and regal hooked nose, the kind everyone imagines Zeus has. After studying his face, she cupped it in her hands and drew herself close to him. She felt her body tingle as the excitement of kissing him increased. She grazed her lips against his and liked that he made no reply.

With a flick of the hand, Artemisia gestured for Vadhut to leave. She began to nibble on Tauron's upper lips. The king appeared ready to speak, but Artemisia put her finger on his lips. She scooted against him and began to lick his lips. He opened his mouth, inviting her in, and she accepted.

Artemisia pressed up against Tauron, until he lay on his back. She laid on him and kissed him hard, loosing herself. When they had kissed for some time, the king rolled her onto her back and pulled up her peplos. She stared into his eyes, hers half closed with desire. She saw that he was overwhelmed by passion and it made her feel beautiful. The intensity of pleasure and pain filled her as she let herself go.

The next day at the meeting Datis spoke first. "This is day five. We can't wait any longer. Food and fresh water will soon become an issue. They are here, but our objective is Athens. I'm going to order our men to load up, horses first. Let's leave them here and race to Athens."

It occurred to Artemisia in a flash. "Spahbed, what if we loaded the horse archers onto the transports, first. We could hold this location, while they landed in a location that would allow them to reach the Athenian rear. Then our men here could attack, while the Athenians were flanked."

Datis' eyes grew large. "Brilliant, Satrap, brilliant! Are there any objections? Hearing none, I'm ordering your plan to go into effect. Say good things, have good thoughts, and do good deeds."

Artemisia returned to her men. The Carians were deployed on the far left. The Athenians and their Plataean allies had edged closer and were about five thousand feet away. Banging echoed along the shore as the horses ran up ramps and onto the triremes. When they were nearly loaded, Artemisia noticed something. There were three Ionians in trees. She leaned over to Ravant. "What are those men doing?"

"I assume they wanted to watch the enemy better."

A moment later the Persian horse transports left their moorings. The Ionians in the trees raised banners into the air. Suddenly horns began to blare from the hills. The Athenians began marching towards the Persian lines. "Those traitors!" Artemisia shouted. "They signaled the Athenians! Ravant, shoot those three men!"

Ravant approached the trees, took aim, and in rapid succession shot each man. One fell out of the tree; the other two hung from the limbs, moaning in pain.

Artemisia ran to Xenocrates. "I don't know about the Ionians. Should we put them on the front line and risk them changing sides, or should we put them in our rear and risk them attacking us from behind?"

"Put them on the front line. At least that way there'll be no surprises."

Artemisia put the Ionians in front, on the right. They were bounded on the right by Persians and Lydians under the command of Artaphernes and on the left by the Halikarnassians. She put everyone else in reserve in ranks behind the Halikarnassians and Ionians. When the redeployment was finished Artemisia was hoisted up onto the shoulders of two men.

"Men of Caria! The enemy is coming. We are going to fight them. This will be the most important battle of your life. If we fight poorly but win, it will reflect badly upon us. Persia will regard us with mistrust. If we fight poorly and lose, Persia will regard us as traitors. If, on the other hand, we fight with glory, whether we win or lose, Persia will forgive all prior indiscretions. The fate of all of Caria is in our hands.

"As your satrap I beseech you to fight your hardest. I'll reward all acts of bravery with acknowledgement before a festival to the Gods in Mylasa. Carians, Ionians, Phoenicians, and Dorians, fight! Fight for all that you hold dearest! Fight for Caria!"

The men shouted, "Caria!"

As Artemisia was set down, she looked towards the enemy, still some seven hundred feet away. Persian archers behind the Carians were readying themselves. She waited to draw her sword to keep her arm fresh.

When the Athenians reached five hundred feet, they began to run. The first explosion of arrows rang out from the Carian lines. They swooshed over Artemisia's head. She felt sorry for the recipients.

Athenians raised their shields, and though the onslaught involved thousands of arrows, few Athenians fell. Their hardened leather breast-plates, helmets, leg greaves, and shields successfully repelled much of the attack.

The enemy ran through a dozen such volleys before they arrived at the Persian army. Artemisia drew her sword after the eleventh salvo, bent her knees, and braced herself. The first Athenian threw a spear as he ran up to Artemisia. She watched his eyes and stepped to the left and jumped. Her powerful thighs sent her forward. Her right arm swung low, just over the spear. The Athenian could not duck fast enough and the blade caught his helmet at the forehead ridge. It came off as he fell hard onto his back.

Artemisia kept her forward momentum as she reached another Athenian. Again, she stepped past the spearhead. He smashed the shaft hard into her side while trying to get to the Halikarnassian behind her. She spun herself low and stabbed him in the back. Then ran back towards Vadhut, stabbing another Athenian in the back on the way.

Artemisia bent down and grabbed the Corinthian helmet she had knocked off. A small crease on the forehead ridge was the only evidence of damage. She put it on. Though it was loose, it did much to make her feel more secure.

The Carian line was already starting to buckle. Artemisia shouted for the middle to back up and ran back through the ranks of her men. She had two men lift her up onto their shoulders. Left and right the Carians were dropping back from the pressure of the onslaught. She could see that the Athenian middle was thin, four ranks, but the flanks were eight men deep. When the men put her down, she pushed her way to King Tauron and the Kosians. "Take your men to our left. We need it bolstered."

Tauron bowed. Artemisia wanted to jump back into the battle, but she knew that the Carians needed a supervisor more than an extra warrior. The Ionians in the middle were starting to fail. Xenocrates' Milesians and the Didymians on the right were holding—it was the Latmosians and Myosians who were faltering.

I could let them get bloodied a bit. The risk isn't good, but their numbers would be reduced. Or I could reinforce them and pretend I trust them. Then it came to her. She turned to the Aphrodisian next to her. "I need you to go to Saroljats. Tell him to pull the Halikarnassians back twenty-five feet. The Athenians will have to readjust their lines." *That'll relieve pressure on the Ionians and it will make our flank less vulnerable.*

As the Aphrodisian left, she had herself lifted again. The Athenians were turning faster than the Halikarnassians. Her maneuver had come just in time to stave off disaster, but it was too little to prevent it. She sent another Aphrodisian to order the Halikarnassians to turn almost ninety degrees.

"The Athenians are outnumbered two and a half to one and yet they are trying to turn our flank! Fight, you bastards! Fight!"

Once the Halikarnassians were turned, Artemisia ordered the Kalyndians and Xanthians to move into position behind the Ionians. Next, she ordered the Ionians to withdraw. The dramatic maneuver pulled Athenians into a bulge between the Halikarnassians and the Persians. "I wish we had horsemen right now!" Artemisia approached the withdrawn Ionians. "Priest Zenodotos of Didyma, how are the men?"

"Your Majesty, we are bloodied and upset."

"Will you continue to fight?"

"It's hard for us to fight Athenians!" The priest admitted.

"I don't like it either, yet we are here! I need to know if I can rely on your men."

Basilon of Latmos arrived. "Your Excellency, I heard your question. My men are yours. We will fight until you tell us to stop."

Artemisia nodded. She turned to another Aphrodisian. "Send the Mylasians to take up a position on the Halikarnassian left. They're to be turned ninety degrees like the Halikarnassians. They must prevent our flank from being passed at all costs!"

Artemisia turned back to Basilon and Zenodotos. "I want to keep the Ionians in reserve. Tell your men to rest. We're going to need them."

It wasn't long before the Halikarnassians fell back on the right, bending their line and straightening out the Athenian lines in the process. Artemisia wondered how much more the Carians could endure.

Then came a messenger. "I bring orders from Spahbed Datis. You're to withdraw back to the beach and board the ships. Datis wants you to take the Carians back through the Persian archers behind you. They are to hold the line until your men are back in ranks. Then they will fall back through your lines. Once they are back in ranks, you'll repeat. Do this until you are safely on the ships!"

Artemisia felt immediate relief. She turned to the Ionian commanders. "I want Ionians and Kosians to go first. Form a rank behind the archers, then the rest of us will follow." She sent a messenger to Saroljats and joined Dibikom. "I'm staying with you."

The signalers blew their trumpeters. The whole Carian army turned and ran. The Athenians and Plataeans gave chase. Artemisia could barely keep up with the men. Persian archers made holes in their lines to let the Carians through.

Once everyone was back in ranks, Artemisia had the trumpeter blare out the signal. The Athenians had only just engaged the Persians when the latter turned and ran. Once they were through the gaps, the Carians braced for the Athenian charge.

In this way the Carians and the Persians archers conducted five entire rotations to cross the five thousand feet to the beach. The Athenians, exhausted from charging and fighting in their armor, were slowed so much that they failed to make contact during the last three rotations.

As the Persians loaded onto the ships, the Carians waited for the Athenians to catch up. Artemisia put the Halikarnassians and Ionians in the front again, but that meant they would load first.

The Athenians crashed into the lines. The grunting was more from despair than savagery. The enemy was too exhausted to fight effectively. The Persians blew their horns, and the Carian fleet came to the shore.

Artemisia sent the Halikarnassians and Ionians to their ships. Once they were on board, more empty ships reached the shore. Artemisia ordered everyone else to the ships. She ran with King Menexenos of Casolaba, towards his ship. She splashed into the gentle waves and then leapt up and grabbed the gunwale. Once on the deck she turned to see that an Athenian had grabbed the gunwale. Startled, she realized that he must have been right behind her the whole time.

Her heart felt hollow for the near call. She drew her sword and hung hard, severing his hand. He cried out as Athenians behind him splashed towards him. The ship pulled away before they could get to him. They lifted their injured comrade out of the water and jeered at the Carians.

"King Menexenos, how long to Athens?"

"I think we have fifty miles and they have twenty-five."

"Surely we can row fifty miles faster than they can run twenty-five!" Artemisia was filled with hope about their chances of taking Athens. The fleet took off at full speed. For nine hours they rowed as hard as possible, traveling around Attica. The peninsula was longer than Menexenos had thought, however, and they traveled sixty-five miles. The rowers were exhausted, but the warriors were rested.

By the time that they reached the Peiraian shore, there was only an hour of sun left. But it was enough sun to see, standing in ranks on the beach, the Athenian army. Artemisia turned to Menexenos. "How did they beat us here?"

"I don't know, Satrap." His voice was filled with awe.

"What was the name of that plains we just fought in?"

"Marathon."

"Marathon!" she repeated.

"Marathon!" the Athenians roared.

Artemisia boarded the *Morning Red* before the fleet set off to find a beach to rest. Worn out, they took four hours to travel sixteen miles in the dark. Several men went ashore and lit torches to guide the ships onto the small sand patches between the rocks.

As the men set up guard shifts and tents, Artemisia went to Datis' war council.

"They traveled twenty-six miles in nine hours, wearing leather armor after a two-hour-long battle!" Satrap Artaphernes declared, awe filling his voice. "In truth they won today because they wanted to win harder than we did."

"Losses?" Datis asked.

"We lost seven ships and five thousand men. They lost two thousand men." Artaphernes went on.

Artemisia was aghast. *How could we be defeated like this?*

"Each side lost one out of five men," Datis declared.

"Yes, Spahbed."

"Supplies?"

"We're critically short on food and fresh water," Artaphernes said. "We have to resupply before we attempt anything else."

"Morale?"

"I'm inclined to think we cannot fight again for a few months."

Datis sighed hard. He made eye contact with each of the officers. When he got to Artemisia he asked, "Satrap, you have been quiet. What do you think?"

"Spahbed, we have to resupply and give our men time to recover, but it breaks my heart. When we were in their harbor, I looked north towards the hills in the heart of Athens. I could barely make it out, but I'm quite certain I saw the Hekatompedon. To be so close and to have to withdraw, that is truly a punishment worthy of Tartarus."

"We will come back, Satrap," Datis declared.

"I'll be right there alongside you," she added.

"You have doubt?" he said.

"Never," she lied.

Before the Boule of 489 BC, Artemisia commissioned the construction of a villa on the north side of the peak of Nisyros. She made a habit of meeting Tauron once per month in Kos, Nisyros, or Halikarnassos.

Upon arriving in Mylasa, Artemisia went straight to Iokaste's chambers. The Queen of Miletos was nursing Hekatomnos, her second child. "Remember when you worried you were sterile?"

"It seems the Gods changed their minds." Iokaste patted a spot next to her. "How are you recovering?"

"Fine."

"Dog shit!" Iokaste was cranky. "You were part of another defeat. Now Damasithymos is going to blame you for it."

Artemisia looked down.

"How about Tauron?"

"What about Tauron?" Artemisia was defensive.

"I know that you slept with him." Iokaste wore a mischievous look.

"How do you know?"

"I've my spies in your court!" Iokaste winked.

"Vadhut!" Artemisia blushed. "He's lovely and strong. I can tell he loves me, but he's careful and that's what I want. He figured out to give me a wide berth, lest our hulls collide. I believe that he knows I want limited contact."

"You're lucky."

Artemisia nodded. "How about Xenocrates?"

"I know that you slept with him, too." Iokaste was snarky.

"No, stupid, I mean how's he treating you."

"He's a dream. I hate politics. He tells me how to vote and handles everything else. He likes sex and so do I. We are well-matched."

Artemisia looked down.

"What?"

"I don't think I like sex as much. I get together with Tauron once a month for five days. We fuck like rabbits, but then I'm happy for the separation."

"Why not?"

"What do you mean?" Artemisia was confused.

"Who cares what you like?" Iokaste beamed unconditional acceptance. "If he's happy, then you aren't hurting anyone."

"But doesn't it reflect on my womanhood?" Artemisia felt small. "I mean if I were a commoner, I'd have no rights. I couldn't simply say, 'I don't feel like it for the next twenty-four days.'"

"It's true that your power allows you to be who you are. That's what power is. Be grateful. You're right. Most women do what they must to get by and carve out some measure of joy."

Artemisia never liked how unfair the world seemed and that moment was no exception.

That night before bed, Artemisia turned to Dryo and Vadhut. "When you dream, what do you look like?"

"I'm a horse!" Dryo said.

"I wear a flowing gown," Vadhut added.

"I'm a boy," Artemisia admitted.

"Really? That's strange, Your Majesty." Vadhut grinned.

"No, I think it's consistent. A boy has no restrictions. He's free to climb trees, punch other boys, throw rocks… I think I want to be free in my dreams."

The Boule began with Damasithymos. "Caria will hear 'Marathon' and cry. Athens will hear it and sing!"

"Are you ascribing our defeat to the satrap?" Menexenos asked. "I was there. I saw the battle from the inside. Men hoisted her onto their shoulders and she moved us around like masons building a wall."

"I know only that it was her leadership that made us part of that disaster."

"We lost one out of ten men. The Athenians and the Persians lost one out of five men. We were on the left flank. The Athenians were going to envelop us, but she prevented it. The right flank was compromised, but the left flank held. She led us brilliantly! Where were you that you do not know these details?"

"As you very well know, I fought alongside the Kalyndians."

Commotion broke out. Artemisia pulled her legs up onto the throne and reclined against its arm. She made eye contact with Iokaste and then Tauron. After some time had passed, she stood. The hall slowly became quiet. "I don't like that we were defeated. Not because of the shame, but rather because the lost lives and lost opportunity. If we'd prevailed, there would now be peace in the Aegean."

She made eye contact with the kings. Most seemed open to her words. "Marathon was not a total disaster. We lost, but in the process, we fought heroically for the empire, especially Ionia." She looked at the Ionian delegates. "I'm proud to be the satrap of Miletos, Didyma, Latmos, and Myos. Tomorrow, as I promised, I'll conduct a ceremony to honor your heroics.

"In addition, I want to reward Miletos with another set of Carian settlers. That said, I'm retiring for the day. Listening to Damasithymos speak poorly of me as part of his clever plan to seduce me is tiring." As she left she heard the Boule descend into shouting. She spent the evening with Pissindelis, Dryo, Iokaste, Aphrodisias, Hekatomnos, Tauron, and Xenocrates.

The next day the satrap conducted the ceremony honoring the heroism at Marathon. Artemisia called out the names of the dead and the living for hours. When she knew details about the man, she told them.

Despite the usual rough start, Artemisia managed to pass a measure to use the plunder from Eretrea to fund the construction of eighteen new triremes. Of those, six would be built and maintained by Halikarnassos, bringing her personal fleet to fourteen.

In spring of 488 BC, after a love session with Tauron on Kos, Artemisia turned to him and said, "I'm going to Attica."

"What?"

"I want to go to Attica...well, Athens."

"Why would you want that? You'll be captured, tried, and executed."

"I won't admit who I am." Artemisia shook her head.

"What if you are recognized?" Tauron was clearly alarmed.

"What are the chances of that?"

"Very high! How many women warriors do you know? Anyone from Marathon will have the details of your face burned into his soul."

"I was wearing a Corinthian helmet. Besides, I'll be in peplos." Artemisia's voice became high-pitched. "I want to go to the City Dionysia and watch a tragedy. I want to walk up the Acropolis to the Hekatompedon."

"What makes you think that you can get away with that? You're a woman! Can a woman even attend the City Dionysia? In Attica, women aren't allowed to have public lives. They collect the water and tie ribbons around the stelae of the graves of their ancestors. They participate in some religious festivals such as the Panathenaia and the Thesmophoria.... Athenians aren't even allowed to use a woman's name in public!"

"I could pretend to be poor. They aren't kept inside. Or maybe I could pretend to be a priestess or a man."

"You don't look much like a man."

Artemisia became sullen and silence set in.

Tauron eventually broke it. "I'm sorry. I don't mean to restrict you. I'm scared. I have this image of you getting recognized or violating some prohibition against women and being killed."

Artemisia continued to pout even though Tauron's words made her feel better. "In Egypt, women are free. They walk the streets, own businesses, haggle, bargain, tell men off, have tampons. They can sleep with whomever they please and can hold positions of high authority. Here I have to fight for the right to go watch a play, and I'm the most powerful person in southwest Anatolia."

"My people call you the Queen of Kos, though we're not married." Artemisia squinted.

"I'm not asking!" Tauron looked genuinely afraid. "I was just adding to how powerful you are. I'm too frightened to ask you to marry."

Artemisia squirmed.

"I'm sorry for bringing it up."

"Please stop apologizing." Artemisia found herself losing respect for Tauron. Her mix of emotions began to feel out of control. She stood.

Tauron looked surprised.

Artemisia left in a huff. She walked out of the king's manor. Her guard scrambled to their feet and gave chase. Artemisia climbed onto the beached *Morning Red*. Godamos opened his mouth to talk, but Artemisia threw up her hand. He held his tongue. She went to the small cabin in the aft and lay on the straw bedding strewn on the deck.

When she awoke, she stepped out of the cabin. There on the deck, sleeping next to Godamos, was Tauron. Artemisia felt another wave of conflicted feelings. *What does it mean that he is here? Is he begging? Or is it a gesture of commitment?*

She decided to err on the side of compassion and lay down in front of Tauron. He stirred and put his arm around her. "It'll take five days to get to Athens," his gravelly morning voice declared. "We could get to Leros on the first day, Ikaria on the second, Delos on the third, Kythnos on the fourth, and our final night before Athens would be spent at Axenia at the foot of Mount Laurion."

Artemisia rolled over and looked into Tauron's eyes. She pulled her arms up between them and crossed them over her breasts. Her sense of vulnerability matched the promise that Tauron was going to take care of her and that she was worth caring for.

Tauron pulled her close, making her feel loved. "The only disguises I can think of are a teenage boy or a female slave. I'm not convinced we can make you appear as a boy. We could put on a false mustache maybe, but those hips… I'm just not seeing it."

Artemisia shuddered. Pretending to be a slave in Attica seemed terrifying.

"We can't take a trireme, of course. I'll pretend to be a merchant trading my wares and catching the City Dionysia in the process."

It was a cool spring day when they left for Athens. Normally Artemisia would have wanted to explore every place they reached, but she couldn't focus—that is until they got to Delos. "This is the island where Leto gave birth to Artemis and Apollo! The island that Zeus fastened to the sea bottom with chains of Adamantine!" She walked into the interior and wondered whether there might be some truth to the story.

When they arrived at the Peiraieus, Artemisia followed Tauron onto the dock. She was dressed in a yellow himation and a blue and yellow scarf on her hair. As her feet touched the dock, she realized that she was actually Tauron's slave. *What's to stop him from turning me over for a hefty reward? Or moving here and keeping me as his slave? My life is in his hands, a man I forced to submit to my will through military force. I must be touched by Lyssa!* Her heart beat hard and her hands became sweaty. Panic began to set in. *I can just turn around and get back on the ship.* Despite this, her feet, as if of their own volition, followed Tauron deeper into the noisy stone city of Peiraieus.

Artemisia could hear the footsteps of Ravant and two Halikarnassian soldiers behind her. This did much to calm her. *But what can five warriors do against a whole city?*

Artemisia's attention moved to a boy in the company of a man. Another man seemed to be reaching out to grab the boy, but his companion blocked the move. The stranger seemed persistent and the companion continued to stop the advances. "What's happening?"

"The boy has a slave to keep men from having sex with him," Tauron said. "The stranger is unusually persistent."

"What!" She thought of Pissindelis and became overwhelmed with a desire to intervene.

"Many Athenian men lust after boys," Tauron clarified. "Fathers who don't want their sons molested will buy a slave to chaperone them. I know what you are thinking, but it won't help. You'd have to fight a quarter of Athens."

As they walked it became increasingly clear that the streets were devoid of women. Only the poor, prostitutes, and an occasional woman carrying water were seen. "We don't hide our women this much," Artemisia observed.

"Athens is severe," Tauron said with a sympathetic voice.

A steady flow of people walked north from Peiraieus towards Athens. A man in his thirties with an entourage of six younger men leaned towards Tauron. "What a lovely creature you keep for a companion, foreigner."

"Thank you. How did you know that we are foreigners?"

"An Attican wouldn't allow even a slave to have her face uncovered. Is she a slave?"

"Yes," Tauron answered.

"I'm a connoisseur of beauty," the stranger went on. "I like her look."

Artemisia squirmed.

"Thank you."

As if you had something to do with my looks!

"Hetaera, of course. She is too regal to be a pornai."

"Yes." Tauron was obviously uncomfortable with the conversation.

I'm reduced to a high-class prostitute! Artemisia thought as she draped her shawl over her head and in front of her mouth.

"Are you here for City Dionysia? You must be! You're heading to Athens."

"Yes."

"We just came back from a day trip to Psyttaleia." The stranger's face seemed contemplative. "I like the quiet there…a chance to ponder the world. It helps me write."

Oh, Dionysus, Tauron! "Yes, yes, yes!" Make conversation with the man! Ask him what he wrote about!

"Where are you from?"

"Kos. I'm here to trade wool from the islands and olive oil from Miletos."

"Oh, you're like Thales come to Attica. Welcome, friend." The man extended his hand.

The gesture looked friendly enough, but Artemisia had no idea what it meant. And clearly neither did Tauron.

The stranger cupped his hand and then jerked it back and forward to demonstrate what he expected from Tauron. "I'm Aeschylus, friend."

The Kosian put his hand out and the two clasped them together. "It's good to meet you."

"What's your name?" Aeschylus asked.

"I'm Thales," Tauron said.

"No!" Aeschylus slapped his thigh and turned to his entourage. "I said it! If I had been born a woman, I should have become the Oracle of Athens."

Artemisia wondered if Tauron had chosen to take the name Thales instead of the alias they had come up with, to disarm Aeschylus.

"And your lovely hetaera?"

"She's Io."

"Oh, a most fitting name for such a lovely creature. Come, Thales, let's dine and then you can stay at my home for the duration of the City Dionysia!"

"Oh no, we couldn't—"

"I insist! You'll be my guests! Your men are welcome as well. Besides, if you haven't already made the arrangements, you'll never find a place to stay within a quarter-day's walk."

Aeschylus' home was a beautiful manor between the Pnyx and the Aeropagus. The lush walled garden adjoining the manor looked up at Acropolis, but to Artemisia's surprise there was no Hekatompedon.

An artist chipped away at an unfinished statue. It was of a surprised man reaching out as if to grab something, only he had no right hand.

Though Artemisia was a hetaera in Aeschylus' eyes, he seated her at the table with the men. She was not sure why or if that was normal. A moment later, servants brought out food.

"Your timing is perfect," Aeschylus said. "We start tomorrow. You'll come with me, of course. I've seats at the front of the Theater of Dionysus. I promised all my seats save one! I'm rich so I buy them for my friends. The Gods gave me wealth, so that I could dedicate my life to art. Can you imagine the tragedy if I were poor?"

Everyone shook their heads.

"Anyway, it's as if the Dionysus wanted you to come with me! Oh, your girl can sit on the ground in front of you, or in your lap if she isn't heavy," he said, answering a question no one asked. "Not many women come, but no one will say anything to you."

It's like a country of Damasithymoi.

They ate lamb and olives and drank a sour white wine. As the evening wore on, Aeschylus became more animated. He insisted that the men with him play a lyre and a drum and sing for him. He stood and danced. Then he grabbed Tauron and made him dance. Soon he took hold of Artemisia's hand and lifted her up to dance. He grabbed her by the hips and pressed against her and moved her. She realized he was erect and found his phallus pressing up against her upsetting, but she didn't know what to do. She looked to Tauron, but fearing that jealousy might lead to violence, she turned away to suffer alone.

Artemisia finally pretended to stumble and hurt her foot. She sat quickly with mock whining while grabbing her ankle.

"Oh, your girl needs training! No matter." He then grabbed a man from his entourage and forced him to dance.

Tauron took the opportunity to sit.

And then Aeschylus cried out. At first, Artemisia didn't know what he said, but he repeated it—*"Kynegeiros!"* He pointed at the unfinished statue. "Kynegeiros! My brother." He raised his mug of wine and then threw it at the marble likeness. "To Tartarus with all of Persia!" He stumbled and collapsed onto the statue, forcing the craftsman to step back. "They killed you—you, the most heroic of us all!"

Their host turned to them. "Do you know? I don't suppose you could. You weren't there... Marathon! Some Persian bitch severed my brother's hand as he grasped a ship."

Artemisia let a loud *Huh* escape her mouth as she recalled severing the hand of the Athenian grabbing the gunwale of Menexenos' ship. She threw her hand over her mouth.

Aeschylus turned to see what Artemisia was doing.

She cried out, "That is horrible! How could they do that to your brother?"

He seemed astonished at the question. "It was war, I guess." He stood and stumbled toward the Carians. He put his hands on both their shoulders. "I should like to sleep with you." It was unclear to Artemisia which one of them he meant. "But I'm too drunk. Maybe before you leave for Kos." He escorted them to their room. Along the way he had Ravant and the two Halikarnassians set up in an adjacent living area.

Artemisia whispered when she was sure that no one was near the door. "I'm too excited to sleep. Is Athens always like this?"

Tauron picked Artemisia up and laid her down on the bed and made love to her.

In the morning, Aeschylus led Artemisia, Tauron, and their entourages to a parade. They walked through Athens in a spiral, until they arrived close to where they started. Before them was the massive Theater of Dionysus stretched up the side of the Acropolis. The crowd was so large they overflowed the theater.

"I wish we had something like this in Halikarnassos," she whispered to Tauron.

The hillside was covered with people all the way to the bottom of the rock face of the Acropolis. And then even more people sat on top of the caprock. But again, Artemisia could see no sign of the Hekatompedon. She dared not ask about it.

After they took their seats, Artemisia sat at Tauron's feet. A group of powerful Athenians, metics, and representatives from Athenian colonies, including Miletos and Ephesos, came in. Artemisia froze. She was glad she had a scarf on her hair and over her mouth, but she studied the Ionians carefully to see if she recognized them or if they would recognize her. But none were familiar to her.

She was soon distracted instead by what they held. Each man held a staff crowned with a phallus made of wood or bronze. Artemisia could not believe it. *A parade of penises!* They walked around in a circle several times.

Then a big brown bull was brought out. He was confident and powerful. Artemisia was a little thrown by how close he was. A priestess walked out carrying a large blade. Artemisia instinctively scooted back.

Six men held the bull. The priestess was quick and cut the animal's throat with a single slash. His eyes grew large, conveying his sense of betrayal, as blood poured out on the stone floor.

Artemisia was splattered. "Oh, that is good luck, Io!" Aeschylus shouted.

She wanted to shout, *Not my first time to wear blood-splattered clothing!*

The bull collapsed to his knees and slowly laid his head on the marble. Blood flooded the floor and then the priestess shouted a blessing. Artemisia stood to avoid getting more blood on her.

"That was the pompe. Tomorrow is the proagon," Aeschylus announced, excitement boiling up. "What would you like to do now? Are you hungry?"

They spent the rest of the afternoon and evening eating and drinking. They also listened to music and the poets whom Aeschylus invited or whom he hired after they came by offering their talent.

The next day they went straight to the Theater of Dionysus. The cobblestone floor had a layer of dried blood. A group of men were queued up on it. Aeschylus joined the queue. He kept winking at Artemisia and Tauron as they sat. Then one by one each man stepped forward and said his name and the name of his play. Aeschylus declared, "Aeschylus, brother of Kynegeiros, *Iphigenia*."

When it was finished, judges were selected by lots.

That evening Aeschylus worked hard to get Tauron and Artemisia apart. The harder he pressed the closer they clung to one another. Finally, he started dancing. Once he got Artemisia up and began pressing against her, she leaned in close. "I had no idea you're a playwright!"

"I'm a playwright and a warrior! I was at Marathon!"

"Oh my!" Artemisia felt a surge of fear course through her veins.

"I'm going to win the City Dionysia!" Aeschylus insisted. "I'm certain my play's the best! You're not a particularly tall woman. Nor are you large, but your muscles are shockingly toned. Like a man's— strong, firm. I must admit I find that very erotic! I really want you."

"I'm sorry, my master's very jealous." Artemisia let the fear she was feeling infect her voice. "Please, for my sake, leave this alone."

"Hmm. I don't know if I can. But I'll try." He kissed her on the lips. Artemisia tensed. He made no effort to insert his tongue, and she was grateful.

Just then she heard a man's voice. "Brother!"

The person slapped a hard hand on his back. She broke off the kiss and looked at a younger version of Aeschylus.

"Ameinias! Thales, Io, this is my glorious brother Ameinias! He was also at Marathon and fought just as bravely!"

"Your whole family is made of warriors of the first class," Tauron said, as he took Artemisia away from Aeschylus.

The rest of the evening was spent listening to the Athenians brag relentlessly about their actions at Marathon. Artemisia knew that some was embellishment because they confirmed they were on the Athenian right flank.

As Artemisia and Tauron went to bed, the king reached over and pulled Artemisia to him. He made no effort to initiate love making. Artemisia was grateful for the break in the lust. She nuzzled up against Tauron and sighed.

The next day, as they sat in the Theater of Dionysus, next to Aeschylus, the choregos walked onto the stage. He was a beautiful man in his thirties. He had a rugged face and a muscular himation. In a powerful voice he declared, "I am Xanthippus, the sponsor of this play! I'm sure this play will win this year's contest! It is my pleasure to introduce to you...*Iphigenia*!"

The play began with Agamemnon stalking a deer in a forest. Artemisia remembered Lobon's cruel servant of the same name. Her last memory of him was at Pedasos, where he lay on the ground, his mouth frozen in a silent shriek, his chest broken open. She shuddered.

A young man wearing a deer skin pretended to nibble on a branch. A black-clad boy ran carrying an arrow to the deer and stuck it into a hole in his costume. In a dramatic fashion, the deer died. Suddenly boys carrying tall, green-dyed, wool-covered logs ran onto the stage and made a circle around Agamemnon and the deer. The Mycenean king looked around at the trees and then said, "Be not true that I have done this here in this place!"

The chorus came out. Then a young man dressed as Artemis was carried onto the floor by four men. They set him down as if she had swooped into the grove. "I am Artemis, Goddess of the hunt, wild animals, and virginity! You have desecrated my sacred grove." The young man's face grimaced as he pointed. "To amend your transgression, you'll sacrifice your oldest daughter to me!"

The audience gasped.

How is that a just!

The Goddess was lifted up by the four black-clad men and swept away. The trees followed as Agamemnon dragged the deer to the shore. The sea was represented by a blue dyed woolen screen held up by more boys. More Mycenaeans showed up and the king ordered the deer cooked. "Brother!"

"Menelaus!"

"My wife has been kidnapped and taken to Troy!"

"We'll sail from Aulis and attack Troy!" Agamemnon howled.

The chorus sang about a strong wind blowing in the wrong direction for days. Stranded, the men of the fleet complained loudly. Soon warriors came to Agamemnon to ask why the Gods had turned on them, but he refused to say.

But eventually Artemis appeared and the chorus sang her demand. Again, each warrior came to the king, but this time they demanded that he sacrifice his daughter, so that Artemis would allow the fleet to sail.

Artemisia was surprised at how stiff the dialogue seemed, but the tension between the king and his men was palpable. She found herself tense and worried for Iphigenia, even though she had already read the book. And she found herself imagining all the different ways she could improve the plays she funded in Halikarnassos.

Agamemnon told his daughter that she would be married to Achilles. Artemisia tensed as Iphigenia and her mother, both played by men, approached the altar. "Father, where is Achilles?"

"He's coming, my dear. Stand here at the altar so that you might receive the blessings of the Goddess."

Iphigenia went to the altar with her eyes closed.

Her father came up from behind her. He raised a blade. The audience gasped. Clytemnestra shouted, "No, Agamemnon!"

With a single stroke he slit his daughter's throat. A black-clad boy threw a bowl of goat's blood and the audience gasped and then wept. Again, Artemisia was splattered.

How horrible men are!

When Aeschylus got up to stand with the actors, Artemisia managed a break from the grief to say to Tauron, "What sort of man would kill his daughter to kidnap another woman? He murdered his daughter so that he could force a woman to remain in a marriage she hated. Are we really so worthless?"

Tauron took her hand and led her out of the theater. They walked with their bodyguards through the streets. Artemisia stared at the ground. "I don't like Athens."

Tauron nodded.

"I want to go home," she said.

"Let's get our things—"

"No, they are just some old clothes, nothing sentimental." She cut him off. "I don't want to take the chance on running into Aeschylus or his brother."

"It's no bother."

"If we live in a tragedy, then we would go there and be caught. Maybe one of them would recognize me as the 'Persian' who killed their brother. Or maybe Aeschylus would rape me. It will lead to bloodshed and some or all of us would be kill or enslaved. I don't want to be part of that tragedy." She looked at the goat and cow blood splattered on her white gown. "This is surely foreshadowing!"

Tauron nodded. They worked their way towards the Peiraieus. Soon they reached the beach. "You could've freed Kos and turned me over to the Athenians."

"I could've," Tauron admitted.

"Why didn't you?" Artemisia asked.

"I don't know," Tauron said, clearly lying.

"Yes, you do."

Tauron lifted Artemisia onto the ship. After he climbed the gunwale, half of the rowers leaped up and pushed the ship into the sea. They scrambled on and rowed towards Axenia.

"Why didn't you turn me in?" Artemisia asked.

"Why did you go with me if you believed I would turn you in?"

"I didn't think it through. The whole thing was an impulsive Lyssa-driven moment." She could feel her heart beating hard. "I can't imagine ever doing something like that again. We weren't pretending that I was your slave. I was in fact your slave!"

Tauron adjusted the zoster on his chiton.

"I want you to say it."

"I don't understand," he pleaded.

Artemisia realized she was pushing too hard, so decided to admit to him what she was feeling. "I'm lucky to have you. That was scary to say, but I can't imagine ever trusting someone else so much." She looked down at her feet. "Nor can I imagine enjoying this trip as much as I did, with anyone else!"

"I like hearing that."

"I can't believe what we saw and did together!" Artemisia's heart continued to beat hard.

"That was one of the wildest things I have ever done or seen!" Tauron's voice was excited.

"It makes me appreciate what I have."

"What you earned!" His eyes filled with pride.

Artemisia accepted the compliment with a smile.

"I'm quite certain that you're the first woman to rule over Hellenes."

"I am?" Artemisia realized he was likely right.

"Do you know of another?" Tauron asked.

Artemisia could think of none. But she also wondered how reliable Homer and the other poets really were. "Maybe there were others and they were written out of history. I'm sure that's what'll happen to me."

"I can't imagine it. You're too glorious!"

Artemisia changed the subject. "Aeschylus was definitely touched by Lyssa!"

"He took his brother's death hard."

"I killed his brother."

"You think so?" Tauron asked.

"I'm certain of it. The man I killed looked like Aeschylus and I saw Aeschylus and the other brother there on the beach."

"Oh, the Gods! What was his name?"

"Kynegeiros!" Artemisia said his name with the most somber voice she could manage. "So why are you with me?"

"Oh, what a horrible question. I mean horrible in the sense of horror. No matter what I say, it'll be wrong."

"Answer anyway. I pardon you in advance."

"Well, I'm physically attracted to you. But obviously if it were just physical I..." He just trailed off.

"You what?"

"You're brilliant. Being around you makes me smarter. I admire you and bask in your glory. And of course, what choice do I have?"

"What do you mean?"

"You conquered me. I'm a king and you let me rule Kos as I see fit, but truly what power do I have?"

"Oh, you could've easily betrayed me in Athens. You're not power-less!"

"I am! You own my heart. I couldn't have betrayed you any more than the moon can betray the Earth."

Artemisia lay against his chest and soaked in the love.

When a month had passed, Artemisia patted her belly. "Tauron, I'm going to need some help over the next few months."

"Why?" He looked at her belly with suspicion.

"I'm pregnant."

Tauron melted before her. The tears were immediate.

Artemisia was shocked. "Are you upset?"

Tauron mumbled. He straightened out and pulled her to him. He kissed her on the belly. "I've never been happier!"

Artemisia suspected that the same was true for her.

In the days that followed, Artemisia sent a trade expedition to Egypt, but though her heart desired it, she did not go. "Would that I could take you there, Tauron! To show you what I have seen! But I dare not leave Caria and pregnant like I am…" Tauron nodded, giving her an understanding look. But she knew he could not comprehend, without seeing it, the glory of Egypt and what he was missing.

As consolation, Artemisia hired the young poet, Panyassis to entertain the court. It did little to sooth the ache in her heart.

Over the months that followed, she allowed herself to fall deeper in love with Tauron and gave birth to a daughter, Eudoxia, on her twenty-ninth birthday, January 26, 486 BC.

In the Boule that year, as Artemisia suckled Eudoxia, nine-year-old Pissindelis sat in the oak throne. Pissindelis was talkative, fearless in the company of strangers, and kind. His studies had gone well, except for reading. He was slow to it. But he spoke Ionian, Persian, Carian, and Dorian fluently and it was obvious he liked sitting in the Boule, except when Damasithymos launched into his tirades.

After the Boule, Thuxra arrived. "Your Highness, Egypt has rebelled."

"Oh, that's most terrible news."

"Indeed, Your Majesty, but when the Emperor brought his armies together to put down the uprising…he died during preparations."

The words stung deep. "I'm never got to see him again. How I wish I could. What would he say now that I'm satrap?" She thought of his face and the kindness he showered upon her.

Three months later Thuxra returned. "Satrap of Caria, Prince Ariabignes has publicly accepted the ascendance of his younger brother, Emperor Khshayarsha!"

Artemisia took in the words. "Emperor Khshayarsha!"

"The emperor sends his regards. He wants you to know he has launched a campaign against Egypt. He fears that Athens will use the opportunity to attack Caria and he counsel's vigilance."

Her thoughts raced to that day when the Khshayarsha lifted her up and kissed her on the lips. *Is he proud of me? Would he still think me beautiful?* "Send the emperor one hundred congratulations! Let him know that Caria is at the ready."

As the Boule of 485 wound down, Thuxra arrived. "Your Majesty, I've been sent to inform you that Babylon has gone into rebellion. After Egypt was secured Khshayarsha moved into Babylon and put down that revolt. It was then that he discovered that Egypt revolted again. Forced back into Egypt, the emperor sends word that he is sure that Athens will attack."

"Tell the emperor that Caria remains ever vigilant and will assist in any way."

Dryo approached Artemisia the next day. "Mistress, I'd like permission to marry."

"I'll grant it, if I like the man."

After Lyxes was interviewed by the satrap, Dryo married him. Artemisia envied Dryo for being able to marry any man she liked.

In 484 Artemisia asked Dryo, "What do you think of King Tauron?"

"It's not my place to think anything of him, Your Majesty."

"I'm ordering you to ignore rank. You are with me most of the time and I trust my children to your care. Though I'm satrap, we're friends."

Dryo looked down.

"It's an order." Artemisia knew that she could not straighten out her feelings without someone's help.

"I like him a lot, mistress. You should marry him right now!"

Artemisia was surprised by such a strong statement. "Marry him?"

"Right now, mistress. He makes you happy."

"How do you know that he makes me happy?"

"You are giddy for the three days before you get together. Then when you're together you're happy. For the first three days you are apart things are still good, but then the next eighteen days you are hard to be around."

"Really?" Artemisia could not believe that Dryo saw her that way.

"Not to mention that your demands are outrageous."

"Outrageous?" *Is she going too far?*

"You make him stay away from you three hundred days per year. What man puts up with that? I'd never accept such an arrangement. Either Lyxes is mine or he's not. And you keep him away from Eudoxia. He loves that girl. Don't keep him separated from her."

Artemisia was surprised at how deeply Dryo's words affected her. Especially the part about Eudoxia.

Dryo went on. "Spend five months in Mylasa, then five months in Halikarnassos and two in Kos and he does the opposite. That way you spend nine months together."

Priam died the next day. Artemisia took the loss hard, but decided to take it as a sign from Myron in the Elysium, to marry Tauron.

Artemisia approached Tauron. "I want to marry you."

He nodded.

"But with conditions."

"Of course."

"I become Queen of Kos, but you never become King of Halikarnassos nor Satrap of Caria."

"I'll sign the contract as soon as you draft it."

Artemisia handed him the papyrus, a reed brush, and ink.

Later that year she gave birth to her second daughter, Eulalia, and Dryo gave birth to a boy, Herodotos. Artemisia held Herodotus and declared, "This one's going to be someone to remember, of that I have no doubt. Look at how he follows me with his eyes. Too much mischief for one so young!"

Not long after, Xenocrates and Iokaste stepped down as the King and Queen of Miletos. Their ten-year term was over. They sailed to Halikarnassos and Artemisia walked out to meet them on the beach. The hugs were tear-filled. "Io, let's promise to never be apart for so long again. Xeno, I never thought that I could miss you so much!"

At the next Boule the new King of Miletos stood up to talk. "I'm Pistokles the Ionian. I represent the end of tyranny and the beginning of better relations with Athens…"

Artemisia rolled her eyes and began considering the possible ways to have Pistokles killed. *But there's no point. They would revere him as a martyr and vote in another such man.*

In 482 Artemisia gave birth to a third daughter, Eupraxia. Though the joy was overwhelming, that same day Simurgh died. She was buried in the courtyard of the Royal Palace, next to her family.

In January 480 BC Artemisia turned thirty-five. Pissindelis was fifteen and Eudoxia turned six. Eulalia was three, and Eupraxia was one. The years of peace, creation, children, love, and family had made Artemisia feel complacent, but space had opened in her heart. She was happy at the prosperity and calm that the unified Caria had managed, even if the plays she funded were still rather bad.

But then Thuxra arrived. "A winter Thuxra, now that's a frightening thought! What brings you to Caria in such dangerous weather, you winged thief of calm?" She noticed how old he looked and it made her feel old.

"Emperor Khshayarsha is on his way. He's bringing an army and a fleet. He asks that you combine your fleet with his. We're going to reduce Athens and bring the Hellenes into the Persian Empire. Be ready in the spring."

Artemisia nodded. The command was clear, but the politics ahead were going to be treacherous. Despite dreading the Boule, the satrap was thrilled. She called the Boule early. Pistokles and Damasithymos railed against the satrap. They made their best arguments against joining the Persian campaign, but to no avail. The vote went down thirty-six to thirty.

"You are disappointed despite your win?" Tauron asked.

"I would've rather the vote have been fifty to sixteen. That result frightens me." She added, "Dryo and Iokaste will stay here in Mylasa with the children until our return."

On the way to Phocaea, Artemisia stopped her fleet in Ephesos. As they walked onto the dock she turned to Tauron, her heart beating hard. "How many years have I wanted to see the Temple of Artemis in Ephesos!"

When they arrived, Artemisia gazed upon the complex statue depicting her namesake. She wore a cylindrical rope hat, flanked by miniature animals. Her dress was covered in more animals and at her feet were two sheep and two beehives. But most important of all were her breasts. Artemisia counted them. "Twenty-four!" she announced proudly. "Tauron, I know that you will think me mad, but I don't think that they are breasts, or eggs, or testicles. I think that they are beehives."

He turned to her and grinned. "It could be."

The hair stood on the back of her neck and goosebumps formed on her arms as she remembered the strange woman on the way to Aphrodisias. "Maybe it was really Artemis. The resemblance is uncanny."

"My dear?" Tauron tilted his head.

"I'm not sure, really. I met a woman... What was her name? Qyris!" Artemisia did not want to explain. She felt it would spoil the moment. "I'll tell you someday." She reached into her purse and counted out twenty-four obols. They were newly struck and oblong. On one side was the front quarter of Pegasos and on the other the front quarter of a goat. Beneath the goat's mouth was an "Λ," her monogram. Artemisia bent low and set them on the offering table. Then she bowed her head and backed out of the temple.

When the Carians arrived in Phocaea, Ionia, Artemisia saw before her that the massive harbor was filled with ships. "Fifteen hundred, I think!" she called out. "Maybe half are triremes!" The men around her nodded.

Khshayarsha stood on the shore, his hands on his hips. He was talking to a spahbed and clearly in his element. The days in Shoosh and Ecbatana came rushing back. Artemisia remembered the first time she saw Khshayarsha. He was handsome and talked to his mother with sweet adoration.

When she reached him, she started to fall to her knees. Khshayarsha ran to her and caught her. He lifted her up and hugged her tightly. "You're never permitted to kneel before me."

Artemisia melted in his arms.

Eventually they pulled apart. As they did the emperor kissed her on the forehead. "Brilliant Satrap of the West! Mother sends her love."

"Atoosa?" Artemisia wiped the tears.

"My mother lives! Your surgery has given her twenty-two years and when I left she was in good health. She's seventy, now!"

Twenty-two! Not three as Demokedes predicted! Artemisia could not contain her joy. It streamed from her eyes. "I'm so happy!"

"I'm so proud of you. Your story got back to Father. He had it told to him a dozen times. Every time he would shake his head in disbelief. Artemisia, the thirteen-year-old who came to us full of fire, she stopped a rebellion on her own terms and made herself into satrap without imperial approval!" He chuckled.

The two stood there for some time, basking in each other's presence, before the emperor asked, "Where's your husband?" Artemisia detected no jealousy in his voice and was at once relieved and disappointed.

"This is King Tauron of Kos."

The king kissed the emperor on the cheek.

"How are the Carians?"

"We're prepared for war, my emperor!"

The army set off by land the next day. The fleet left on the second day. They paralleled each other north along the Anatolian coast. It took two days for the fleet to arrive at the Dardanelles. A flurry of activity erupted. Pentekonters and merchant vessels moved between the two shores of the Dardanelles in two places.

Artemisia stood next to Khshayarsha and watched. Hundreds of ropes were used to tie the ships together. Then ten-foot split logs were put onto the aft and bow of each ship and lashed together. "A bridge?"

"Two." The emperor's pride was overwhelming.

It took a week, and when completed one bridge was made up of 360 ships and the other 314. The ropes curved under the power of the water current bowing each bridge towards the Aegean. The men of Marduniya's command began to cross.

Later when she saw Marduniya, Artemisia stood, glaring. "I still hate him."

"Why?" Tauron asked.

"I don't know."

"I do," Vadhut declared. "He stole Artemisia's best friend and nearly stole her!"

Khshayarsha led the fleet west, camping on the fourth night at the Isthmus of Acte. To their left was Mount Athos.

At the war council Khshayarsha said, "You'll remember that twelve years ago, Spahbed Marduniya sent the fleet around Mount Athos. A storm sank three hundred ships, killing twenty thousand men. We're not going to let something like that happen again." He pointed at an earthen mound. "I sent men here three years ago." He led the war council to the mound.

When they climbed to the top and looked down, Artemisia saw a canal.

"We cut a canal through the isthmus."

"Like the Egyptians did to the Red Sea!" Artemisia blurted out.

"Yes, Satrap."

She was stunned, "The very notion that the Persians can do such a thing…it must be impossible that we can lose! You've shaped the shore and, in the process, you've shaped the sea!"

Khshayarsha grinned with pride.

The entire command staff wore expressions of awe.

The canal was one and a quarter miles long and straight. It was one hundred feet wide and ten feet deep. It took three years to build, but just hours for the fleet of nine hundred ships to pass through it. When the fleet was through, two earthen dams were erected to keep out the silt.

They traveled to Therma and waited for the army to catch up. At the war council Artemisia stood across from Ariabignes. Even though Artemisia remembered that awkward moment with the see-through gown that Iokaste got her to wear, seeing Ariabignes' gentle face brought back pleasant memories. A warm smile automatically emerged on her lips.

He smiled back. At first, the polite smile given to a stranger. Then his eyes grew wide and his smile wider still. It warmed Artemisia's heart.

Khshayarsha spoke and all became silent. "From here I'll lead the army. Marduniya, you'll be my second-in-command. Ariabignes, you'll take the title of artanavpati and command the fleet. Satraps Haxamanis, Xactaron, and Artemisia, you'll each take the rank of navpati and act as my older brother's second, third, and fourth in command, respectively."

Artemisia could not believe it. *Navpati! I'm an admiral!*

After the council was over Ariabignes summoned Haxamanis, Xactaron, and Artemisia. "Xactaron, you will command the 147-ship Phoenician and Syrian fleet and the fifty-eight ships from Kilikia. Haxamanis, you'll command the ninety-eight ships from Egypt, the seventy-seven Cypriot ships, and the twenty-four ships from Lycia. Artemisia, I am putting you in command of the rest. The Pamphylians have brought twenty-one. There are forty-two Ionian ships, your fifty-six ships from Caria, twelve from the Cyclades, thirty-three Aeolian ships, and forty-seven Pontic ships. In this way you'll each command approximately two hundred triremes."

The army left two days later. The navy spent eleven days stocking up on supplies before they finally departed on August 3. As it traveled south Artemisia looked west. "Mount Olympus towering above all else! Home of the Gods!"

The next day, after they'd traveled forty miles, a northeasterly summer gale, a Hellesponter, struck. It came on so quickly that all were caught off guard. Artemisia shouted at Godamos, "Which way should we go?"

"To shore!"

"Signal my fleet to make for the shore!"

The crews battled the wind and currents. Bail boys and marines frantically threw out the water. When, finally, the shore came into view, Artemisia's heart sank. It was a maze of rocks with tiny patches of beach. "A fleet of six hundred triremes and three hundred supply ships isn't going to find enough sand to beach!" She struggled to speak as the wind and rain blasted into her mouth. "What if we had the first ships go in on a swell?"

"Why?"

"Won't it beach our ships high?"

"Navpati, that's brilliant!" Godamos shouted the orders to the *Morning Red* and then signaled Artemisia's fleet. The crew of the *Morning Red* perched precariously on the crest of a tall wave. The ship didn't fit. It hung behind the wave, the bow sticking out over the crest. Steering was nearly impossible.

As the swell started to break, the bow began to tip downward. The sensation was exhilarating, but Artemisia feared she had doomed the ship. The keel hit the beach high and bounced, throwing half the crew up as it shot forward. The trireme made a ferocious sound before coming to a halt and tipping to the side. Artemisia ran along the sloped deck to the aft and watched as more ships came in.

Another was aimed right at them. The rain struck Artemisia hard in the face and the wind chilled her to the bone, but she could not turn away. As the ship closed in she sat hard on a bench and grabbed it with all her might. The ship struck, but it was a glancing blow and merely shoved the *Morning Red* to the right.

Artemisia leaped off and looked for Tauron's ship. Though it was day, all was dark. The fear of losing Tauron replaced all discomfort. Artemisia ran until she saw his ship and ran through it. *Please be alive!* When she climbed the gunwale, she saw Tauron on the deck ordering his men to secure everything. She ran to him and buried herself in his arms.

For a day and half the winds tormented the fleet. They fought to secure the ships and supplies. Artemisia ordered them to begin repairs in the storm. To their dismay two hundred ships were damaged; however, more than half were put back into service. All total the Carians had lost nine ships. Two were sunk and seven were too heavily damaged to go on. Fifty men were missing.

Artemisia picked through the coins. She found a Kindyan coin. On the back was a deep, circular dent with eight spokes webbed together with raised lines. "Fishing net?" On the front was the roaring head of a ketos—a large serpent monster with a full set of teeth and a long tongue. "I've a lot of doubt about all of this, but there've been so many storms! Maybe Zeus is angry. I need help. Ketos if you could intercede in this matter, maybe you could give us a fighting chance!"

The day after the storm had passed they completed repairs and set off towards the Gap of Skiathos. In the morning the fleet landed at Aphete. During the war council Ariabignes said, "Xactaron, take your command around the east of the island of Euboea. If we attack the Hellenes now, they will simply retreat, but if we have a fleet in their rear, they will have no escape and we can wipe them out once and for all."

Artemisia nodded, thinking the plan made sense.

Haxamanis spoke. "Spahbed, it seems to me that we're taking a great risk with such a maneuver. If the Hellenes understand what we have done, then they should go after Xactaron and destroy him."

After no other objections were received, Ariabignes declared, "I've considered the matter and wish to take the risk. Xactaron, leave immediately."

The rest of the Persian fleet sailed into the strait. They waited until the Athenians showed up. It was then that Artemisia noticed that an Ionian ship was missing. "Godamos, I can't see Skyllias' ship. Was it the Milesian ship that we lost?"

"No, Navpati." He recounted the nine missing ships.

"Do you think he has gone to the enemy?" Artemisia was reminded of the Ionians in the trees at Marathon.

"I didn't see it, but he has fled."

"We can't worry about that now, but from now on let's keep our eyes on the Ionians." Artemisia ordered her ships to approach the Hellenic fleet. It was already late in the afternoon, but she and her men were eager for the fight.

Once the Persians deployed, Godamos came to Artemisia. "Look how they are formed up!"

"A half-circle nearly the width of the strait. Why?"

"The curve will make doing an end-around on them more difficult. However, I believe their real goal is to negate our diekplous maneuver."

"Will it work?" Artemisia asked.

Godamos shrugged. "We've got better crews."

Ariabignes ordered an advance. Just as the Persian fleet began closing in on the Hellenes, the latter suddenly blew their horns and put their ship at full speed. Artemisia watched in horror. The Persian fleet made no effort to react. She had Godamos order her ships to pull back, but it was too late. The battle was engaged. The *Morning Red* was in the rear. Artemisia heard horns sound *retreat*. She turned around in surprise as if to discern who sent the withdrawal order. "What's happening?"

"Ariabignes appears to have lost his nerve, Navpati."

"We can't win battles if we don't fight."

The battle was over. The Hellenes let them withdraw.

When the Persian fleet had returned to Aphete, Artemisia could see the effect that the storm and the retreat had on the morale of her men. *Sullen and confused faces, all.*

At the war council, Ariabignes was somber. "What are the numbers?"

Artemisia cleared her throat. "We lost eighteen ships. Thirteen were captured and five sunk. We sank three ships."

"What are the final numbers?"

"The Persian fleet is down from 342 to 324. They are up from 280 to 290."

Ariabignes seemed sullen. "We outnumber them now only by thirty-four ships."

Artemisia felt sorry for Ariabignes. "Spahbed, everyone is thinking, if we had Xactaron's 171 ships, we would have an incredible advantage. However, if we had those ships, then the Athenians would never have engaged! They fought us today because we have reduced our numbers. We should take advantage of that. We have the better crews."

"How did they know our numbers were reduced?" Ariabignes asked.

"My Prince," Artemisia looked down in shame, "we are missing a Milesian ship commanded by Skyllias. I believe that he snuck away with Xactaron's fleet and then broke off and told our enemy."

"Did you see that ship amongst the enemy fleet?"

"No, Spahbed."

"I want extra watch put on our ships," Ariabignes said in frustration.

Artemisia felt guilty. She might not have noticed the missing Ionian ship had the captain not made such an effort to repair after the storm.

As she said to Tauron, "And it was from my fleet and from the Satrapy of Caria! That stings!" They were in a tent. The sun was setting behind a massive tree with a large branch covered in brown leaves. A howling wind shook the tent. Ropes smacked against masts. Artemisia felt the chill in the air and snuggled closer to Tauron. Then drops of rain fell. She could here men scrambling to put an oiled tarp over their tent.

"Another storm?" Tauron asked. He moved to go out.

Artemisia put her hand on his leg to stop him. She watched the tent deform. "A southeasterly, it seems. I cannot get what happened today out of my mind."

"The men are shook up."

Artemisia pulled the covers over her and wondered if they had picked a good spot or if the tent would flood. A flash. Then a few moments later the ground shook as a rumble washed over them. An intense thunderstorm kept Artemisia awake. Soon she felt wet. She stood up and sighed.

Tauron grabbed the blankets. "Lower deck?"

The two ran to the *Morning Red* and crawled in and slept on the top level, under a bench, with the men. Artemisia was not sure what was worse—the snoring of one hundred men, being wet, or the thunder.

"Do you know the name of the strait we fought for today?" Tauron asked.

"No."

"Artemision."

"What?"

"Yes, we have to win. Surely the Gods have sent us here to honor you!"

In the morning, Ariabignes ordered more repairs. Artemisia was antsy. She wanted to get the battle underway, but knew that her men were shaken. She looked at Tauron. "The thunderstorm was like a tap on a pine tree, but instead of resin it produced superstition. Even I'm worried about its portends."

Artemisia stood on the bow of the *Morning Red*. "Men of Caria!"

Slowly her men began to put down their tools or stop their jokes. Thousands of mouths became silent in a wave that promulgated away from her. "You have eaten dinner, but you're wet and sullen. I don't blame you. We have been hit by two storms. The second we were already on shore." She liked the echoing of her speech in the voices of men as it traveled away from her in waves, as conveyers shouted her speech towards men too far to hear her.

"That engagement yesterday didn't go well. I too have been affected by all of this. I have taken out a Kindyan Ketos coin to keep close to me. But it's all nonsense."

Grumbling propagated back.

"It's nonsense, because you are focusing on only one set of signs." She knew asking sailors, rowers, and marines to set aside their superstition was impossible. Even she didn't know how. "When we left Caria, there were dolphins off our prow. Remember the sunset when we left Phocaea? The bridge of ships! The canal at Mt. Athos! Remember that those are all signs, too. Mount Olympus on our starboard. The clear sky over the mountain in all its full splendor!

"That evening we camped near Leibethra, the town were Orpheus was buried and the mouth of the Pineios River. We slept in the shadow of Mount Olympus. To our southwest was the famed Vale of Tempe. A favorite haunt for Apollo and the Muses. The Persian army and Khshayarsha had traveled through it in the days prior.

"That tree!" She pointed at the large, half-alive giant. "It endures though half of it has suffered! And I bring you one more sign. This strait, the strait that we will fight for tomorrow. It is called the Strait of Artemision!"

The men remained silent as they took it in. Then suddenly a roar began in the south from the Pamphylians. The Carians began chanting, "Artemisia! Artemision!" Soon her whole fleet was roaring. Artemisia could not hear what Tauron said to her, but she imagined he said, "Good speech." A moment later, the whole Persian navy was chanting. Artemisia had never heard a sound like that before. *Tens of thousands of men are chanting my name.* And then she heard Khshayarsha's name. *My name and the emperor's name in the same chant!* It was all she could do to contain her pride.

That evening sixty-two ships arrived. Artemisia ran to the beach to see who they were.

"We're the survivors of the Xactaron's fleet."

"Survivors?" Artemisia asked, alarmed.

"A thunderstorm—"

"Oh Zeus! How can this be?" Artemisia talked over the captain.

"It sent our ships into the Euboean hollows, smashing them against the rocks. Then as we returned, the Athenians met us. They took another thirty ships."

At the war council, Ariabignes turned to Artemisia. "I'm assigning the thirteen remaining Kilikian ships to your fleet. Haxamanis, I am giving you the remaining forty-nine Phoenician and Syrian ships.

Xactaron's death and our losses are heavy, but we mustn't despair. We outnumber the enemy and have the advantage of experience. These extra ships are exactly what we need to win tomorrow.

"Haxamanis and Artemisia, you won't be allowed to engage your personal ships. I want you to direct the battle, only. With Xactaron dead, we cannot afford to lose another navpati. Understand me?"

Both nodded.

The Persian navy set out in the morning. Artemisia's fleet took the right. Ariabignes' ship stayed in the back in the middle. The fleet formed a half-circle with the opening facing the Hellenes. Artemisia did a quick count and estimated that the Hellenes had 340 ships, fifty ships more than had been anticipated. She sighed hard and whispered to Godamos, "Thank Poseidon and Zeus for the extra sixty-two ships from Xactaron's fleet—386-340 seems awfully close, considering how poorly we've been performing."

"Indeed, Navpati."

After the Persian fleet neared the Hellenes, the latter finally moved forward to engage. Artemisia was heartened to see so many of her ships conduct the diekplous. In an instant, four dozen enemy ships were hit midsection. A cheer rose up from the Persian fleet.

The Athenian ships were sluggish, moving and turning slowly. The crunching sounds of the breaking hulls rang out one after another in rapid succession. Artemisia was impressed by the performance of her men. However, she paid special attention to the Ionians and kept all twelve of the Halikarnassian and Kosian ships in reserve. *I swear by Zeus, I'll sink all Ionian ships if you misbehave!*

Despite the brutal start of the battle, and the immediate loss of so many Athenian ships, the fighting soon locked into hand-to-hand combat. Before she knew it, an hour had passed, then another. Artemisia looked on as the Persians and Hellenes bloodied each other, marine on marine, rower against rower. It soon became impossible to imagine how either fleet could come out with anyone left.

She wanted to commit the Halikarnassians but knew she couldn't. *The time will come.* And as the battle dragged on it became clear that the Ionians were not fighting as hard as the rest of her fleet, neither the Ionians of Caria nor from the Satrapy of Ionia. "Godamos is it my imagination, but are the Ionians faltering?"

He squinted as he examined that portion of the battle. Artemisia and the trierarch stood on a small tower erected just to observe the battle.

"In fact, Navpati, Damasithymos and Pistokles appear to be falling backwards even as the rest of our fleet slowly pushes forward."

"Bitchfaces!"

Artemisia took the *Morning Red* to Haxamanis and Ariabignes. "Spahbed, there's a bulge in my lines where the Ionians having been fighting without conviction. I would like to take the Lycians, who have been kept in reserve by Haxamanis, and swing around our starboard flank. I want to get behind that bulge and see if I can't affect its capture."

"Right now?"

"I want to take them right now, but I want to let the bulge grow first."

Ariabignes nodded. "Very well."

Ariabignes' rapid agreement with Artemisia made her realize that she truly was a navpati. A grin formed as she turned around. She wondered if it cheapened the moment a little, but whether he saw it or not, it was what she felt. *He accepted my audacious plan without second guessing me, without consulting Haxamanis.*

The bulge in the line grew over the next two hours. An exhausting stalemate had set in everywhere, except in the middle of Artemisia's lines where the Hellenic alliance appeared to be winning.

She remained patient and let the battle rage for yet another two more hours. *Even if the Ionians are fighting halfheartedly, they are still taking casualties. They are tiring the Athenians.* With the arrows long since exhausted, she took the nineteen Lycian and twelve Halikarnassian triremes and led them far to the right. Her flanking force had arrows and were fully rested.

When the flankers reached the extreme northern edge of the battle, Artemisia slipped around the tip of the Hellenic line. From the rear the thirty-one ships, with the *Morning Red* in the lead, charged. Tauron was on her starboard. She looked over at her husband's ship—*Eurotas*. "He's a good man."

"Yes, Navpati." Godamos was quick to agree.

Artemisia blushed from having expressed her feelings out loud.

The Athenian ships tried to break away from their Pontic opponents to confront their flankers, but it was too late. Artemisia's ships had no trouble executing the diekplous. A moment later a terrible crunching sound rang out. Athenian marines were assailed by arrows as they attempted to board the *Morning Red*.

Artemisia ran towards a tall Athenian with an arrow in his shoulder. He brought his sword down hard on hers. Melanthios' steel prevailed over the iron blade, which broke with a sickening crack. The Athenian threw down the hilt and knelt. Artemisia pushed passed him, but her own marines blocked her way, forcing her to wait.

The marine in front of her was cut on the arm and fell back. Ducking, she raised her scorpion shield and charged, slashing low as she did. She cut an Athenian in the leg and came up behind him, surprising the hoplite on the other side. He had a terrified look as he raised his sword. She stabbed at his belly, but he reacted fast enough to block it.

Then Artemisia caught something coming at her in her peripheral; she ducked as a javelin swooshed over her. It splashed into the water, but she was forced to pull back to avoid a sword. She ran into the man she cut in the leg. As her opponent stabbed at her, she dropped to a knee. The Athenian stabbed the man behind her in the back. She stood, plunging the Pegasos blade into his gut.

The *Morning Red* lurched backwards. Artemisia pulled back to Vadhut. "Please, Your Highness, don't get so far ahead!" A moment later the *Morning Red* had pulled free and was moving towards the bulge. Panic set in as the Athenian ships began to turn.

Soon Artemisia and her flankers reached the rear of the bulge. Ship after ship crashed into the Hellenes. Artemisia held her marines back to let Godamos withdraw the *Morning Red*. The Athenian ship broke in half, and the men on board threw down their weapons. Then when the *Morning Red* struck the next ship, the satrap led the marines forward onto the deck of a damaged Athenian ship.

Artemisia's charge through the Athenians was met with pockets of resistance and chaos. In places Athenians surrendered, ran, or fought. She wasted no time on such pockets. Marines were left behind to deal with them as she continued forward. Artemisia jumped the gunwale and soon was on a second ship. Then a third. The tightly packed ships in the bulge had formed an island where the naval battle had become a land battle.

A group of Athenians formed into an oval spread out over four ships. Artemisia ordered her archers to fire upon them until they surrendered. Volley after volley fell. To her horror they shouted in pain, but refused to surrender. She wondered how many mothers, sisters, daughters, wives, and sons were going to grieve.

The satrap looked back towards the rest of the fleet and saw that the Hellenic alliance was breaking off and racing towards the horizon. She looked towards the bulge and discovered that she had captured it. The last ship surrendered.

With heavy casualties and exhausted men, the Persian fleet limped back to Aphete with its bounty of captured ships, prisoners, and wounded.

Artemisia was filled with a powerful sense of ownership. She knew her flanking maneuver had broken the Athenian left and contributed strongly to their defeat. *I won the battle of Artemision.* "Vadhut, we won the Battle of Artemision!"

"How many ships have we lost?"

Artemisia cleared her throat. "We lost 126 ships and we captured forty-eight. Around fifteen thousand men were killed or severely wounded."

"And the Hellenes?"

"They lost only slightly more men, but 171 ships, including the forty-eight we captured."

"The way you used the weakness in your own lines to our advantage was brilliant," Ariabignes declared as the rest of the council nodded. "I'm proud to declare that we won the battle of Artemision, because of Navpati Satrap Artemisia of Caria. You have done a great service to the empire on this day. The emperor will be proud."

Later a scout ship reported to the war council that the Hellenes had withdrawn. Surprised, Ariabignes sent Artemisia with the least damaged one hundred ships to Phokis to reestablish communication with the Persian army.

When she reached the shore, she saw the Persian army swarming along the beach and understood why the Hellenes had withdrawn. She turned to Godamos. "Our army passed their navy. They'll fall back now to the Isthmus of Corinth. In Hecataeus' book he said that the neck of land there is skinny. It's where they'll make their last stand."

"But our fleet."

"Exactly, for the defense at the Isthmus to work, they must at least stop us. Otherwise we go around the defenses on the isthmus and land our men behind them."

Godamos nodded.

"308 to 170? I like those odds." Artemisia added.

She leaped from the ship and walked across the beach towards the Persian command. When she reached it, she saw Khshayarsha standing in front of the blood red horizon. His hands were on his hips as he watched his men march by.

As she approached from behind, an aid nodded to the emperor and pointed to her. Artemisia could not help but smile when she saw his face. *Always at ease.* "King of Kings, we have won the Battle of Artemision!" She leaned in and kissed Khshayarsha on the cheek.

"We've named it for you?" His voice was deep, loud, and playful.

"No, my emperor, it was named after the city that the Hellenes were stationed at and the strait that we fought in."

"If I believed in such things, I would say it was a sign."

Artemisia smiled.

"What are our losses?"

"Unfortunately, Your Excellency, we lost half our fleet and they did as well."

He sighed hard.

"We've lost twenty-five thousand men and they have lost fifteen thousand. But many of our losses were due to the two storms."

"Ah, we got those storms as well. If I believed in such things, I would surely believe that was a bad omen." He cleared his throat. "We had to dig the Spartans out of a well-fortified position. We brought 120,000 men against seven thousand, and by the time it was over we killed two thousand but lost ten thousand. They call that place Thermopylae."

"Master, I'm sad for our losses."

"Don't be sad. This is the way of war."

Artemisia ate a late dinner with Khshayarsha and his adjutants. She frowned at Marduniya when he looked at her, but otherwise enjoyed her time with the army staff. She found it hard to separate. "I should get back to Ariabignes."

"Indeed."

Artemisia hesitated.

Khshayarsha smiled through the false beard. She backed up slowly, as if pulling away from a lion about to pounce. He leaned back and belted out a loud guffaw and left.

Halfway between the Imperial camp and the beach, Artemisia stood and stared at the emperor. *That man occupies a large space in my heart.*

Not long after the fleet regrouped, 241 reinforcing ships arrived. Ariabignes took the Phoenicia ships in Haxamanis' command and added them to 118 ships from Thrake and forty-seven newly arrived Phoenician reinforcements to form a renewed third command under his direct supervision. The rest were divided between Haxamanis and Artemisia.

During Artemisia's war council, Kharax of Kaunos spoke up. "Some of us are here because we have no choice. Some of us are here because we believe that fighting for Persia is the right thing to do. We've seen inscriptions left at the springs by Themistocles addressed to the Ionians." Kharax paused for dramatic effect.

"Artemisia has demonstrated leadership unequaled in our country's history. Though I'm no Ionian, I've some sympathy for the Ionia. I'm a mix of Phoenician, Carian, Dorian, and Lycian. The satrap is Carian, Dorian, and Cretan. Regardless we speak Ionian and some of you are Ionian. Caria is a mix of five proud nations. But in the end, we're Carians and Caria fights for Persia! Don't disgrace Caria in the face of the Gods! We've put our eyes upon Mount Olympus; you can be sure they're looking back!"

Artemisia was happy with Kharax's speech. She hoped it would inspire the Ionians as much as it inspired her, but she'd never take her eyes off them.

A week later, they reached Peiraieus. The city was abandoned. Artemisia casually pulled her fleet into the fantastic harbor and unloaded. After they secured the vacant walls, she led one thousand marines to

Athens and took them to Aeschylus' manor.

Tauron looked at her when he realized where they were going. "Remember how crowded the streets were?"

"I can't comprehend what I'm looking at. Athens without people." She looked around. "I recognize the buildings, but I might as well be in India."

"Why are we going to Aeschylus' home?"

"I'm not sure, really. I felt like I need to." She walked into the walled courtyard and shuddered. "The whole thing was so strange. I haven't been able to truly understand what happened."

"He wanted to have sex with you. What's there to understand?"

"Maybe I want to understand why we stayed as long as we did." Artemisia studied the home.

"Ah, well, isn't that why we were here? Curiosity?"

Artemisia nodded and began going through Aeschylus' things. She took a small statue to Apollo, a small golden goat, a stack of papyrus, and a large ornate wooden box. She looked through the papyrus and realized that they were his plays.

When she was done looting, she gathered the men and approached the Acropolis. At the Theater of Dionysus, she waited. Only when she saw Persians at the top did she begin to climb the steep hill.

At the top, Artemisia saw that the Hekatompedon had been torn down and a new temple was being built in its place. Khshayarsha beamed as he looked over the city. A sense of victory surged through Artemisia's veins. She was vindicated. She turned to look at Damasithymos. He was bewildered. His eyes asked an unheard question. She wondered what it might be when she spotted a stela dedicating the new temple:

> This is the Parthenon, dedicated to the Goddess Athena and her companion Nike, for our victory in the Battle of Marathon.

Artemisia pushed against it without thinking. It wobbled. She put her back into it and pushed until it became unbalanced and fell. The stela smashed against the limestone with a thud, cracking into a dozen pieces. Suddenly the Acropolis came alive as the Persians and Carians demolished the partially built temple.

A woman came scrambling out from under a pile of columns. Artemisia instinctively gave chase. She was of similar age and build, but had no chance against the Amazon's battle-hardened thighs. Artemisia leaped through the air and tackled the stranger. She sat on the woman and raised a fist.

The captive turned her head and drew her hands up to protect her face. "Please! I am a priestess of Athena."

"Why are you here?"

"I couldn't bear to leave the Goddess unattended."

"Why didn't the Athenians defend their city?"

"The words of the Oracle of Delphi and Priestess of Athena Polias."

"What did they say?" Artemisia stood and offered the woman her hand.

The priestess stood and straightened out her peplos.

"No one will hurt you." Artemisia turned to Vadhut. "Bring her some wine."

"When the oracle came out she said, 'Only the wooden palisades may save you.' Some people believed that meant we should build wooden palisades and fight for the Acropolis." She pointed at some hastily built wooden walls.

Artemisia was surprised that anyone could have thought those structures would have sufficed to defend anything.

"Others understood it as an exhortation to get into ships and flee to Sicily. Many have left. And the rest believe that Apollo will give them a naval victory."

"I see. What did the Priestess of Athena Polias tell them?" She looked at the skinny temple of Athena, next to where the Hekatompedon had been.

"She came out of the temple and declared, 'Athena's sacred snake has failed to eat its honey cake! This is certainly a sign that the Goddess has already left Athens!' At that point, even those up here fled."

"Save you." Artemisia took it all in and was ready to let her go, when a contradiction came to her mind. "Wait, you said that the snake didn't eat the honey cake. Now this is a riddle!"

"Yes. You are the female satrap?" The priestess strained.

"I'm Satrap Artemisia of Caria, Queen of Halikarnassos and Kos." Artemisia squinted. "But that means that the Goddess is gone?" She was not about to let the mystery go.

"Yes, Your Highness."

"But you said, 'I couldn't bear to leave the Goddess unattended.'" Artemisia put her hand on her hilt. "Who are you?"

"I'm Leto, and you really shouldn't kill me, Your Majesty."

"Why not?"

"I'm named after the mother of Artemis and Apollo, who gave birth to them on Delos. Leto, herself, was born on Kos, the Island you are queen of."

Artemisia grew a look of understanding. "I see, you're the High Priestess of Athena Polias."

"Yes."

"And the Goddess hasn't left. You lied to them to get them to abandon this foolish defense."

"Yes." The High Priestess of Athena nodded. "I'm practiced in seeing; if you kill me, something awful is going to happen to Your Excellency."

"Oh, the Gods! No one's going to kill you." Artemisia turned to Vadhut. "See to it that the high priestess is taken care of. Before we leave the Peiraieus, you are to bring her to me." She turned back to Leto. "Thanks for the riddle!"

That night Artemisia and Tauron made love in Aeschylus' bed. In the morning they ate his food. After their plunder was packed and they were ready to leave, Artemisia lit a torch and dropped it on the playwright's bed. When she was sure that the fire was going, she left.

The Persian military marched to the Peiraieus. Artemisia looked back at Athens. Small fires sent up columns of smoke across the horizon. "What a waste!"

"Satrap?" Vadhut asked.

"Burning Athens. Maybe we should have left it intact and given it to people from elsewhere."

"What will happen to the Athenians?"

"The Ionians debated leaving Anatolia when defeat seemed certain. They were thinking of settling in Sicily. I assume that Athenians will do the same. The Spartans will fight until there are few men left. But they'll never give up Lakedemonia. They will be a great addition to the empire."

"I'll admit something to you, Your Majesty. I admire the Athenians. I think they should stay and become part of the Empire."

Artemisia found herself conflicted. "When I came here...well...it's hard to imagine such a people fitting in. Maybe, but after some changes. Let's fall back and go to the army's baggage train."

When she turned around, she saw the flames of Athens had grown taller and were merging.

Vadhut followed Artemisia as they walked against the flow of the army. "What are we doing?"

"Marduniya's here."

"Mistress?"

"She's here. We're looking for a Persian princess." Artemisia looked around at the massive army and baggage train. "What an incredible thing that we are part of."

"Look, Your Grace!" Vadhut pointed at the soldiers in front of them.

"What?"

"Look at the men."

Artemisia saw it. The Persian army gave her deference and opened up as Artemisia walked through their columns. "Are they doing this for me?"

"They know who you are, mistress."

Artemisia couldn't believe it. She stared at their dusty and kind faces. They bowed their head slightly as they passed. "Do they really know me?"

"Yes, mistress."

Then she saw her on a fancy wagon. Artazostreh held a one-year-old girl. Her face had changed in only one way over the twenty years— it was filled with sadness. Tears fell instantly and her legs moved quickly. At first Artazostreh didn't seem to recognize the Amazon standing in front of her.

"*Zoster.*"

Artazostreh's eyes grew large. "Only one person ever called me that!" She came out of the wagon still holding her daughter and fell into Artemisia's open arms. Both women cried for a long moment. They squeezed the young girl between them.

"Zoster, I am thirty-five now! I was thirteen when I met you! I was sixteen when you were stolen from me!"

"I am thirty-seven. Were we together for only three years?"

"It felt like my entire childhood." Artemisia could barely speak. "I've never stopped thinking about you. I can't believe we are together again!" They did not let go.

"By the way, I know what a 'zoster' is now!" Artazostreh chuckled. It's a wide belt worn with a chiton."

Artemisia wanted to catch up, but she knew that she couldn't. "*Zoster*," she said for emphasis, "your brother has called for a war council in the Peiraieus. I can't be late, but I'll see you again. I promise!"

Artazostreh nodded.

Though it was painful Artemisia pulled away and ran back to the Peiraieus.

At the war council, Khshayarsha asked, "What's our next step?"

Marduniya enthusiastically said, "Sparta!"

Khshayarsha waved his open hand to indicate, *Thanks for stating the obvious. How do we get there?*

Silence set in. Artemisia had the answer but feared speaking. *Why do I still feel like an imposter! I've earned this rank! Armies part before me!* She inhaled deep. "My emperor."

Khshayarsha turned to Artemisia. "Navpati Artemisia, what's your opinion?"

She liked the sound of her title. *Satrap-queen-navpati! I'd never have done it were it not for the training your father gave me!*

"Everything depends on the fleet, Your Excellency. The Hellenes will use the Isthmus of Corinth to block the army. According to Hecataeus there is a stele facing Megara that says, 'Here is not Peloponnesus, but Ionia,' and another which faces southwest: 'Here is Peloponnesus, not Ionia.' I believe that's where the Lakedemonians and the Atticans will erect the barriers for their final stand. They'll fight as hard as at Thermopylae, but with more men. We need the fleet to get around that position. If we can, they might see the futility in resistance and quit. If they don't, at least they will no longer have the terrain on their side."

"Should we send a portion of the fleet around Salamis to trap the Athenians and their allies, as was tried at Artemision?"

Ariabignes answered. "In principle I like the idea of making it impossible for their navy to escape, but it failed last time."

"How do you feel about this, Artemisia?"

"We don't have to destroy the Athenians' navy. We just need to be able to go past it. Let them run. Let them run all the way to Sicily if they want!"

"Clearly, Navpati, you have given this thought. So be it. Ariabignes, prepare the fleet for action. We won't send anyone to cut off their retreat!"

The preparations took several days. They included the emperor putting four hundred Immortals on the island of Psyttaleia. "What a coincidence," she said to Tauron. "Wasn't this the island that Aeschylus said he was coming from?"

"Honestly, I don't remember. I think the details of that event are more interesting to you."

"I'm going to come get these men if we lose too many marines."

When they returned to the Peiraieus, Immortals were loaded up onto the ships to make up for the marines lost at Artemision.

High Priestess Leto was brought before Artemisia. The satrap held the large ornate wooden box. She indicated that Leto should come to her. "These are Aeschylus' plays. When this is over, you must give them back to him. I'm leaving you here with the protection of the Persian Empire."

"Why are you giving him back his plays?" Tauron asked.

"Not all of them. I destroyed *Iphigenia*. I'm not here to be cruel. He put his heart into these works. But *Iphigenia*, that had to be destroyed."

"You are a good person, Artemisia." Tauron's eyes filled with admiration.

At dawn, the fleet sailed out of the deep harbor to a spot just south of Psyttaleia, where it formed into ranks. Ariabignes put Artemisia on the left. He put his own command on the right and Haxamanis in the middle. They sailed into the Strait of Salamis.

Artemisia could not imagine losing. She looked at Damasithymos and his ship and thought, *Despite all his doubts, here we are on the verge of our greatest victory.*

Then she saw the Hellenes. They had been reinforced. She made the best count she could and guessed they numbered 310. She turned to Godamos. "We still have a two to one advantage." The Spartans were on the left, the allies were in the middle, and the Athenians were on the right. "At least the Gods put us against the Spartans. I bet my Ionians will fight Spartans."

The Hellenes were stretched out in a one-and-a-quarter-miles-long arch in two ranks. The Persians were four ranks deep as they moved into place. Artemisia realized it was brilliant to fight in such a narrow strait. The number of ships facing each other was equal. This did much to eliminate the two to one advantage that the Persians had and it would make a flanking maneuver impossible.

Artemisia began to have second thoughts. She realized that the straits were a trap, but she knew it was too late. *Maybe we should've gone the other way around Salamis and landed south of the Isthmus of Corinth? Ariabignes would never agree to all the shame turning back would create.*

Then she heard the Hellenes:

> *O sons of the Hellen, go,*
> *Liberate your country, liberate*
> *Your children, your women, the seats of your fathers' gods,*
> *And the tombs of your forebears:*
> *now is the struggle for all things.*

The Persians responded:

> *Children of all nations,*
> *Warriors of light,*
> *Defenders of order,*

Champions of the many faiths,
Do good deeds!
Say good things!
Think good thoughts!

The two chants stirred Artemisia's heart. She climbed to the top of the mast and watched as the Persian fleet charged and the Hellenes rowed backwards. Shocked at what she saw, she began shouting, "Tighten up the lines!" The Persian navy, including her own fleet, was charging individually towards the withdrawing ships. There was no cohesion in the ranks. Combined with the narrow straits and unbridled Persian enthusiasm, chaos emerged before her eyes.

Artemisia ordered the ships under her command to slow and reform ranks. But as the Hellenes withdrew faster, her own ships failed to obey. Furious, she shouted into the wind. "We're being pulled into the strait. It's a trap!" She turned the *Morning Red* and managed to get the Halikarnassians, the Mylasians, Kalyndians, Lycians, and Kilikians formed into orderly ranks.

From the mast, however, she could see that the Hellenes had stopped their withdrawal. She ordered the signal men to get the rest of her fleet back in order, but to no avail. "Who are you that you ignore me! If we survive this, I'll punish you!"

The Hellenes began their orderly charge.

"My trierarchs act out of hubris!" Artemisia lamented to Godamos.

He shook his head in despair.

The first collisions that rang out were heart-wrenching. Piecemeal pockets of Persian ships were overrun by the orderly Hellenic fleet. She looked on in horror as Phoenicians on the far right crowded until they fouled up their oars. This was especially distressing, since they were the best sailors in the world.

"Where is Ariabignes? Why doesn't he straighten out his command?"

She watched with horror as the Xanthians and other forward Carian ships were sunk or overwhelmed. Kharax and Terpander's ships were lost in the opening moments. "Two kings, gone! Two suitors from those days of innocence!"

After an hour of fighting, Artemisia realized that the disarray amongst the Phoenicians was not improving. The Persian right flank was collapsing so badly that Phoenician ships were running aground. She began to consider sending the reserve that she had created to that flank.

And then it happened.

The Hellenes in the middle, led by the Corinthians, punched a hole between the Egyptians and Phoenicians. Artemisia climbed down from the mast. "Godamos, the fleet is falling into utter chaos. We're facing collapse in the middle. If we don't shore up our right flank, we'll be destroyed. I'm ordering our reserve to cut through their salient and join the right flank."

Godamos ordered the signalers into action. The ships of the Mylasa, Kalynda, Halikarnassos, Kilikia, and Lycia moved into place. When it was done, the *Morning Red* was in the middle with Tauron's ship in front, Damasithymos' ship on the starboard, and Parydik's ship two ships behind Damasithymos'. *How strange that these last two living suitors are here in this moment.*

Artemisia's seventy-one ships raced behind the Egyptian fleet. Twelve Egyptian ships peeled off and joined hers. Then the collisions rang out as her ships smashed into the base of the salient. She watched as they destroyed one enemy craft after the other. Soon Artemisia's counter-force had successfully cut off the Hellene salient in two. However, the enemy sent reinforcements and Artemisia's ships began to get overwhelmed.

"Godamos, we must get to Ariabignes and get him back in command. We need to take twenty ships to the Phoenicians."

Tauron's ship collided with an Athenian ship. Then to her horror Artemisia realized that second Athenian ship was charging the *Eurotas*.

"Godamos, belay that order! We have to help them!"

The *Morning Red* collided with the second Athenian with a sickening crunch. Men on all four ships fell. But Artemisia kept her feet and led the still-standing marines onto the Athenian ship. A hoplite, confused by her Corinthian helmet or her gender, took no action against her. She ran up to him and stuck him in the side, then pushed past him to attack a spearman. He stabbed at her.

She stepped aside, but put her shield into the path of the tip. It stuck hard and penetrated. She turned her arm as hard as she could while turning her body in the same direction. The spearman was stronger, but the act of resisting unbalanced him and left him vulnerable. She slashed his throat and dropped her scorpion shield.

As she pushed forward, she came upon a Kosian marine struggling hard against two hoplites. Artemisia attacked the closer one, drawing him away.

Vadhut charged on her left and cut the swordsman's arm. He dropped. Artemisia ducked behind the Kosian and came upon Tauron. He was on the ground, a spear through his side. He made no attempt to remove it, but was struggling to break the shaft. Artemisia dropped down next him. She lifted the king slightly. The spear went all the way through. She sat back and looked at Tauron. Grief filled her heart.

Tauron tried to move, but the spear was too big. "I'm finished. The Athenians are going to overrun the *Eurotas*. Save my men and withdraw."

"My love."

"Give me a kiss, break this spear, and get out of here."

He scouted to gunwale and she helped him prop the spear against it. Then with all her might she brought her foot down hard on the shaft. Her instep was bruised and in stinging pain, but the shaft broke. She offered him a hand.

"I'm going to die with five of my men. We'll hold them off. Save the rest of my men. Go!"

"No—"

"I've never made a demand of you. But today you listen to me! Go!"

She kissed him. She wanted to lose herself in him.

But he pushed her away. "If you die, then my death is in vain." His eyes pleaded with her. "We've three daughters. They and Pissindelis need their mother. Caria needs its satrap. I need you to live!"

Artemisia found the strength to pull away. She grabbed the Kosian crew and fought her way back to the *Morning Red*. Two Athenians came forward. Using Tauron's crab-decorated shield, she batted a slashing sword and parried the other. Then she dropped and slid between the two men. She stood before either could turn around and bashed the one on her left with the shield. Then with the snap of her wrist, she struck the other in the kidney.

By the time she had killed another two men, she reached the *Morning Red*.

Godamos shouted, "Your Highness, a ship charging to ram us! Your orders!"

She looked off the port and saw an Athenian ship coming straight for them. To her starboard was Damasithymos' ship. It was locked in combat between a Corinthian ship on the aft and an Athenian ship on the bow. "Can we ram either of those ships?"

"No, but we could ram Damasithymos' ship. We have enough space to make the diekplous. Because it's held fast, we would cut it in half."

When she looked back, she recognized the trierarch of the Athenian closing in on them. It was none other than Ameinias, Aeschylus' brother. Next to him was Aeschylus himself. Artemisia couldn't believe her eyes, but she knew that she didn't want to get caught by those men. "Execute the maneuver against Damasithymos!"

The skilled Halikarnassian crew turned the ship hard and fast. They gained speed rapidly and executed the maneuver like she had never seen it done. Upon colliding with Damasithymos' ship, a terrible vibration shot through the *Morning Red*. The crunching sound was followed by cracking and splintering. The Kalyndian ship broke in half just as Godamos had predicted. The *Morning Red* ground between the two halves.

Artemisia made eye contact with Damasithymos. He began to move towards her ship. She ran to a marine and said, "Shoot him."

The marine pulled back an arrow and let it sail. The arrow struck the stunned Damasithymos in the throat.

Artemisia waved, her fingers rolling them up and down. "You won't drown after all! The Oracle was wrong!" She turned back to see that Ameinias and Aeschylus had turned their ship starboard. "They must think we are Corinthians!"

Then she looked at the *Eurotas*. "Tauron!" To her shock he was still on his feet with one remaining Kosian marine. They were backed into a corner and fighting five Athenians. As if hearing his name gave him permission, he charged forward, stabbing an Athenian as another plunged his sword into his side.

Artemisia turned, finding it hard to watch him die. Tears overwhelmed her. "He was a good man."

"Yes, mistress, the best of men." Vadhut hugged her.

Artemisia took it. She leaned against the warrioress' shoulder and let out a silent cry that was so overwhelming it felt like she would die.

Vadhut's voice was gentle and loving. "Satrap, your grief must wait. Your people need you, now."

Artemisia pulled away. She wiped the tears and watched. Once they were clear of Damasithymos' sinking ship halves and the rowers put their oars back into the water, she ordered Godamos to fly to the Phoenicians. Bodies floated everywhere. Bits of wood littered the sea. Then she saw a cape that she recognized. "There! That man floating face down!"

A marine used an oar to pull his body over. They pulled him out to reveal Ariabignes. Artemisia stared frozen for a long moment. "Haxamanis is in command now." She bent down and kissed the prince on the forehead. "I'm glad you won't have to endure your defeat. You were too kind to deserve such an ignominious end." She turned to Godamos. "Let's find Haxamanis."

When they found the Satrap of Egypt's ship, the trierarch of that ship shouted, "Haxamanis is severely wounded. We're without orders!"

"I'm in command?" Artemisia asked, knowing the answer. She turned to Godamos. "Each section is to withdraw as orderly as possible. We have to put the surviving ships back into ranks and conduct a fighting withdrawal. If the Hellenes counterattack, the Persian navy will at least be in a position to give a solid last stand." It took two hours to disengage. Artemisia was not entirely sure why the Hellenes didn't push harder as she withdrew, but was grateful for it.

Once the last surviving ship was in place she looked out at the Hellenes. They were back in ranks. She made a quick count with the help of Vadhut and Ravant. They concluded that the Persian fleet was down to 294 ships and that the Hellenes still had 270. "We couldn't defeat them when we outnumbered them two to one and believed there was no way to lose. We must admit defeat. Take the fleet to the port of Phalerum. I fear that the harbor at Peiraieus will be too easy to blockade."

As the wounded were pulled off, Artemisia looked back at the *Morning Red*. It was the only ship in the fleet that didn't have a red deck.

"Godamos, begin repairs immediately with every able-bodied man. Let's assume that the Hellenes are coming. Send patrols. I want to make sure we know what they're doing."

"What about those immortals on Psyttaleia?"

Artemisia shook her head.

Not long after unloading the wounded, Khshayarsha and Marduniya arrived from their perch on Mount Aigaleo. "Artemisia, I'm calling for my war council. Where are the rest of the officers?"

"We have suffered terrible losses amongst the command staff. Pistokles, Menexenos, Parydik, and Khaires of Myos are the only kings left from Caria." Artemisia felt numb. "We have several commanders from Lycia, Thrake, Kilikia, Phoenicia, and Egypt left. Haxamanis is in the care of a physician, fighting for his life."

"Artemisia, give me the numbers."

"Yes, Your Excellency. By my count the Hellenes have 270 ships and we have one of 294. We lost 302 ships and they suffered a net loss of forty. I think that we sank 120 of their ships; however, they captured eighty of ours. Ariabignes' command was reduced to eighty-two ships. Haxamanis has one hundred, and I have 112."

"Where's my brother?"

Artemisia nodded to Ravant. Several warriors brought Ariabignes' body.

The ranking Phoenician spoke. "Emperor, we lost because of the Ionians!"

"I saw the battle from the top of Mount Aigaleo." Khshayarsha's voice filled with anger. "I saw how foolish you were! I watched as your commands fell apart as you chased the enemy, believing them to be in retreat. Hubris! I watched as Artemisia tried to bring her command back together. And did so finally, to stave off utter ruin. You'd all be dead or captured if she hadn't been there. In fact, the Ionians fought gallantly. If you say any such nonsense again, I'll have you executed!"

All became silent. Finally, Marduniya broke the silence. His speech was long and tiring. Artemisia ignored him until he reached the end. "Salamis is no reflection on Persia. It was fought by non-Persians. The defeat is not Persian. My emperor, you will return to Asia, but if you leave men with me, I'll fight on. I don't need the navy to destroy the Hellenes! If you leave me even three thousand men, I'll prevail!"

Artemisia rolled her eyes.

Khshayarsha nodded. "I'll have an audience with the Artanavpati, alone."

When everyone save Artemisia had left, the emperor walked up to her. He hugged her and kissed her on top of her head. "I'm saddened by the death of Tauron."

The words cut through her heart as surely as that spear through cut through Tauron's gut. "I'm sad for the loss of your brother."

"My father was a genius for seeing greatness in you." Khshayarsha's voice was deep and calm. "I was there when we debated replacing you with a man. It was after you had killed Lobon. He said that if you were brilliant enough to take the satrapy, then you were brilliant enough to rule. He said that there would be only one test of loyalty—if you told the truth about Daurises." Khshayarsha gave a warm smile. "When I saw you in action today I said, 'My men have become women; and my women, men.' You were brilliant to behold."

Artemisia looked at her feet. "I'm sorry that I couldn't turn our defeat around."

"Victory was my brother's to give. You gave me the next best thing, half of my navy. Caria is small, but its satrap is a titan."

Artemisia was overwhelmed by the surge of pride.

"I should have put you in charge of the fleet after Artemision."

"And bypass your brother?" Artemisia loved the compliment, but wanted to reassure the emperor. "When we make a decision, we make a memory for the future."

"How can we make a memory for the future?" Khshayarsha grew a thin grin.

"Are not memories and imagined future made of the same substance? When you conjure them in your mind, the only difference is that one is truer."

Khshayarsha nodded. "I suppose."

"So, when the effect of your decisions becomes known, you compare the memory you generated in the past to the memory that has happened. If the latter memory is better than the former, then you are pleased. If the former memory is better, then you're disappointed. But in truth it's all illusion.

"There was no way that anyone of us could've predicted the hubris of our trierarchs. It wouldn't have mattered who was in charge. Your disappointment is because we both imagined that tomorrow we *were* going the Peloponnesos, celebrating the glory of Ariabignes and Tauron, not retreating to Asia to bury them."

"You're right." Khshayarsha made direct eye contact. "Well, I want your opinion. Should we fight on?"

"No, Your Excellency. We are defeated; our morale is in ruins."

"Marduniya wants to stay and fight," the emperor said.

Artemisia turned away.

"You hate him?"

"I hate him for what he has done to your sister," Artemisia admitted.

"They were properly married."

"He's a pig. A pig cannot marry a glowing star." Artemisia thought for a moment. "Our lack of armor and abundance of hubris were mistakes of our doing. The rebellions in Egypt and Babylon and the storms were not our fault." She knew that if she told him that the Battle of Salamis was itself a mistake, it would break his heart. "If we fight on, then we'll add folly to our list."

He looked off towards the west. "Maybe I should stay?"

"No, master. We can't hope to get over the Isthmus of Corinth. We should quit this country. Let them have Europe, and we keep Asia."

"And Marduniya? Should I leave him here to try on his own?"

"I wouldn't, but if you must, then leave him as many men as you are willing to let die. If he fails, then the defeat is on him."

"I've decided the matter. I'll leave eighty thousand men and evacuate the rest. You'll take the fleet to Asia with my sons."

"Emperor, I've a request."

"My horse, my crown, Babylon, you name it." Khshayarsha grinned.

"I want Artazostreh."

"My sister?" He was surprised.

"Send her and her children with me to Caria. Whatever happens to Marduniya, she and her children will be safe."

"Done."

In fall of 479, Artemisia reclined on a couch next to Artazostreh, in the Royal Palace. At their feet Eudoxia, Eulalia, and Eupraxia played with Aphrodisias, Hekatomnos, Herodotos, and Artazostreh's five children. Pissindelis, Iokaste, and Xenocrates carried on about the latest court drama, but Artemisia heard none of what they said. All around her was warmth. She was happy save the absence of Tauron. *Tauron, if I had one more Imperial wish... The girls, Pissindelis, and I miss you!*

Then the door opened and Vadhut let in Thuxra.

"Destroyer of joy and calm!" Artemisia was genuinely upset to see the messenger. "You've come to steal this moment from me."

He looked at his feet.

"Oh Zeus!" She cried out in frustration.

"I'm sorry, Your Majesty." Thuxra bowed his head low.

"Let's hear it."

"Empress Amestris has died."

Artemisia tried to hide her pleasure, but she knew that she failed.

Before she could say anything, Thuxra went on. "The Hellenes have destroyed the Persian army in the Battle of Mycale. The Ionians changed sides during the battle and are now in rebellion, again."

"All our work!" Artemisia lamented. "You may go now."

"Your Excellency, there's more."

Artemisia sighed hard.

"Marduniya and the Persian army were wiped out at the Battle of Plataea."

Artemisia looked at Artazostreh and the two shared the moment of mixed feelings. *To think that such a terrible defeat would bring me some pleasure!*

In the days that followed Artemisia readied her army for a possible Ionian or Athenian invasion. She prepared herself for the fight in the Boule, but was grateful that Damasithymos and the Ionians wouldn't be there.

On the third day, as the sun was nearing the western horizon, she stared out at the Great Harbor. Her fleet was repaired and new ships were being built. Artemisia relived the moment when she realized that the Battle of Salamis was careening towards disaster, but was startled out of her thoughts by the blaring of a horn. It came from the Mylasa Gate. She looked towards the north and saw soldiers east of the city marching down the Mylasa Road.

Alarmed, the satrap ran to the livery. Vadhut chased after her. They mounted horses and road out of the palace towards the Mylasa Gate. Soldiers ran to man the walls. "Open the gate!" Artemisia shouted as she spurred her young stallion into a gallop.

She wove him through the narrowly opened gate and down the slope. As the road bent north, turning uphill, she saw banners fluttering in the wind: red, purple, turquoise, and yellow. *Persians!* She shouted at the soldiers marching in front of the army. "Who are you that you bring an army to Halikarnassos!"

An officer shouted "Halt!" and the army stopped.

The satrap stopped, Vadhut by her side.

All became quiet save for the sound of a single horse walking between the ranks of men. The two columns parted to make space for stallion and rider.

Artemisia strained through the banners to get a look. Then she saw a shock of curly black hair. Her stallion shifted to the right. Next, she saw the top of what appeared to be the Imperial Crown. Artemisia jammed her spur into her mount's haunch. He galloped towards the Persian soldiers.

As she rode between the two columns, she saw the emperor. He was regal, wearing his massive false beard. When she reached Khshayarsha, her heart sped up.

"Does the sea shape the shore?" she called out to him.

Suddenly he spurred his stallion into a gallop. He stretched out his right arm and reached behind her. With a tug she came up and out of her saddle. Startled, Artemisia kicked her right leg up and over his horse's head, as he swung his arm back towards himself. She threw her arms around the emperor's neck as he set her down on the pommel of his saddle and asked, "Or does the shore shape the sea?"

Artemisia laughed out loud.

Khshayarsha pulled her against him and pressed his lips against hers.

The End

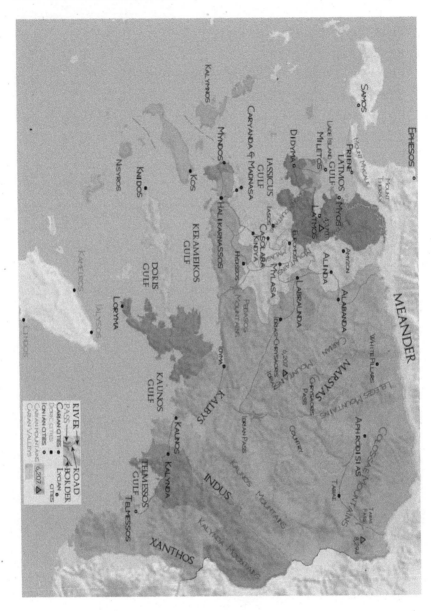

Caria 485 BC

Obverse: Pegasos forepart left charging

Reverse: Goat forepart left, Λ below goat's mouth, all within incuse circle.

Artemisia I*: 496-479 BC. Silver Obol, minted in Halikarnassos, 7mm diameter, 0.71g.

SNG Keckman 39; SNG Kayhan 757-8. Very Fine.

*Note: Numismatists believe that this coin was struck between 500 and 480 BC. That period corresponds very closely to Artemisia I's reign (496-479 BC). In my research, I have not come across a numismatist who attributes this coin to Artemisia I, but I believe that the Λ beneath the goat's mouth is in fact Artemisia I's monogram.

Roy Casagranda

Photo by Blake Weaver

Roy Casagranda is a professor of political science
in Austin, Texas, where he gives monthly public
lectures on politics, history, and philosophy.
http://www.casagranda.com
https://www.facebook.com/RoyCasagrandaBooks/

Cover design by JD Mossburg